PAST TENSE

www.**penguin**.co.uk

PAST TENSE

Lee Child

BANTAM PRESS

LONDON · TORONTO · SYDNEY · AUCKLAND · JOHANNESBURG

TRANSWORLD PUBLISHERS
61–63 Uxbridge Road, London W5 5SA
www.penguin.co.uk

Transworld is part of the Penguin Random House group of companies
whose addresses can be found at global.penguinrandomhouse.com

Penguin
Random House
UK

First published in Great Britain in 2018 by Bantam Press
an imprint of Transworld Publishers

A CIP catalogue record for this book
is available from the British Library.

ISBNs 9780593078198 (cased)
9780593078204 (tpb)

Typeset in 11/15½pt Century Old Style by Falcon Oast Graphic Art Ltd.
Printed and bound by Clays Ltd, Bungay, Suffolk.

Penguin Random House is committed to a sustainable
future for our business, our readers and our planet. This book
is made from Forest Stewardship Council® certified paper.

MIX
Paper from
responsible sources
FSC
www.fsc.org   FSC® C018179

1 3 5 7 9 10 8 6 4 2

In Memoriam

John Reginald Grant, 1924–2016
Norman Steven Shiren, 1925–2017
Audrey Grant, 1926–2017

ONE

J ack Reacher caught the last of the summer sun in a small town on the coast of Maine, and then, like the birds in the sky above him, he began his long migration south. But not, he thought, straight down the coast. Not like the orioles and the buntings and the phoebes and the warblers and the ruby-throated hummingbirds. Instead he decided on a diagonal route, south and west, from the top right-hand corner of the country to the bottom left, maybe through Syracuse, and Cincinnati, and St Louis, and Oklahoma City, and Albuquerque, and onward all the way to San Diego. Which for an army guy like Reacher was a little too full of navy people, but which was otherwise a fine spot to start the winter.

It would be an epic road trip, and one he hadn't made in years.

He was looking forward to it.

He didn't get far.

He walked inland a mile or so and came to a county road and stuck out his thumb. He was a tall man, more than six feet five in his shoes, heavily built, all bone and muscle, not particularly good-looking, never very well dressed, usually a little unkempt. Not an overwhelmingly appealing proposition. As always most drivers slowed and took a look and then kept on going. The first car prepared to take a chance on him came along after forty minutes. It was a year-old Subaru wagon, driven by a lean middle-aged guy in pleated chino pants and a crisp khaki shirt. Dressed by his wife, Reacher thought. The guy had a wedding ring. But under the fine fabrics was a workingman's body. A thick neck and large red knuckles. The slightly surprised and somewhat reluctant boss of something, Reacher thought. The kind of guy who starts out digging post holes and ends up owning a fencing company.

Which turned out to be a good guess. Initial conversation established the guy had started out with nothing to his name but his daddy's old framing hammer, and had ended up owning a construction company, responsible for forty working people, and the hopes and dreams of a whole bunch of clients. He finished his story with a little facial shrug, part Yankee modesty, part genuine perplexity. As in, how did *that* happen? Attention to detail, Reacher thought. This was a very organized guy, full of notions and nostrums and maxims and cast-iron beliefs, one of which was at the end of summer it was better to stay away from both Route One and I-95, and in fact to get out of Maine altogether as fast as possible, which meant soon and sideways, on Route Two, straight west into New Hampshire. To a place just south of Berlin, where the guy knew a bunch of back roads that would get them down to Boston faster than any other way. Which was where the guy was going, for a meeting about marble countertops. Reacher was happy. Nothing wrong with Boston as a starting point. Nothing at all. From there it was a straight shot to Syracuse. After which Cincinnati was easy, via Rochester and Buffalo and Cleveland. Maybe even via Akron, Ohio. Reacher had been in worse places. Mostly in the service.

2

They didn't get to Boston.

The guy got a call on his cell, after fifty-some minutes heading south on the aforementioned New Hampshire back roads. Which were exactly as advertised. Reacher had to admit the guy's plan was solid. There was no traffic at all. No jams, no delays. They were bowling along, doing sixty miles an hour, dead easy. Until the phone rang. It was hooked up to the car radio, and a name came up on the navigation screen, with a thumbnail photograph as a visual aid, in this case of a red-faced man wearing a hard hat and carrying a clipboard. Some kind of a foreman on a job site. The guy at the wheel touched a button and phone hiss filled the car, from all the speakers, like surround sound.

The guy at the wheel spoke to the windshield pillar and said, 'This better be good news.'

It wasn't. It was something to do with an inspector from a municipal buildings department, and a metal flue liner above a fireplace in an entrance lobby, which was properly insulated, exactly up to code, except that couldn't be proved visually without tearing down the stonework, which was by that point already three storeys high, nearly done, with the masons booked on a new job starting the next week, or alternatively without ripping out the custom walnut millwork in the dining room on the other side of the chimney, or the millwork in the closet above, which was rosewood and even more complicated, but the inspector was being a hardass about it and needed to see for himself.

The guy at the wheel glanced at Reacher and said, 'Which inspector is it?'

The guy on the phone said, 'The new one.'

'Does he know he gets a turkey at Thanksgiving?'

'I told him we're all on the same side here.'

The guy at the wheel glanced at Reacher again, as if seeking permission, or offering an apology, or both, and then he faced front again and said, 'Did you offer him money?'

3

'Five hundred. He wouldn't take it.'

Then the cell signal ran out. The sound went garbled, like a robot drowning in a swimming pool, and then it went dead. The screen said it was searching.

The car rolled on.

Reacher said, 'Why would a person want a fireplace in an entrance lobby?'

The guy at the wheel said, 'It's welcoming.'

'I think historically it was designed to repel. It was defensive. Like the campfire burning in the mouth of the cave. It was intended to keep predators at bay.'

'I have to go back,' the guy said. 'I'm sorry.'

He slowed the car and pulled over on the gravel. All alone, on the back roads. No other traffic. The screen said it was still searching for a signal.

'I'm going to have to let you out here,' the guy said. 'Is that OK?'

'No problem,' Reacher said. 'You got me part of the way. For which I thank you very much.'

'You're welcome.'

'Whose is the rosewood closet?'

'His.'

'Cut a big hole in it and show the inspector. Then give the client five commonsense reasons why he should install a wall safe. Because this is a guy who wants a wall safe. Maybe he doesn't know it yet, but a guy who wants a fireplace in his entrance lobby wants a wall safe in his bedroom closet. That's for damn sure. Human nature. You'll make a profit. You can charge him for the time it takes to cut the hole.'

'Are you in this business too?'

'I was a military cop.'

The guy said, 'Huh.'

Reacher opened the door and climbed out, and closed the door again behind him, and walked far enough away to give the guy space to swing the Subaru around, gravel shoulder to gravel shoulder, across the whole width of the road, and then to take off back the way he had come. All of which the guy did, with a brief gesture Reacher took to be a rueful good-luck wave. Then he got smaller and smaller in the distance, and Reacher turned back and continued walking, south, the way he was headed. Wherever possible he liked to maintain forward momentum. The road he was on was a two-lane, wide enough, well maintained, curved here and there, a little up and down. But no kind of a problem for a modern car. The Subaru had been doing sixty. Yet there was no traffic. None at all. Nothing coming, either way. Total silence. Just a sigh of wind in the trees, and the faint buzz of heat coming up off the blacktop.

Reacher walked on.

Two miles later the road he was on curved gently left, and a new road of equal size and appearance split off to the right. Not exactly a turn. More like an equal choice. A classic Y-shaped junction. Twitch the wheel left, or twitch the wheel right. Your call. Both options ran out of sight through trees so mighty in places they made a tunnel.

There was a road sign.

A tilted arrow to the left was labelled Portsmouth, and a tilted arrow to the right was labelled Laconia. But the right-hand option was written in smaller writing, and it had a smaller arrow, as if Laconia was less important than Portsmouth. A mere byway, despite its road being the same size.

Laconia, New Hampshire.

A name Reacher knew. He had seen it on all kinds of historic family paperwork, and he had heard it mentioned from time to time. It was his late father's place of birth, and where he was raised, until he escaped at age seventeen to join the Marines. Such was the vague family legend. Escaped from what had not been specified.

5

But he never went back. Not once. Reacher himself had been born more than fifteen years later, by which time Laconia was a dead detail of the long-ago past, as remote as the Dakota Territory, where it was said some earlier ancestor had lived and worked. No one in the family ever went to either place. No visits. The grandparents died young and were rarely mentioned. There were apparently no aunts or uncles or cousins or any other kind of distant relatives. Which was statistically unlikely, and suggested a rift of some kind. But no one other than his father had any real information, and no one ever made any real attempt to get any from him. Certain things were not discussed in Marine families. Much later as a captain in the army Reacher's brother Joe was posted north and said something about maybe trying to find the old family homestead, but nothing ever came of it. Probably Reacher himself had said the same kind of thing, from time to time. He had never been there either.

Left or right. His call.

Portsmouth was better. It had highways and traffic and buses. It was a straight shot to Boston. San Diego beckoned. The Northeast was about to get cold.

But what was one extra day?

He stepped right, and chose the fork in the road that led to Laconia.

At that same late-afternoon moment, nearly thirty miles away, heading south on a different back road, was a worn-out Honda Civic, driven by a twenty-five-year-old man named Shorty Fleck. Next to him in the passenger seat was a twenty-five-year-old woman named Patty Sundstrom. They were boyfriend and girlfriend, both born and raised in Saint Leonard, which was a small faraway town in New Brunswick, Canada. Not much happened there. The biggest news in living memory was ten years previously, when a truck carrying twelve million bees overturned on a

6

curve. The local paper reported with pride that the accident was the first of its kind in New Brunswick. Patty worked in a sawmill. She was the granddaughter of a guy from Minnesota who had slipped north half a century earlier, to beat the draft for Vietnam. Shorty was a potato farmer. His family had been in Canada for ever. And he wasn't particularly short. Maybe he had been once, as a kid. But now he figured he was what any eyewitness would call an average-looking guy.

They were trying to make it non-stop from Saint Leonard to New York City. Which by any standard was a hardcore drive. But they saw a big advantage in doing it. They had something to sell in the city, and saving a night in a hotel would maximize their profit. They had planned out their route, looping west to avoid the summer people heading home from the beaches, using back roads, Patty's blunt finger on a map, her gaze ranging ahead for turns and signs. They had timed it out on paper, and figured it was a feasible course of action.

Except they had gotten a later start than they would have liked, due a little bit to general disorganization, but mostly due to the Honda's ageing battery not liking the newly crisp autumnal temperatures blowing in from the direction of Prince Edward Island. The delay put them in a long line at the U.S. border, and then the Honda started overheating, and needed nursing along below fifty miles an hour for an extended spell.

They were tired.

And hungry, and thirsty, and in need of the bathroom, and late, and behind schedule. And frustrated. The Honda was overheating again. The needle was kissing the red. There was a grinding noise under the hood. Maybe the oil was low. No way of telling. All the dashboard lights had been on continuously for the last two and a half years.

Shorty asked, 'What's up ahead?'

Patty said, 'Nothing.'

Her fingertip was on a wandering red line, which was labelled with a three-digit number, and which was shown running north to south through a jagged shape shaded pale green. A forested area. Which matched what was out the window. The trees crowded in, still and dark, laden down with heavy end-of-summer leaves. The map showed tiny red spider-web lines here and there, like the veins in an old lady's leg, which were presumably all tracks to somewhere, but nowhere big. Nowhere likely to have a mechanic or a lube shop or radiator water. The best bet was about thirty minutes ahead, some ways east of south, a town with its name printed not too small and semi-bold, which meant it had to have at least a gas station. It was called Laconia.

She said, 'Can we make another twenty miles?'

Now the needle was all the way in the red.

'Maybe,' Shorty said. 'If we walk the last nineteen of them.'

He slowed the car and rolled along on a whisker of gas, which generated less new heat inside the engine, but which also put less airflow through the radiator vanes, so the old heat couldn't get away so fast, so in the short term the temperature needle kept on climbing. Patty rubbed her fingertip forward on the map, keeping pace with her estimate of their speed. There was a spider-web vein coming up on the right. A thin track, curling through the green ink to somewhere about an inch away. Without the rush of air from her leaky window she could hear the noises from the engine. Clunking, knocking, grinding. Getting worse.

Then up ahead on the right she saw the mouth of a narrow road. The spider-web vein, right on time. But more like a tunnel than a road. It was dark inside. The trees met overhead. At the entrance on a frost-heaved post was nailed a board, on which were screwed ornate plastic letters, and an arrow pointing into the tunnel. The letters spelled the word *Motel*.

'Should we?' she asked.

The car answered. The temperature needle was jammed against

8

the stop. Shorty could feel the heat in his shins. The whole engine bay was baking. For a second he wondered what would happen if they kept on going instead. People talked about automobile engines blowing up and melting down. Which were figures of speech, surely. There would be no actual puddles of molten metal. No actual explosions would take place. It would just conk out, peacefully. Or seize up. It would coast gently to a stop.

But in the middle of nowhere, with no passing traffic and no cell signal.

'No choice,' he said, and braked and steered and turned in to the tunnel. Up close they saw the plastic letters on the sign had been painted gold, with a narrow brush and a steady hand, like a promise, like the motel was a high-class place. There was a second sign, identical, facing drivers coming the other way.

'OK?' Shorty said.

The air felt cold in the tunnel. Easily ten degrees colder than the main drag. Last fall's leaf litter and last winter's mud were mashed together on the shoulders.

'OK?' Shorty asked again.

They drove over a wire laid across the road. A fat rubbery thing, not much smaller than a garden hose. Like they had at gas stations, to ding a bell in the kiosk, to get the pump jockey out to help you.

Patty didn't answer.

Shorty said, 'How bad can it be? It's marked on the map.'

'The track is marked.'

'The sign was nice.'

'I agree,' Patty said. 'It was.'

They drove on.

TWO

The trees cooled and freshened the air, so Reacher was happy to keep up a steady four miles an hour, which for his length of leg was exactly eighty-eight beats a minute, which was exactly the tempo of a whole bunch of great music, so it was easy time to pass. He did thirty minutes, two miles, seven classic tracks in his head, and then he heard real sounds behind him, and turned around to see an ancient pick-up coming crabwise towards him, as if each of the wheels wanted to go in a different direction.

Reacher stuck out his thumb.

The truck stopped. An old guy with a long white beard leaned across inside and wound down the passenger window.

He said, 'I'm going to Laconia.'

'Me too,' Reacher said.

'Well, OK.'

Reacher got in, and wound the window back up. The old guy pulled out and wobbled back up to speed.

He said, 'I guess this is the part where you tell me I need new tyres.'

'It's a possibility,' Reacher said.

'But at my age I try to avoid large capital expenditures. Why invest in the future? Do I even have one?'

'That argument is more circular than your tyres.'

'Actually the frame is bent. I was in a wreck.'

'When?'

'Close on twenty-three years ago.'

'So this is normal to you now.'

'Keeps me awake.'

'How do you know where to point the steering wheel?'

'You get used to it. Like sailing a boat. Why are you going to Laconia?'

'I was passing by,' Reacher said. 'My father was born there. I want to see it.'

'What's your last name?'

'Reacher.'

The old guy shook his head.

He said, 'I never knew anyone in Laconia named Reacher.'

The reason for the previous Y-shaped fork in the road turned out to be a lake, wide enough to make north–south drivers pick a side, right bank or left bank. Reacher and the old guy squirmed and shuddered along the right bank, which was mechanically stressful, but visually beautiful, because the view was stunning and the sun was less than an hour from setting. Then came the town of Laconia itself. It was a bigger place than Reacher expected. Fifteen or twenty thousand people. A county seat. Solid and prosperous. There were brick buildings and neat old-fashioned streets. The low red sun made them look like they were in an old-time movie.

The squirming pick-up truck wobbled to a stop at a downtown corner. The old guy said, 'This is Laconia.'

Reacher said, 'How much has it changed?'

'Around here, not much.'

11

'I grew up thinking it was smaller than this.'

'Most people remember things bigger.'

Reacher thanked the guy for the ride, and got out, and watched the truck squeal away, each tyre insisting the other three were wrong. Then he turned away and walked random blocks, getting a sense for what might be where, in particular two specific destinations for start of business the next day, and two for immediate attention that evening, the first being a place to eat, and the second being a place to sleep.

Both were available, in a historic-downtown kind of way. Healthy food, no place more than two tables wide. No motels in town, but plenty of inns and plenty of bed and breakfasts. He ate at a narrow bistro, because a waitress smiled at him through the window, after a moment of embarrassment when she brought his order. Which was some kind of salad with roast beef in it, which was the menu choice he felt would be most nutritious. But when it came it was tiny. He asked for a second order, and a bigger plate. At first the waitress misunderstood. She thought there was something wrong with the first order. Or the size of the plate. Or both. Then she caught on. He was hungry. He wanted two portions. She asked if there was anything else he needed. He asked for a bigger cup for his coffee.

Afterwards he tracked back to lodgings he had seen, on a side street near the city offices. There was room at the inn. Vacation time was over. He paid a premium price for what the innkeeper called a suite, but what he called a room with a sofa and way too many floral patterns and feather pillows. He shovelled a dozen off the bed and put his pants under the mattress to press. Then he took a long hot shower, and climbed under the covers, and went to sleep.

The tunnel through the trees turned out to be more than two miles long. Patty Sundstrom traced its curves with her finger on the

12

map. Under the Honda's wheels was greyed and pitted blacktop, the finished surface completely washed away in places by runoff water, leaving shallow potholes the size of pool tables, some of them bare ribbed concrete, some of them gravelled, some of them full of leaf mould slop still wet from springtime, because overhead the leafy canopy was thick and unbroken, apart from one spot where no trees grew for twenty-some yards. There was a bar of bright pink open sky. Maybe a narrow seam of different dirt, or a sudden underground escarpment of solid rock, or a hydraulic oddity with no ground water, or too much. Then the sliver of sky was behind them. They were back in the tunnel. Shorty Fleck was going slow, to save the shocks and nurse the motor. He wondered if he should put his headlights on.

Then the canopy thinned for a second time, with the promise of more to come, like a big clearing was on its way, like they were arriving somewhere. What they saw was the road ahead coming out of the trees and running in a straight line through a couple acres of flat grassland, the thin grey ribbon suddenly naked and exposed in the last of the daylight. Its destination was a group of three substantial wooden buildings, laid out one after the other on a sweeping right-hand curve, maybe fifty yards between the first and the last. All three were painted dull red, with bright white trim. Set against the green grass they looked like classic New England structures.

The closest building was a motel. Like a picture in a kid's book. Like learning your ABCs. M is for Motel. It was long and low, made of dull red boards, with a pitched roof of grey asphalt shingle, and a red neon *Office* sign in the first window, and then a louvred door for storage, and then a repeating pattern, of a broad window with an HVAC grille and two plastic lawn chairs under it, and a numbered door, and another broad window with the same grille and the same chairs, and another numbered door, and so on, all the way to the end. There were twelve rooms in total, all in a line.

But there were no cars parked out front of any of them. Looked like zero occupancy.

'OK?' Shorty said.

Patty didn't answer. He stopped the car. In the distance on the right they saw the second building was shorter from end to end, but much taller and deeper from front to back. Some kind of barn. But not for animals. The concrete ramp to the door was conspicuously clean. There was no shit, to put it bluntly. It was a workshop of some kind. Out front were nine quad-bike ATVs. Like regular motorcycles, but with four fat tyres instead of two slicks. They were lined up in three ranks of three, with exact precision.

'Maybe they're Hondas,' Patty said. 'Maybe these guys would know how to fix the car.'

On the end of the line the third building was a regular house, of plain construction but generous size, with a wraparound porch, which had rocking chairs set out on it.

Shorty rolled the car forward, and stopped again. The blacktop was about to end. Ten yards short of the motel's empty lot. He was about to bump down on to an owner-maintained surface that his expert potato-farmer eye told him was made up of equal parts gravel, mud, dead weeds, and live weeds. He saw at least five species he would rather not have in his own dirt.

The end of the blacktop felt like a threshold. Like a decision.

'OK?' he said again.

'The place is empty,' Patty said. 'There are no guests. How weird is that?'

'The season is over.'

'Like flicking a switch?'

'They're always complaining about it.'

'It's the middle of nowhere.'

'It's a getaway vacation. No hustle, no bustle.'

Patty was quiet a long moment.

Then she said, 'I guess it looks OK.'

14

Shorty said, 'I think it's this or nothing.'

She traced the motel structure left to right, the plain proportions, the solid roof, the heavy boards, the recent stain. Necessary maintenance had been performed, but nothing flashy. It was an honest building. It could have been in Canada.

She said, 'Let's take a look.'

They bumped down off the blacktop and rattled across the uneven surface and parked outside the office. Shorty thought a second and shut the motor down. Safer than letting it idle. In case of molten metal and explosions. If it didn't start up again, too bad. It was already near enough where it needed to be. They could ask for room one, if necessary. They had one huge suitcase, full of the stuff they planned to sell. It could stay in the car. Apart from that they didn't have much to haul.

They got out of the car and stepped into the office. There was a guy behind the reception counter. He was about Shorty's own age, and Patty's, mid-twenties, maybe a year or two more. He had short blond hair, combed neatly, and a good tan, and blue eyes, and white teeth, and a ready smile. But he looked a little out of place. At first Shorty took him to be like a summer thing he had seen in Canada, where a well-bred kid is sent to do a dumb job in the countryside, for the purposes of building his résumé, or expanding his horizons, or finding himself, or some such. But this guy was five years too old for that. And behind his greeting he had a proprietorial air. He was saying welcome, for sure, but to my house. Like he owned the place.

Maybe he did.

Patty told him they needed a room, and that they wondered if whoever looked after the quad bikes could take a look at their car, or failing that, they would surely appreciate the phone number of a good mechanic. Hopefully not a tow truck.

The guy smiled and asked, 'What's wrong with your car?'

He sounded like every young guy in the movies who worked on

15

Wall Street and wore a suit and tie. Full of smooth confidence. Probably drank champagne. Greed is good. Not a potato farmer's favourite type of guy.

Patty said, 'It's overheating and making weird banging noises under the hood.'

The guy smiled a different kind of smile, this one a modest but commanding junior-master-of-the-universe grin, and he said, 'Then I guess we should take a look at it. Sounds low on coolant, and low on oil. Both of which are easy to fix, unless something is leaking. That would depend on what parts are needed. Maybe we could adapt something. Failing that, as you say, we know some good mechanics. Either way, there's nothing to be done until it cools right down. Park it outside your room overnight, and we'll check it first thing in the morning.'

'What time exactly?' Patty asked, thinking about how late they were already, but also thinking about gift horses and mouths.

The guy said, 'Here we're all up with the sun.'

She said, 'How much is the room?'

'After Labor Day, before the leaf-peepers, let's call it fifty bucks.'

'OK,' she said, although not really, but she was thinking about gift horses again, and what Shorty had said, that it was this or nothing.

'We'll give you room ten,' the guy said. 'It's the first we've refurbished so far. In fact we only just finished it. You would be its very first guests. We hope you will do us the honour.'

THREE

Reacher woke up a minute after three in the morning. All the clichés: snapped awake, instantly, like flicking a switch. He didn't move. Didn't even tense his arms and legs. He just lay there, staring into the dark, listening hard, concentrating a hundred per cent. Not a learned response. A primitive instinct, baked deep in the back of his brain by evolution. One time he had been in Southern California, fast asleep with the windows open on a beautiful night, and he had snapped awake, instantly, like flicking a switch, because in his sleep he had smelled a faint wisp of smoke. Not cigarette smoke or a building on fire, but a burning hillside forty miles away. A primeval smell. Like a wildfire racing across an ancient savannah. Whose ancestors outran it depended on who woke up fastest and got the earliest start. Rinse and repeat, down hundreds of generations.

But there was no smoke. Not at one minute past three that particular morning. Not in that particular hotel room. So what woke him? Not sight or touch or taste, because he had been alone in bed with his eyes shut and the drapes closed and nothing in his mouth. Sound, then. He had heard something.

He waited for a repeat. Which he considered an evolutionary weakness. The product was not yet perfect. It was still a two-step process. One time to wake you up, and a second time to tell you what it was. Better to do both together, surely, first time out.

He heard nothing. Not many sounds were lizard-brain sounds any more. The pad or hiss of an ancient predator was unlikely. The nearest forest twigs to be ominously stepped upon and loudly broken were miles away beyond the edge of town. Not much else scared the primitive cortex. Not in the audio kingdom. Newer sounds were dealt with elsewhere, in the front part of the brain, which was plenty vigilant for the scrapes and clicks of modern threats, but which lacked the seniority to wake a person up from a deep and contented sleep.

So what woke him? The only other truly ancient sound was a cry for help. A scream, or a plea. Not a modern yell, or a whoop or a cackle of laughter. Something deeply primitive. The tribe, under attack. At its very edge. A distant early warning.

He heard nothing more. There was no repeat. He slid out from under the covers and listened at the door. Heard nothing. He took a feather pillow and held it over the peephole. No reaction. No gunshot through the eye. He looked out. Saw nothing. A bright empty hallway.

He lifted the drapes and checked the window. Nothing there. Nothing on the street. Pitch dark. All quiet. He got back in bed and smacked the pillow into shape and went back to sleep.

Patty Sundstrom was also awake at one minute past three. She had slept four hours and then some kind of subconscious agitation had forced its way through and woken her up. She didn't feel good. Not deep inside, like she knew she should. Partly the delay was on her mind. At best they would get to the city halfway through the next day. Not prime trading hours. On top of which was the fifty extra bucks for the room. Plus the car was an unknown quantity.

18

It might cost a fortune. If parts were required. If something had to be adapted. Cars were great until they weren't. Even so, the engine had started when they came out of the office. The motel guy didn't seem too worried about it. He made a reassuring face. He didn't come to the room with them. Which was good too. She hated people crowding in, showing her where the light switch was, and the bathroom, judging her stuff, acting all obsequious, wanting a tip. The guy did none of that.

But still she didn't feel good. She didn't know why. The room was pleasant. It was newly refurbished, as promised, every inch. The wallboard was new, and the ceiling, and the trim, and the paint, and the carpet. Nothing adventurous. Certainly nothing flashy. It looked like an apples-for-apples update of what tradition would have had there before, but newly straight and true and smooth and solid. The AC was cold and quiet. There was a flat-screen television. The window was an expensive unit, with two thick panes of glass sealed in thermal gaskets, with an electric roller blind set in the void between. You didn't tug on a chain to close it. You pressed a button. No expense spared. Only problem was, the window itself didn't open. Which she would worry about in a fire. And generally she liked a breath of night air in a room. But overall it was a decent place. Better than most she had seen. Maybe even worth fifty bucks.

But she didn't feel good. There was no phone in the room, and no cell signal, so after half an hour they had walked back to the office to enquire about using the motel's land line for hot food delivery. Pizza, maybe. The guy at the desk had smiled a rueful smile and said he was sorry, but they were way too remote for delivery. No one would come. He said most guests drove out to a diner or a restaurant. Shorty looked like he was going to get mad. As if the guy was saying, most guests have cars that work. Maybe something to do with the rueful smile. Then the guy said, but hey, we've got pizzas in the freezer down at the house. Why don't you come eat with us?

19

Which was a weird meal, in a dark old residence, with Shorty and the guy and three others just the same. Same age, same look, with some kind of same-wavelength connection between them. As if they were all on a mission. There was something nervous about them. After some conversation she concluded they were all maxed-out investors in the same new venture. The motel, she assumed. She assumed they had bought it and were trying to make a go of it. Whatever, they were all extremely polite and gracious and talkative. The guy from the reception desk said his name was Mark. The others were Robert, Steven and Peter. They all asked intelligent questions about life in Saint Leonard. They asked about the hardcore drive south. Again Shorty looked like he was going to get mad. He thought they were calling him dumb for setting out in a bad car. But the guy who said he looked after the quad bikes, who was Peter, said he would have done exactly the same thing. Purely on a statistical basis. The car had run for years. Why assume it would stop now? The odds said it would keep on going. It always had before.

Then they said goodnight and walked back to room ten, and went to sleep, except she woke up again four hours later, agitated. She didn't feel good, and she didn't know why. Or maybe she did. Maybe she just didn't want to admit it. Maybe that was the issue. Truth was, deep down, she guessed she was probably mad at Shorty himself. The big trip. The most important part of their secret plan. He set out in a bad car. He was dumb. He was dumber than his own potatoes. He couldn't invest a buck upfront? What would it have cost, at a lube shop with a coupon? Less than the fifty bucks they were paying for the motel, that was for sure, which Shorty was also pestering her to agree was a creepy place run by creepy people, which was a conflict for her, because really she felt like a bunch of polite young men were rescuing her, like knights in shining armour, from a predicament caused entirely by a potato farmer too dumb to check his car before setting out on about a

20

thousand-mile trip to, oh yeah, a foreign country, with, oh yeah, something very valuable in the trunk.

Dumb. She wanted air. She slipped out of bed and padded barefoot to the door. She turned the knob, and pressed her other hand on the frame for balance, so she could ease the door open without a sound, because she wanted Shorty to stay asleep, because she didn't want to deal with him right then, as mad as she was.

But the door was stuck. It wouldn't move at all. She checked it was properly unlocked from the inside, and she tried the knob both ways, but nothing happened. The door was jammed. Maybe it had never been adjusted properly after installation. Or maybe it had swelled with the summer heat.

Dumb. Really dumb. Now was the one time she could use Shorty. He was a strong little fireplug. From throwing hundred-pound bags of potatoes around. But was she going to wake him up and ask him? Was she hell. She crept back to bed and got in alongside him and stared at the ceiling, which was straight and true and smooth and solid.

Reacher woke again at eight o'clock in the morning. Bright bars of hard sun came past the edges of the drapes. There was dust in the air, floating gently. There were muted sounds from the street. Cars waiting, and then moving off. A light at the end of the block, presumably. Occasionally the dulled blare of a horn, as if a guy in front had looked away and missed the green.

He showered, and retrieved his pants from under the mattress, and dressed, and walked out in search of breakfast. He found coffee and muffins close by, which sustained him through a longer reconnaissance, which brought him to a place he figured might have good food hiding under multiple layers of some kind of faux-retro irony. He figured it would take a smarter guy than him to decode them all. The basic idea seemed to be someone's modern-day notion of where old-time lumberjacks might have dined, on whatever it was that old-time lumberjacks ate, which in the modern day seemed to be interpreted as one of every fried item on the menu. In Reacher's experience lumberjacks ate the same as any other hard-working person, which was all kinds of different things. But he had no ideological objection to fried food as such, especially not in generous quantities, so he played along. He went in and sat down, briskly, he hoped, as if he had thirty minutes before he had a tree to fell.

The food was fine, and the coffee kept on coming, so he lingered longer than thirty minutes, watching out the window, timing the hustle and the bustle, waiting until the people in the suits and the skirts were safely at work. Then he got up and left his tip and paid his check, and walked two of the blocks he had scouted the night before, towards the place he guessed he should start. Which was the records department of the city offices. Which had a suite number all its own, on a crowded multi-line floor directory, outside a brick-built multi-purpose government building, which because of its age and its shape Reacher figured had once contained a courtroom. Maybe it still did.

The suite he was looking for turned out to be one of many small rooms opening off a grand mezzanine hallway. Like a corridor in an expensive hotel. Except the doors were half glass, which was reeded in an old-fashioned style, with the department name painted on it in gold. Over two lines, in the case of the records department. Inside the door was an empty room with four plastic chairs and a waist-high enquiry counter. Like a miniature version of any government office. There was an electric bell push screwed to the counter. It had a thin wire that ran away to a nearby crack, and a handwritten sign that said *If Unattended Ring For Service*. The message was carefully lettered and protected by many layers of clear tape, applied in strips of generous length, some of which were curled at the corners, and dirty, as if picked at by bored or anxious fingers.

22

Reacher rang for service. A minute later a woman came through a door in the rear wall, looking back as she did so, with what Reacher thought was regret, as if she was leaving a space dramatically larger and more exciting. She was maybe thirty, slim and neat, in a grey sweater and a grey skirt. She stepped up to the counter but she glanced back at the door. Either her boyfriend was waiting, or she hated her job. Maybe both. But she did her best. She cranked up a warm and welcoming manner. Not exactly like in a store, where the customer was always right, but more as an equal, as if she and the customer were just bound to have a good time together, puzzling through some ancient town business. There was enough light in her eyes Reacher figured she meant at least some of it. Maybe she didn't hate her job after all.

He said, 'I need to ask you about an old real estate record.'

'Is it for a title dispute?' the woman asked. 'In which case you should get your attorney to request it. Much faster that way.'

'No kind of dispute,' he said. 'My father was born here. That's all. Years ago. He's dead now. I was passing by. I thought I would stop in and take a look at the house he grew up in.'

'What's the address?'

'I don't know.'

'Can you remember roughly where it is?'

'I've never been there.'

'You didn't visit?'

'No.'

'Perhaps because your father moved away when he was young.'

'Not until he joined the Marines when he was seventeen.'

'Then perhaps because your grandparents moved away before your father had a family of his own. Before visits became a thing.'

'I got the impression my grandparents stayed here the rest of their lives.'

'But you never met them?'

23

'We were a Marine family. We were always somewhere else.'

'I'm sorry.'

'Not your fault.'

'But thank you for your service.'

'Wasn't my service. My dad was the Marine, not me. I was hoping we could look him up, maybe in a register of births or something, to get his parents' full names, so we could find their exact address, maybe in property tax records or something, so I could drop by and take a look.'

'You don't know your grandparents' names?'

'I think they were James and Elizabeth Reacher.'

'That's my name.'

'Your name is Reacher?'

'No, Elizabeth. Elizabeth Castle.'

'I'm pleased to meet you,' Reacher said.

'Likewise,' she said.

'I'm Jack Reacher. My dad was Stan Reacher.'

'How long ago did Stan leave to join the Marines?'

'He would be about ninety now, so it was more than seventy years ago.'

'Then we should start eighty years ago, for a safety margin,' the woman said. 'At that point Stan Reacher would be about ten years old, living at home with his parents James and Elizabeth Reacher, somewhere in Laconia. Is that a fair summary?'

'That could be chapter one of my biography.'

'I'm pretty sure the computer goes back more than eighty years now,' she said. 'But for property taxes that old it might just be a list of names, I'm afraid.'

She turned a key and opened a lid in the countertop. Under it was a keyboard and a screen. Safe from thieves, while unattended. She pressed a button, and looked away.

'Booting up,' she said.

Which were words he had heard before, in a technological

context, but to him they sounded military, as if infantry companies were lacing tight ahead of a general advance.

She clicked and scrolled, and scrolled and clicked.

'Yes,' she said. 'Eighty years ago is just an index, with file numbers. If you want detail, you need to request the actual physical document from storage. Usually that takes a long time, I'm afraid.'

'How long?'

'Sometimes three months.'

'Are there names and addresses in the index?'

'Yes.'

'Then that's really all we need.'

'I guess so. If all you want to do is take a look at the house.'

'That's all I'm planning to do.'

'Aren't you curious?'

'About what?'

'Their lives. Who they were and what they did.'

'Not three months' worth of curious.'

'OK, then names and addresses are all we need.'

'If the house is still there,' he said. 'Maybe someone tore it down. Suddenly eighty years sounds like a real long time.'

'Things change slowly here,' she said.

She clicked again, and scrolled, fast at first, scooting down through the alphabet, and then slowly, peering at the screen, through what Reacher assumed was the R section, and then back up again, just as slowly, peering just as hard. Then down and up again fast, as if trying to shake something loose.

She said, 'No one named Reacher owned property in Laconia eighty years ago.'

FOUR

Patty Sundstrom also woke again at eight in the morning, later than she would have liked, but finally she had succumbed to exhaustion, and she had slept deeply for almost five more hours. She sensed the space in the bed next to her was empty. She rolled over and saw the door was open. Shorty was out in the lot. He was talking to one of the motel guys. Maybe Peter, she thought. The guy who looked after the quad bikes. They were standing next to the Honda. Its hood was up. The sun was bright.

She slipped out of bed and crept bent-over to the bathroom. So Peter or whoever it was by the Honda wouldn't see. She showered, and dressed in the same clothes, because she hadn't brought enough for an extra day. She came out of the bathroom. She was hungry. The door was still open. The sun was still bright. Now Shorty was there on his own. The other guy had gone.

She stepped out and said, 'Good morning.'

'Car won't start,' Shorty said. 'The guy messed with it and now it's dead. It was OK last night.'

'It was not OK, exactly.'

'It started last night. Now it won't. The guy must have messed it up.'

'What did he do?'

'He poked around some. He had a wrench and a pair of pliers. I think he made it worse.'

'Was it Peter? The guy that looks after the quad bikes?'

'So he says. If it's true, good luck to them. Probably that's why they need nine bikes in the first place. To make sure they always have one that works.'

'The car started last night because it was hot. Now it's cold. That makes a difference.'

'You're a mechanic now?'

'Are you?' she said.

'I think the guy broke something.'

'And I think he's trying to help us the best he can. We should be grateful.'

'For getting our car broken?'

'It was already broken.'

'It started last night. First turn of the key.'

She said, 'Did you have a problem with the room door?'

He said, 'When?'

'When you came out this morning.'

'What kind of problem?'

'I wanted some air in the night but I couldn't get it open. It was jammed.'

'I didn't have a problem,' Shorty said. 'It opened right up.'

Fifty yards away they saw Peter come out of the barn, with a brown canvas bag in his hand. It looked heavy. Tools, Patty thought. To fix their car.

She said, 'Shorty Fleck, now you listen to me. These gentlemen are trying to help us, and I want you to act like you appreciate it. At the very minimum I don't want you to give them a reason to stop helping us before they're finished. Do I make myself clear?'

'Jesus,' he said. 'You're acting like this is my fault or something.'

'Yeah, something,' she said, and then she shut up and waited for Peter, with the bag of tools. Who clanked up to them with a cheerful smile, as if he was just itching to clap the dust off his hands and get straight to work.

She said, 'Thanks so much for your help.'

He said, 'No problem at all.'

'I hope it's not too complicated.'

'Right now it's dead as a doornail. Which is usually electrical. Maybe a wire melted.'

'Can you fix that?'

'We could splice in a replacement. Just enough to bypass the bad part. Sooner or later you would want to get it properly repaired. It's the kind of thing that could shake loose eventually.'

'How long does it take to splice?'

'First we need to find where it melted.'

'The engine started last night,' Shorty said. 'Then we ran it two minutes and shut it off again. It got cooler and cooler, all night long. How would anything melt?'

Peter said nothing.

'He's just asking,' Patty said. 'In case the melting thing is a wild goose chase. We wouldn't want to take up more of your time than we had to. It's very nice of you to help us.'

'It's OK,' Peter said. 'It's a reasonable question. When you stop the engine you also stop the radiator fan and the water pump. So there's no forced cooling and no circulation. The hottest water rises passively to the top of the cylinder head. Surface temperatures can actually get worse in the first hour. Maybe there was a wire touching the metal.'

He ducked under the hood and pondered a moment. He traced circuits with his finger, checking the wires, tugging things, tapping things. He looked at the battery. He used a wrench to check the clamps were tight on the posts.

28

He backed out and said, 'Try it one more time.'

Shorty put his butt on the seat and kept his feet on the ground. He twisted to face front and put his hand on the key. He looked up. Peter nodded. Shorty turned the key.

Nothing happened. Nothing at all. Not even a click or a whirr or a cough. Turning the key was the same thing as not turning it. Inert. Dead as a doornail. Dead as the deadest thing that ever died.

Elizabeth Castle looked up from her screen and focused on nothing much, as if running through a number of possible scenarios, and the consequent next steps in all the different circumstances, starting, Reacher assumed, with him being an idiot and getting the town wrong, in which case the next step would be to get rid of him, no doubt politely, but also no doubt expeditiously.

She said, 'They were probably renters. Most people were. The landlords paid the taxes. We'll have to find them somewhere else. Were they farmers?'

'I don't think so,' Reacher said. 'I don't remember any stories about having to go outside in the freezing dawn to feed the chickens before walking twenty miles through the snow to school, uphill both ways. That's the kind of thing farmers tell you, right? But I never heard that.'

'Then I'm not sure where you should start.'

'The beginning is often good. The register of births.'

'That's in the county offices, not the city. It's a whole different building, quite far from here. Maybe you should start with the census records instead. Your father should show up in two of them, when he was around two years old and twelve years old.'

'Where are they?'

'They're in the county offices too, but a different office, slightly closer.'

'How many offices have they got?'

'A good number.'

She gave him the address of the particular place he needed, with extensive turn-by-turn directions how to get there, and he said goodbye and set out walking. He passed the inn where he had spent the night. He passed a place he figured he would come back to for lunch. He was moving south and east through the downtown blocks, sometimes on worn brick sidewalks easily eighty years old. Even a hundred. The stores were crisp and clean, many of them devoted to cookware and bakeware and tableware and all kinds of other wares associated with the preparation and consumption of food. Some were shoe stores. Some had bags.

The building he was looking for turned out to be a modern structure built wide and low across what must have been two regular lots. It would have looked better on a technology campus, surrounded by computer laboratories. Which was what it was, he thought. He realized in his mind he had been expecting shelves of mouldering paper, hand-lettered in fading ink, tied up with string. All of which still existed, he was sure, but not there. That stuff was in storage, three months away, after being copied and catalogued and indexed on a computer. It would be retrieved not with a puff of dust and a cart with wheels, but with a click of a mouse and the whirr of a printer.

The modern world.

He went in, to a reception desk that could have been in a hip museum or an upscale dentist. Behind it was a guy who looked like he was stationed there as a punishment. Reacher said hello. The guy looked up but didn't answer. Reacher told him he wanted to see two sets of old census records.

'For where?' the guy asked, like he didn't care at all.

'Here,' Reacher said.

The guy looked blank.

'Laconia,' Reacher said. 'New Hampshire, USA, North America, the world, the solar system, the galaxy, the universe.'

'Why two?'

'Why not?'

'What years?'

Reacher told him, first the year his dad was two, and then the next census ten years later, when his dad was twelve.

The guy asked, 'Are you a county resident?'

'Why do you want to know?'

'Funding. This stuff ain't free. But residents are entitled.'

'I've been here a good while,' Reacher said. 'At least as long as I lived anywhere else recently.'

'What is the reason for your search?'

'Is that important?'

'We have boxes to check.'

'Family history,' Reacher said.

'Now I need your name,' the guy said.

'Why?'

'We have targets to meet. We have to take names, or they think we're inflating the numbers.'

'You could make up names all day long.'

'We have to see ID.'

'Why? Isn't this stuff in the public domain?'

'Welcome to the real world,' the guy said.

Reacher showed him his passport.

The guy said, 'You were born in Berlin.'

'Correct,' Reacher said.

'Not Berlin, New Hampshire, either.'

'Is that a problem? You think I'm a foreign spy sent here to disrupt what already happened ninety years ago?'

The guy wrote *Reacher* in a box on a form.

'Cubicle two, Mr Reacher,' he said, and pointed through a door in the opposite wall.

Reacher stepped in, to a hushed square space, with low lighting, and long maple workbenches divided by upright partitions into separate stations. Each station had a muted tweed chair, and a flat-screen computer on the work surface, and a freshly sharpened pencil, and a thin pad of paper with the county's name printed at the top, like a hotel brand. There was thick carpet on the floor. Fabric on the walls. The woodwork was excellent quality. Reacher figured the room as a whole must have cost a million dollars.

He sat down in cubicle two, and the screen in front of him came to life. It lit up blue, a plain wash of colour, apart from two small icons in the top right corner, like postage stamps on a letter. He was not an experienced computer user, but he had tried it once or twice, and he had seen it done many more times. Now even cheap hotels had computers at reception. Many times he had waited while a clerk clicked and scrolled and typed. Gone were the days when a person could slap down a couple of bills and get a big brass key in instant exchange.

He moved the mouse and sent the arrow up towards the icons. He knew they were files. Or file folders. You had to click on them, and in response they would open. He was never sure whether you had to click once or twice. He had seen it done both ways. His usual habit was to click twice. If in doubt, et cetera. Maybe it helped, and it never seemed to hurt. Like shooting someone in the head. A double tap could do no harm.

He put the arrow centre mass on the left-hand icon and clicked twice, and the screen redrew to a grey colour, like the deck of a warship. In the centre was a black and white image of the title page from a government report, like a bright crisp Xerox, printed with prissy, old-fashioned writing in a government-style typeface. At the top it said: U.S. Department of Commerce, R. P. Lamont, Secretary, Bureau of the Census, W. M. Steuart, Director. In the middle it said: Fifteenth Census of the United States, Returns Extracted for the Municipality of Laconia, New Hampshire. At the bottom it said: For Sale by the Superintendent of Documents, Washington, D.C., Price One Dollar.

Reacher could see the top of a second page peeking up from the bottom of the screen. Scrolling would be required. That was clear. Best accomplished, he imagined, with the little wheel set in the top surface of the mouse. Between about where its shoulder blades would be. Under the pad of his index finger. Convenient. Intuitive. He skimmed the introduction, which was mostly about many and various improvements made in methodology since the fourteenth census. Not boasting, really. More of a one-geek-to-another kind of a thing, even back then. Stuff you needed to know, if you loved counting people.

Then came the lists, of plain names and old occupations, and the world of nearly ninety years before seemed to rise up all around. There were button makers, and hat makers, and glove makers, and turpentine farmers, and labourers, and locomotive engineers, and silk spinners, and tin mill workers. There was a separate section titled *Unusual Occupations For Children*. Most were optimistically classified as apprentices. Or helpers. There were blacksmiths and brick masons and engine hostlers and ladlers and pourers and smelter boys.

There were no Reachers. Not in Laconia, New Hampshire, the year Stan was two.

He wheeled his way back to the top and started again, this time paying particular attention to the dependent children column. Maybe there had been a gruesome accident, and orphan baby Stan had been taken in by unrelated but kindly neighbours. Maybe they had noted his birth name as a tribute.

There were no dependent children separately identified as Stan Reacher. Not in Laconia, New Hampshire, the year he was supposed to be two.

Reacher found the place in the top left of the screen, with the three little buttons, red, orange, green, like a tiny traffic signal laid on its side. He clicked twice on red and the document went away. He opened up the right-hand icon, and he found the sixteenth census, different Secretary, different Director, but the same substantial improvements since the last time around. Then came the lists, now just eighty years old instead of ninety, the difference faintly discernible, with more jobs in factories, and fewer on the land.

But still no Reachers.

Not in Laconia, New Hampshire, the year Stan Reacher was supposed to be twelve.

He clicked twice on the little red button and the document went away.

FIVE

Shorty tried the key one more time, but again nothing happened. There was nothing but a soft mechanical click, which was just the physical key itself, turning inside the barrel on the steering column. A soft little click no one ever heard, because normally it was drowned out instantly by the sounds of a car bursting into life. Same thing with the click of a trigger, ahead of a gunshot.

But not that morning. The Honda felt dead. Like a sick old dog, gone in the night. A whole different condition. No response at all. Some kind of charge gone out of it.

Patty said, 'I think we better call a mechanic.'

Peter looked over her shoulder. She turned, and she saw the other three guys walking up towards them. From the house, or the barn. The main man was in the lead, as always. Mark, who had checked them in the night before. Who had invited them to dinner. The guy with the smile. Behind him was Steven, and then Robert. They arrived and Mark said, 'How are we doing this morning?'

Peter said, 'Not great.'

'What's wrong with it?'

'Can't tell. It's dead as a doornail. I guess something fried.'

'We should call a mechanic,' Patty said. 'We don't want to take up any more of your time.'

'It started last night,' Shorty said. 'First turn of the key.'

Mark smiled and said, 'Yes, it did.'

'Now it's dead. Just saying. I know this car. I've had it a long time. It has good days and bad days, but it never dies.'

Mark was quiet for a long moment.

Then he smiled again and said, 'I'm not sure what you're suggesting.'

'Maybe poking around in there made it worse.'

'You think Peter broke it?'

'Something did, between last night and right now. That's all I'm saying. Maybe it was Peter, and maybe it wasn't. Doesn't even matter any more. Because the thing is, you guys poking around in there is pretty much the same thing as you guys assuming responsibility for it. Because you're a motel. I'm sure there are innkeeper laws. Safekeeping of guest property, all that kind of issue.'

Again Mark went quiet.

'He doesn't mean it,' Patty said. 'He's upset, is all.'

Mark just shook his head, hardly moving at all, as if he was shrugging off the smallest of things. He looked at Shorty and said, 'Stress is a hard thing to deal with, I agree. I think we all know that. But equally I think we all know the smart play here is to es-tablish a minimum amount of courtesy, in all our mutual dealings. Wouldn't you say? A little respect. Maybe a little humility, too. Maybe a little acceptance of responsibility. Your car hasn't been well looked after, has it?'

Shorty didn't answer.

'The clock is ticking,' Mark said. 'Midday is on its way. Which is when last night becomes tonight, in the motel business, at which time you will owe us another fifty dollars, which I can see in Patty's face you don't want to pay, or can't pay, so a speedy reply would help you much more than it would help me. But fast or slow, the choice is yours.'

Patty said, 'OK, our car is not well maintained.'

'Hey,' Shorty said.

'Well it isn't,' she said. 'I bet this is the first time the hood was up since you bought it.'

'I didn't buy it. I got given it.'

'Who by?'

'My uncle.'

'Then I bet this is the first time the hood was up since it left the factory.'

Shorty said nothing.

Mark looked at him and said, 'Patty sees things from a third-party perspective. Which implies a measure of objectivity. So I'm sure she's absolutely right. I'm sure it's that simple. You're a busy man. Who has the time? Some things get neglected.'

'I guess,' Shorty said.

'But you need to say it out loud. We need to hear it from your own lips, in your own words.'

'What?'

'So we can all get off on the right foot.'

'The right foot of what?'

'We need to establish a friendly relationship, Mr Fleck.'

'Why?'

'Well, for instance, last night we fed you dinner. And, also for instance, about an hour from now you're going to ask us to feed you breakfast. Because what other choice do you have? All we ask in return is that you give as well as take.'

'Give what?'

'An honest account of your own part in your predicament.'

37

'What for?'

'It would be like putting some chips on the table, I suppose. At the start of the game. It would be like an emotional stake in our friendly relationship. We opened ourselves to you, when we had you at our table, and now we ask that you return the favour.'

'We don't want breakfast.'

'Not even coffee?'

'We can get water from the bathroom tap. If that's OK with you.'

'You'll ask us to feed you lunch. Pride can make you skip one meal, but not two.'

'Just give us a ride to town. We'll send a tow truck for the car.'

'A ride to town is not on offer.'

'Then call a mechanic for us.'

'We will,' Mark said. 'Immediately after you've spoken.'

'You want a public confession?'

'Do you have something to confess?'

'I guess I could have done better,' Shorty said. 'Some guy told me Japanese motors could take it. Like you could skip a year. Then I guess some years I couldn't remember what year I was up to. So overall I guess some years got missed, that shouldn't have.'

'Only some?'

'Maybe all of them. Like you said, I didn't have the time.'

'Good policy in the short term.'

'It was easiest.'

'But not in the long term.'

'I guess not,' Shorty said.

'A mistake, in fact.'

'I guess so.'

'That's the part we want you to say out loud, Mr Fleck. We want to hear you say you made a dumb mistake that is causing all kinds of people all kinds of trouble. And we want to hear you say you're sorry about that, to Patty especially, who we think is being touchingly loyal. You've got a good one there, Mr Fleck.'

'I guess so.'

'We need to hear you say it out loud.'

'About Patty?'

'About the mistake.'

No response.

Mark said, 'A moment ago you asked us to assume responsibility. But it's you that must do that. We didn't neglect your car. We didn't treat a fine machine like a piece of shit, and then set out on a long important journey without so much as kicking the tyres. It was you that did all that, Mr Fleck. Not us. All we're trying to do is make that clear.'

No response.

The sun was bright. It was hot on the top of Patty's head.

She said, 'Just say it, Shorty. It won't be the end of the world.'

Shorty said, 'OK, I made a dumb mistake that is causing all kinds of people all kinds of trouble. I apologize to all concerned.'

'Thank you,' Mark said. 'Now we'll go call a mechanic.'

Reacher walked back the way he had come, past the stores with the bags, and the shoes, and the wares, past the place he had picked out for lunch, past the place he had spent the night, back to the records department, inside the city offices. The waist-high counter was once again unattended. He rang the bell for service. There was a short delay, and then Elizabeth Castle came in.

'Oh,' she said. 'Hello again.'

'Hello,' he said.

'Any luck?'

'Not so far,' he said. 'They weren't in either census.'

'You sure you got the right town? Or state, even. There could be a Laconia somewhere else. New Mexico, or New York or New Jersey. There are a lot of N-states.'

'Eight,' Reacher said. 'Between New and North and Nevada and Nebraska.'

'Then it might not have been N-H you saw. It might have been N-something else. Old-time handwriting can be weird.'

'I saw it typed,' Reacher said. 'Mostly by Marine Corps clerks. Who usually get things right. And I heard him say it, a dozen times. My mother would be ribbing him about something, most likely a missing romantic gesture, and he would say, well hell, I'm just a plain New Hampshire Yankee.'

Elizabeth Castle said, 'Huh.'

Then she said, 'I guess every census misses people. All kinds of geeky reasons. They're forever trying to improve the methodology. There's a guy here you should talk to. He's a census enthusiast.'

'Is that a new thing?'

'Probably not,' she said, a little sharply. 'I'm sure it's a serious pursuit with a long and honourable history.'

'I'm sorry.'

'For what?'

'I think I offended you.'

'How could you? I'm not a census enthusiast.'

'If the census enthusiast was your boyfriend, for instance.'

'He isn't,' she said, with an indignant gasp, as if the idea was absurd.

'What's his name?'

'Carter,' she said.

'Where will I find him?'

'What time is it?' she said, suddenly looking around for her phone, which wasn't there. Reacher had noticed many fewer people wearing watches. Phones did everything.

'Nearly eleven o'clock,' he said. 'Four minutes to, plus a few seconds.'

'Seriously?'

'Why not? I took it as a serious question.'

'Plus a few seconds?'

'You think that's too exact?'

'Most people would say five to. Or about eleven o'clock.'

'Which I would have, if you had asked me what time it was approximately. But you didn't. You asked me what time it was, period. Three minutes and change, now.'

'You're not looking at your watch.'

'I don't wear one,' he said. 'Like you.'

'Then how do you know what time it is?'

'I don't know.'

'For real?'

'Now it's two minutes and maybe fifty seconds before eleven in the morning.'

'Wait,' she said. She went back out through the door in the rear wall. A long moment later she came back in with her phone. She laid it on the counter. The screen was dark.

She said, 'What time is it now?'

'Wait,' he said.

Then he said, 'Three, two, one, it's the top of the hour. Eleven o'clock exactly.'

She pressed the button on her phone.

The screen lit up.

It showed 10:59.

'Close,' she said.

It changed to 11:00.

'How do you do that?' she said.

'I don't know,' he said again. 'Where will I find your friend Carter, the census enthusiast?'

'I didn't say he was my friend.'

'Co-worker?'

'Different department entirely. In the back office. Not part of the customer-facing ecology, as they say.'

'Then how do I get to see him?'

'That's why I asked the time. He takes a coffee break at a quarter past eleven. Every day, regular as clockwork.'

'He sounds like a man of sound character.'

'He takes thirty minutes exactly, in the place across the light. In the garden, if the sun is shining. Which it might or might not be. We can't tell in here.'

'What's Carter's first name?' Reacher asked, thinking about baristas calling out to customers. He figured the place could be crowded with office workers taking thirty-minute breaks, all of them looking pretty much the same.

'Carter is his first name,' Elizabeth Castle said.

'What's his last name?'

'Carrington,' she said. 'Check back and tell me how it went. Don't give up. Family is important. There will be other ways to find out.'

SIX

Patty and Shorty were alone in room ten, sitting together on the unmade bed. Mark had invited them to breakfast after all. He had turned to go and then turned back with a forgiving grin on his face, all-friends-together, let's-not-be-stupid. Patty had wanted to say yes. Shorty said no. They had gone inside and drunk toothbrush glasses of tepid water, standing at the bathroom sink.

Patty said, 'You'll only feel worse when you have to ask him to give us lunch. You should have gotten it over with right away. Now it's going to build up in your mind.'

Shorty said, 'You got to admit that was weird.'

'What was?'

'All of what just happened.'

'Which was what?'

'You saw it. You were there.'

'Tell me in your own words.'

'From my own lips? You sound like him. You saw what happened. He started up with some weird vendetta against me.'

43

'What I saw was Peter voluntarily donating his time to help us out. He got to work right away. I wasn't even awake yet. Then what I saw was you kicking him in the teeth by saying he had made it worse.'

'I agree yesterday the car was not running great, but now it's not running at all. What else can have happened? Obviously he did something.'

'There was plenty wrong with your car already. Maybe starting it up last night was the straw that broke the camel's back.'

'It was weird, what he made me do.'

'He made you tell the truth, Shorty. We would have been in New York City by now. The deal would have been done. Now we could be driving to one of those lots where they take anything in trade. We could have gotten something better. We could have gone the rest of the way in style.'

'I'm sorry,' Shorty said. 'I mean it.'

'Maybe the mechanic can fix it.'

'Maybe we should just dump it and walk away. Before we have to pay another fifty bucks for the room.'

'What do you mean, walk away?'

'On our own two feet. We could walk back to the road and thumb a ride. You said there was some place twenty miles ahead. They might have a bus.'

'The track through the trees was more than two miles long. You'd be carrying the suitcase. It's bigger than you are. We can't leave it here. And then all we got anyway is a back road. With no traffic. We planned it that way, remember? We could wait there all day for a ride. Especially with a big suitcase. That kind of thing puts people off. They don't stop. Maybe their trunk is already full.'

'OK, maybe the mechanic will fix it. Or at least he could give us a ride to town. In his truck. With the big suitcase. We could figure something out from there.'

'Another fifty bucks will surely make a dent.'

'It's worse than that,' Shorty said. 'Fifty bucks is a drop in the ocean. We could stay here all week, compared to what the mechanic will cost. Those guys get a call-out charge, can you believe that? Which is basically like getting paid for still being alive. It's not like that when you grow potatoes, let me tell you. Which mechanics eat, by the way. They love potatoes. French fries, hash browns, twice baked with cheese and bacon. What if I asked them to pay me just to think about growing them a potato?'

Patty got up suddenly, bouncing the bed, and she said, 'I'm going out for some air.'

She crossed to the door and turned the handle and pulled. Nothing happened. It was jammed again. She checked the lock.

She said, 'This is what happened in the night.'

Shorty got off the bed and stepped over.

He turned the handle.

The door opened.

He said, 'Maybe you're turning the handle wrong.'

She said, 'How many ways are there to turn a handle?'

He closed the door and stood back.

She stepped up and tried again. She used the same grip as before, the same turn, the same pull.

The door swung open.

She said, 'Weird.'

The sun was shining on downtown Laconia, a little low in the sky, like the first days of fall, but it was still as warm as summer. Reacher got to the coffee shop across the light at ten past eleven, five minutes ahead of schedule, and he got a seat at a small iron table in the corner of the garden, where he could see the sidewalk coming down from the city office door. He wasn't sure what kind of a person he expected Carter Carrington to be. Although there were a number of clues. One, Elizabeth Castle found it absurd to imagine the guy as her boyfriend. Two, she had taken pains to

45

point out he wasn't even her regular friend. Three, the guy was banished to a back office. Four, he was kept away from customers. Five, he was enthusiastic about census methodology.

The signs were not good.

The garden had a side gate also, for the parking lot. People came and went. Reacher ordered regular black coffee, in a go-cup, not because he was planning on rushing away, but because he didn't like the look of the table service alternatives, which were about the size and weight of chamber pots. Poor cups for coffee, in his opinion, but other people must have been satisfied, because the garden was filling up. Pretty soon there were only three spare seats. One of which was opposite Reacher, inevitably. A fact of his life. People didn't find him approachable.

First in from the direction of the city office was a woman about forty, bustling, competent, probably in charge of some big department. She said hey and hi to a couple of customers, routine co-worker courtesies, and she dumped her bag on an empty seat, not the one opposite Reacher, and then she went in to the counter to get whatever it was she wanted. Reacher watched the sidewalk. In the distance he saw a guy come out of the city office, and start walking down the block. Even far away it was clear he was tall and well dressed. His suit was fine, and his shirt was white, and his tie was neat. He had fair hair, short, but a little unruly. Like he tried his best with it. He was tan and he looked fit and strong and full of vigour and energy. He had presence. Against the old brick he looked like a movie star on a film set.

Except he walked with a limp. Very slight, left leg.

The woman who had been to the counter came back with a cup and a plate, and she sat where she had saved her place, which left just two empty spaces, one of which was immediately taken by another woman, probably another department head, because she said hey and hi to a whole different bunch of people. Which left the only spare chair in the garden directly across from Reacher.

46

Then the movie star guy stepped in. Up close and personal he was everything Reacher had seen from a distance, and also good-looking, in a rugged kind of way. Like a cowboy who went to college. Tall, rangy, capable. Maybe thirty-five years old. Reacher made a small bet with himself the guy was ex-military. Everything said so. In a second he constructed a whole imaginary bio for the guy, from ROTC at a western university to a wound in Iraq or Afghanistan, and a spell at Walter Reed, and then separation and a new job in New Hampshire, maybe an executive position, maybe something that required him to go argue with the city. He was holding a go-cup of coffee and a paper bag slightly translucent with butter. He scanned the garden and located the only empty seat. He set out towards it.

Both department heads called out, 'Hey, Carter.'

The guy said hey back, with a smile that probably killed them dead, and then he continued on his way. He sat down across from Reacher.

Who said, 'Is your name Carter?'

The guy said, 'Yes, it is.'

'Carter Carrington?'

'Pleased to meet you. And you are?'

He sounded more curious than annoyed. He spoke like an educated man.

Reacher said, 'A woman named Elizabeth Castle suggested I speak to you. From the city records department. My name is Jack Reacher. I have a question about an old-time census.'

'Is it a legal issue?'

'It's a personal thing.'

'You sure?'

'The only issue is whether I get on the bus today or tomorrow.'

'I'm the town attorney,' Carrington said. 'I'm also a census geek. For ethical reasons I need to be absolutely certain which one you think you're talking to.'

47

'The geek,' Reacher said. 'All I want is background information.'

'How long ago?'

Reacher told him, first the year his father was two, and then the year he was twelve.

Carrington said, 'What's the question?'

So Reacher told him the story, the family paperwork, cubicle two's computer screen, the conspicuous absence of Reachers.

'Interesting,' Carrington said.

'In what way?'

Carrington paused a beat.

He said, 'Were you a Marine too?'

'Army,' Reacher said.

'That's unusual. Isn't it? For the son of a Marine to join the army, I mean.'

'It wasn't unusual in our family. My brother did it too.'

'It's a three-part answer,' Carrington said. 'The first part is all kinds of random mistakes were made. But twice in a row makes that statistically unlikely. What were the odds? So we move on. And neither part two or part three of the answer reflects all that well on a theoretical person's theoretical ancestors. So you need to accept I'm talking theoretically. In general, as in most of the people most of the time, the vast majority, nothing personal, lots of exceptions, all that kind of good stuff, OK? So don't get offended.'

'OK,' Reacher said. 'I won't.'

'Focus on the count when your dad was twelve. Ignore the earlier one. The later one is better. By then we'd had seven years of the Depression and the New Deal. Counting was really important. Because more people equalled more federal dollars. You can be sure that state and city governments tried like crazy not to miss anyone that year. But they did, even so. The second part of the answer is that the highest miss percentages were among renters, occupants of multi-family dwellings or overcrowded quarters, the unemployed, those of low education and income levels,

48

and those receiving public assistance. Folks on the margins, in other words.'

'You find people don't like to hear that about their grand-parents?'

'They like it better than part three of the answer.'

'Which is?'

'Their grandparents were hiding from the law.'

'Interesting,' Reacher said.

'It happened,' Carrington said. 'Obviously no one with a federal warrant would fill out a census form. Other folks thought laying low might help them in the future.'

Reacher said nothing.

Carrington said, 'What did you do in the army?'

'Military police,' Reacher said. 'You?'

'What makes you think I was in the army?'

'Your age, your appearance, your manner and bearing, your air of decisive competence, and your limp.'

'You noticed.'

'I was trained to. I was a cop. My guess is you have an artificial lower leg. Barely detectable, therefore a really good one. And the army has the best, these days.'

'I never served,' Carrington said. 'I wasn't able to.'

'Why not?'

'I was born with a rare condition. It has a long and complicated name. It meant I had no shin bone. Everything else was there.'

'So you've had a lifetime of practice.'

'I'm not looking for sympathy.'

'You're not getting any. But even so, you're doing OK. Your walk is close to perfect.'

'Thank you,' Carrington said. 'Tell me about being a cop.'

'It was a good job, while it lasted.'

'You saw the effect of crime on families.'

'Sometimes.'

'Your dad joined the Marines at seventeen,' Carrington said. 'Got to be a reason.'

Patty Sundstrom and Shorty Fleck sat outside their room, in the plastic lawn chairs under the window. They watched the mouth of the track through the trees and waited for the mechanic to come. He didn't. Shorty got up and tried the Honda one more time. Sometimes leaving a thing switched off for a spell fixed it. He had a TV set like that. About one time in three it came on with no sound. You had to shut it down and try again.

He turned the key. Nothing happened. On, off, on, off, silently, no difference at all. He went back to his lawn chair. Patty got up and took all their maps from the glove box. She carried them back to her own chair and spread them out on her knee. She found their current location, at the end of the inch-long spider-web vein, in the middle of the pale green shape. The forested area. Which seemed to average about five miles across, and maybe seven from top to bottom. The tip of the spider-web vein was off-centre in the space, two miles from the eastern limit but three from the western. It was about equal north and south. The green shape had a faint line around it, as if it was all one property. Maybe the motel owned the forest. There was nothing much beyond it, except the two-lane road they had turned off, which wandered east and south, to the town with its name printed semi-bold. Laconia, New Hampshire. Nearer thirty miles away than twenty. Her guess the day before had been optimistic.

She said, 'Maybe the best bet will be what you said. We should forget the car and get a ride in the tow truck. Laconia is near I-93. We could hitch a ride to the cloverleaf. Or take a taxi, even. For less money than another night here, probably. If we can get to Nashua or Manchester we can get to Boston, and then we can get the cheap bus to New York.'

'I'm sorry about the car,' Shorty said. 'I mean it.'

'No use crying over spilt milk.'

'Maybe the mechanic can fix it. It might be easy. I don't get how it can be so dead. Maybe there's a loose connection, simple as that. I had a radio once, wouldn't light up at all. I was banging and banging on it, and then I saw the plug had fallen out of the wall. It felt the same kind of dead.'

They heard footsteps in the dirt. Steven stepped around the corner and walked towards them. He passed room twelve, and eleven, and came to a stop.

'Come to lunch,' he said. 'Don't take what Mark said to heart. He's upset, that's all. He really wants to help you, and he can't. He thought Peter would fix it in two minutes. He got frustrated. He likes things to turn out right for everybody.'

Shorty said, 'When is the mechanic coming?'

'I'm afraid we haven't called him yet,' Steven said. 'The phone has been down all morning.'

SEVEN

Reacher left Carrington in the garden, and walked back to the city office. He pressed the record department's bell, and a minute later Elizabeth Castle came in through the door.

He said, 'You told me to check back.'

She said, 'Did you find Carter?'

'He seems like a nice guy. I don't see why you wouldn't want to date him.'

'Excuse me?'

'When I wondered if he was your boyfriend, and you were incredulous.'

'That he would want to date me. He's Laconia's most eligible bachelor. He could have anyone he wants. I'm sure he has no idea who I am. What did he tell you?'

'That my grandparents were either poor or thieves, or poor thieves.'

'I'm sure they weren't.'

Reacher said nothing.

She said, 'Although I know both those things were frequent reasons.'

'Either one is a possibility,' he said. 'We don't need to walk on eggs.'

'Probably they didn't register to vote, either. Would they have had driver's licences?'

'Not if they were poor. Not if they were thieves, either. Not in their real names, anyway.'

'Your dad must have had a birth certificate. He must be on paper somewhere.'

The customer door from the corridor opened, and Carter Carrington stepped inside, with his suit and his smile and his unruly hair. He saw Reacher and said, 'Hello again,' not surprised at all, as if he had expected no one else. Then he turned towards the counter and stuck out his hand and said, 'You must be Ms Castle.'

'Elizabeth,' she said.

'Carter Carrington. Really pleased to meet you. Thanks for sending this gentleman my way. He has an interesting situation.'

'Because his dad is missing from two consecutive counts.'

'Exactly.'

'Which feels deliberate.'

'As long as we're sure we're looking at the right town.'

'We are,' Reacher said. 'I saw it written down a dozen times. Laconia, New Hampshire.'

'Interesting,' Carrington said. Then he looked Elizabeth Castle in the eye and said, 'We should have lunch sometime. I like the way you saw the thing with the two counts. I'd like to discuss it more.'

She didn't answer.

'Anyway, keep me in the loop,' he said.

She said, 'We figure he must have had a birth certificate.'

'Almost certainly,' he said. 'What was his date of birth?'

Reacher paused a beat.

He said, 'This is going to sound weird. In this context, I mean.'

'Why?'

'Sometimes he wasn't sure.'

'What does that mean?'

'Sometimes he said June, and sometimes he said July.'

'Was there an explanation for that?'

'He said he couldn't remember because birthdays weren't important to him. He didn't see why he should be congratulated for getting another year closer to death.'

'That's bleak.'

'He was a Marine.'

'What did the paperwork say?'

'July.'

Carrington said nothing.

Reacher said, 'What?'

'Nothing.'

'I already agreed with Ms Castle we don't need to walk on eggs.'

'A child uncertain of its birth date is a classic symptom of dysfunction within a family.'

'Theoretically,' Reacher said.

'Anyway, birth records are in date order. Could take some time, if you're not sure. Better to find another avenue.'

'Such as?'

'The police blotter, maybe. Not to be insensitive. Purely as a percentage play. If nothing else it would be nice to eliminate the possibility. I don't want them to be hiding from the law, any more than you do. I want a more interesting reason than that. And it won't take long to find out. As of now our police department is computerized back about a thousand years. They spent a fortune. Homeland Security money, not ours, but still. They also built a statue of the first chief.'

'Who should I go see?'

'I'll call ahead. Someone will meet you at the desk.'

'How cooperative will they be?'

'I'm the guy who decides whether the city goes to bat for them. When they do something wrong, I mean. So they'll be plenty cooperative. But wait until after lunch. You'll get more time that way.'

Patty Sundstrom and Shorty Fleck went to lunch over at the big house. It was an awkward meal. Shorty was by turns stiff and sheepish. Peter was silent. Either offended or disappointed, Patty couldn't tell. Robert and Steven didn't say much of anything. Only Mark really talked. He was bright and blithe and chatty. Very friendly. As if the events of the morning had never occurred. He seemed determined to find solutions to their problems. He apologized to them over and over about the phone. He made them listen to the dead handset, as if to share his burden. He said he was concerned people would be worried about them, either back home, or at their destination. Were they missing appointments? Were there people they needed to call?

Patty said, 'No one knows we're gone.'

'Really?'

'They would have tried to talk us out of it.'

'Out of what?'

'It's boring up there. Shorty and I want something different.'

'Where do you plan to go?'

'Florida,' she said. 'We want to start our own business there.'

'What kind of business?'

'Something on the ocean. Watersports, maybe. Like windsurfer rentals.'

'You would need capital,' Mark said. 'To buy the windsurfers.'

Patty looked away, and thought about the suitcase.

Shorty asked, 'How long will the phone be out?'

Mark asked back, 'What am I, clairvoyant?'

'I mean, usually. On average.'

'They usually fix it in half a day. And the mechanic is a good friend. We'll ask him to put us first in line. You could be back on the road before dinnertime.'

'What if it takes longer than half a day?'

'Then it just does, I guess. I can't control it.'

'Honestly, the best thing would be just give us a ride to town. Best for us, and best for you. We'd be out of your hair.'

'But your car would still be here.'

'We would send a tow truck.'

'Would you?'

'From the first place we saw.'

'Could we trust you?'

'I promise I would take care of it.'

'OK, but you have to admit, you haven't proved a hundred per cent reliable about taking care of things so far.'

'I promise we would send a truck.'

'But suppose you didn't? We're running a business here. We would be stuck with getting rid of your car. Which might be difficult, because strictly speaking it isn't ours to get rid of in the first place. There wouldn't be much we could do without a title. We couldn't donate it. We couldn't even sell it for scrap. No doubt pursuing alternatives would cost us time and money. But needs must. We couldn't have it here for ever, dirtying up the place. Nothing personal. A business like ours is all about image and kerb appeal. It needs to entice, not repel. A rusty old wreck of a car front and centre would send the wrong message. No offence. I'm sure you understand.'

'You could come with us to the tow company,' Shorty said. 'You could drive us there first. You could watch us make the arrangements. Like a witness.'

Mark nodded, eyes down, now a little sheepish himself.

'Good answer,' he said. 'The truth is we're a little embarrassed ourselves, at the moment, when it comes to rides to town. The investment in this place was enormous. Three of us sold our cars. We kept Peter's, to share, because as it happened it was the oldest and therefore the least valuable. It wouldn't start this morning. Just like yours. Maybe it's something in the air. But in practical terms, as of right now, I'm afraid we're all stuck here together.'

Reacher ate at the place he had picked out earlier, which served upscale but recognizable dishes in a pleasant room with table-cloths. He had a burger piled high with all kinds of extras, and a slice of apricot pie, with black coffee throughout. Then he set out for the police station. He found it right where Carrington said it would be. The public lobby was tall and tiled and formal. There was a civilian desk worker behind a mahogany reception counter. Reacher gave her his name and told her Carter Carrington had promised he would call ahead and arrange for someone to speak with him. The woman was on the phone even before he got through the first part of Carrington's name. Clearly she had been warned he was coming.

She asked him to take a seat, but he stood instead, and waited. Not long, as it turned out. Two detectives pushed through a pair of double doors. A man and a woman. Both looked like solid profes-sionals. At first Reacher assumed they weren't for him. He was expecting a file clerk. But they walked straight towards him, and when they arrived the man said, 'Mr Reacher? I'm Jim Shaw, chief of detectives. I'm very pleased to meet you.'

The chief of detectives. Very pleased. They'll be plenty coopera-tive, Carrington had said. He wasn't kidding. Shaw was a heavy guy in his fifties, maybe five-ten, with a lined Irish face and a shock of red hair. Anyone within a hundred miles of Boston would have made him as a cop. He was like a picture in a book.

'I'm very pleased to meet you too,' Reacher said.

'I'm Detective Brenda Amos,' the woman said. 'Happy to help. Anything you need.'

Her accent was from the south. A drawl, but no longer honeyed. It was roughed up by exposure. She was ten years younger than Shaw, maybe five-six, and slender. She had blonde hair and cheekbones and sleepy green eyes that said, don't mess with me.

'Ma'am, thank you,' he said. 'But really, this is no kind of a big deal. I don't know exactly what Mr Carrington told you, but all I need is some ancient history. Which probably isn't there anyway. From eighty years ago. It's not even a cold case.'

Shaw said, 'Mr Carrington mentioned you were an MP.'

'Long ago.'

'That buys you ten minutes with a computer. That's all it's going to take.'

They led him back through thigh-high mahogany gates, to an open area full of plain-clothed people sitting face to face at paired desks. The desks were loaded with phones and flat screens and keyboards and wire baskets of paper. Like any office anywhere, except for a weary air of grime and burden, that made it unmistakably a cop shop. They turned a corner, into a corridor with offices either side. They stopped at the third on the left. It was Amos's. She ushered Reacher in, and Shaw said goodbye and walked on, as if all appropriate courtesies had been observed, and his job was therefore done. Amos followed Reacher inside and closed the door. The outer structure of the office was old and traditional, but everything in it was sleek and new. Desk, chairs, cabinets, computer.

Amos said, 'How can I help you?'

He said, 'I'm looking for the surname Reacher, in old police reports from the 1920s and 30s and 40s.'

'Relatives of yours?'

'My grandparents and my father. Carrington thinks they dodged the census because they had federal warrants.'

'This is a municipal department. We don't have access to federal records.'

'They might have started small. Most people do.'

Amos pulled the keyboard close and started tapping away. She asked, 'Were there any alternative spellings?'

He said, 'I don't think so.'

'First names?'

'James, Elizabeth, and Stan.'

'Jim, Jimmy, Jamie, Liz, Lizzie, Beth?'

'I don't know what they called each other. I never met them.'

'Was Stan short for Stanley?'

'I never saw that. It was always just Stan.'

'Any known aliases?'

'Not known to me.'

She typed some more, and clicked, and waited.

She didn't speak.

He said, 'I'm guessing you were an MP too.'

'What gave me away?'

'First your accent. It's the sound of the U.S. Army. Mostly southern, but a little mixed up. Plus most civilian cops ask about what we did and how we did it. Because they're professionally curious. But you aren't. Most likely because you already know.'

'Guilty as charged.'

'How long have you been out?'

'Six years,' she said. 'You?'

'Longer than that.'

'What unit?'

'The 110th, mostly.'

'Nice,' she said. 'Who was the CO when you were there?'

'I was,' he said.

'And now you're retired and into genealogy.'

'I saw a road sign,' he said. 'That's all. I'm beginning to wish I hadn't.'

She looked back at the screen.

'We have a hit,' she said. 'From seventy-five years ago.'

EIGHT

Brenda Amos clicked twice and typed in a passcode. Then she clicked again and leaned forward and read out loud. She said, 'Late one September evening in 1943 a youth was found unconscious on the sidewalk of a downtown Laconia street. He had been beaten up. He was identified as a local twenty-year-old, already known to the police department as a loudmouth and a bully, but untouchable, because he was the son of the local rich guy. Therefore I guess there would have been much private celebration inside the department, but obviously for the sake of appearances they had to open an investigation. They had to go through the motions. It says here they went house to house the next day, not expecting to get much. But actually they got a lot. They got an old lady who had seen the whole thing through binoculars. The victim started an altercation with two other youths, clearly expecting to win, but the way it turned out he got his butt kicked instead.'

Reacher said, 'Why was the old lady using binoculars late in the evening?'

'It says here she was a birdwatcher. She was interested in night-time migration and continuous flight. She said she could make out the shapes against the sky.'

Reacher said nothing.

Amos said, 'She identified one of the two other youths as a fellow member of a local birdwatching club.'

Reacher said, 'My dad was a birdwatcher.'

Amos nodded. 'The old lady identified him as a local youth personally known to her, name of Stan Reacher, then just sixteen years old.'

'Was she sure? I think he was only fifteen in September of 1943.'

'She seems to be sure about the name. I guess she could have been wrong about the age. She was watching from an apartment window above a grocery store, looking directly down the street towards a good-sized patch of night sky in the east. She saw Stan Reacher with an unidentified friend about the same age. They were walking towards her, away from the centre of downtown. They passed through a pool of light from a street lamp, which allowed her to be confident in her identification. Then walking towards them in the other direction she saw the twenty-year-old. He also passed through a pool of light. The three youths all met face to face in the gloom between two lamps, which was unfortunate, but there was enough spill and scatter for her to see what was going on. She said it was like watching shadow puppets. It made their physical gestures more emphatic. The two smaller boys were still facing her. The bigger boy had his back to her. He seemed to be demanding something. Then threatening. One of the smaller boys ran away, possibly timid or scared. The other smaller boy stayed where he was, and then suddenly he punched the bigger boy in the face.'

Reacher nodded. Personally he called it getting your retaliation in first. Surprise was always a good thing. A wise man never counted all the way to three.

Amos said, 'The old lady testified the smaller kid kept on hitting the bigger kid until the bigger kid fell down, whereupon the smaller kid kicked him repeatedly in the head and the ribs, and then the bigger kid struggled up and tried to run, but the smaller kid caught him and tripped him up, right in the next pool of light, which was apparently quite bright, which meant the old lady had no trouble seeing the smaller kid kicking the bigger kid a whole lot more. Then he quit just as suddenly as he had started, and he collected his timid pal, and they walked away together like nothing had happened. The old lady made contemporaneous notes on a piece of paper, plus a diagram, all of which she gave to the visiting officers the following day.'

'Good witness,' Reacher said. 'I bet the DA loved her. What happened next?'

Amos scrolled and read.

'Nothing happened next,' she said. 'The case went nowhere.'

'Why not?'

'Limited manpower. The draft for World War Two had started a couple of years before. The police department was operating with a skeleton staff.'

'Why hadn't the twenty-year-old been drafted?'

'Rich daddy.'

'I don't get it,' Reacher said. 'How much manpower would they need? They had an eyewitness. Arresting a fifteen-year-old boy isn't difficult. They wouldn't need a SWAT team.'

'They had no ID on the assailant, and no manpower to go dig one up.'

'You said the old lady knew him from the birdwatching club.'

'The unknown friend was the fighter. Stan Reacher was the one who ran away.'

They gave Patty and Shorty a cup of coffee, and they sent them on their way, back to room ten. Mark watched them go, until they

63

were halfway to the barn, until they looked like people who weren't coming back. Whereupon he turned around and said, 'OK, plug the phone back in.'

Steven did so, and Mark said, 'Now show me the problem with the door.'

'The problem is not with the door,' Robert said. 'It's with our reaction time.'

They crossed an inner hallway and opened a back parlour door. The room beyond it was small by comparison, but still a decent size. It was painted flat black. The window was boarded over. All four walls were covered with flat-screen televisions. There was a swivel chair in the centre of the room, boxed in by four low benches pushed together, loaded with keyboards and joysticks. Like a command centre. Patty and Shorty were on the screens, live pictures, past the barn now, walking away from one bunch of hidden cameras, towards another, some focused tight and head-on, others set wider, with the strolling couple tiny in the distance.

Robert stepped over a bench and sat down in the chair. He clicked a mouse and the screens changed to a dim night-vision shot.

He said, 'This is a recording from three o'clock this morning.'

The picture was hyped up and misty because of the night-vision enhancements, but it was clearly of room ten's queen-sized bed, which clearly had two sleeping people in it. It was the camera in the smoke detector, wide enough to be called a fisheye.

'Except she wasn't asleep,' Robert said. 'Afterwards I figured she slept about four hours, and then she woke up. But she didn't move at all. Not a muscle. She gave absolutely no sign. By that point I was kind of lying back, frankly, taking it easy, because the last four hours had been pretty boring. Plus at that point as far as I knew she was still asleep. But actually she was lying there thinking. About something that must have made her mad. Because, watch.'

64

On the screens the scene stayed the same, and then it changed, fast, with no warning at all, when Patty suddenly flipped the covers aside and slid out of bed, controlled, neat, decisive, exasperated.

Robert said, 'By the time I sat up and got my finger near the unlock button, she had already tried the door once. I guess she wanted air. I had to make a decision. I decided to leave it locked, because it felt more consistent. I left it locked until Peter went up there to fix the car. I unlocked it then because I figured one of them would want to come out to talk to him.'

'OK,' Mark said.

Robert clicked the mouse again and the screens changed to a daylight shot from a different angle. Patty and Shorty were sitting side by side on room ten's unmade bed.

'This took place while we were eating breakfast,' Robert said.

'I was on duty,' Steven said. 'Watch what happens.'

Robert pressed play. There was audio. Shorty was deflecting attention from his own shortcomings by ranting on about mechanics getting call-out charges. He was saying, 'Which is basically like getting paid for still being alive. It's not like that when you grow potatoes, let me tell you.'

Robert paused the recording.

Steven asked, 'Now what happens next?'

Mark said, 'I sincerely hope Patty points out the two trades are massively dissimilar in the economic sense.'

Peter said, 'I sincerely hope Patty punches him in the face and tells him to shut up.'

'Neither one,' Steven said. 'She gets exasperated again.'

Robert pressed play again. Patty got up suddenly, bouncing the bed, and she said, 'I'm going out for some air.'

Steven said, 'She's really abrupt and jumpy. Right there she was zero to sixty in one-point-one seconds. I counted the video frames. I couldn't get to the button in time. Then I saw Shorty was going to give it a go, so I unlocked it late. I thought if he got it open, where she couldn't, she would somehow blame herself more than the door.'

'Is there a fix for this?' Mark asked.

'Forewarned is forearmed. I guess we need to concentrate harder.'

'I guess we'll have to. We don't want to spook them too soon.'

'How long before we make the final decision?'

Mark paused a long moment.

Then he said, 'Make the final decision now, if you like.'

'Really?'

'Why wait? I think we've seen enough. They're as good as we could ever hope to get. They're from nowhere and no one knows they're gone. I think we're ready.'

'I vote yes,' Steven said.

'Me too,' Robert said.

'Me three,' Peter said. 'They're perfect.'

Robert clicked back to the live feed and they saw Patty and Shorty in their lawn chairs, on the boardwalk under their window, catching the wan rays of the afternoon sun.

'Unanimous,' Mark said. 'All for one and one for all. Send the e-mail.'

The screens changed again, to a webmail page peppered with translations in foreign alphabets. Robert typed four words.

'OK?' he asked.

'Send it.'

He did.

The message said: Room Ten Is Occupied.

NINE

Reacher said, 'I still don't get it. The birdwatcher lady supplied the ID on Stan, and Stan could have been leaned upon to ID his mysterious friend, surely. Just one extra step. One extra visit to his house. Five minutes at most. That's no kind of a manpower problem. One guy could have done it on the way to the doughnut shop.'

Amos said, 'Stan Reacher was listed as resident outside the jurisdiction. That's a whole lot of paperwork right there. All they had was typewriters back then. Plus they must have figured he was likely to clam up anyway, no matter how hard they leaned on him, which couldn't have been very hard in any case, because they would have been on foreign turf, probably with a local guy sitting in, and maybe lawyers or parents too. Plus they must have figured the mystery friend would be in the wind already and out of the state by then. Plus they weren't shedding any tears for the victim anyway. No doubt the easy decision was to let it all go.'

'Stan Reacher was resident outside of what jurisdiction?'

'Laconia PD.'

'The story was he was born and grew up here.'

'Maybe he was born here, in the hospital, but then maybe he grew up out of town, on a farm or something.'

'I never got that impression.'

'In a nearby village, then. Close enough to be in the same bird-watching club as a woman living above a downtown grocery store. He would put Laconia as his birthplace, because that's where the hospital was, and he would probably say he grew up in Laconia, too. Like shorthand for the general area as a whole. Like people say Chicago, even though a lot of the suburbs aren't technically in Chicago at all. Same thing with Boston.'

'The Laconia metro area,' Reacher said.

'Things were more dispersed back then. There were little mills and factories all over. Couple dozen workers in four-flats. Maybe a one-room schoolhouse. Maybe a church. All considered Laconia, no matter what the postal service had to say about it.'

'Try Reacher on its own,' he said. 'No first names. Maybe I have cousins in the area. I could get an address.'

Amos pulled her keyboard close again and typed, seven letters, and clicked. Reacher saw the screen change, reflected in her eyes.

'Just one more hit,' she said. 'More than seventy-some years after the first. You must be a relatively law-abiding family.' She clicked again, and read out loud, 'About a year and a half ago a patrol car responded to the county offices because a customer was causing a disturbance. Yelling, shouting, behaving in a threatening manner. The uniforms calmed him down and he apologized and it went no further. He gave his name as Mark Reacher. Resident outside the jurisdiction.'

'Age?'

'Then twenty-six.'

'He could be my distant nephew, many times removed. What was he upset about?'

'He claimed a building permit was slow coming through. He claimed he was renovating a motel somewhere out of town.'

After thirty minutes in the sun Patty went inside to use the bathroom. On her way back she stopped at the vanity opposite the end of the bed. She looked in the mirror and blew her nose. She balled up the tissue and lobbed it towards the trash can. She missed. She bent down to correct her error. She was Canadian.

She saw a used cotton bud in the dent where the carpet met the wall. Not hers. She didn't use them. It was deep in the shadows, at the back of the knee hole under the vanity, beyond the legs of the stool. Imperfect housekeeping, no question, but understandable. Maybe even inevitable. Maybe it had been pressed deeper into its hiding place by the wheels of the vacuum cleaner itself.

Except.

She called out, 'Shorty, come take a look at this.'

Shorty got up out of his chair and stepped in the room.

He left the door wide open.

Patty pointed.

Shorty said, 'It's for cleaning your ears. Or drying them. Maybe both. They have two ends. I've seen them in the drugstore.'

'Why is it there?'

'Someone missed the trash can. Maybe it bounced off the rim, and rolled out of sight. Happens all the time. The maids don't care.'

She said, 'Go back to your lawn chair, Shorty.'

He did.

A long minute later she joined him.

He said, 'What did I do?'

She said, 'It's what you didn't do.'

'What didn't I do?'

'You didn't think,' she said. 'Mark told us this is the first room they've refurbished so far. He said in fact they only just finished it.

69

He asked us to do them the honour of being its very first guests. So why does it have a used cotton bud in it?'

Shorty nodded. Slow but sure. He said, 'The story about their car was weird, too. Peter must be some kind of saboteur. When are they going to catch on?'

'Why would they lie about the room?'

'Maybe they didn't. Maybe a painter used the cotton bud. To touch up a last-minute ding in the wood stain. That happens, too. Maybe when they moved the furniture in. Hard to avoid.'

'Now you think they're OK?'

'Not about the car, no. If theirs wouldn't start this morning, why hadn't they already called the mechanic anyway?'

'The phone was out.'

'Maybe not then. Maybe not first thing in the morning. We could have tagged on. We could have split the call-out charge. That would have made it more reasonable.'

'Shorty, forget the call-out charge, OK? This is more important. They're acting weird.'

'I told you that at the beginning.'

'I thought you just didn't like them.'

'For a reason.'

'What are we going to do?'

Shorty glanced around. First at the mouth of the track through the trees, and then at the dead Honda's load space, where their suitcase was weighing down the springs.

'I don't know,' he said. 'Maybe we could tow the car with a quad bike. Maybe the keys are in them. Or on a hook inside the barn.'

'We can't steal a quad bike.'

'It wouldn't be stealing. It would be borrowing. We could tow the car two miles to the road, and then bring the quad bike back again.'

'Then what? All we would have is a dead car on the side of the road.'

'Maybe a wrecker would come by. Or we could get any kind of ride and forget about the car. The county would come along and junk it sooner or later.'

'Do we have a tow rope?'

'Maybe there's one in the barn.'

'I don't think a quad bike would be strong enough.'

'We could use two. Like tugboats pulling an ocean liner to the harbour mouth.'

'That's crazy,' Patty said.

'OK, maybe we could use a quad bike to haul just the suitcase.'

'You mean drag it along?'

'I think they have a platform on the back.'

'Too small.'

'Then we could balance it on the gas tank and the handlebar.'

'They won't like it if we leave our car here.'

'Too bad.'

'Do you even know how to drive a quad bike?'

'It can't be that hard. We would want to go slow anyway. And we couldn't fall off. Not like a regular motorbike.'

'It's a possibility,' Patty said. 'I suppose.'

'Let's wait until after dinner,' Shorty said. 'Maybe the phone is back on and the mechanic will show up and everything will work out fine. If not, we'll take a look at the barn after dark. OK?'

Patty didn't answer. They stayed where they were, slumped down in their lawn chairs, keeping the low sun on their faces. They left their room door wide open.

Fifty yards away in the command centre in the back parlour, Mark asked, 'Who missed the cotton bud?'

'All of us,' Peter said. 'We all checked the room and we all signed off on it.'

'Then we all made a bad mistake. Now they're agitated. Way too soon. We need to pace this better.'

71

'He thinks it was the painter. She'll believe him eventually. She doesn't want to worry. She wants to be happy. She'll talk herself around. They'll calm down.'

'You think?'

'Why would we lie about the room? There's no possible reason for it.'

Mark said, 'Bring me a quad bike.'

TEN

Reacher walked back to the fancy county office with the census scans and the million-dollar cubicles, and he found the same surly guy on duty at the desk. Once again Reacher asked for two censuses, the first when Stan was two, and the second when he was twelve, but this time for the rest of the county that lay outside of Laconia's technical city limit.

The guy said, 'We can't do that.'

'Why not?'

'You're asking for a doughnut shape. With a hole in the middle, which is Laconia, which you already saw. Am I right?'

'You got it in one.'

'That's not how the extracts are done. There are no doughnut shapes. You can have an area, or a bigger area, or a bigger-still area. Which would be the city, the county, and the state. But the bigger area always includes the smaller area all over again. And the bigger-still area includes both of them all over again. Which is logical, if you think about it. There are no holes in the middle. The city is in the county, and the county is in the state.'

'Understood,' Reacher said. 'Thank you for the explanation. I'll take the whole county.'

'Are you still a resident?'

'You agreed I was this morning. And here I am again. Clearly I didn't leave town with all my worldly possessions. I would say my status as a resident is more secure than ever.'

'Cubicle four,' the guy said.

Patty and Shorty heard an engine start up in the distance, deafening like a motorcycle, and they got up and walked to the corner to take a look. They saw Peter riding a quad bike back to the house. Now only eight were neatly parked.

'First turn of the key,' Shorty said. 'I hope they're all like that.'

'Way too noisy,' Patty said, disappointed. 'We can't do it. They would know.'

Peter parked at the distant house. He killed the engine and silence came back. He got off and went inside. Patty and Shorty went back to their lawn chairs.

Shorty said, 'The land is pretty flat around here.'

'Does that help us?'

'We could push the quad bike. With the engine off. With the suitcase balanced on it. We could use it like a furniture dolly.'

'Could we?'

'They can't be that heavy. You see people wheeling motorbikes all the time. We wouldn't even have to keep it upright, and there are two of us. I bet we could do it dead easy.'

'Two miles there and two miles back? Which would leave the suitcase by the side of the road, and us back here. So then we would have another two miles to walk. Altogether six, four of them pushing a quad bike. It would take a good long time.'

'I figure about three hours,' Shorty said.

'Depends how fast we could push. We don't know yet.'

'OK, call it four hours. We should time it to finish at dawn.

74

Maybe we might see a farmer heading to market. There has to be traffic sometimes. So we should start in the middle of the night. Which is good. They'll be asleep.'

'It's a possibility,' Patty said. 'I suppose.'

They heard the distant quad bike start up again, fifty yards away, then closer. It sounded like it was passing the barn and coming straight towards them.

They stood up.

The engine got loud and the machine roared around the corner, with Mark riding it, scattering dirt. There was a cardboard carton strapped to the rack on the back. Mark braked to a stop, and tapped the gear change into neutral, and shut the motor down. He smiled his master-of-the-universe smile.

'Good news,' he said. 'The phone is back on. The mechanic will be here first thing in the morning. We were too late to get him today. But he knows what the problem is. He's seen it before. Apparently there's an electronic chip close to where the heater hoses go through the back of the dashboard. The chip fries when the water in the hoses gets too hot. He's bringing a replacement chip he got from a wrecker's yard. He wants five dollars for it. Plus fifty for labour.'

'That's great,' Shorty said.

Patty said nothing.

Mark said, 'And I'm afraid I want another fifty for the room.'

There was silence for a second.

Mark said, 'Guys, I would love to tell you just forget it, but the bank would kick my ass. This is a business, I'm afraid. We have to take it seriously. And from your point of view it's not so terrible. A hundred for the motel and fifty-some to fix your car, and you're out of here for less than two hundred dollars all in. Could have been a whole lot worse.'

'Come take a look at this,' Patty said.

Mark climbed off the quad bike and Patty led the way inside

the room. She pointed down into the void under the vanity.

Mark said, 'What am I looking for?'

'You'll see.'

He looked.

He saw.

He said, 'Oh, dear.'

He bent down and came back up with the cotton bud.

'I apologize most sincerely,' he said. 'This is unforgivable.'

'Why did you tell us we were the first guests in this room?'

'What?'

'You made a big deal out of it.'

'You are the first guests in this room. Most definitely. This is something else entirely.'

'The painter?' Shorty said.

'No.'

'Then who?' Patty asked.

'The bank told us to improve our marketing. We hired a photographer to take pictures for a new brochure. He brought a model from Boston with him. We let her do her make-up in here, because it's the nicest room. I suppose we were trying to impress her. She was very good-looking. I thought we cleaned up after her. Obviously we didn't succeed completely. Again, I apologize most sincerely.'

'So do I,' Patty said. 'I guess. For jumping to conclusions. How did the pictures come out?'

'She was dressed as a hiker. Very big boots and very short shorts. A hiker on a warm day, clearly, because her top wasn't huge either. The motel was behind her. It looked pretty good.'

Patty gave him fifty of her hard-earned bucks.

She said, 'What do we owe you for the meals?'

'Nothing,' Mark said. 'That's the least we can do.'

'Are you sure?'

'Absolutely. That's just housekeeping money. The bank doesn't see those numbers.' He put the fifty bucks and the cotton bud in his pants pocket. He said, 'And kind of on the same subject I have something for you.'

He led the way out to the lot again, back to the quad bike, to the carton strapped to its rack.

He said, 'You are absolutely invited to dinner tonight, of course, and breakfast tomorrow, but equally all of us would absolutely understand if you preferred to eat alone, just the two of you. Everyone knows making conversation can be stressful. We put together some ingredients for you. Either join us at the house, or help yourselves from the box. No pressure either way.'

He undid the straps and hefted the box in his arms. He half turned and slid it into Shorty's waiting hands.

'Thank you,' Patty said.

Mark just smiled, and climbed aboard the quad bike, and started up its ferocious engine. He turned a wide circle in the stony lot and disappeared around the corner, heading back to the house.

Cubicle four was the same as cubicle two, except in a different place. Otherwise it was identical. It had the same tweed chair, and a flat screen, and a sharpened pencil, and a pad of paper with the county name at the top, like a hotel brand. The flat screen was already lit up blue, with two icons already top right, like stamps on a letter, the same as before. Reacher double-clicked on the first, and saw the same battleship-grey background, and a title page in the same government writing, saying all the same things he had seen before, except for the centre line, which said this time the returns were extracted for the county as a whole.

He scrolled down, with the wheel between the mouse's shoulder blades. The same introduction was there, with the same long disquisition about improvements in methodology. He skipped it all and went straight to the list of names. He got a rhythm going, flicking at the wheel with the tip of his finger, using some kind of elastic inbuilt momentum, spooling through the A section, and the B section, and the C section, then speeding to a blur, and then letting the list settle and slow and come to a stop among a short run of Q-names. There was a Quaid family, and a Quail, and a Quattlebaum, and two Queens.

He rolled on to the R section.

And there they were. Near the top. James Reacher, male, white, twenty-six years old, a tin mill foreman, and his wife Elizabeth Reacher, female, white, twenty-four years old, a bed sheet finisher, and their thus-far only child Stan Reacher, male, white, two years old.

Two years old in April, when the census was taken. Which would make him three years old in the fall, which would make him sixteen years old late on a September evening in 1943. Not fifteen. The old birdwatching lady was right.

Reacher said, 'Huh.'

He read on. Their address was given as a number and a street in a place named Ryantown. Their home was rented, at a cost of forty-three dollars a month. They didn't own a radio set. They didn't work on a farm. James had been twenty-two and Elizabeth twenty when they married. Both could read and write. Neither had any Indian tribal affiliation.

Reacher double-clicked on the tiny red traffic light at the top of the document, and the screen went back to the blue wash with the two postage stamps. He double-clicked on the second of them, and the census from ten years later opened up. He scrolled down, swooping through most of the alphabet, once again rolling to a stop among the Q-names. The Quaids were still there, and the Quails, and the two Queen families, but the Quattlebaums had gone.

The Reachers were still there. James, Elizabeth, and Stan, in that April thirty-six, thirty-four, and twelve years old respectively. Apparently there had been no further children. No siblings for

78

Stan. James had changed his employment to labourer on a county road grading crew, and Elizabeth was out of work altogether. Their address was the same, but the rent had dropped to thirty-six bucks. Seven years of Depression had taken its toll, on workers and landlords alike. James and Elizabeth were still listed as literate, and Stan was in daily attendance at school. The household had acquired a radio set.

Reacher wrote the address with the sharpened pencil on the top sheet of the branded notepaper, which he then tore off, and folded up, and stuck in his back pants pocket.

Mark parked the quad bike back at the barn, and walked on down to the house. The phone rang as soon as he got in the door. He picked it up and said his name, and a voice told him, 'There was a guy here, name of Reacher, checking out his family history. A big guy, pretty rough. He won't take no for an answer. So far he's looked at four different censuses. I think he's searching for an old address. Maybe he's a relative. I thought you should know.'

Mark hung up without replying.

ELEVEN

Reacher walked back to the city office and got there a half hour before the close of business. He went up to the records department and pressed the bell. A minute later Elizabeth Castle came in.

'I found them,' he said. 'They lived beyond the city limit, which is why they didn't show up the first time around.'

'So no federal warrants.'

'Turned out they were relatively law-abiding.'

'Where did they live?'

'A place called Ryantown.'

'I'm not sure where that is.'

'That's a shame, because I came here especially to ask you.'

'I'm not sure I ever heard of it.'

'Can't be far away, because his birdwatching club was here in town.'

She took out her phone, and did things to it, with spread fingers. She showed him. It was a map, expanded. She spread her fingers some more, and smaller places popped into view. Then she moved the magnified image around, circling Laconia's boundary, examining the nearby hinterland.

No Ryantown.

'Try further out,' he said.

'How far would a kid go for a birdwatching club?'

'Maybe he had a bike. Maybe Ryantown was boring. The cops told me there were all kinds of little spots, each with a couple dozen families and not much else. Maybe it was a place like that.'

'It would still have birds, surely. Maybe more than here, if it was quiet.'

'The cops said there were all kinds of mills and little factories. Maybe the atmosphere was smoky.'

'OK, wait,' she said.

She started over with her phone. This time typing and tapping, not swooping around. Maybe a search engine, or a local history site.

'Yes,' she said. 'It was a tin mill. Belonged to a man named Marcus Ryan. He built worker accommodations and called the place Ryantown. The mill finally closed in the 1950s and the town died, such as it was to begin with. Everyone left and the name fell off the map.'

'Where was it?'

'Supposedly north and west of here,' she said. She dabbed the map back on her phone, and spread and pinched and moved her fingers around.

'About here, possibly,' she said.

There was no name on the map. Just a blank grey shape, and a road.

'Zoom out,' he said.

She did, and the grey shape receded to a pinprick, north and west of Laconia, maybe eight miles out. Between ten and eleven on a clock face. It was one of many similar pinpricks. Like busy planets around a sun, held close in by gravity or magnetism or some other kind of strong attraction. Like Detective Brenda Amos had predicted, for all practical purposes Ryantown had been part of Laconia, no matter what the postal service said. The road that passed it by went onward towards nowhere in particular. It just meandered north and west, ten or more miles, and then another ten through a wood, and then onward. A back road, like the one he had been on with the guy in the Subaru. He could picture it.

He said, 'I guess there won't be a bus.'

'You could rent a car,' she said. 'There are places here in town.'

'I don't have a driver's licence.'

'I don't think a cab would want to go out there.'

Eight miles, he thought.

'I'll walk,' he said. 'But not now. It would be dark as soon as I got there. Tomorrow, maybe. You want to get dinner tonight?'

'What?'

'Dinner,' he said. 'The third meal of the day, generally eaten in the evening. Can be functional, or social, or sometimes both.'

'I can't,' she said. 'I'm having dinner with Carter Carrington tonight.'

Shorty carried the cardboard carton into the room and placed it on the dresser in front of the TV screen. Then he sat with Patty, side by side in their lawn chairs, through the last of the afternoon sun. She didn't talk. She was thinking. She often was. He knew the signs. He guessed she was processing the information she had received, examining it, turning it this way and that, until she was satisfied. Which would be soon, he thought. Surely. He really didn't see much of a problem any more. The thing with the cotton bud had a simple explanation. And the phone was back on. The mechanic was coming first thing in the morning. Total damage, less than two hundred dollars. A drag for sure, but not a disaster.

Patty said, 'Let's not go to the house for dinner. I think he was kind of hinting they didn't want us to.'

'He said we were invited.'

'He was being polite.'

'I think he meant it. But he was also looking at it from our point of view.'

'Now he's your best friend for ever?'

'I don't know,' Shorty said. 'Most of the time I think he's a weird asshole who needs a smack. But I have to admit he did good with the mechanic. He explained the problem and got a solution. That shows he's taking it seriously. Maybe we were both right, way back at the beginning. They're weird, but also they're doing their best for us. I guess they could be both things at once.'

'Whichever, let's eat just the two of us.'

'Works for me. I'm sick of answering their questions. It's like the third degree.'

'I told you,' Patty said. 'They're being polite. It's considered polite to take an interest.'

They got up and stepped inside the room. They left the door wide open. They shifted the cardboard box to the bed. Patty slit the tape with her thumbnail. Shorty lifted the flaps. Inside was an assortment of items, densely and meticulously packed. There were cereal bars and power bars and energy bars, and bottles of water, and packets of dried apricots, and tiny red boxes of raisins. Everything was arranged in a specific pattern that repeated twelve times over. Like twelve identical meals, all neatly laid out. Each one had a bottle of water, and then an equal one-twelfth share of the rest of the stuff.

There were also two flashlights in the box, standing on their ends, crammed in among the food.

'Weird,' Patty said.

'I think this place is for hikers,' Shorty said. 'Like in the photograph they took with the model. Why else would they dress her up like that? I bet they give this stuff out as box lunches. Or sell it. It's the kind of thing a hiker likes to carry.'

'Is it?'

'It's compact and high energy. Easy to put in a pocket. Plus water.'

'What are the flashlights for?'

'I suppose in case you're out late and have to eat in the dark.'

'A lantern would be better.'

'Maybe hikers prefer flashlights. I'm sure there's consumer feedback. I think this is part of their stock of supplies.'

'He said ingredients.'

'It's probably a balanced diet. Probably quite healthy. I bet hikers worry about that kind of thing.'

'He said they put some ingredients together. They didn't put this together. It's pre-packaged. Like you said, off their storeroom shelf.'

'We could still go eat at the house.'

'I told you, I don't want to. They don't want us there.'

'Then we got to eat this stuff.'

'Why does he make such grandiose statements? He could have said he brought the same iron rations he sells the hikers for lunch. I would have been happy with that. It's not like we're paying for it.'

'Exactly,' Shorty said. 'They're weird. But kind of helpful too. Or the other way around.'

Reacher ate dinner alone in Laconia, at a greasy hole-in-the-wall with no tablecloths. He didn't want to risk a fancier place, in case Carter Carrington and Elizabeth Castle picked the same spot. They would feel obliged to at least come over and say hello. He didn't want to disturb their evening. Afterwards he spent an hour walking random blocks, looking for a grocery store with an apartment window above it, that faced east down the length of a street. He found one plausible possibility. It was dead ahead as he walked away from the centre of downtown. The apartment was now an attorney's office. The store now sold pants and sweaters. He stood with his back to its window. He looked down the street. He saw a good-sized patch of night sky in the east, and below it the camber of the blacktop, humped between two gutters, flanked by two kerbs and two sidewalks, lit up here and there by widely spaced street lamps.

He walked the same direction the twenty-year-old had walked. He stopped thirty yards out. Any closer than that, he felt the old lady wouldn't have used the binoculars. She would have trusted the naked eye. He turned around and looked up at her window. Now he was the smaller boys. He imagined the big guy in front of them, demanding, and then threatening. Technically no big deal. For Reacher himself, anyway. At sixteen he had been bigger than most twenty-year-olds. He had been bigger at thirteen. Biology had been good to him. He was fast, and nasty. He knew all the tricks. He had invented some of them. He had grown up in the Marine Corps, not in Ryantown, New Hampshire. And Stan had been a normal-sized person by comparison. Compact, even, in some respects. Maybe six-one in dress shoes, maybe 190 after a four-course dinner.

Reacher looked down at the bricks in the sidewalk, and imagined his father's footsteps there, inching backward, and then turning and running.

Patty and Shorty ate outside, under their window, in their lawn chairs. They took meal number one and meal number two, which left ten in the box, and they dutifully drank their bottles of water. Then it got cold and they moved inside. But Patty said, 'Leave the door open.'

Shorty said, 'Why?'

'I need the air. Last night I felt like I was choking.'

'Open the window.'

'It doesn't open.'

'The door might blow.'

85

'Wedge it with your shoe.'

'Someone might get in.'

'Like who?' Patty said.

'A passer-by.'

'Here?'

'Or one of them.'

'I would wake up. Then I would wake you up.'

'Promise?'

'Count on it.'

Shorty kicked off his shoes, and wedged one between the outer face of the door and the jamb, and he bent the other into a pliable shape, and propped it against the inner face, to push back against gentle night-time breezes. Potato-farmer engineering, he knew, but it looked like it might work.

TWELVE

Steven called to Robert, who called to Peter, who called to Mark. They were all in different rooms. They got together in the back parlour, and stared at the screens.

'It's a pair of shoes,' Steven said. 'In case you're wondering.'

'Why did they do it?' Mark asked. 'Did they say?'

'She wants air. It's consistent behaviour. She's mentioned it before. I don't think it's a problem.'

Mark nodded. 'I told her a story about a supermodel doing her make-up. I think she believed it. I told her a mechanic will be riding to the rescue in the morning. I even made up some technical stuff about the heater hoses. I think she believed all of it. I think she's calm now. Doesn't matter about the door.'

'We need to lock it pretty soon.'

'But not tonight. Let sleeping dogs lie. They're relaxed now. They have nothing to worry about.'

Reacher preferred to move on whenever possible, so he found a new place to sleep, one street away from the previous night. It was a fancy bed and breakfast, in a narrow house built of brick, with its trim newly painted in faded colours. He got a top-floor room, through a low door at the head of a steep and dog-legged stair. He took a long hot shower, and fell asleep, still warm and damp.

Until one minute past three in the morning.

Once again he snapped awake, instantly, like flicking a switch. The same thing exactly. Not touch or taste or sight or smell. Therefore sound. This time he got out of bed immediately, and he pulled his pants out from under the mattress, and dressed fast, and tied his shoes. Then he headed out through the low door and down the winding stair to the street.

The night air was cool, and the silence was hard and brittle, all brick and glass and narrow spaces and humming electricity in the wires. He stood still. A minute later he heard a brief scrape of feet on the sidewalk. Ahead and half left. Maybe thirty yards away. Not going anywhere. Just shuffling in place. Maybe two people. Nothing visible.

He waited.

Another minute later he heard a muted yelp. A woman's voice. Maybe joy. Or ecstasy. Or maybe not. Maybe outrage or anger. It was hard to tell. But it was definitely muted. It was suppressed, in a particular way. It was the sound of clamped lips.

Nothing visible.

He moved left, and saw a gap between a bag store and a shoe store. It was pedestrian access to a narrow alley that divided two buildings. The alley had doors both sides for walk-up apartments above the stores. Two people were standing next to one of the doors. A man and a woman, in a full-on clinch. Like wrestling standing up. They were half lit by a harsh bulb above the door. The guy was young. Not much more than a kid. But he was big and solid. The woman was a little older. She had blonde hair, and she was wearing high heels and black nylons under a short black coat, which was getting rucked up by the wrestling.

Good or bad?

Hard to tell.

He didn't want to ruin anyone's evening.

He watched.

Then the woman squirmed her face away and said, 'No,' in a sudden low and breathy tone, like spitting, as firm as talking to a dog, but also with what Reacher took to be feelings of shame and embarrassment and disgust. She pushed against the guy's chest, and tried to get away. The guy wouldn't let her.

Reacher said, 'Hey.'

They both turned their faces towards him.

He said, 'Take your hands off her, kid.'

The boy said, 'This is none of your business.'

'It is now. You woke me up.'

'Get lost.'

'I heard her say no. So step back.'

The kid half turned. He was wearing a sweatshirt embroidered with the name of a famous university. He was a big solid boy. Maybe six-three, and 220 pounds. Maybe an athlete. He was rippling with youth and excitement. He had a look in his eye. He thought he was a hell of a guy.

Reacher looked at the woman and said, 'Miss, are you OK?'

She asked, 'Are you a cop?'

'I was once upon a time, in the army. Now I'm just a guy passing through.'

She didn't reply. She was close to thirty, Reacher thought. She looked like a nice person. But sad.

'Are you OK?' he asked her again.

She pushed away from the boy and stood a yard apart. She didn't speak. But she looked at Reacher like she didn't want him to leave.

He said, 'Did this happen last night too?'

She nodded.

'Same place?'

She nodded again.

'Same exact time?'

'It's when I get home from work.'

'You live here?'

'Until I get on my feet.'

Reacher looked at her heels and her hair and her nylons and said, 'You work in a cocktail bar.'

'In Manchester.'

'And this guy followed you home.'

She nodded.

'Two nights running?' Reacher said.

She nodded again.

The boy said, 'She asked me to, man. So butt out and let nature take its course.'

'That's not true,' the woman said. 'I did not ask you.'

'You were all over me.'

'I was being polite. That's what you do when you work in a cock-tail bar.'

Reacher looked at the boy.

'Sounds like a classic misunderstanding,' he said. 'But easily fixed. All you need to do is apologize most sincerely and then go away and never come back.'

'It's her who won't come back. Not to that bar, anyway. My father owns a big chunk of it. She'll lose her job.'

Reacher looked at the woman, and said, 'What happened last night?'

'I let him,' she said. 'He agreed one time only. So I got it over with. But now he's back for more.'

'I'll discuss it with him, if you like,' Reacher said. 'Meanwhile you go inside now, if you want. And think no more about it.'

'Don't you dare go inside,' the boy said. 'Not without me.'

The woman looked from him to Reacher, and back again. And

again, as if choosing. As if down to her last twenty bucks at the racetrack. She made her decision. She took her keys from her bag, and unlocked her door, and stepped inside, and closed her door behind her.

The boy in the sweatshirt stared first at the door, and then at Reacher. Who jerked his head towards the mouth of the alley, and said, 'Run along now, kid.'

The boy stared a minute longer, apparently thinking hard. And then he went. He walked out of the alley and turned out of sight. To the right. Which made him right-handed. He would want to set up his ambush so that Reacher would walk face first into a free-swinging right hook. Which pretty much defined the location. About three feet around the corner, Reacher thought. Level with the edge of the bag shop's window. Because of the pivot point for the right hook. Basic geometry. Fixed in space.

But not fixed in time. Speed was under Reacher's control. The kid would be expecting a normal kind of approach, plus or minus. Maybe a little tense and urgent. Maybe a little cautious and wary. But mostly average. He would trigger the hook at the first glimpse of Reacher coming around the corner. Any kind of normal walking pace would bring it home good and solid. The kid wasn't dumb. Possibly an athlete. Probably had decent hand to eye coordination.

Therefore nothing would be done at normal or average speed.

Reacher stopped six paces short of the corner, and waited, and waited, and then he took another pace, a slow, sliding scrape across grit and dirt, and then he paused, and waited, and took another step, slow, sliding, ominous. And then another long wait, and another slow step. He pictured the kid around the corner, tensed up, his fist cocked, holding his position. And holding. Holding too long. Getting too tensed. Getting all cramped and shaky.

Reacher took another step, long and slow. Now he was six feet from the corner. He waited. And waited. Then he launched fast, at

91

a run, his left hand up, palm open, fingers spread like a baseball glove. He burst around the corner and saw the kid sputtering to life, confused by the change of pace, locked into slow-motion waiting, so that his triumphant right hook was so far coming out like a herky-jerky feeble squib, which Reacher caught easily in his left palm, like a soft liner to second. The kid's fist was big, but Reacher's open hand was bigger, so he clamped down and squeezed, not hard enough to crush the bones, but hard enough to make the kid concentrate on keeping his mouth shut, so no whines or squeals came out, which obviously he couldn't afford, being a hell of a guy.

Then Reacher squeezed harder. Mostly as an IQ test. Which the kid failed. He used his free hand to claw at Reacher's wrist. The wrong move. Unproductive. Always better to go straight to the source of the problem, and use your free hand to hit the squeezer in the head. Or thumb out his eye, or otherwise get his attention. But the kid didn't. A missed opportunity. Then Reacher added a twist to the squeeze. Like turning a door knob. The kid's elbow locked up and he dropped a shoulder to compensate, but Reacher kept on twisting, until the kid got so lopsided he had to take his hand off Reacher's wrist and hold his whole arm straight out for balance.

Reacher said, 'Want me to hit you?'

No reply.

'It's not a difficult question,' Reacher said. 'A yes or no answer will do it.'

By that point the kid was shuffling in place, trying to find a bearable position, huffing and gasping. But not squealing yet. He said, 'OK, sure, I got her signals wrong. I'm sorry, man. I'll leave her alone now.'

'What about her job?'

'I was kidding, man.'

'What about the next new waitress, down on her luck, in need of secure employment?'

The kid didn't answer.

Reacher clamped down harder, and said, 'Want me to hit you?'

The kid said, 'No.'

'No means no, right? I expect they teach you that now, at your fancy university. Kind of theoretical, I guess, from your point of view. Until now.'

'Come on, man.'

'Want me to hit you?'

'No.'

Reacher hit him in the face, with a straight right, maximum force, crashing and twisting. Like a freight train. The kid's lights went out immediately. He went slack and gravity took over. Reacher kept his left hand rock solid. All the kid's weight fell on his own locked elbow. Reacher waited. One of two things would happen. Either the strength and elasticity in the kid's ligaments would roll him forward, or they wouldn't.

They didn't. The kid's elbow broke and his arm turned inside out. Reacher let him fall. He landed on the bricks outside the bag shop, one arm right and the other arm wrong, like a swastika. He was breathing. A little bubbly, from the blood in his throat. His nose was badly busted. Cheekbones too, maybe. Some of his teeth were out. Upper row, mostly. His dentist's kid was going to be just fine for college.

Reacher walked away, back to his lodgings, up the winding stair and through the low door to his room, where he took a second shower and got back in bed, once again warm and damp. He punched the pillow into shape, and went back to sleep.

At which moment Patty Sundstrom woke up. A quarter past three in the morning. Once again a pulse of subconscious disquiet had forced its way through to the surface. What were the flashlights for? Why two of them? Why not one, or twelve?

The room was blissfully cool. She could smell the night air, rich, like velvet. Why pack two flashlights with twelve meals? Why pack them at all? What did flashlights have to do with food? They weren't natural partners. No one ever said, do you want a flashlight with that? And what Shorty suggested was nonsense. No one ate lunch in the dark. Which was all it was. It was lunch, for fellow rich guys up from Boston, who wanted to feel rugged for a week. No one paying before-Labor-Day or leaf-peeper rates would accept granola bars for dinner. Or breakfast. Lunch only, surely, as part of a manly outdoor fantasy. So why the flashlights? Lunch was eaten in the middle of the day. Generally speaking the sun was out. Unless the rich guys were spelunkers. In which case they would have flashlights of their own, surely. Expensive specialist items, probably strapped to their heads.

Why would flashlights be packed in a carton of food, as if they were somehow integral, like silverware or napkins would be?

Were they packed?

Maybe they were just shoved in there as afterthoughts. She kept her eyes closed and pictured the scene when they opened the box. She had slit the tape with her nail, and Shorty had lifted the flaps. What had been her impression?

Two flashlights in the box, standing on their ends, crammed in among the food.

Crammed in.

Therefore not packed as integral components. Added later.

Why?

Two flashlights for two people.

They had each been given a flashlight and six subsistence meals. Why?

We put together some ingredients for you. Either join us at the house, or help yourselves from the box. Which was kind of phony. Which they didn't mean.

What else didn't they mean?

She flipped the covers back and slid out of bed. She padded over

94

to the dresser, where the carton sat in front of the TV screen. She lifted the flaps and felt inside. The first flashlight had fallen over in the void where the first two meals had been. She lifted it out. It was big and heavy. It felt cold and hard. She pressed it against her palm and switched it on. She rolled her palm a fraction and let a sliver of light spill out. It was pink from her skin. The flashlight was a famous make. It felt like it had been machined out of a solid billet of aerospace-grade aluminium. It had a cluster of tiny LED bulbs, like an insect's eye.

She looked back in the box. The other flashlight was where it had started, rammed down into the crux between lunches nine, ten, eleven and twelve. Some of the granola bars around it were cracked and splintered. One of the raisin boxes was crushed. Added later, for sure. She looked at the tape she had slit. Two layers. One from the wholesaler, and one from them, when they resealed the box, after they added the flashlights.

What else didn't they mean?

She padded towards the door, and she nudged Shorty's bent shoe aside with her toe, and opened a gap wide enough to slip outside. She took her hand off the flashlight lens. It cast a bright white beam of light. She minced towards the Honda, with bare feet on the stones. She opened the passenger door. The hood release was where her shin would be. She had seen it a million times. A broad black lever. She tugged on it. The hood sprang up an inch with a *thunk* that in the still of the night sounded like a wreck on the highway.

She turned off the flashlight and waited. No one came. No windows in the house lit up. She turned the beam on again. She walked around to the front of the hood. She jiggled the catch and raised it up. She propped it with the bent metal rod that fit in the hole. She worked in a sawmill. She knew her way around machinery. She moved left and right, and ducked her head, until she could see what she wanted to see.

The acid test.

He knows what the problem is. He's seen it before. Apparently there's an electronic chip close to where the heater hoses go through the back of the dashboard.

She leaned forward. She held the flashlight in her fingers, like a medical probe. She angled the beam this way and that.

THIRTEEN

Patty Sundstrom identified the back of the dashboard easily
enough. It was a bare panel, pressed and dimpled with
strengthening reinforcements, grey and dirty, partially
covered by a thin and peeling sheet of sound-deadening material.
All kinds of wires and pipes and tubes went through it. Mostly
electrical, she thought. The hot water for the heater would be in
a thick hose. Maybe an inch or so in diameter, serious and re-
inforced. By convention black, she expected, clamped to a port
on the engine block, which was where the hot water came from.
And obviously it would be twinned with an identical black hose,
for the return feed. Circulation, around and around. Because
of the water pump. Which stopped when the engine stopped,
Peter said.

She craned her neck and moved the flashlight beam.

She found two black hoses connected to the engine block. There
were no other candidates. She followed them with the flashlight
beam. They stayed low in the bay. They passed through the bulkhead into the passenger compartment very low down. Directly

behind where the floor console was, with the gearshift lever. The heater was right above it.

The heater hoses go through the back of the dashboard.

No they don't, Patty thought. She double-checked. They went nowhere near the back of the dashboard. They went through level with the bottom of the footwell. Much lower down. And there was nothing near them anyway. Just thick metal components, all caked with dirt. No wires. Nothing vulnerable. Nothing that would fry from excessive temperatures. Certainly no black boxes that might contain electronic chips.

She backed away and straightened up. She looked at the house. All quiet. The barn was ghostly in the moonlight. All nine quad bikes were neatly parked. She killed the flashlight beam and minced back to the room. She stepped to the bed and nudged Shorty awake. He sat up in a panic and looked all around for passers-by or other intruders.

He saw none.

He said, 'What?'

She said, 'The heater hoses don't go through the back of the dashboard.'

He said 'What?' again.

'In the car,' she said. 'They go through real low down, about level with the bottom of the gearstick.'

'How do you know?'

'I looked,' she said. 'With one of the flashlights they gave us.'

'When?'

'Just now.'

'Why?'

'I woke up. Something is not right.'

'So you ripped the console out of the car?'

'No, I looked under the hood. From the other side. I could see the connection. And there's no electronic chip nearby.'

'OK, maybe the mechanic got it wrong,' Shorty said. 'Maybe he was thinking of a different year. Ours is a pretty early model. Or maybe Hondas are different in Canada.'

'Or maybe the mechanic doesn't exist. Maybe they never called one.'

'Why wouldn't they?'

'Maybe they're keeping us here.'

'What?'

'How else do you explain it?'

'Why would they? Seriously. You mean, like an occupancy thing? Because of the bank? They want our fifty bucks?'

'I don't know why.'

'Hell of a way to do business. We could go on TripAdvisor.'

'Except we can't go on anything. There's no wifi and no cell signal and no phone in the room.'

'They can't just keep people here, against their will. Someone would miss them eventually.'

'We as good as told them no one knows we're gone.'

'We also as good as told them we're broke,' Shorty said. 'How long can they expect us to pay fifty bucks?'

'Two days,' Patty said. 'Breakfast, lunch, and dinner. Six meals each.'

'That's crazy. Then what? Then they call the mechanic?'

'We have to get out of here. We have to do the thing you said with the quad bike. So get dressed. We have to go.'

'Now?'

'This minute.'

'It's the middle of the night.'

'Like you said. They're asleep now. We have to do it now.'

'Because a mechanic was wrong on the phone?'

'If there was a mechanic at all. And because of everything.'

Shorty said, 'Why did they give us flashlights?'

Patty said, 'I don't know that either.'

'It's like they knew we might want to leave in the dark.'

'How could they?'

Shorty got out of bed. He said, 'We should take some food. Can't count on getting anywhere before lunchtime, earliest. We'll miss breakfast for sure.'

They got dressed, hopping from foot to foot in the half dark, with nothing but moonlight coming in the open door. They packed their stuff by feel and put their bags outside near the car.

'You sure about this?' Shorty said. 'Never too late to change your mind.'

'I want to go,' Patty said. 'Something isn't right here.'

They walked down to the barn on the grass, not the dirt, because they felt it would be quieter. They were cautious across the last of the gravel, to the near corner of the perfect square of bikes, to the one Peter had driven away for Mark to use. Its engine was still faintly warm. Shorty wanted that exact one, because he had seen how to put its gearbox in neutral, and he knew it rolled along OK, but most of all because it was closest. Who wanted to push extra yards? Not him. He clicked the lever to neutral, and pushed back on the handlebars, kind of weak and sideways at first, but even so the machine rolled back obediently, getting faster and faster as Shorty got more and more head-on in his pushing.

'This is not too bad,' he said.

He dragged the machine to a stop and took up a new position and pushed it forward again, in a tight curve, a perfect neat man-oeuvre, like reversing out of a parking space and turning and driving away. Patty joined in on the other side, and they pushed together and got up to a decent speed, steering along the centre of the track towards the motel building, pretty much silently, apart from the scrape of their shoes on the dirt, and a lot of close-up squelching and popping from stones under the bike's soft rubber tyres. They pushed on, breathing hard, around room twelve's corner, and onward to the Honda, two bays down, outside room

100

ten. They stopped the bike right behind the car. Shorty popped the hatch.

'Wait,' Patty said.

She walked back to the corner and watched the house. No lights, no movement. She came back to the Honda and said, 'OK.'

Shorty turned to face the open hatch square on, and he bent forward with his arms spread wide, and he wriggled his fingers under the suitcase, both ends, and he heaved it up at the front, and dragged it forward until it rested at an angle on the lip of the hatch. He grabbed the handle and hauled, intending to balance the case weightless on the lip, so he had time to change his position and adjust his grip, ready for the clean-and-jerk, and the turn towards the bike.

But the handle tore off the suitcase.

Shorty tottered back a step.

He said, 'Damn.'

'Proves we couldn't have carried it anyway,' Patty said. 'That would have happened sooner or later.'

'How are we going to get it on the bus?'

'We'll have to buy a rope. We could wrap it around a couple of times, and make a new handle. So we need a gas station or a hardware store. For the rope. First place we see.'

Shorty stepped forward again and bent down and got his fingers under the case. He grunted and lifted and gasped and turned and set it down on the bike, lengthways, the top corners resting on the handlebar, the bottom edge digging into the padded seat. He nudged it a little and got it balanced. It ended up pretty solid. Better than he thought it would. He was pleased, overall.

He shut the Honda's hatch, and they strapped their overnight bags on the bike's rear rack. Then they took up position, Shorty on the left and Patty on the right, each of them with one hand clamped tight on the short length of handlebar visible either side beyond the suitcase's corners, and the other hand close to it, partly pushing, partly juggling a flashlight. Which gave them twin makeshift headlight beams, and it made steering easy, and it meant they could steady the suitcase between them, with Shorty's right forearm and Patty's left at the top end, and with his right hip and her left at the bottom end, assuming they both walked kind of bent over at the waist, which clearly they would need to, because the weight of the load made pushing a whole different thing than before. Getting started required a full-on effort, both of them straining like a strongman show on cable television, and then keeping going afterwards required nearly as much, although it got a little better when they bumped up out of the stony lot and on to the blacktop, at the very end of the road through the trees.

More than two miles to go. They entered the tunnel. The air was cool, and it smelled of rotten leaves and damp earth. They gasped and trudged. Through trial and error they learned it was best to keep their speed as high as they could bear, so that momentum alone would carry them through the long shallow potholes. It meant a lot of effort all of the time, but it was better than starting over whenever the front wheels bumped down into a pit. They kept on going, almost running against the weight, very quickly no fun at all, just grinding it out.

'I need to rest,' Patty said.

They let the bike coast to a stop. They nudged the suitcase left and right to perfect its balance. Then they stepped away, and arched their backs, and clamped their palms low down on their spines. They huffed and puffed, and eased their necks.

Shorty said, 'How much further?'

Patty looked back, and then forward.

'About a mile and a half to go,' she said.

'How long have we taken so far?'

'Maybe twenty minutes.'

'Damn, that's slow.'

102

'You said four hours. We're about on schedule.'

They took up their positions again, and forced the thing to roll. Like a bobsled team at the top of the hill, going harder and harder with every step. They got it up to speed and kept it there, jamming their forearms against the trembling suitcase, ducking their heads, breathing deep, glancing up again to check their direction. They did another half mile, and rested again. And another. A whole hour had gone by.

'Coming back will be easier,' Patty said. 'Without the weight.'

They passed through the section where no trees grew. They saw a belt of sky, full of stars.

'Getting close,' Patty said.

Then she said, 'Wait,' and she hauled back on the handlebar and dug her heels in, way out in front, like a kid stopping a home-made cart.

Shorty said, 'What?'

'There was a wire. Like at the gas station. For ringing a bell. Lying across the road. It probably rings in the house.'

Shorty hauled the bike to a dead stop. He remembered. As fat and rubbery as a garden hose. He searched ahead with his flash-light. They saw nothing. They rolled on, half speed, which was a pain through the potholes, with one beam ranging far, and the other sweeping close.

A hundred yards later they saw it.

Fat and rubbery and lying across the road.

They stopped four feet short.

Patty said, 'How does it work?'

'I guess inside there are two metal strips. Somehow held apart. But when a wheel goes over, they get pressed together and a bell rings. Like a push switch.'

'So we can't let a wheel go over.'

'No.'

Which was a problem. Shorty couldn't lift the quad bike. Not at either end. Maybe an inch for a second, but not enough to ease it over the wire and set it down again.

'How much further?' he said.

'About three hundred yards.'

'I'll carry the suitcase.'

'Wait,' she said again.

She ducked down and eased her fingers under the fat rubber wire. She lifted it. It came up easily, an inch, a foot, as much as she wanted. She tested it side to side, and pulled and tugged to make it equally loose.

'Get ready,' she said.

She lifted it up, gently, on open palms, head high, arms wide. Shorty ducked low and pushed the bike under it. She held it until he was clear. She felt like she was performing a dance ceremony at a hippy's wedding.

'OK,' Shorty said.

She laid the wire back down, gently, like she was bowing. Then they pushed on, energized. Safe. On the last lap. Not far to go. Their flashlight beams bounced and swayed, first showing nothing but trees and the track between, but then a different kind of void loomed up ahead. The two-lane road. Where they had turned in, what felt like a thousand years ago. Shorty had said, OK? Patty hadn't answered.

Now she said, 'We need to find a place to hide the suitcase. But not too far from the road. So we can load it easy when we get a ride.'

They let the bike slow to a stop where the mouth of the track widened out to meet the road. Hiding places looked to be in short supply. Tree trunks crowded in either side. The last yard of shoulder was thick with underbrush. Although maybe a little thinner where the frost-heaved posts were set. Maybe the ground had been disturbed many years earlier. Maybe the brush was coming back slower. Maybe there was a suitcase-sized hole behind one or the other.

Patty went to check. In the end she figured the right-hand hole was better than the left. They huffed and puffed and got the bike as close as possible. Shorty spread his arms wide and lifted the suitcase off the bike, and then he grunted and gasped and turned and dropped it in the bushes, where it scraped and crackled through the lower branches and came to rest pretty well hidden. Patty walked up the road a spell and used her flashlight like an approaching headlight beam, and said she saw nothing much. Certainly nothing anyone would stop for. Just a dark shape, way low down, behind the base of the post. It could have been the corpse of a deer. She was satisfied.

Then her voice changed and she said, 'Shorty, come here.'

He went. They stood together on the county blacktop and looked back the way he had come, back along her flashlight beam, which was wavering on a wide area centred on the frost-heaved post, with the dark shape low and behind it. Which you couldn't really see unless you knew it was there. He was satisfied too.

He said, 'What am I looking for?'

'Think, Shorty,' she said. 'What did we see when we turned in?'

He thought. He visualized. He took two sideways steps left, nearer the centre line of the road, where the Honda's wheel had been. He squatted down a little, to approximate the level of the driver's seat. What had he seen? He had seen a frost-heaved post, on which was nailed a board, on which were screwed ornate plastic letters, and an arrow pointing into the woods. The letters had spelled out the word *Motel*.

He compared his memory with the scene in front of him.

He was pretty sure it was different.

He stared. Then he saw. Now there was no board. No letters, no word, no arrow. Now there was just a post. Nothing on it. Same both sides of the track.

'Weird,' he said.

'You think?'

'So is it a motel or not? Sure feels like one to me. They're taking our money.'

'We have to get out of here.'

'We are. First car that comes.'

'After we take the bike back to the barn.'

'We don't owe them that,' Shorty said. 'We don't owe them diddly. Not any more. Not if they're pulling weird shit on us now, with the motel signs. We should dump the bike here and let them come get it themselves.'

'They get up with the sun,' Patty said. 'If there's a bike missing they'll know right away. But if it's back in its proper place, they might not think about us for hours. They'll assume we're eating breakfast on our own, in our room. They'll have no reason to come by until later in the morning.'

'It's a gamble.'

'It could buy us a lot of time later. They'll come looking for us as soon as they find us gone. We need to delay that moment as long as possible. We need to be miles away by then. We definitely can't afford to be still stuck down here with our thumbs out. I think we should buy ourselves as much time as we can get.'

Shorty said nothing. He looked along the dark and silent road, first one way, and then the other.

'I know it feels weird to go back,' Patty said. 'Now that we just got here. But there are no cars coming anyway. Not yet. We'll do better closer to dawn.'

Shorty was quiet another long moment.

Then he said, 'OK, we'll take the bike back to the barn.'

'As fast as we can,' Patty said. 'Now it's all about speed.'

They unstrapped their overnight bags from the rack and stashed them close to the suitcase, and then they eased the bike around a wide circle on the blacktop. The air smelled sweeter in the open. They got the bike pointed back down the track. They took up their

106

positions. They set off. The same two-plus miles all over again, in the reverse direction. But Patty had been right. Pushing was much easier without the weight of the suitcase. The bike felt buoyant. Like it was floating. They did the hippy dance under the wire again, and then they got it going and kept it up at a fast walk with what felt like barely any effort at all. They didn't stop and they didn't rest.

FOURTEEN

It took them a fraction more than thirty minutes to push the two-plus miles. They rolled to a stop where the track came out of the trees. It ran on ahead of them, grey and ghostly in the moonlight, through the flat two acres, to the curve of buildings in the distance. The motel, dark and quiet. The barn, dark and quiet. The house, dark and quiet. Five-thirty in the morning, by Patty's watch. Easily an hour before the first hint of daylight.

All good.

They pushed on, as quiet as they could, nothing but the hiss of the tyres and the slap of their soles on the last of the blacktop. Then they bumped down into the motel lot, and their progress got louder, with crunching steps and squelching stones, past the office, past room one, and two, all the way to the dead Honda, and onward, past room twelve's corner, straight towards the barn. They could see eight ghostly shapes, neatly parked, and the ninth slot empty, like a punched-out tooth in a smile. Shorty pointed and gave Patty a thumbs-up. She was right. The first daylight glance out the window would have raised the alarm.

They cut the last corner across the grass, and rolled real slow on the parking area's gravel. Putting the bike back in place was easy. Just a question of lining it up and pushing it in, nose first, and then nudging it dead level with the others, and stepping away. Job done. Perfect. Undetectable. They tiptoed across the gravel, and they walked away on the grass, back to the track, where they stood for a second and took a breath. Ahead of them were the same two-plus miles. All over again. But this time they had nothing to push. This time they would be walking, plain and simple. Walking away, for ever.

Behind them a door opened. Over at the house. Relatively distant. A faraway voice called out, 'Hey guys, is that you?'

Mark.

They stood still.

'Guys?'

A flashlight beam lanced beyond them, with their shadows cut out, which meant light was playing on their backs.

'Guys?' Mark called again.

They turned around.

Mark was walking through the dark towards them. He was fully dressed. His day had already begun. He was keeping his flashlight low, and so were Shorty and Patty, all three beams acting polite, trying to illuminate, but not dazzle.

They waited.

Mark arrived.

He said, 'This is the most amazing coincidence.'

Along with the flashlight he was carrying a blank sheet of paper and a pencil.

Patty said, 'Is it?'

'I'm sorry, I should have asked, is everything OK?'

'We're fine.'

'Just out for a walk?'

'Why is it a coincidence?'

'Because literally at this very moment I have the mechanic on the phone. He starts work at five, to be ready for rush hour. This morning he woke up with a sudden thought. He remembered we had mentioned you drove down from Canada. He realizes at the time he instinctively assumed you were Americans returning home. Then this morning he realized it was equally likely you were Canadians visiting the other way around. In which case you would have a Canadian-spec car. In which case you would have the mandatory winter package, which back then was a different heater and no AC. In which case his diagnosis was wrong. That's a US-spec problem. In Canada it's the starter motor relay that fries. He needs to know which part to pick up at the scrapyard. He's heading there now. He literally just sent me out to get the ID number off your windshield.'

He held up the paper and pencil, as if in proof.

Then he said, 'But obviously it will be a lot quicker for all concerned if you come in and answer his questions yourselves.'

He mimed the relative distances by chopping his palms closer together and further apart, first showing the long way to go to the Honda, plus the even longer way back again, versus a short sharp one-way trip from where they were standing to the phone in the house. A dramatic difference. Impeccable logic. Shorty looked at Patty. She looked at him. All kinds of questions.

Mark said, 'We could make a pot of coffee. We could ask the guy to call us back when he's actually got the part he needs in his hot little hand. And then again, when he's actually in his truck and on his way to you. I want you to hear it from the horse's mouth. I feel at this point a little reassurance is in order. I feel that's the least we can do. You folks have been messed around enough already.'

He held out his hand, in a courtly after-you gesture.

Patty and Shorty walked towards the house. Mark walked with them. All three flashlight beams bounced along in the

110

same direction. At the end Mark speeded up and then waited at the kitchen door, ushering them in. He flicked on a light and pointed ahead to the inner hallway, where the dead phone had been demonstrated at lunch the day before. Now the receiver was lying tethered by its cord on the seat of a chair. On hold, the old-fashioned way.

Mark said, 'His name is Carol. Probably spelled different. He's from Macedonia.'

He held out his hand, towards the phone, in a courtly help-yourself gesture.

Patty picked up the receiver. She put it to her ear. She heard a kind of spacy noise. A cell connection somewhere, doing its best.

She said, 'Carol?'

A voice said, 'Mark?'

'No, my name is Patty Sundstrom. My boyfriend and I own the Honda.'

'Oh man, I didn't mean for Mark to wake you guys up. That isn't polite.'

The voice had an accent that sounded like wherever it came from deserved a name like Macedonia. Eastern Europe, she thought. Or Central. Somewhere between Greece and Russia. The kind of guy who should shave twice a day but didn't. Like a sinister bad guy in the movies. Except his voice was friendly. Light in tone. Helpful, and full of concern. Full of energy, too, first thing in the morning.

She said, 'We were awake anyway.'

'Were you?'

'We were taking a walk, as a matter of fact.'

'Why?'

'Something else woke us up, I suppose.'

'Listening to your voice I'm guessing you're Canadian.'

'So is our car.'

'Yeah,' the voice said. 'I made an assumption and thereby nearly made a mistake. I learned my trade in the old Yugoslav army. Like armies everywhere they taught us assuming things made an ass out of you and me. This time it's all me, I'm afraid. I apologize. But let's be certain. Have you ever had cause to change out the heater hoses?'

'I know they go low down,' Patty said.

'OK, that's Canadian for sure. Good to know. I'll pick up a starter motor relay. Then I got to pay the bills. I'll head out to the highway for a spell. Maybe I'll get lucky with a wreck. If not, I'll get to you all the sooner. Call it two hours minimum, four hours maximum.'

'You sure?'

'Ma'am, I cross my heart,' the voice said, with its accent. 'I promise I'll get you on your way.'

Then the call went dead and Patty hung up the phone.

Mark said, 'The coffee is ready.'

Patty said, 'He'll be here between two hours and four hours from now.'

'Perfect.'

Shorty said, 'Really?'

'He promised,' she said.

They heard a vehicle on the track outside. The crunch of stones, and the thrash of an engine. They looked out the window and saw Peter in a battered old pick-up truck. He was coming close. He was slowing to a stop. He was parking.

Shorty said, 'Whose truck?'

'His,' Mark said. 'He gave it another try late last night. Maybe the warmth of the day helped the battery. He got it going. Now he's been down to the road and back, to charge it up and blow the cobwebs away. Maybe that was what woke you up. He can give you a ride to your room, if you like. Better than walking. It's the least we can do. I'm sure you're tired.'

They said they didn't want to impose, but Peter wouldn't take no for an answer. His truck was a crew cab, so Shorty rode in front, and Patty sat in back. Peter parked next to the Honda. Room ten's door was closed. Which Patty thought was weird. She was pretty sure they had left it open. Maybe it had blown. Shorty's shoes were back on his feet, after all. Although she didn't remember wind. She had been outdoors most of the night. She remembered the air as still and oppressive.

They got out of the truck. Peter watched them to their door. Patty turned the handle and opened up. She went in first. Then she came straight back out again. She pointed at Peter in his truck and she yelled, 'You stay there.'

She stepped aside. Shorty looked in the room. In the centre of the floor was their luggage. Back again. Their suitcase and their two overnight bags. Neatly placed, in a precise arrangement, as if a bell boy had left them. Their suitcase was now tied up with rope. There were complicated knots on the upper face, with a doubled thickness of rope between them. Like an improvised handle.

Patty said, 'What the hell is this?'

Peter got out of his truck.

'We sincerely apologize,' he said. 'We are very, very sorry about this, and very, very embarrassed that you should get caught up in it.'

'In what?'

'It's the time of year, I'm afraid. College semesters are starting. Undergraduates are everywhere. Their fraternities set them challenges. They steal our motel signs all the time. Then they started a new thing. Some kind of initiation rite. They had to steal everything out of a motel room while the guest was temporarily absent. Stupid, but it was what it was. We thought it was finished a couple of years ago, but now it seems to be back again. I found your stuff in the hedge, down by the road. It's the only possible explanation. They must have gotten in while you were taking your walk. We apologize for the inconvenience. Please let us know if anything is damaged. We're going to make a police report. I mean, OK, everyone likes high spirits, but this kind of thing is ridiculous.'

Patty said nothing.

Shorty didn't speak.

Peter got back in his truck and drove away. Patty and Shorty stood still for a moment. Then they went inside. They stepped around their luggage and sat down together on the bed. They left the door open.

The breakfast part of Reacher's bed and breakfast deal was located in a pretty room that was half a storey below the street but level with the small rear garden, which was just as pretty as the room. Reacher took an inside table at a quarter to eight in the morning, ready for coffee. He was the only person in there. The season was over. He was showered and dressed and felt good and looked respectable, all except for a cut knuckle. From the kid in the night. His teeth, no doubt. Not a serious injury. Just a short worm of crusted blood. But a distinctive shape. Reacher had been a cop for thirteen years, and then not a cop for longer, so he saw things from both points of view. As a result wherever possible he liked to avoid confusion. He ordered his meal and then got up and stepped out to the garden. He squatted down and made a fist with his right hand and tapped and scraped it on the brick of a flower-bed wall. Just enough to make the tooth mark one of many. Then he went back to his table and dipped the corner of his napkin in his water glass, and sponged the grit off his knuckles.

Fifteen minutes later Detective Brenda Amos stepped into the room. She was writing in her notebook. At her shoulder was a man in a suit. His posture and his manner said he was showing her around. Therefore he was the bed and breakfast's manager. Or its owner. Reacher half lip-read and half heard him say, 'This gentleman is the only guest still on the premises.'

Amos glanced up from her notebook, routinely, and glanced away again. Then she looked back. A classic slow-motion double

114

take, like something out of an old-time television show. She stared. She blinked.

She said to the man in the suit, 'I'll talk to him now.'

'May I bring you coffee?'

'Yes, please,' Reacher called out to him. 'A pot for two.'

The guy nodded politely, after a fractional delay. To bring coffee to a police detective was one thing. To a guest was another. Beneath his station. But on the other hand, the customer was always right. He backed out of the room and Amos came all the way in. She sat down at Reacher's table, in the empty seat across from him.

She said, 'As a matter of fact I already had coffee this morning.'

'It doesn't have to be a once-a-day thing,' he said. 'There's no law that says you ever have to stop.'

'Also as a matter of fact I think Dunkin' is spiking it with LSD today.'

'How so?'

'Or else as a matter of fact this is the biggest déjà vu in history.'

'OK, how so that?'

'You know what déjà vu literally means?'

'It literally means already seen. It's French. My mother was French. She liked it when Americans used French phrases. It made her feel part of things.'

'Why are you telling me about your mother?'

'Why are you asking me about LSD?'

'What did we do yesterday?'

'Do?' he said.

'We dug up an old case from seventy-five years ago, in which a youth was found unconscious on the sidewalk of a downtown Laconia street. He was identified as a local twenty-year-old, already known to the police department as a loudmouth and a bully, but untouchable, because he was the son of the local rich guy. Remember?'

115

'Sure,' Reacher said.

'What happened when I got to work this morning?'

'I have no way of knowing.'

'I was told that a youth had just been found unconscious on the sidewalk of a downtown Laconia street. He had been identified as a local twenty-year-old, already known to the police department as a loudmouth and a bully, but untouchable, because he was the son of the local rich guy.'

'Seriously?'

'And I walk into the hotel across the street and here you are.'

'I guess that seems like a coincidence.'

'You think?'

'Not really. Clearly such crimes happen all the time.'

'Seventy-five years apart is all the time?'

'I'm sure there were many similar incidents in between. All rich bullies get a smack sooner or later. You could have picked any old case at random, and it could have been the same kind of match. And obviously I'm here, because I'm the guy who asked you about the non-random old case in question. So instead of a coincidence, it's really a mathematical certainty, especially because you know I don't live here, so where else would I be, except a hotel?'

'Directly across the street from the crime scene.'

'Are you going house to house for witnesses?'

'That's what we do.'

'Did anyone see anything?'

'Did you?'

'I'm not a birdwatcher,' Reacher said. 'More's the pity. Migration has started. My dad would have been excited.'

'Did you hear anything?'

'What time?'

'The kid was still unconscious at seven. Assuming his assailant was a human being and not an eighteen-wheel truck, call it no earlier than five o'clock.'

'I was asleep at five o'clock,' Reacher said. 'Didn't hear a thing.'

'Nothing at all?'

'Something woke me up the night before. But that was three o'clock, and a different hotel.'

'What was it?'

'It woke me up but it didn't happen again. I couldn't get a fix on it.'

'The kid also has a broken arm,' Amos said.

'That can happen,' Reacher said.

A waitress came in with two pots of coffee and two fresh cups. Reacher poured, but Amos didn't. She closed her notebook. He asked her, 'How is this investigation viewed inside the department?'

She said, 'We have low expectations.'

'Are tears not being shed?'

'It's complicated.'

'Who was the kid?'

'The kid is a lout and a bully and a predator. The kind who gets the best of everything, including victims and lawyers.'

'Doesn't sound all that complicated to me.'

'We're worried about what happens next.'

'You think he's going to get up a posse?'

'The problem is his father already has a posse.'

'The local rich guy? Who is he?'

'I paraphrased a little. He's really from Boston. But he lives in Manchester now.'

'And what kind of posse does he have?'

'He makes financial arrangements for clients who can't risk paper trails. In other words he launders money for the kind of people who need money laundered. I imagine he could borrow pretty much any kind of posse he wants. And we think he will. These guys have a culture. Someone attacked his family. Got to be made an example. This guy can't look weak. So we know sooner or later his people will show up here in town, asking around. We don't want trouble here. That's why it's complicated.'

Reacher poured another cup of coffee.

Amos watched.

She said, 'How did you hurt your hand?'

'I punched the garden wall.'

'That's an odd way to put it.'

'Can't really blame the wall.'

'It makes it sound deliberate.'

He smiled. 'Am I coming across as the kind of guy who would deliberately punch a wall?'

'When did it happen?'

'About twenty minutes ago.'

'Were you bending down to look at the flowers?'

'I like flowers as much as the next guy.'

Her phone dinged, and she read a message.

She said, 'The kid woke up but doesn't remember a thing about his attacker.'

'That can happen,' Reacher said again.

'He's lying. He knows but he's not telling us. He wants to tell his father instead.'

'Because they have a culture.'

'I hope whoever did it knows what's coming.'

'I'm sure whoever did it will leave town. Just like seventy-five years ago. Déjà vu all over again.'

'What are your own movements today?'

'I guess technically I'm leaving town.'

'Where are you going?'

'I'm going to Ryantown,' Reacher said. 'If I can find it.'

He bought a paper map at an old edge-of-town gas station. It showed the same kind of vagueness as Elizabeth Castle's phone. Certain roads headed in certain directions, as if for a purpose, and

118

certain destinations were shaded grey, as if once developed, but none of them had names any more, and there was no way of telling one from the other. He wasn't entirely sure what kind of geographic setting a tin mill would require. Truth was, he wasn't entirely sure what a tin mill did. Did it make tin out of ore? Or did it make cans and whistles and toys out of tin? Either way he guessed heat was involved. All kinds of fires and furnaces. Maybe a steam engine, to drive belts and tools. Which meant trucking in wood or coal. Plus water would be necessary, to make the steam. He looked at the map again, for roads, and rivers, and streams, all meeting at a place shaded grey. North and west of Laconia, according to Elizabeth Castle's historical research.

There were two possibilities. One was eight miles out, and the other was ten. Both had roads coming in off the main drag and stopping right there, for no apparent modern-day reason. Both had water, in what looked like broad tributaries both flowing towards the same larger river. The streams met the roads in tiny triangles, both printed as fine as the mapmaker could get them, both set in dots shaded grey. Little mills and factories, a couple dozen workers in four-flats, maybe a one-room schoolhouse, maybe a church, Amos had said. Either spot would fit the bill. Except the access road in and out of the ten-mile place curved gently north. Away from Laconia. Whereas the road in and out of the eight-mile place curved gently south. Towards Laconia. As if part of it. Not turning its back. Reacher pictured a boy on a bike, rattling eagerly away from home, his binoculars bouncing around his neck. From the ten-mile place he would first waste a couple of miles on the wrong bearing, and then he would have to make an awkward against-the-flow tight right turn. Whereas from the eight-mile place he would be heading the right way from the get-go, accelerating around the curve and then launching straight towards the heart of town. Which boy would say he lived in Laconia?

Which was good. Eight miles not ten would save an hour on the round trip. Plus a quarter of the effort. He folded the map and stuck it in his pocket. He set out walking.

He didn't get far.

FIFTEEN

Mark and Peter and Steven and Robert were together in the back parlour, watching the screens. They all showed Patty and Shorty still on their bed. Different angles, and different zooms. Some were wide shots, and some were close-ups.

Their door was still open.

'But no shoes this time,' Steven said. 'He's still got them on.'

'We should have used a self-closing mechanism,' Robert said.

'How could we have known?' Peter said. 'Normal people close their doors.'

'Relax,' Mark said. 'They're not going anywhere. Not right now. Bringing that suitcase back broke their hearts. Anyway, now they believe in the mechanic again.'

'We need that door shut pretty soon. We need to start warming them up. Their emotional state is important. Pacing is crucial now.'

'Then think of something.'

Peter turned back to the screens.

Reacher got a mile beyond the old edge-of-town gas station, around a long New England curve through woods as deep as a fairytale setting. Then behind him he heard tyres on the blacktop. He heard them slow to a walk. He heard them keep pace, ten yards back.

He stopped and turned around.

He saw a dark sedan. Medium in size and crisp in appearance. But poverty spec. There was paint where chrome might have been, and plain hubs, and mouse-fur upholstery. There was a sprung antenna on the trunk lid. An unmarked squad car. In it was Jim Shaw, of the Laconia Police Department. Chief of detectives. The guy from the police station lobby, the day before, with Brenda Amos. The redheaded Irish guy. In action he looked brisk and confident. He was alone at the wheel. He let his window down. Reacher walked closer, but stopped six feet away.

He said, 'Can I help you?'

Shaw said, 'Brenda told me you were headed this way.'

'You going to offer me a ride?'

'If I do it will be back to town.'

'How so?'

'The house-to-house turned up a woman who lives in the alley. She works in a cocktail bar in Manchester. Which is half owned by the folks the kid's father works for. We asked a lot of pointed questions and eventually she told us exactly what happened last night. From beginning to end. Soup to nuts. Everything except a physical description of her saviour. She claims she was so stressed her mind has gone blank.'

'That can happen, I guess,' Reacher said.

'She's lying. Why wouldn't she? She's protecting someone who did her a favour. But we have other evidence. She was saved real good, believe me. The kid looks like he was run over by a freight train. Therefore we're not looking for a small guy. We're looking

122

for a big guy. Probably right-handed. Probably woke up this morning with damage to his knuckles. Got to be something. A hit like that leaves a mark, believe me.'

'I scraped my hand on a wall,' Reacher said.

'Brenda told me.'

'Just one of those things.'

'A smarter man than me might start putting it all together. The woman from the cocktail bar gets home in the middle of the night, at an exactly predictable time, because of no night-time traffic, and the kid is waiting there for her, so she yells for help, which wakes a guy up, within a certain narrow radius, who then gets out of bed and goes to check, and who ends up dragging the kid away and smacking him around.'

'You told me she already said all that. Soup to nuts. You don't need to put it together.'

'The interesting part is the narrow radius. How close would the guy need to be, for the sound to travel clearly, and for him to get there as fast as he did? Pretty close, we think. The woman said she didn't yell real loud. The kid was trying to get his hand over her mouth at the time. It was definitely not a scream. So the guy asleep had to be close by. He was on the scene more or less immediately. Maximum one block, we think.'

'I'm sure there are many variables involved,' Reacher said. 'Maybe it's all down to how well people hear and how fast they get dressed. Maybe there's a link between the two. You could conduct a series of experiments. You could get the university involved. You could write a paper for a criminology journal.'

Shaw said, 'Common sense would indicate a woman's low-volume cry for help would be heard only through windows over the street. On a one-block radius. The house-to-house lists only six such rooms as occupied last night. A lot of apartments are offices now. Empty during the night. But still, we had six people to look at. And what did we find?'

'I have no way of knowing.'

'Five were ruled out immediately, two for being women and three of the men for age and infirmity and slightness of build. One of the men was over ninety. Two of them were over sixty. None of them could have hit that kid. Not the way it must have happened.'

'I was asleep at five o'clock,' Reacher said.

'Brenda told me. And because once upon a time you were a brother cop, we believe you. And because the kid was a scumbag, we don't care anyway. Not even enough to point out that five o'clock doesn't matter any more. The woman from the cocktail bar got home at three o'clock. She told Brenda the same thing happened the night before. You told Brenda you woke up the night before. At three o'clock. But we don't care. Except Brenda also told me she told you the scumbag's father is obliged to react.'

'She did.'

'That's my point. You should think carefully. OK, maybe the kid really is woozy. Maybe he truly can't remember his attacker. But you can't rely on that. If we can figure it out without eyewitness testimony, so can they. They'll be looking for a big guy with a damaged hand. You can't beat their forensics by rubbing your knuckles on a wall, not because they don't have walls, but because they don't have forensics. They have other methods. They're going to send whoever it takes to get this job done. We don't want trouble here.'

'Has the kid called his father yet?'

'First he called his lawyer. No doubt the lawyer called his father. By now they've known for thirty minutes. They're scrambling. Burner phones are burning up in more than one state, at this very moment, believe me. Presumably nothing is decided yet. But it won't be long. They'll be arriving soon. Better if they didn't find you here. Better if you took a look at the old homestead, and then kept on walking. Better if you didn't come back.'

'Because you don't want trouble?'

'Would you?'

'No,' Reacher said. 'Generally speaking, I think trouble is best avoided. You could almost call it a rule.'

'So we're on the same page?'

'We're in the same book. Maybe a difference in emphasis.'

'I'm not kidding,' Shaw said. 'I don't want trouble.'

'Relax,' Reacher said. 'I'll keep on walking. It's what I do. Assuming I find Ryantown first.'

'Don't give me terms and conditions. Don't tell me what you got to do first. I'm serious. I don't want trouble in my town.'

'Ryantown ain't yours. If you don't believe me, check with the kid at the census archive. He'll set you straight.'

'It's all Laconia to guys up from Boston. They'll be here tomorrow, asking around. Anyone seen a big guy with a banged-up hand?'

Reacher said, 'Tomorrow?'

'They won't let this go.'

'But until tomorrow walking on county roads is still pretty much a legal activity.'

'That's the problem with terms and conditions. You'll still be walking tomorrow. You could be walking for ever. They could have ten guys in town before you finally figure out you'll never even know if you find Ryantown or not. Those old places are nothing more than holes in the ground now. Who the hell can tell which was which a hundred years ago? So do me a big favour, OK? Find any old hole in the ground, go right ahead and call it Ryantown, and then get the hell out, and keep on getting, preferably in a straight line, preferably east, north, or west.'

Reacher nodded, and turned, and walked on, waving once but not looking back, and behind him he heard the hiss and squeal of the squad car's power steering, and then the sound of its tyres rolling away, back to town. He kept up a steady pace, four miles an hour, easy in the cool of the morning. The road was entirely in

125

shadow. He checked his map as he passed a left turn that led to a place with grey shading but no water. It was right where it should have been. He was on track. The map was good. He had about six more miles to go.

He walked on.

Patty and Shorty were still on the bed long after dawn. They had stared for hours at their luggage, as if hypnotized. The sudden and capricious reversal of its epic and hard-won voyage was hard to process. It was as if the long two-plus miles spent pushing the heavy load had never happened. But it had. Hours and hours, wasted. Maximum effort, bent at the waist. For no net result. Zero yards gained. A bitter pill.

Patty said, 'Do you think the story about the undergraduates is true?'

'Are you crazy?' Shorty said. 'You know we took it down there ourselves.'

'I don't mean this time. I mean undergraduates ever doing that.'

'I don't know,' Shorty said. 'I got no experience. But I guess it could be true. In a logical kind of way. Because Peter didn't know we took our stuff down there ourselves. All he knew was he found it in the hedge. How could he explain that? It must have reminded him of a thing from the past, which he assumed was happening again. Actually it wasn't, but it kind of proves the original thing must have been real, or how else could he have been reminded?'

'That's a circular argument.'

'Is it?'

'But it doesn't matter anyway. What matters is what he said. And what he said was weird.'

'Was it?'

'He said students steal their motel signs all the time.'

'Maybe they do. Maybe that's why they're gone now.'

'But to say all the time means over and over again, year after year.'

'I guess.'

'Like you would say your bottom ten-acre floods all the time.'

'Well, it does. Like you said, over and over, year after year.'

'Exactly. To say all the time means you're speaking from a certain length of experience. And then he said they thought the bag-stealing thing was finished a couple of years ago. And to know something is finished means you must have suffered it first. Let's say at least for a year. A whole cycle through both semesters. I'm sure students do different kinds of crazy stuff at different times.'

'OK,' Shorty said. 'Call it three years minimum. One year of suffering it and two years of not.'

'Except everything else they've said makes this feel like a brand new start-up. Like this could be their very first season. The stories don't match at all.'

Shorty was quiet a long moment.

Then he said, 'But you spoke to the mechanic.'

'Yes,' Patty said. 'I did.'

'And the mechanic was real.'

'Yes,' Patty said. 'He was.'

'Tell me again.'

'He sounded bright and wide awake and on the ball. He sounded friendly but courteous. He was knowledgeable but not domineering. He was an immigrant. Maybe one of those guys who takes a step down in terms of employment. Compared to the old country, I mean. He said something about the Yugoslav army. Maybe once he was a master sergeant in an armoured division, and now he drives a tow truck. That kind of thing. But he's going to make the best of it. It's going to be the shiniest tow truck you ever saw. He's going to work his way back. He's going to be a classic story.'

'You got all that from his voice?'

'It's what I felt. He asked mechanic questions. He knew what he should about us. He was worried in case Mark had woken us up. He was apologetic.'

'Total worst case?' Shorty asked, like a ritual between them.

'Would be he was one of those smooth-talking busy guys who pay no attention at all until an appointment actually rolls around. Deep down I think he was apologizing for not figuring it out yesterday.'

'That sounds real,' Shorty said.

'We'll know soon enough,' Patty said. 'He promised four hours maximum.'

After another mile the woods stopped and the vista opened out to a patchwork of horse fields and cow fields. Reacher walked on, conscious of the distance, thinking about a boy on a bike. It felt like a long way. But maybe it wasn't. Times had changed. In the past a five-mile walk or a twenty-mile cycle ride would have been considered routine. For a boy with a hobby, eight miles was nothing. Or nine, to be exact, to the downtown streets. Which was where he had been seen, late one September evening in 1943. Doing what? The birdwatcher lady made no mention of binoculars around his neck. Reacher felt she would have noticed. He was there for some other purpose. Which theoretically could have been many and various, for a sixteen-year-old. Except that 1943 was a serious year. The war was nearly two years old. Everything was rationed or in short supply. Everyone was dour and worried and working long hours. Hard to imagine any kind of giddy excitement going on good enough to attract a sixteen-year-old nine miles to the centre of a stiff little New Hampshire town on a fall evening during tough times.

No mention of a bicycle, either. Maybe he had parked it. Maybe he was walking back to get it. With his friend. Maybe his friend's bike was parked too. Then they met the big kid.

Reacher walked on. Coming up ahead on his left he saw his

general target area. He scoped it out, from the middle distance to the far horizon. Ryantown was in there somewhere. Possibly. He checked the map. The road he wanted was a shallow left turn about a mile ahead. Some distance short of it was shown a thinner spur. Same basic direction, but shorter and narrower. Not much more than a farm track. Which might or might not be useful. Best case, it would lead to a stern old farmhouse, ideally in continuous occupation by the same family for two centuries or more, ideally with a very old farmer sitting in a wheelback chair by the stove in the kitchen, with a rug on his knees, ready to talk for hours about his long-ago neighbours a mile to the north.

Hope for the best, plan for the worst, was Reacher's motto.

He walked on, and he took the turn into the narrow track. Very quickly he saw it didn't lead to a stern old farmhouse. What it led to was a pleasant split level, about as old as he was. Therefore built long after Ryantown was already gone. Therefore no good. No old geezer sitting there with his memories. Unless the house was a replacement. Which was possible. Plenty of houses were. Maybe they had torn down the stern old structure. Maybe it was no longer livable, in the modern era. Or maybe it had burned down. Maybe the wiring was bad. Possibly original, with silk insulation. But they all got out in time and they built a new house, which meant the very old farmer with the rug on his knees was no longer in a wheelback chair in the kitchen, but in a vinyl recliner in the family room. But it would be the same guy. With the same stories. Still willing to talk.

Hope for the best.

He walked on. The house was harmoniously designed and lovingly maintained, even pampered, like it got painted a year early every time. It had sensible plants around the foundation, neatly trimmed. It had a car port, shading a clean domestic pick-up truck from the pale midmorning sun. It had a white picket fence, running all the way around, enclosing a neat quarter acre, like a suburban garden.

Behind the fence was a pack of dogs.

There were six of them. Not barking yet. All mutts, all scruffy. Nothing huge, nothing tiny. Maybe a hundred different breeds, all mixed together. They came close and stood inside the picket gate. He was going to have to wade through them. He wasn't scared of dogs. He believed a measure of mutual trust solved most problems. He didn't plan to bite them. Why assume they planned to bite him?

He opened the gate. The dogs sniffed around him. They followed him down the path. He found the front door and pressed the bell. He stepped back and waited in the sun. The dogs pooled around his knees. A long minute later the front door opened and a man appeared behind the screen. He was a lean person, with a sensible expression on his face, and buzzed grey hair on his head. He was wearing blue jeans from a farm store, and a plain grey T-shirt. He was old enough to get a discount at the movies, but a long way from needing a cane. He too had a pool of dogs around his knees. Six more. Maybe the previous generation. Some had fur frosted grey.

Reacher watched the guy test out a bunch of alternative greetings in his mind, as if trying to find one to match his particular circumstances, in which a random pedestrian had shown up silently and magically on his doorstep in the middle of nowhere. But evidently failing to find one, because in the end all he said was, 'Yes?'

Reacher said, 'Sir, I'm sorry to disturb you, but I was passing by, and I have a question about some real estate north of here, and I wondered if you might be in a position to fill in the gaps in my information.'

The guy said, 'Are you a salesman?'

'No sir, I am not.'

'Insurance?'

'No sir.'

'Any kind of lawyer?'

'Not guilty.'

'Are you from the government?'

'No sir, not that either.'

'I believe you're obliged to tell me, if you are.'

'Understood, but I'm not.'

'OK,' the guy said.

He opened the screen door to shake hands.

'Bruce Jones,' he said.

'Jack Reacher.'

Jones closed the screen again.

Maybe to keep the old dogs in and the young dogs out.

He said, 'What real estate?'

'Where the next road on the left meets the stream,' Reacher said. He pointed in what he thought was a rough crow-flies direction, west and north. He said, 'Maybe a mile or two from here. The abandoned remains of a tiny industrial hamlet. Probably nothing left above ground level. Probably nothing to see except ruined foundations.'

'Nothing like that on my land.'

'How long have you lived here?'

'You're quick with the questions, mister. You should state your business.'

'My father grew up there. I want to go take a look. That's all.'

'Then I'm sorry. I can't help you. Sounds like the kind of thing you would need to stumble across accidentally. I never heard any mention. How long ago was it abandoned?'

'At least sixty years,' Reacher said. 'Maybe more.'

'I don't know whose land it is now, over by the stream. Maybe they know there are ruins, maybe they don't. If they were railed off for grazing sixty years ago, they would be completely over-grown by now. How big would they be?'

'Some acres, I suppose.'

'Then they could be under any copse of trees you see.'

131

'OK,' Reacher said. 'Good to know. I'll check a few out. Thank you for your time.'

Jones nodded, with the same sensible expression he had used before. Reacher turned to go, and got a couple of paces off the porch, followed by six patient dogs, and then behind him he heard the door change direction and open again, a stiff sound against a diligent draught excluder, and this time the screen door opened too. He turned back and saw Jones leaning one shoulder out and looking around the edge of the frame, as if to see him better, while simultaneously blocking his dogs with his leg.

He called out, 'Did you say industrial?'

'Small scale,' Reacher said.

'Would it have had something to do with pollution?'

'Possibly. It was a tin mill. There was probably a certain amount of crap leaking out.'

'You better come in,' Jones said.

The screen door creaked all the way open ahead of him, and slapped all the way shut behind him, which were in his limited experience the eternal sounds of a New England summer. Dog nails clicked on the floors. All six came in with him. He stepped into the unique smell of someone else's home. It was as clean and well maintained inside as outside. Jones led him to an alcove off an open-plan kitchen and dining room. Twelve dogs foamed around them. There was no family room. No vinyl recliner, no old geezer with a rug on his knees. The alcove was in use as a home office area. It was a decent size, but by that point the house was two generations old, and it looked like every member of both of them had kept every scrap of paper they ever saw. First Jones opened a sliding file drawer and thumbed through one of several fat and bulging folders suspended between sagging steel rods. Apparently he came up short, because he turned away and pushed and shoved a stack of bankers' boxes around, until he got the one he wanted, which was full of archived folders just as fat and bulging

132

as the current items. He thumbed through the first, and part of the way through the second.

Then he stopped.

He said, 'Here.'

He pulled out a faded sheet of paper. Reacher took it from him. It was a photocopied newsletter, dated eight years previously. Clearly one of a sequence of several, covering an issue in feverish detail, with a clear assumption of some prior knowledge. But it was easy enough to follow. The issue was Ryantown.

A little prior history was referred to, with the first appearance of the mill in the historical record, and then much later its period of peak production, which by implication seemed to be universally accepted as a horrific tableau of clouds of smoke and raging fires and boiling metals, like a miniature hell, like something the old poet Dante would have been proud of. Except that the next sentence, in brackets, was a grudging apology that the photograph used to illustrate the same point in an earlier edition had not actually been of Ryantown itself, but was a stock library image of a mill town in Massachusetts a decade earlier than the newsletter suggested, but which was nevertheless chosen with absolutely no intention to deceive, but rather in a spirit meant to be taken as purely mood-based, as such a tragic subject surely demanded, not literally, as indeed most histories were all too often written, usually to their detriment.

After the apology the narrative cut to the then-current chase, which seemed to be equal parts political, legal, and deranged. Apparently it was not yet definitively proved that the slow decomposition of Ryantown's ancient mineral runoff had harmed anyone's ground water. But it surely would be proved, and soon. Some of the world's top scientists were working on it. It was only a matter of time. Therefore readiness was everything. In which connection there was splendid news. Old Marcus Ryan's long chain of heirs and assigns had finally been untangled, and it was now certain beyond a reasonable doubt that the remaining stock in his company had been bundled with other near worthless assets and swept up in a sixty-year tornado of big-fish-eat-little-fish deals, which as of that moment had left the stock technically in the hands of a giant mining corporation based in Colorado. It was a breakthrough of enormous significance, because at last the tragic Ryantown ecological disaster had an identifiable owner. The lawsuits were typed up and ready to go.

At the bottom of the newsletter was a call for all concerned citizens to attend a meeting. Below that was an obvious pseudonym as the writer's name, and an e-mail address.

Reacher handed the paper back to Jones.

He said, 'What did you think of this at the time?'

'There's nothing wrong with our water,' Jones said. 'Never has been. I remember at first I figured this guy was probably a lawyer, jumping on a bandwagon. I figured he had identified a big corporation to go after with a class action suit. Maybe the company would settle just to make him go away. Bad ground water is never good PR. The lawyer would get a third. But I never heard about it again. I guess it fizzled out. I guess he never got his proof. Which he couldn't ever anyway, because the water is fine.'

'You said at first you thought he was a lawyer.'

'Later someone told me he was just a crazy old coot about five miles north of here. Then I met him, and he seemed harmless enough. He's not looking for money. He wants them to acknowledge their wrongdoing. Like a public confession. That seems to mean a lot to him.'

'You didn't go to the meeting?'

'Meetings are not my thing.'

'Pity,' Reacher said.

'Why?'

'One very important fact about Ryantown was not in the newsletter.'

134

'What?'

'Where it is.'

'I thought you knew. You said the side road and the river.'

'That was a best guess. Plus now you tell me it's going to look like a patch of primeval forest anyway. Which at first glance would seem to include about two-thirds of the state. I don't want to spend all day.'

'To see the place your father grew up? Some folks would spend all day.'

'Where did your father grow up?'

'Right here.'

'Which is a lovely place, I can see. But we just agreed Ryantown is an overgrown hole in the ground. There's a difference.'

'It might be of sentimental value. People like to know where they come from.'

'Right now I would rather know what a guy who wants to build a mill would need. He would need the road and the water. Is there anything else he would need?'

'How would I know?'

'You know how land is used.'

'I guess where the river meets the road would make sense. Look for a stand of trees with straight edges. The neighbours would have wanted safe grazing. They would have railed off the falling-down buildings long before the saplings came up, from seeds blowing in. The copse will have grown the same shape as the fences. Usually it's the other way around.'

'Thank you,' Reacher said.

'Good luck,' Jones said.

The screen door creaked open ahead of him, and slapped shut behind him.

He walked away. All twelve dogs followed him to the picket gate.

SIXTEEN

Patty and Shorty had moved out to their lawn chairs. Patty was staring at the view, which contained the dead Honda in the stony lot, and then the flat two acres, and then the dark belt of trees beyond, implacable, like a wall.

She looked at her watch.

She said, 'Why is it when someone says between two hours and four hours it's always nearer four hours than two hours?'

'Parkinson's disease,' Shorty said. 'Work expands to take up as much time as there is.'

'Law,' Patty said. 'Not disease. That's when you get the shakes.'

'I thought that was when you quit drinking.'

'It's a lot of things.'

'How much longer has he got?'

Patty looked at her watch again, and did a sum in her head.

'Thirty-three minutes,' she said.

'Maybe he didn't mean to be exactly precise.'

'He said two hours minimum and four hours maximum. That

sounds exactly precise to me. Then he said, I promise I'll get you on your way, cross my heart. With his accent.'

Shorty watched the dark space where the track came out of the woods.

He said, 'Tell me about the mechanic things he told you.'

'Best part was he said he had to pay the bills. He said he was going to head out to the highway and maybe he would get lucky with a wreck. The way he said it sounded professional. It was the kind of thing only a mechanic would say. Who else would say lucky about a wreck?'

'He sounds real,' Shorty said.

'I think he's real,' Patty said. 'I think he's coming.'

They watched the track. The sun was higher and the front rank of trees was lit up bright. Solid trunks, packed together, with more behind, with brush between, and brambles, and fallen branches propped at crazy angles.

Shorty said, 'How long has he got now?'

Patty checked her watch.

'Twenty-four minutes,' she said.

Shorty said nothing.

'He promised,' she said.

They watched the track.

And he came.

They felt it before they saw it. There was gradually a deep bass presence in the air, in the distance, like a shuddering, like a tense moment in a movie, as if huge volumes of air were being bludgeoned aside. Then it resolved into the hammer-heavy throb of a giant diesel engine, and the subsonic pulse of fat tyres and tremendous weight. Then they saw it drive out of the trees. A tow truck. A huge one. Industrial size. Heavy duty. It was the kind of thing that could haul an eighteen-wheeler off the highway. It was bright red. Its engine was roaring and it was grinding along in low gear.

Patty stood up and waved.

The truck bumped down off the blacktop into the lot. She had said it would be the shiniest truck you ever saw, purely from the guy's voice alone, and she had guessed exactly right. It was as bright as a carnival float. The red paint was waxed and polished. It had pinstripes and coachlines painted in gold. There were chrome lids and levers, all polished to a blinding shine. The guy's name was written on the side, proudly, a foot high, in a copperplate style. It was Karel, not Carol.

'Wow,' Shorty said. 'This is great.'

'Sure seems to be,' Patty said.

'Finally we're out of here.'

'If he can fix it.'

'We're out of here either way. He doesn't leave here without us. OK? Either he fixes our car or he gives us a ride. No matter what the assholes say. Deal?'

'Deal,' Patty said.

The truck came to a stop behind the Honda, and it settled back to a grumbling idle. Way up high the door opened and a guy used one step of the ladder and then jumped the rest of the way down. He was medium sized and wiry, bouncing on his toes, full of get-up-and-go. He had a shaved head. He looked like a photo in a war crimes trial. Like a stone-faced lieutenant behind a renegade colonel in a black beret. But he was smiling. He had a twinkle in his eye.

'Ms Sundstrom?' he said. 'Mr Fleck?'

Patty said, 'Call us Patty and Shorty.'

He said, 'I'm Karel.'

She said, 'Thank you so much for coming.'

He pulled an object from his pocket. It was a dirty black box the size of a deck of cards, with stubs of disconnected wires coming out. He said, 'We got lucky with a wreck. Way in the back of the junkyard. Same model as yours. Same colour, even. Rear-ended by a gravel truck six months ago. But the front part was still OK.'

Then he smiled encouragingly and shooed them towards their door.

'Go inside and pack your stuff,' he said. 'This is a two-minute job.'

'We packed already,' Patty said. 'We're good to go.'

'Really?'

'We packed early this morning. Or late last night. We wanted to be ready.'

'Have you not enjoyed your stay?'

'We're anxious to get going. We should be somewhere else by now. That's all. Apart from that, it's a great place. Your friends have been very kind to us.'

'No, I'm the new guy. They're not my friends yet. I think the last guy they used was their friend. But I think they had a falling out. So they started calling me instead. Which was great. I wanted the business. I'm an ambitious guy.'

Shorty said, 'I wouldn't want to work for them.'

'Why not?'

'I think they're weird.'

Karel smiled.

'They're clients on a list,' he said. 'The longer the list, the better I get through the hungry months.'

'I still wouldn't,' Shorty said.

'It's nine quad bikes and five cars. Guaranteed work. I can put up with a little weirdness in exchange for that.'

'Five cars?'

'As of now. Plus a ride-on lawnmower.'

'They told us one car,' Shorty said. 'We saw it.'

'Which one?'

'An old pick-up truck.'

'That's the beater they use around the property. On top of that they got Mercedes-Benz SUVs, one apiece.'

'You're kidding.'

'Totally loaded.'

'Where are they?'

'In the barn.'

Shorty said nothing.

Patty said, 'I have a question.'

Karel said, 'Go ahead.'

'How long have they been here?'

'This was their first season.'

She said, 'Please fix our car now.'

'That's why I'm here,' Karel said.

He opened the Honda's hood, with deft and practised movements. He leaned forward and held the new black box down low, as if trying it for size. Then he backed off an inch and squinted, as if trying to get a better look. He extricated himself and stood up straight.

He said, 'Actually your relay is in good shape.'

Patty said, 'Then why won't it start?'

'Must be a different problem.'

Karel put the black box with the disconnected wires back in his pocket. He shuffled around the fender and approached from a different angle.

'Try the key one more time,' he said. 'I want to hear how dead it is.'

Shorty got in behind the wheel and flipped the key, on, off, on, off, click, click, click, click. Karel said, 'OK, I get it.'

He shuffled a full 180, all the way around to the opposite fender, and he bent down again, where the battery was bolted into a skeletal cradle. He stuck his face right down and twisted his neck so he could see underneath. He brought his hand down and felt with his fingertip. Then he backed out and straightened up and stood still for a second. He glanced at the woods, and then the other way, at room twelve's corner. He stepped out until he could see beyond it. To the barn, and the house. He came back and shooed Patty and Shorty up on their boardwalk, over towards their door, looking back all the time as he came, as if checking they were all safely out of some theoretical line of vision.

He said, quietly, 'Did any of these guys work on your car?'

'Peter did,' Shorty said.

'Why?'

'He said he looked after the quad bikes, so we asked him to take a look.'

'He doesn't look after the quad bikes.'

'Did he screw it up?'

Karel looked left and right.

'He cut the main positive feed coming out of the battery.'

'How? By accident?'

'Not possible by accident,' Karel said. 'It's a pure copper wire thicker than your finger. You would need a big pair of pliers with a wirecutter blade. It would take some strength. You would definitely know you were doing it. It would be an act of deliberate sabotage.'

'Peter had a pair of pliers. Yesterday morning. I saw him.'

'It's like disconnecting the battery completely. Zero electrical activity anywhere. The vehicle is paralysed. Which is exactly your symptom.'

'I want to see,' Shorty said.

'Me too,' Patty said.

Karel said, 'Look underneath.'

They took it in turns, leaning deep over the engine bay, ducking down, twisting their necks. They saw a stiff black wire, clearly chopped in half, the ends displaced, the cut faces gleaming as fresh as new pennies. They walked back to where Karel was standing. He said, 'I'm sorry, but I don't know what to tell you. I don't really know these guys very well. I have to assume this was their idea of a practical joke. But it's a really stupid one. It won't be cheap

141

to fix. That kind of wire is almost rigid. It's like plumbing. You have to remove a whole bunch of other components just to get near it.'

'Don't fix it,' Patty said. 'Don't even think about it. Just get us out of here this minute. Give us a ride right now.'

'Why?'

'It wasn't a practical joke. They're keeping us here. They won't let us leave. We're like prisoners.'

'That sounds pretty weird.'

'But it's true. They're stringing us along. Everything they tell us is lies.'

'Like what?'

'They said we were the first guests in this room, but I don't think we are.'

'That's totally weird.'

'Why?'

'There were people in this room a month ago. I know that for sure, because I had to bring a tyre to a guy in room nine.'

'They said you were their good friend.'

'That was the second time I ever met them.'

'They implied they had been here at least three years.'

'That's not right. They showed up a year and a half ago. There was a big fight over a building permit.'

'They said their phone was out yesterday. But I bet it wasn't. They just wanted to keep us here.'

'But why would they? Money?'

'We thought of that,' Shorty said. 'We were about to run out. Anyone would run out sooner or later. Then what would they do?'

'This is very weird,' Karel said.

He stood there, uncertain.

'Please give us a ride,' Patty said. 'Please. We have to get out of here. We'll pay you fifty bucks.'

'What about your car?'

'We'll leave it here. We were going to sell it anyway.'

'It wouldn't be worth much.'

'Exactly. We don't care what happens to it. But we've got to go. We have to get out. Right now, this minute. You're our only hope. We're prisoners here.'

She stared at him. He nodded, slowly. Then again, taking charge. He stepped back, and looked left and right, craning over both his shoulders. He glanced at his giant truck, and the dimensions of the lot, measuring it, scoping it out, and then he glanced into the room, at the neat arrangement of luggage.

'OK,' he said. 'Time to arrange a jailbreak.'

'Thank you,' Patty said.

'But first I need to ask an embarrassing question.'

'What?'

'Did you pay your bill? I would get in trouble if I helped you skip out in secret. There are innkeeper laws here.'

'We paid last night,' Shorty said. 'We're good until noon.'

'OK,' Karel said. 'So let's think for a minute. We should err on the side of caution. We should assume the worst case. We don't know how they're going to react to this. Therefore it's probably better if they don't see it happening. Agreed?'

'Much better,' Patty said.

'So you guys stay out of sight, while I turn the truck around, so it's facing in the right direction, then you guys grab your bags and hop on board, and away we go. By which time nothing will be able to stop us. Even a Mercedes-Benz would bounce right off. OK?'

'We're good to go,' Shorty said.

Karel looked in the door at the suitcase.

'That's pretty big,' he said. 'Can you lift it? Want me to come back and help?'

'I can do it.'

'Show me. A delay could screw this up.'

Patty went in first. She picked up the overnight bags, one in

143

each hand, and stood out the way, so Shorty could get to the main attraction. He wrapped both fists around the new rope handle, and hauled, and the case came up six inches in the air. Karel watched from the doorway, as if judging.

He said, 'How fast can you move with it?'

'Don't worry,' Shorty said. 'I won't screw up.'

Karel looked at him, and then at Patty, she with a small bag in each hand, he with the big bag in both, the two of them standing there side by side in the space between the bed and the AC. He said, 'OK, wait there, and don't come out until I get turned around. Then Patty comes out first. She throws the small bags up in the cab and climbs in after them. Then Shorty comes out and boosts the suitcase up and Patty leans down and hauls it in, and then Shorty climbs up. Does that make sense?'

'Sounds good,' Shorty said.

'OK,' Karel said. 'Be ready.'

He leaned in the doorway and grabbed the knob and closed the door on them. Through the window they saw him hustle across the dirt and climb the ladder to the cab. They heard the engine roar and saw the truck jerk into gear and move slowly away, right to left, out of sight.

They waited.

It didn't come back.

They waited.

Nothing.

No sound, no movement. Nothing out the window except the view as before. The Honda, the lot, the grass, the wall of trees.

Shorty said, 'Maybe he got hung up for a minute. Maybe the assholes came out and started talking to him.'

'He's been gone longer than a minute,' Patty said. She put her bags down and stepped closer to the window. She craned her neck and peered out.

'Can't see anything,' she said.

144

Shorty put the suitcase down. He joined her at the window. He said, 'I could go check from the corner.'

'They might see you. They're probably all standing around talking. What else can they be doing? How long does it take to turn a truck around?'

'I'll be careful,' Shorty said.

He stepped to the door. He turned the knob and pulled. But the door was stuck. It wouldn't move at all. He checked it was properly unlocked from the inside, and he tried the knob both ways. Nothing happened. Patty stared at him. He pulled harder. He put one meaty palm flat on the wall and hauled.

Nothing.

'They locked us in,' Patty said.

'How?'

'They must have a button in the house. Like remote control. I think they've been messing with it all along.'

'That's completely crazy.'

'What isn't, here?'

They stared out the window. The Honda, the lot, the grass, the wall of trees. Nothing else.

Then the window blind motored down in front of them and the room went dark.

SEVENTEEN

Karel stepped into the back parlour and the others crowded around and whooped and hooted and slapped him on the back. Steven ducked away and pattered at a keyboard and the video on the screens rewound at high speed, three jerky figures racing around, doing everything fast and backward. He put on a TV voice and said, 'Folks, let's go to the action replay, and let's ask the man of the hour how it felt to hit that big grand slam.'

He changed to forward motion and normal speed, and on the screens Karel was seen smiling encouragingly and shooing Patty and Shorty towards their door. The audio caught him saying, 'Go inside and pack your stuff. This is a two-minute job.'

'But it's a swing and a miss,' the real Karel said, in a TV voice of his own, like a scratchy signal coming in all the way from the Balkans. 'The first at-bat is a strikeout.'

On the screens Patty said, 'We packed already.'

In the parlour Karel said, 'And from that point onward I was just making it up as I went along. I figured something might happen sooner or later. I knew all I needed to do was manoeuvre them into the room and close the door. In the end I got lucky.'

The others hooted and hollered again, but Mark said, 'There was no luck involved. That was a virtuoso performance. We should save this video for ever. We should learn it by heart. It was like hearing a maestro play the violin. You've done this before, haven't you, Karel?'

The parlour went quiet.

On the screens the video ran on, with the three figures huddled between the Honda and the boardwalk, talking low.

Mark said, 'You distanced yourself from us, by pretending not to be our friend, which purely by default generated a closer bond with them. They fell right into it. They did this to themselves. They became almost intimate. Which you then built on by confirming their worst fears about certain inconsistencies they had noticed. Then you doubled down even more by slowly agreeing to help them escape. It was a masterpiece of emotional manipulation. It was a perfectly constructed rollercoaster. They were worried all morning, then suddenly filled with intense hope, which then increased to actual euphoria, as they stood there, bags in hand, waiting to go, and now they're suddenly sick with utter defeat.'

Steven clicked to a live feed. Patty and Shorty were sitting on their bed, in the dark, not moving at all.

'It works better this way,' Karel said. 'I promise. It's better when they're in touch with their feelings. It marinates their brains. It makes them more fun later, cross my heart.'

Then he said, 'I'll see you soon,' and walked out the door.

Reacher saw the left turn coming up. It was a hundred yards ahead. It met the main drag at an oblique angle and curved gently away, as if reluctant. Then it ran onward through apple orchards. He walked on towards it. Halfway there he had to step up on the

147

grass shoulder to let a giant tow truck blow by. It was huge and bright red and spotlessly clean. It had gold pinstripes all over it. It shook the ground under his feet. He watched it go. Then he walked on again and took the turn.

The side road was narrower than the main drag, but wide enough and hard enough for the kind of primitive trucks they might have used long ago, for hauling wood or coal or tin. On either side in the orchards the apple trees were bending over with heavy fruit. He could smell it in the air. He could smell hot dry grass. He could hear the buzz of insects. Overhead a hawk rode the thermals.

Then half a mile after its reluctant turn away from Laconia, the road turned again, as if definitively, due west. After that it ran straight into the distance, through more apple orchards, towards a small shiny dot, which Reacher figured might be a parked car. Beyond that seemed to be trees of a different green. He walked on. As he got closer he saw the dot was indeed a car. Shiny because of the power of the sun, not because of the paint on the car. It looked like a battered old lump. Eventually he saw it was a Subaru, a little like the one he had ridden in with the contractor with the inspector problem, genetically related, but twenty years older. Like an ancestor. It was parked head-on against a wooden fence that ran side to side where the blacktop ended. Beyond the fence was another acre of apple orchard, and then another fence, beyond which were wild trees with bigger leaves.

There was a guy in the Subaru.

He was sitting behind the wheel. Reacher could see the collar of a blue denim jacket, and a long grey ponytail. The guy wasn't moving. He was just staring ahead through the windshield.

Reacher walked the length of the car on the passenger side and stopped with his back to the guy and his hips against the fence. The next fence was a hundred yards away. The trees beyond it looked like regular New England species, densely but randomly scattered, twisted and competing. Which might be what happened when seeds blew in.

Also, the fence looked straight.

Promising.

Behind him he heard a car door open, and a voice said, 'You're the man who talked to Bruce Jones.'

Reacher turned around and said, 'Am I?'

The guy from the Subaru was a reedy character maybe seventy years old, tall but cadaverous. Under his jacket his shoulders looked like a coat hanger.

He said, 'He showed you the newsletter I wrote.'

'That was you?'

'The very same. He called me. He thought I might be interested that you were interested. I was, so I came out to meet you.'

'How did you know where?'

'You're looking for Ryantown,' the guy said.

'Have I found it?'

'Straight ahead.'

'Those trees?'

'They thin out in the centre. You can see pretty well.'

'Sure I won't get poisoned?'

'Tin has the potential to be dangerous. More than a hundred milligrams of tin per cubic metre of air is immediately injurious to life and health. What's worse is when tin bonds with certain hydrocarbons to make organotins. Some of those compounds are more lethal than cyanide. That's what I was worried about.'

'What happened with that in the end?'

'The chemistry didn't say what it needed to say.'

'Even though top scientists were working on it?'

'In the end the corporation in Colorado banned me from trespassing on what I insisted was their land. They took out a restraining order to keep me away. I can't go beyond this fence.'

'Pity,' Reacher said. 'You could have shown me around.'

'What's your name?'

'Reacher.'

The guy said an address. A street number and a street name. The same name and the same number Reacher had seen in cubicle four, on the screen, from the census when his father was two.

'It was on the ground floor,' the guy said. 'Some of the tile is still there. In the kitchen. It was still there eight years ago, anyway.'

'You haven't been back?'

'You can't fight city hall.'

'Who would know?' Reacher said. 'Just this once.'

The guy didn't answer.

Reacher said, 'Wait.'

He looked ahead, across the hundred yards of orchard, to the second fence, and the trees beyond.

He said, 'If that's Ryantown over there, why does the road stop here?'

'It used to go all the way,' the guy said. 'Technically the apple farmer is only squatting on this part of his land. About forty years ago a cold winter froze the blacktop off, and the next winter broke the base up, so in the spring the farmer borrowed a bulldozer and planted some more apple trees. Then in the summer the county came by and fixed what it could see. In the fall the farmer threw up this fence, and from that point onward it was a done deal. But good luck ever selling that parcel. The title search won't come back pretty.'

'OK,' Reacher said. 'Maybe I'll see you later.'

He hitched up on the fence, and swung his legs over, and stepped down in the orchard.

'Wait,' the guy said. 'I'll come with you.'

'You sure?'

'Who will know?'

'Live free or die,' Reacher said. 'I saw it on your licence plate.'

The guy stepped up on the bottom rail of the fence and from

150

there performed a manoeuvre similar to Reacher's. They walked together past shiny green eye-level apples, all of them bigger than baseballs, some of them bigger than softballs, stumbling now and then on uneven ground, where maybe forty years earlier the clandestine winter cleanup had been a little hasty. A hundred yards later they arrived at the second fence, where ahead of them were trees of a different kind, not decorous or orderly or smelling sweetly of ripe fruit, but rank weeds, basically. They were thinner and unhealthier dead ahead, because there they were growing through where the old road resumed, without the benefit of either a bulldozer or planting. Therefore dead ahead would be the practical way in. No machete required. Or at least less pushing and shoving. The guy with the ponytail agreed. He was looking at it eight years later, but it was still the best option.

'How long before we see anything?' Reacher asked.

'Right away,' the guy said. 'Look down. You're walking on the old road. Nothing has been done to it, except by nature, and weather.'

Which was plenty. They climbed the fence and pushed through thin trunks and halfhearted bushes, over terrain broken up by sixty years of rain and roots, with cobblestones thrust upward and turned over and rolled aside. Soon they were in an inner ring, like the hole in a doughnut, where the trees were thin everywhere, because the ground was bad everywhere. The road itself could be traced ahead, curving towards where Reacher could hear water. The stream. Maybe the mill was down there. Built next to it, or even over it.

The guy with the ponytail started pointing things out. First up on the left was a rectangular foundation the size of a single garage. The church, the guy said. Facing away from everything else, as if from temptation and wickedness. Next up on the right was the same kind of thing. The nub of a stone foundation, just inches high, mostly mossy and covered, crisply enclosing an area of early and vigorous growth, because it had been a crawl space, with no

151

cobblestones, or flagstones, or stones of any other kind. Just beaten earth, which after a couple of rains was raring to go. This was the schoolroom, the guy said. Better than you might expect. All the kids could read and write. Some of them could think. Teachers were respected then.

'Were you a teacher?' Reacher asked.

'For a time,' the guy said. 'In an earlier life.'

The mill was where the road met the stream. It had been built half in and half out of the water. All that was left was a complex matrix of blocky foundations made of mossy stone, half overgrown by damp riverbank species. One of the foundations was solid and the size of a chimney. One was solid and the size of a room. Perhaps to support heavy machinery. Cauldrons, and crucibles, and ladles. The guy showed Reacher a drain in the floor, open to the water below.

The workers' housing was across the street, in two buildings laid out in a line. Just the foundations remained. Both would have had a central lobby with stairs, with left-hand and right-hand apartments up and down. Two four-flats. A total of eight residences. Ryantown, New Hampshire. Population, possibly less than thirty.

The guy said, 'The Reacher address would have been the ground-floor apartment on the extreme right-hand end. Nearest the mill. Traditionally the foreman lived there. Your grandfather, perhaps.'

'For a time he graded roads for the county. But his address didn't change.'

'The mill closed for a couple of years late in the Depression. No point throwing him out in the street. It wasn't like they fired him and needed his house. The mill was idle. It was World War Two that got it going again.'

Reacher looked up at the sky. It was full of bird life. Then in his mind he subtracted the new trees and rebuilt the old chimney, and

152

he wondered how it was back in the fall of 1943, with the mill running night and day, and the sky full of smoke.

The guy said, 'I better get going. I shouldn't be here at all. You stay, if you want. I'll wait in the car. I could give you a ride, if you like.'

'Thanks,' Reacher said. 'But don't wait any longer than you want to. I'm always happy to walk.'

The guy nodded, and slipped away through the trees, back the way they had come. Reacher walked over to the right-hand four-flat. Nothing was left of where the shared entrance would have been, except for a stone doorstep. It was wide and deep. It bridged a gutter on the side of the road. The gutter was made from cobble-stones laid in a deep U-shaped contour, now mostly broken up and displaced by growth. He stepped over it into the one-time lobby. The floor was cement, broken up by time into random slabs, canted this way and that like ice floes on a winter river. Every split and seam had been colonized by something growing.

Nothing remained of the lobby's right-hand wall except for stubs of broken brick, low down at floor level. They looked like teeth smashed down to the gum. In the centre was a stone saddle, no taller, but intact. The right-hand ground-floor apartment's front door. Reacher stepped inside. The hallway floor had three trees growing through it. Their trunks were no thicker than his wrist, but they had raced twenty feet high, looking for light. Beyond them and either side were low lines of smashed brick, showing where the rooms had been, like an architect's floor plan come to life, slightly three-dimensional. Two bedrooms, he thought, plus a living room and a dine-in kitchen. All small. Mean and pinched, by modern standards. No bathroom. Maybe out back.

The surviving patch of tile was on a tipped-up slab of what must have been the kitchen floor. It looked like a standard old-fashioned commercial product, and the cement under it looked crusty and full of air, but it had clung on by some miracle of

153

adhesive chemistry. The pattern in the tile was faded and washed out by sixty years of exposure, but it looked like once upon a time it had been some kind of a late Victorian riot of bright tangled colours, with acanthus leaves, and marigolds, and artichoke blossoms. Reacher imagined it close up, from a kid's point of view, crawling around, with the colours bobbing in and out of focus. As he remembered it the only colour Stan had grown up to care about was olive drab. Maybe why.

He left by squeezing past the hallway trees again and going out through the lobby. Which was pointless, because he could have stepped out of the building anywhere he chose. No wall was more than four inches high. But he wanted to feel he was retracing steps. He paused at the street door, which wasn't there, and sat down on the step, which still was, like a kid might, maybe after a rainstorm, with the gutter running like a river under his feet.

Then he heard a sound, way off to his right.

It was a yelp. A man's voice. Definitely not joy or ecstasy. Not really outrage or anger either. Just pain. Distant. About where the orchard was, on the way back to the car. Reacher stood up, and picked his way over the heaved and tumbled stones as fast as he could, slipping between trees, following the old road, past the schoolroom, past the church, back to the fence.

Where fifty yards away he saw the old guy with the ponytail, exactly halfway across the orchard. Another guy less than half his age and maybe twice his weight was standing behind him, twisting his arms.

Reacher stepped over the fence and set out towards them.

EIGHTEEN

Fifty yards would have been five or six seconds for an athlete, but Reacher was aiming nearer thirty. A slow walk. But purposeful. Intended to communicate something. He kept his strides long and his shoulders loose and his hands away from his sides. He kept his head up and his eyes hard on the big guy. A primitive signal, learned long ago. The guy glanced away to the south. For help, maybe. Maybe he wasn't alone.

Reacher got close.

The big guy turned to face him. He wrestled the old guy around in front, and used him like a human shield.

Reacher stopped six feet away.

He said, 'Let him go.'

Just three words, but in a tone also learned long ago, with whole extra paragraphs hidden in the dying vowel sound at the end of the phrase, about the inevitable and catastrophic result of attempted resistance. The big guy let the old guy go. But he wasn't quitting. No sir. He wanted Reacher to be sure about that. He made it like he wanted to free up his hands anyway. For more important purposes. He shoved the old guy aside and stepped right into Reacher's space, not more than four feet away. He was twenty-some years old, dark-haired and unshaven, more than six feet and two hundred pounds, tanned and muscled by outdoor labour.

He said, 'This is none of your business.'

Reacher thought, what is this, Groundhog Day?

But out loud he said, 'You were committing a crime on public land. I would be failing in my duty as a citizen if I didn't point it out. That's how civilization works.'

The guy glanced away to the south, and back again.

He said, 'This ain't public land. This is my granddaddy's apple farm. And neither of you should be here. Him because he ain't allowed and you because you're trespassing.'

'This is the road,' Reacher said. 'Your granddaddy stole it from the county forty years ago. Back when he was a brave young fellow. Like you are now.'

The guy glanced south again, but this time he didn't glance back. Reacher turned and saw another guy approaching, walking fast between two lines of trees, where the orchard came down a slope. He looked the same as the first guy, except a generation older. Not more. The daddy, perhaps. Not the granddaddy. Better jeans than his son. Cleaner T-shirt. Deeper tan, greyer hair. Built the same, but fifty-something.

He arrived, and said, 'What's going on here?'

Reacher said, 'You tell me.'

'Who are you?'

'Just a guy standing on the public road asking you a question.'

'This is not the public road.'

'That's the problem with denial. Reality doesn't care what you think. It just keeps rolling along. This is the road. Always was. Still is.'

'What's your question?'

'I saw your boy physically assaulting this much older gentle-

156

man. I guess my question is how well you think that reflects on your parenting skills.'

'In this case, pretty damn well,' the new guy said. 'What are our apples worth if people think our water is poisoned?'

'That all was eight years ago,' Reacher said. 'It came to nothing anyway. The top scientists in the world said your water is OK. So get over it. With a little humility. Probably you said some dumb thing eight years ago. Should I twist your arm today?'

The old guy with the ponytail said, 'Technically they have a contract with the corporation in Colorado. There was a rider on the restraining order. It said they get paid if they can prove I was here. I hoped they had forgotten the arrangement. Apparently they hadn't. They saw my car.'

'How do they prove it?'

'They just did. They texted a picture. That's where he went. No cell signal, except up on the rise.'

'Law and order,' the daddy said. 'It's what this country needs.'

'Except for the part about stealing the county road to grow more apples.'

'I'm getting sick of hearing you say that, over and over.'

'It's the sound of reality, rolling along.'

'Why were you in the woods anyway?'

'None of your business,' Reacher said.

'Maybe it is our business. We have a relationship with the land-owner.'

'You can't text a picture of me.'

'Why not?'

'You would have to take your phone out of your pocket. Where-upon I would take it away from you and break it. I guess that's why you can't.'

'There are two of us. Two phones.'

'Still not enough. You should call for reinforcements. But oh dear, you can't. No cell signal, except up on the rise.'

'You're a cocky son of a bitch, aren't you?'

'I prefer realistic,' Reacher said.

'Want to put it to the test?'

'I would have an ethical dilemma. It might scar the boy for life to see his daddy laid out in front of him. Equally it might scar you to see your boy laid out. After being unable to protect him, I mean. You might feel bad about that. I believe it's a parenting thing. I wouldn't know for sure. I'm not a father myself. But I can imagine.'

The guy didn't reply.

Reacher said, 'Wait.'

He looked south, between the two lines of trees, where the orchard came down the slope.

'You were on your way back,' he said. 'The text was already sent, from the top of the hill. The photograph must have been taken some moments before that. So why was our mutual friend still here, with his arms behind his back?'

No answer.

The guy with the ponytail said, 'I was to get a beating. So I would learn my lesson. Just as soon as the text was sent and their money was guaranteed. At that point they didn't know you were in the woods too.'

'That shouldn't really make a difference,' Reacher said. 'Should it? Not to men of conviction, surely.'

He looked at the daddy, and then at the son, full in the eye.

He said, 'Time is wasting, guys. Go ahead and give him his beating.'

No one moved.

Reacher looked at the young guy.

He said, 'It's OK. He won't hurt you. He's seventy years old. You could push him over with a feather. He's nothing to be scared of.'

The guy moved his head, like a dog sniffing the air.

'It's a binary choice now,' Reacher said. 'Either you hit him, or you're scared of him.'

No response.

'Or maybe it's conscience trouble. Maybe that's it. You don't want to hit an old guy. You really don't. But hey, think about the apples. You have a job to do. I get it. In fact I could help you out. You could give me a beating first. That way you would feel you had earned it, when you start in on the old guy. It might make you feel less troubled.'

No response.

'Why not?' Reacher said. 'You scared of me too? Scared I'm going to hurt you? I have to tell you, it's a possibility. Full disclosure. You need to make an informed decision. Because now it really is a binary choice. Either you hit me, or you're scared of me.'

No answer.

Reacher stepped in close. The opposite of risky. Better to crowd him. If the kid was dumb enough to throw a punch, it was better to smother it early, before it had speed and development and direction. Which would be easy enough. If the kid was dumb enough. Reacher was thirty pounds heavier and three inches taller and probably five inches longer in the arm. That much was visible.

The kid was dumb enough.

His shoulder jerked back in what Reacher took to be the early warning stages of what was no doubt intended to be a short clubbing right to his face. Which gave him a choice. Either instantaneous reaction, involving a wide outward-sweeping gesture with his left forearm, designed to deflect the incoming short right, while his own short right crashed home. Which would be in any realistic sense the best move to make. It would be fast, hard, and elegantly abrupt. But it wouldn't be forensic. Reacher felt like he was in front of a jury. Like he was giving evidence. Or being asked to explain it, like an expert witness. He felt in order to be effective he should let the narrative unspool a little longer than an instant. A crime required both intent and action, and he felt he should let both components become plainly visible, all the way to where they were provable beyond a reasonable doubt.

So he jerked his head sideways and let the short right fizz past his ear, in all its glory, a big punch now, right there for every eye to see, unmistakable, obvious in its intent, and then he waited for the kid to drag his fist back unrequited, and then he waited again, for what felt to him like a very long interval, purely to allow adequate time for jury-room deliberations, and then he hit the kid under the chin with a solid right-hand uppercut. The kid went up weightless in his boots, and then collapsed backward on the grass, with a bristly thump, with all kinds of dust and pollen puffing up in the sunshine. The kid's limbs went slack and his head lolled to the side.

Reacher gave the guy with the ponytail a let's-go nod.

Then he looked at the kid's daddy.

'Parenting tip,' he said. 'Don't leave him lying in the road. He could get run over.'

'I won't forget this.'

'That's the difference between us,' Reacher said. 'I already have.'

He caught up to the old guy, and they walked the second fifty yards together, back to the ancient Subaru.

Eventually Patty got up off the bed. She walked to the door, where the light switch was. Three steps. Through the first she was certain the power would still be on. Through the second she was sure it would be off. If they could lock the door and shade the window by remote control, surely they could kill the electricity. Then she changed her mind again. Why would they? Through the third step she was once again convinced it would be on. Because of the meals. Why would they give them meals and then expect them to eat in the dark? Then she remembered the flashlights. What were they for? She remembered Shorty's comment. *In case you have to eat in the dark.* Maybe not so dumb.

160

She tried the switch.

It worked. The lights came on. Hot and yellow. She hated electric light in the daytime. She tried the door. Still locked. She tried the buttons for the window blind. Nothing. Shorty sat still in the brassy glare, and watched her. She turned and looked all around the room. At the furniture. At their bags, still where they had dropped them, when the truck didn't come back. At the walls, and the slim moulding where they met the ceiling. At the ceiling itself. It was a snowy expanse of perfectly smooth old-fashioned New England white, containing nothing except a smoke alarm and a bulkhead light, both above the bed.

Shorty said, 'What?'

Patty looked back at their bags.

She said, 'How well were they hidden?'

'Where?'

'In the hedge, Shorty.'

'Pretty well,' he said. 'The big one is heavy. It squashed right down. You saw.'

'And then Peter got lucky and got his truck started and took it down the track to warm it up. There and back, real quick. Yet he had time to spot our luggage.'

'Maybe it was his headlights as he turned. Maybe it was more visible from behind. It was on the right. He would have turned counterclockwise. Different view than you got with the flashlight. You checked from the road.'

'He had time to make a rope handle.'

Shorty said nothing.

'Using rope he just happened to have with him,' she said.

'What are you thinking?'

'There were other things too,' she said. 'We made fun of Karel for saying he might get lucky with a wreck, and then he said it right back to us, practically the first thing out of his mouth. In the back of the junkyard.'

161

'Maybe he says it a lot.'

'Why did they make a rope handle?'

'I thought they were maybe helping us.'

'Are you kidding?'

'I suppose. I didn't understand it.'

'They were taunting us.'

'Were they?'

'We talked about getting a rope to make a handle, so that's exactly what they did. They got a rope and made a handle. To demonstrate their power. And to show us how they're secretly laughing up their sleeves at us.'

'How could they know what we talked about?'

'They're listening to us,' Patty said. 'There's a microphone in this room.'

'That's crazy.'

'You got another explanation?'

'Where is it?'

'Maybe in the light.'

They both squinted at it, hot and yellow.

Shorty said, 'Mostly we talked outside. In the chairs.'

'Then there must be a microphone out there too. That's how Peter found our luggage. They heard us talking about where to put it. They heard the whole plan. Back and forth with the damn quad bike. Which is why Mark said we must be tired. Which was a weird remark otherwise. But he knew what we had been doing. Because we told him ahead of time.'

'What else did we say?'

'Lots of things. You said maybe Canadian cars are different, and the next thing we hear is, hey, Canadian cars are different. They were listening all along.'

'What else?'

'Doesn't matter what else. What else we said is not what matters. What matters is what we say next.'

162

'Which is what?'

'Nothing,' Patty said. 'We can't even plan what to do. Because they'll hear us.'

NINETEEN

Reacher and the guy with the ponytail climbed the fence and walked to the Subaru. The guy said, 'You were pretty rough back there.'

'Not really,' Reacher said. 'I hit him once. There is no smaller number. It was the irreducible minimum. It was almost kind-hearted. I assume he has a dental plan.'

'His father meant what he said. He won't forget. That family has a reputation to keep up. They'll have to do something.'

Reacher stared at him.

Déjà vu all over again.

The guy said, 'They think they're top dogs around here. They'll worry that word will get out. They won't want people laughing at them behind their backs. So they'll have to come looking for you.'

'Who?' Reacher said. 'The granddad?'

'They offer a lot of seasonal work. They get a lot of loyalty in exchange.'

'How much more do you know about Ryantown?'

The guy paused a beat.

He said, 'There's an old man you should talk to. I was debating whether to mention him at all. Because honestly I think you should get going instead.'

'Pursued by a large and hostile crowd of fruit pickers?'

'These are not pleasant people.'

'How bad can they be?'

'You should get going.'

'Where is the old man I should talk to?'

'You couldn't see him before tomorrow. It would have to be arranged.'

'How old is he?'

'I guess more than ninety now.'

'From Ryantown originally?'

'His cousins were. He spent time there.'

'Does he remember people?'

'He claims to. I interviewed him about the tin. I asked him about kids who got sick. He came up with a list of names. But they were just regular childhood ailments. Nothing conclusive.'

'That was eight years ago. Maybe his memory got worse.'

'Possible.'

'Why tomorrow?'

'He's in a home. Deep in the countryside. Visiting hours are limited.'

'I would need a motel tonight.'

'You should go to Laconia. It would be safer. More people around. You would be harder to find.'

'Maybe I prefer the rural ambience.'

'There's a place twenty miles north of here. It's supposed to be good. But maybe not for you. It's deep in the woods. No bus. Too far to walk. You would be much better off in Laconia.'

Reacher said nothing.

The guy said, 'Better still if you moved on altogether. I could

165

drive you somewhere, if you like. As a way of saying thank you for rescuing me back there.'

'That was my fault anyway,' Reacher said. 'I persuaded you to come. I got you in trouble.'

'I would still drive you somewhere.'

'Drive me to Laconia,' Reacher said. 'Then make the arrangements with the old guy.'

Reacher got out on a downtown corner, and the guy with the ponytail drove away. Reacher looked left and right and got his bearings. He smiled. He was halfway between where two separate twenty-year-olds had been discovered unconscious on the sidewalk, seventy-five years apart. He checked the passers-by. There were a few folks who could have been up from Boston. But none of them looked wrong. Couples, mostly. Some grey hair. Shoppers, probably, looking for end-of-season bargains on whatever it was Laconia had to offer. Nothing suspicious. Not yet. Tomorrow, Shaw had said. The chief of detectives. He should know.

Reacher took a side street, where he had seen an inn, no better or worse than all the others. It was another narrow three-floor building, painted an artful faded colour. He paid for a room, and went up to take a look at it. The window faced out back. Which he was happy about. It decreased the effective radius. He might get a quiet night. A raccoon or a coyote, maybe, looking for trash in the alley. Or a neighbour's dog. But nothing worse.

Then he went out again, because it was still full daylight. He was hungry. He had skipped lunch. He should have been eating it about the time he was gazing at the fragment of old kitchen tile. All that remained. Not a large room. Probably not well equipped. Therefore a simple menu for lunch. Peanut butter, maybe, or grilled cheese. Or something out of a can. A tin can.

He found a coffee shop a block away which offered all-day

breakfast, which in his experience usually implied all-day everything. He went inside. There were five booths. Four were occupied. The first three by what looked like out-of-town shoppers refreshing themselves after an exhausting spree, and the fourth by a familiar face.

Detective Brenda Amos.

She was deep in a salad. No doubt a long-awaited meal much delayed by ongoing chaos. Reacher had been a cop. He knew what it was like. Running here, running there, phones ringing, eat when you can, sleep when you can.

She looked up.

At first she looked surprised, just for a second, and then she looked dismayed. He shrugged and sat down on the bench across from her.

He said, 'Shaw told me I'm legal until tomorrow.'

She said, 'He told me you agreed to move on.'

'If I found Ryantown.'

'Didn't you?'

'Apparently there's a guy I should talk to. A very old man. Same age my father would be. An exact contemporary.'

'Are you going to talk to him today?'

'Tomorrow.'

'This is exactly what we were afraid of. You're going to be here for ever.'

'Look on the bright side. Maybe no one is coming. The kid was an asshole. Maybe they think he deserved it. Tough love, or whatever they call it now.'

'No chance whatsoever.'

'The very old man I should talk to had cousins in Ryantown. He used to visit on a regular basis. Maybe they all got up a game in the street. All the neighbourhood kids. Stickball, or whatever. Maybe they played catch across the stream.'

'With all due respect, major, do you really care about that stuff?'

167

'I guess a little bit,' Reacher said. 'Enough to stick around one more night, anyway.'

'We don't want trouble here.'

'Always best avoided.'

'They have the rest of the day to plan. They'll mobilize before midnight. They'll be here by morning. The distances are not great. They'll have your description with them. Therefore Shaw is going to dial it up to eleven before first light. He's going to treat this place like a war zone. Where does this very old man live?'

'In a home somewhere out of town. A guy I met is going to pick me up.'

'What guy?'

'Eight years ago he thought the water was contaminated.'

'Was it?'

'Apparently not. It's a sore point.'

'Where is he going to pick you up?'

'Where he let me out.'

'At an agreed-upon time?'

'Nine-thirty on the dot. Something about visiting hours.'

Amos paused a beat.

'OK,' she said. 'You're authorized to do that. But you'll do it my way. You don't leave your room at any point, no one ever sees you, and at nine-thirty in the morning exactly you run straight to the car with your head down. And you drive away. And you don't come back. That's the deal I'm offering. Or we run you out now.'

'I already paid for my room,' Reacher said. 'Running me out now would be an injustice.'

'I'm serious,' she said. 'This is not the O.K. Corral. This is collateral damage just waiting to happen. If they miss you, they'll hit two other people instead. Watch my lips. We are not going to allow drive-by shootings in our town. No way. This is Laconia, not Los Angeles. And with respect, major, you should support our

168

position. You should know better than to put innocent bystanders at risk.'

'Relax,' Reacher said. 'I support your position. I support it big time. I'll do everything your way. I promise. Starting tomorrow. Today I'm still legal.'

'Start when it gets dark tonight,' Amos said. 'Play it safe. For my sake.'

She took out a business card and handed it to him.

She said, 'Call me if you need me.'

TWENTY

P atty took off her shoes, because she was Canadian, and stepped up on the bed, and stood upright on the bouncy surface. She shuffled sideways and tilted her face up towards the light.

She said, loudly, 'Please raise the window blind. As a personal favour to me. I want to see daylight. What possible harm could it do? No one ever comes here.'

Then she climbed down, and sat on the edge of the mattress to put her shoes back on. Shorty watched the window, like he was watching a ball game on a television screen. The same kind of close attention.

The blind stayed down.

He shrugged.

'Good try,' he mouthed, silently.

'They're discussing it,' she mouthed back.

They waited again.

And then the blind rolled up. The motor whirred and a blue bar of bright afternoon light came spilling in, narrow at first, but widening all the time, until it filled the room with sunshine.

Patty glanced up at the ceiling.

'Thank you,' she said.

She walked to the door, to kill the hot yellow bulb. Three steps. The first felt good, because she liked the daylight. The second felt better, because she had made them do something for her. She had established a line of communication. She had made them understand she was a person. But then the third step felt worse again, because she realized she had given them leverage. She had told them what she feared to lose.

She put her elbows on the sill and her forehead on the glass and stared out at the view. It was unchanged. The Honda, the lot, the grass, the wall of trees. Nothing else.

In the back parlour over at the house Mark finished a phone call and put the receiver down. He checked the screens. Patty was happy. He turned to face the others.

'Listen up,' he said. 'That was a neighbour on the phone. Some old apple farmer twenty miles south of here. They had a guy there today, making trouble. They want us to keep an eye out for him. In case he happens to come by, looking for a room. They'll send folks up to get him. Apparently they need to teach him a lesson.'

'He won't come by,' Peter said. 'We took the signs down.'

'The apple farmer said this was a big rough guy. Which is exactly what our friend at the county office said too. About a big rough guy named Reacher, who was researching his family history. Who looked at four separate censuses. At least two of which must have had a Ryantown address. Which is a place where theoretically I had distant relatives. And which is a place right there in the corner of the apple farm in question. This guy is mapping out Reacher real estate. He's going from parcel to parcel. He must be some kind of mad hobbyist.'

'You think he'll come here?'

171

'My grandfather's name is still on the deed. But that was after Ryantown. It was after they got rich.'

'We don't need this now,' Robert said. 'We have bigger fish to fry. The first arrival is less than twelve hours away.'

'He won't come here,' Mark said. 'He must be a different branch of the family. I never heard about anyone like that. He'll stick to his own lineage. Surely. Everyone does. No reason why he would come here.'

'We just rolled their blind up.'

'Leave it up,' Mark said. 'He won't come here.'

'They could signal for help.'

'Watch the track and listen for the bell.'

'Why would we need to, if he won't come here?'

'Because someone else might. Anyone could. We need maximum vigilance now. Because this is where we earn it, guys. Attention to detail today pays dividends tomorrow.'

Steven switched out the screens either side of centre to two alternate views of the mouth of the track, where it came out of the trees, one close up, one wide angle.

Nothing was moving.

Reacher did it Amos's way. He went back to his room and holed up for the rest of the afternoon. No one saw him. Which was good. Except dinner was going to be a problem. The place he had picked to stay was just a bijou little inn. There was no room service. Probably no catering at all, except bought-in muffins for the breakfast buffet. Free, in the lobby. But not yet. Not for another twelve hours, at the earliest. Probably closer to fourteen. A person could starve to death.

He looked out the window, which was a waste of time, because it showed him nothing but the back of the next street. But he knew the place with the all-day breakfast was only a block away. If he went there, who would see him? Maximum two or three

172

passers-by on a single downtown block, in a town like Laconia, at sundown. Plus the customers in the coffee shop. Plus the wait staff. Who had already seen him once, at lunch time. Not long before. Which was not good. Yes, they could say, he's in here all the time. He's practically a regular. Which would then focus any subsequent search on the immediate neighbourhood. The bijou inn with the faded colours would be target number one. Front and centre. The obvious location. Perhaps worthy of an immediate visit. Maybe first thing in the morning, before a civilized person was up and about.

Not good.

Better to go further afield. He turned away from the window and made a mental map in his head, of what he had seen so far. His first hotel, the city office, the county office, the police station, his second hotel, and all the establishments in between, where he had eaten and gotten coffee and window-shopped for shoes and bags and cookware. For dinner he wanted a place he hadn't been before. He figured two sightings were ten times worse than one. Call it a rule. Always better to be a first-time stranger. He recalled a particular single-wide storefront bistro, with a half-curtained window, and old-fashioned light bulbs inside, like glowing tangles of heated wire. Probably a small staff, and a small and discreet clientele. He had passed it by, but not gone in. Six blocks away, he thought. Or seven. Which was more than ideal, but he figured he could zigzag through the side streets, which would be quieter.

Safe enough.

He went downstairs and stepped out to the fading light and set out walking. His mental map worked well enough. One time he hesitated, but in the end he guessed right. The bistro came up dead ahead. Eight blocks out, not seven or six. Further than he thought. He had been exposed a long time. He had counted eighteen passers-by. Not all of them had seen him. But some had. No one suspicious. All regular folk.

173

On the sidewalk outside the bistro he stood up tall on tiptoes, so he could see inside over the half curtain. So he could make an assessment. He had no real taste in food. Anything would do. But he liked a corner table with his back to the wall, and a little hustle but not too much, and a few other customers but not too many. Whatever it took to be served fast and not remembered. The place looked like it would fit the bill. There was an empty two-top in the far rear corner. The waitresses looked brisk and on the ball. The room was about half full. Six people eating. All good. Ideal in every way. Except that two of the six people eating were Elizabeth Castle and Carter Carrington.

A second date. Possibly delicate. He didn't want to ruin their evening. They would feel obliged to ask him to join them at their table. Saying no wouldn't help. Then he would be eating two tables away, and they would feel self-conscious and scrutinized. The whole atmosphere would feel weird and strained and artificial.

But he owed Amos. She was out on a limb. *You don't leave your room at any point. No one ever sees you.* How much more walking around could he afford to do?

In the end the decision made itself. For some reason Elizabeth Castle looked up. She saw him. Her mouth opened in a little *O* of surprise, which then changed instantly to a smile, which looked totally genuine, and then she waved, at first just an excited greeting, but then an eager come-in-and-join-us gesture.

He went in. At that point it was the path of least resistance. He crossed the room. Carrington stood up to shake hands, courteous, a little old-fashioned. Elizabeth Castle leaned across and scraped out a third chair. Carrington held out his palm towards it, like a maître d', and said, 'Please.'

Reacher sat down, his back to the door, facing a wall.

The path of least resistance.

He said, 'I don't want to wreck your evening.'

Elizabeth Castle said, 'Don't be silly.'

174

'Then congratulations,' he said. 'To both of you.'

'For what?'

'Your second date.'

'Fourth,' she said.

'Really?'

'Dinner last night, coffee break this morning, lunch break, dinner tonight. And it was your predicament that introduced us. So it's lovely you were passing by. It's like an omen.'

'That sounds bad.'

'Whatever the good version is.'

'A good omen,' Carrington said.

'I found Ryantown,' Reacher said. 'It all matched up with the census. The occupation was listed as tin mill foreman, and the address was right across the street from a tin mill. Which was mothballed for a spell, which explains why later he was labouring for the county. I assume he went back to being foreman when the mill started up again. I didn't look at the next census. My father had left home by then.'

Carrington nodded, and said nothing, in a manner Reacher thought deliberate and reluctant, as if actually he had plenty to say, but he wasn't going to, because of some fine point of manners or etiquette.

Reacher said, 'What?'

'Nothing.'

'I don't believe you.'

'OK, something.'

'What kind of something?'

'We were just discussing it.'

'On a date?'

'We're dating because of you. Obviously we're going to discuss it. No doubt we'll discuss your case for ever. It will be of sentimental value.'

'What were you discussing?'

'We don't really know,' Carrington said. 'We're a little embarrassed. We can't pin it down. We looked at the original documents. They're both lovely censuses. You develop a feel. You can see patterns. You can recognize the good takers, and the lazy ones. You can spot mistakes. You can spot lies. Mostly about reading and writing for men, and age for women.'

'You found a problem with the documents?'

'No,' Carrington said. 'They rang true. They were beautifully done. Among the best I ever saw. The 1940 in particular was a hall of fame census. We believed every word.'

'Then it sounds pinned down pretty good to me.'

'Like I said, you develop a feel. You're in their world, right there with them. You become them, through the documents. Except you know what happens next, and they don't. You stand a little apart. You know the end of the movie. So you're thinking like them, but you're also noticing which ones will be proved wise or foolish by future events.'

'And?'

'There's something wrong with the story you told me.'

'But not in the documents.'

'Some other part.'

'But you don't know what.'

'Can't pin it down.'

Then the waitress came by and took their orders, and the conversation moved on to other things. Reacher didn't turn it back. He didn't want to ruin their evening. He let them talk about whatever they felt like, and he joined in wherever he could.

He ate a main course only, and got up to go. He wanted them to have dessert on their own. It seemed the least he could do. They didn't object. He made them take a twenty. They said it was too much. He said tell the waitress to keep the change.

He stepped out the door, and turned right, back the way he had

come. The dark was noticeably darker. The streets were noticeably quieter. Traffic was light. No one was walking. The stores
were all closed. A car came by from behind, and it drove on ahead,
maybe a little slower than it wanted to, like night-time cars in
towns everywhere. Nothing to worry about, the back part of his
brain told him, after computing a thousand points of instinctive
data about speed and direction and intent and consistency, and
coming up with a result right in the centre of normal.

Then it saw something that wasn't.

Headlights, coming towards him. A hundred yards away. Big
and blinding and spaced high and wide. A large vehicle. Dead
level, as if it was driving in the middle of the road. As if it was strad-
dling the line. And it was driving slow. Which is what rang the
bell. Neither one speed or another. Wrong for the context. Like a
cautious rush hour creep, but one click slower, as if the driver was
also preoccupied with something else. A modern person might
have guessed his phone, but Reacher thought the guy was searching for something. Visually. Hence the central position. Hence the
bright lights. He was sweeping both sidewalks at once.

Searching for what?

Or searching for who?

It was a large vehicle. Maybe a cop car. Cops were allowed to
drive slow in the middle of the road. They were allowed to search
for whatever or whoever they wanted.

He was pinned by the lights. They washed over him, hard and
blue and bright, and then they slid past him, and suddenly he was
in a half grey world, half lit by the bright lights' reflection off the
night mist ahead. He turned and saw a pick-up truck, high and
shiny and handsome, immensely long, with two rows of seats
and a long, long bed, and big chrome wheels turning slow, just
rolling along, relaxed as can be.

It was on the inside where the action was happening.

It looked like an explosion of incredulous joy, like a crazy bet

177

was paying out. The impossible had happened. Five faces were swivelling towards him. Five pairs of eyes were locked on his. Five mouths were open. One of them was moving.

It was saying, 'That's him.'

The guy with the moving mouth was the daddy from the apple farm.

TWENTY-ONE

The guy from the apple farm was in the second row, behind the driver. Not a natural squad leader position. Not a throne of authority, like the front passenger seat. Maybe the guy saw himself more as an active-duty soldier. Just one of the boys. Which was encouraging. It might indicate a low bar. At least a lowered average. Like looking at the opposition batting order. It was nice to know there was a guy you could get out.

The other four were a generation younger. Not so different from the kid in the orchard. Same kind of build, same kind of muscle, same kind of tan. The same human species. But poorer. Different kind of grandfather. No one said life was fair. But they looked happy to help. Picking time was coming up. Maybe baby needed shoes.

The truck squelched to a stop, and all four doors opened, in a ragged sequence. Five men jumped down. Boots clattered on the blacktop. Two guys came around the hood and formed up shoulder to shoulder with the other three, with the older guy right in the middle, all of them grey and ghostly in the reflected half light.

They looked like a faded billboard for an old-time black and white movie. Some sentimental story. Maybe their mother died young and the old guy raised them all solo. Now they're grateful. Or now for the first time ever a fractured family is seeing eye to eye, because of a terrible external threat. Some kind of dramatic hokum. They were acting it out.

Reacher was thinking about Brenda Amos.

We don't want trouble here.

But she was talking about collateral damage. Which in this case was likely to be very minor. Even non-existent. The street was empty. There were no guns. There was no action at all. Not yet. Just a staring competition. And posing. Which Reacher guessed he was, too. He was acting relaxed and unconcerned, standing easy, almost smiling, but not quite, as if he had just found out an irksome task might need attention, before an otherwise excellent day came finally to a close. Opposite him the other five were still giving it the full-on shoulder to shoulder thing, with high crossed arms and hard tilted-up stares, and slowly it dawned on Reacher that their display was not after all intended to be seen as a narrative tableau, with a poignant implied backstory explaining their sudden new solidarity. It was intended to be seen as a much less subtle message. It was a raw statement of numbers. Nothing more. It was five against one.

The guy from the apple farm said, 'You need to come with us.'

Reacher said, 'Do I?'

'Best to come quietly.'

Reacher said nothing.

The guy said, 'Well?'

'I'm trying to figure out where that would fall, on a scale of likelihood. Where ten means it's extremely likely to happen, and one means it ain't going to happen in a million years. I have to tell you, right now the numbers popping up in my mind are all fairly small.'

'Your choice,' the guy said. 'You could save yourself a couple of bruises. But you're coming with us one way or the other. You put your hands on my son.'

'Only one hand,' Reacher said. 'And only briefly. Not much more than a tap. The kid's got a glass jaw. You should look after him better. You should explain to him why he can't play with the grown-ups. It's cruel not to. You're doing him a disservice.'

The guy didn't answer.

Reacher said, 'Are these new boys any better? I sure hope so. Or you need to explain to them, too. This is the big leagues now.'

A ripple ran down the line, like a little spasm. Sharply drawn breaths rustled arms against chests, and jabbed glares jerked heads above shoulders.

We don't want trouble here.

Reacher said, 'We don't have to do this.'

The guy from the farm said, 'Yes, we do.'

'This is a nice town. We shouldn't make a mess.'

'Then come with us.'

'Where to?'

'You'll see.'

'We already discussed that part. Right now the likelihood is still close to zero. But hey, I'm open to offers. You could sweeten the deal.'

'What?'

'You could pay me. Or offer me something.'

'We're offering you the chance to save yourself a couple of extra bruises.'

Reacher nodded.

'You mentioned that before,' he said. 'It raised a number of questions.'

He looked left and right and back again, at the four younger guys.

He asked, 'Where were you born?'

None of them answered.

'You should tell me,' he said. 'It's important to your futures.'

'Around here,' one of them said.

'And then you grew up around here?'

'Yes.'

'Not Southie or the Bronx or South-Central LA?'

'No.'

'Not in a shantytown outside of Rio de Janeiro? Or in Baltimore or Detroit?'

'No.'

'Any law enforcement experience?'

'No.'

'Have you done time in prison?'

'No.'

'Any military service?'

'No.'

'Any secret clandestine training by Mossad? Or the SAS in Britain? Or the French Foreign Legion?'

'No.'

'You understand this is going to be different than picking apples, right?'

The boy didn't answer.

Reacher turned back to the guy from the apple farm.

'See the problem?' he said. 'This whole thing with the bruises just doesn't work. It has no internal logic. It's an optical illusion. You're offering the absence of something you can't deliver anyway. Not with this crew. You need to do better than that. Use your imagination. An inducement is required. Maybe a large cash payment would be tempting. Or the keys to the truck. Or maybe one of these boys could introduce me to his sister. Just one night. He could tear himself away.'

He knew they would all react, which was exactly what he wanted, but he didn't know which one of them would react first

182

and fastest, so he stayed loose, already winding up his counter-measures, but keeping his aim flexible, as long as he could, hoping he would know before the point of no return, when finally he had to commit to a direction. And he did, because the kid to the left of centre started forward a foot ahead of the others, enraged by the abuse and derision, so Reacher lined him up and threw his punch. Legend had it the fastest hands in boxing could move at thirty miles an hour, much faster than Reacher, who was happy with twenty, but even at that slower speed his fist crossed the yard of air in front of him in a tenth of a second. Virtually instantaneous. It hit the kid in the face, and then Reacher snapped it back just as fast, like a crisp parade ground move, and he stood upright and easy, like nothing had happened, like you had blinked and missed it.

Just for the drama.

The kid fell down.

Fifty yards away Elizabeth Castle and Carter Carrington stepped out of the bistro. He said something and she laughed. The sound was loud in the empty street. The guys from the truck turned to look. Not the guy on the ground. He wasn't doing anything.

Fifty yards away Carrington took Elizabeth Castle's hand, and they turned together and set out walking. Head-on. Approaching. They were lit flat and bright by the stopped truck's lights, like Reacher had been. He watched them for a second, and then he turned to the farm guy and said, 'Now you got a choice of your own. The city attorney is coming. A credible witness, if nothing else. I'm prepared to stick around and slug it out. Are you?'

The guy from the farm glanced down the street. At the approaching couple. All lit up. Now forty yards away. Their heels were loud on the brick. Elizabeth Castle laughed again.

The guy from the farm said nothing.

Reacher nodded.

'I understand,' he said. 'You don't like letting things go. Because you're the top dog. I get it. So I'll make it easy for you. I'll make sure we meet again. Tomorrow or the next day. One day soon. I'll come back to Ryantown. I'm sure I'll want to. Keep an eye out for me.'

He walked away. He didn't look back. Behind him he heard nothing for a second, and then he heard muttered commands and scuffling feet, and the truck backing up, and thumps and gasps as the groggy guy was hauled up off the ground and stuffed in a seat. He heard a door slam. Then he turned in on a side street, and heard nothing more, all the way back to his room. Where he stayed the rest of the night. He caught most of a meaningless late-season Red Sox game out of Boston, and then the late local news, and then he went to bed, where he slept soundly.

Until one minute past three in the morning.

TWENTY-TWO

Patty was still awake at one minute past three in the morning, having not slept at all. Shorty had kept her company most of the time, but finally he had closed his eyes. Just a nap, he said, which had so far lasted an hour. He was snoring. They had eaten the fourth of their six meals. They had drunk the fourth of their six bottles of water. They had two of everything left. Breakfast and lunch the next day. Then what? She didn't know. Which was why she was still awake at one minute past three in the morning. Having not slept at all. She didn't understand.

They were in a warm and comfortable room, with electricity and hot and cold running water. There was a shower and a toilet. There were towels and soap and tissues. They had not been assaulted, or abused, or threatened, or leered at, or touched, or treated inappropriately in any way. Apart from being locked up against their will. Why? What was the reason? What was the purpose? Who was she, and who was Shorty, in the grand scheme of things? What good were they to anybody?

She took the question seriously. They were poor, and everyone

185

they knew was poor. A ransom note would be a joke. They knew no industrial secrets. They had no specialized knowledge. People had been growing potatoes and sawing wood in North America for hundreds of years. Maybe thousands. Both processes were pretty much figured out by that point.

So why? They were twenty-five and healthy. For a time she thought about organ harvesting. Maybe their kidneys were about to be auctioned on the internet. Or their hearts, or their lungs, or their corneas. Plus whatever else was good. Bone marrow, maybe. The whole long list, like on their driver's licences. But then she thought not. No attempt had been made to check their blood types. No casual questions, no accidental nicks or scrapes or cuts. No first aid. No bloodstained gauze. You couldn't sell a kidney without a blood type. It was the kind of thing people needed to know.

She relaxed, for a moment. But not for long. She didn't understand. Who was she, and who was Shorty? What were they good for?

Reacher woke up at one minute past three in the morning. Same deal. He snapped awake, instantly, like flicking a switch.

Same reason.

A sound.

Which he didn't hear again.

Nothing.

He padded naked out of bed and checked the alley through the window. Nothing. No glint of raccoon, no ghostlike coyote, no eager dog. A quiet night. Except apparently not, and once again at exactly one minute past three in the morning. He doubted the cocktail waitress would have gone to work that night. Probably fired, or afraid of reprisals. And a new gig in a new place wouldn't have gotten her home at precisely the same time. Plus the kid wasn't waiting at her door any more. He was in the hospital. Plus now the alley where she lived was more than four blocks away. On a diagonal, with plenty of stuff in between. Outside the radius. He wasn't close enough for a cry to carry.

Therefore the timing was a coincidence. He heard Amos's voice in his head: *They'll mobilize before midnight. They'll be here by morning. The distances are not great.*

Was it morning? Technically, he supposed. He pictured midnight in Boston, and a car gassing up, and slipping away in the dark. Could it be in Laconia three hours and one minute later? Easily. Probably two times over. He pictured the guy taking his time, prowling, getting the lay of the land, maybe rousing a clerk or an innkeeper here or there, asking his question about a big guy with a cut hand, apologizing when the answer was no, shoving a fifty in a shirt pocket, moving on, back to the car, looking for the next place. Until sooner or later he found the innkeeper who would say, sure, top floor, the room in the back.

Reacher pulled his pants out from under the mattress and put them on. He buttoned his shirt and laced his shoes. He collected his toothbrush from the bathroom glass, and he put it in his pocket. He was good to go.

He walked downstairs to the lobby. Still three hours before the buffet. He waited inside the street door and listened. He heard nothing. He stepped out. He heard the swish of a distant car. He saw no one. He walked to the corner. Nothing there. He heard the car again. Same sound, different position. Far away. Then nearer. As if it had turned in, one block closer. Going nowhere in particular. Just around and around, on a new tighter radius.

For the sake of it Reacher walked the four diagonal blocks and found the alley between the bag store and the shoe store. Where the waitress lived. It was all quiet. No one was there. No disturbance. Just dark blank windows, and mist, and silence.

He heard the car again. Behind him, in the distance. The faint hiss of its tyres, the breathing of its engine, a *pock* as it hit a join in the blacktop. Three blocks away, he thought. No direct line of sight. There was a dogleg in the cross street.

He turned back towards the inn. He walked through cones of yellow light. Once he stopped in the shadows and listened. He could still hear the car. Rolling slow. Still three blocks away. Turning right every now and then, going around and around.

He walked on. The car stepped another block closer. It turned right one street early. Now it was only two blocks away. Going around and around. A giant map-sized spiral. A search pattern. But a lazy one. It proved nothing. There could be a whole football team of big guys with cut hands running around, and a slow spiral could miss every one of them, every time. Not missing one of them would be a random chance.

Therefore maybe not a search pattern. Not yet. Maybe still a lay-of-the-land reconnaissance. It was still very early. Thorough preparations were always to be recommended. A degree of professionalism could be anticipated. Exit routes could be planned. Difficult turns could be noted. Alleys could be inspected, for width and destination.

The car turned right, two blocks behind him.

He walked on. Two blocks to go. Which presented a problem with four dimensions. Where would he be, when the car next passed close to the inn? Where would the car be, when he arrived at its door? Which was the same question. Time, and distance, and direction. Like deflection shooting. Where will the running man be, when the bullet gets there?

He stopped walking. The timing was going to be wrong. Better to wait it out a quarter turn. Better to get there right after the guy drove on, not right before he was due to arrive. Common sense, surely. He strolled to the corner and waited. The street was deserted. Still the dead of night. All good.

Except right then the car chose to step in another block closer. Way early, compared to its previous pattern. Not remotely predictable. It came rolling down the cross street on Reacher's left, with its bright lights on, sweeping both sidewalks at once. Reacher was lit up like a movie star. The car stopped fifteen feet away. Idling engine, blinding light. Behind it a door opened. Reacher planned to dive down and to the right of the sound. But forward. Into the light. Safer that way. The guy was probably right-handed. A panic spasm caused by the sudden dive would jerk his gun up and away, not down and in.

If he had a gun.

Behind the light a voice said, 'Laconia Police Department.'

Then it said, 'Raise your hands.'

'I can't see you,' Reacher said. 'Kill the lights.'

Which was a test, of sorts. A real cop might, and a fake cop wouldn't. He was still planning on the dive to the right. Then any kind of contact with the open door would get the job done. It would smack back into the guy, and after that it would be a fair fight.

The lights went out.

Reacher blinked a couple of times, and the yellow night-time glow came back, soft through the misty air, harsh where the streets were wet. The car was a Laconia PD black and white, clean and new, glowing orange inside with technology. The guy behind its open door was in a patrolman's uniform. His nameplate said Davison. He was maybe in his middle twenties. Maybe a little skinnier than he wanted to be. But bright and alert and resolved. His creases were crisp. His hair was brushed. His equipment belt was in excellent order. He was ready. For once a routine night patrol had turned out interesting.

'Raise your hands,' he said again.

'Not really necessary,' Reacher said.

'Then turn around and I'll cuff you.'

'Not really necessary either.'

'It's for your safety as well as mine,' Davison said.

Which Reacher figured had to come from a role play class.

189

Maybe led by a psychologist. Maybe the task of the day was to find a line that could inhibit further resistance simply by stunning vital cortexes in the brain with its blatant opacity. How could putting him in handcuffs help his safety?

But out loud he said, 'Officer, I don't see a lot of probable cause here.'

Davison said, 'None is required.'

'Was there a constitutional crisis I didn't hear about?'

'You're already a person of interest. You were mentioned in the start-of-watch briefing. A sketch was distributed. You're not supposed to be seen in public.'

'Who conducted the briefing?'

'Detective Amos.'

'What else did she say?'

'Report immediately if we see a Massachusetts licence plate.'

'Did you?'

'Not yet.'

'She's taking it seriously,' Reacher said.

'She has to. We can't let anything bad happen. We'll be crucified.'

'I'm heading back to my hotel now.'

'No sir, you need to come with me.'

'Am I under arrest?'

'Sir, Detective Amos informed us of your prior service in the MPs. We're happy to extend every courtesy.'

'Yes or no?'

'You're about an inch away,' the kid said, bright and alert and resolved. And sure of himself. And sure of his orders, and the law, and his bosses.

Happy days.

Reacher thought about coffee. Nearly three hours in the future, in the innkeeper's lobby. No doubt an ever-present fixture in the police station.

'An arrest won't be necessary,' he said. 'I'll ride with you of my own free will. But in the front. Call it a rule.'

They got in the car, and they drove on, at the same speed Reacher had heard in the distance, slow and deliberate, nosing around corners, dutifully completing whichever lap it was of the night-long patrol. Reacher's seat was cramped by an overspill of equipment from the centre console. There was a laptop computer on a gooseneck stalk. There were holders and holsters for small specialist items. The vinyl on the dash was shiny and clean. The air smelled new. The car could have been a month old.

Then whichever lap it was on ended, and Davison turned a corner near the city office, and set out on a wider street, in a direction that Reacher recognized led to the station. A straight shot. About half a mile. Davison drove it a little faster than before. With panache. With a certain swagger. The master of the night-time universe. He pulled in outside the lobby doors. He got out. Reacher got out. They went inside together. Davison explained the situation to the night guy. Who was unclear on only one point.

He said, 'Until nine-thirty, do I need to lock him up?'

Davison looked at Reacher.

He said, 'Does he?'

'Not really necessary.'

'You sure?'

'I don't want anything bad to happen either. All I want is coffee.'

Davison turned back to the night guy.

He said, 'Find him an office to wait in, and get him a cup of coffee.'

Then ahead of them the double doors swung open and Brenda Amos walked through.

'We'll use my office,' she said.

TWENTY-THREE

The first arrival happened well before dawn. A repeat customer. He lived in the far northern part of Maine, in a wooden house in the centre of eighty square miles of forest, all of which he owned. As always he drove only by night, in a beat-up old Volvo wagon, not worth a second glance, but just in case it got one, it was also fitted with fake Vermont plates made up with an unissued number. His phone told him where to turn, but of course he remembered the place anyway. From his first visit. How could he forget? He recognized the mouth of the track, and the sketchy blacktop, and the fat rubber wire. Which rang a bell somewhere, to scare up a welcome.

Which this time was offered in the motel office. By Mark only. The others were nowhere to be seen. Watching the security cameras, the new guest assumed. And hoped. Mark offered him room three, and he took it. Mark watched him as he parked the wagon. Watched him as he carried his bags inside. He was wondering which bag held his money, the new guest assumed. He set his stuff down near the closet and stepped outside again, to the predawn darkness. To the soft misty air. He couldn't contain himself. He crept along the boardwalk, past room four, past five, towards a dead-looking Honda Civic, crouching blackly in the moonlight. He stepped out into the lot at that point and looped around behind it, so he could take in the whole of room ten from a distance. The first look. It was occupied. The e-mail said so. But it was currently blank and quiet. The window blind was down. There was no light inside. No sound. Nothing was happening.

The new guest stood for a minute, and then he walked back to room three.

Reacher took coffee from the squad room pot, and then Amos walked him back to her office. The same as before. The old structure, the new contents. The desk, the chairs, the cabinets, the computer.

She said, 'I asked you to play it safe, for my sake.'

He said, 'Something woke me up.'

'Is there a law that says therefore automatically you have to get up?'

'Sometimes.'

'They could have been arriving right then.'

'Exactly. I thought I should at least get my pants on. Then I went out to take a look. Nothing doing, except an excellent performance from Patrolman Davison. With which I had no problem. I'm happy to wait here. All good. Except I'm sorry you had to get up early.'

'Yeah, me too,' Amos said. 'You also went out for dinner.'

'How do you know?' he asked.

'Take a guess.'

Because of blood on the street, he thought, or a random traffic stop a block or two later, or both. The guys from the apple farm. Had to be.

But out loud he said, 'I don't know.'

'Carter Carrington told us,' she said. 'You walked eight blocks

193

to the same bistro he was in. And eight blocks back. That wasn't playing it safe.'

'At the time I thought it was, in a roundabout way.'

'You should have called me. I gave you my card. I would have brought pizza to your room.'

'Why did you ask Carrington about me?'

'We didn't. We needed a legal opinion. Your dinner plans came up in the subsequent conversation.'

'What kind of legal opinion?'

'Who we can detain, before they've actually done anything wrong.'

'And what was the answer?'

'These days, practically anybody.'

'Maybe no one is coming,' Reacher said. 'The kid was an asshole.'

'No chance whatsoever.'

'OK, but maybe it's not top of their list. Maybe they have to pick up the dry cleaning first. I'll be out of here at half past nine. They'll find me gone.'

'I sincerely hope every part of what you just said is true.'

'Let's hope some of it is.'

'We got some news,' she said. 'Slightly encouraging for us. Not so much for you.'

'What is it?'

'Current thinking has downgraded the risk of drive-by casualties. Now we think they're somewhat unlikely. Chief Shaw was on the phone with the Boston PD. They think the attempt will not be made here. They think their preferred tactic will be to get you in their car, so they can drive you back to Boston, where they'll throw you off an apartment building. That's what they do. Like a signature. Like a press release. Makes a splash, in every way. I would prefer that didn't happen to you.'

'Are you worried about me?'

'Purely as a professional responsibility.'

'I won't get in the strange man's car,' Reacher said. 'I think I can pretty much guarantee that.'

Amos didn't reply.

Her door opened a crack and a head stuck in and said, 'Ma'am, we have reports on the radio of a Massachusetts plate incoming from the southwest, on a black Chrysler 300 sedan, which according to Mass DMV seems to be registered to a freight forwarding operation based out of Logan Airport, in Boston.'

'What are the demographics on a black Chrysler 300?'

'Some limo companies, some rentals, but definitely a go-to gangster car.'

'Where is it now?'

'Still south of downtown. With a squad car right behind it.'

'Can he see inside?'

'The windows are tinted.'

'Dark enough to pull him over?'

'Ma'am, we can play this any way you tell us.'

Amos said, 'Not yet. Stay with him. Make it obvious. Show the flag.'

The head ducked out and the door closed again.

'So,' Amos said. 'Here we go.'

'Not yet,' Reacher said. 'Not with this guy.'

'How many more clues do you need?'

'That's my point,' Reacher said. 'It's a big black sedan with tinted windows. It's a shiny object. It's immediately traceable back to Boston. It's owned by a freight forwarding company at a major international airport. It might as well carry a neon sign. It's a decoy. They want you to follow it. It's going to drive around all day at exactly twenty-nine miles an hour. It's going to signal every turn, and you can bet your ass its tail lights are in working order. Meanwhile the real guy is in an electrician's van. Or a plumber. Or flowers. Or whatever. We have to assume a certain amount of

195

common sense. The real guy is going to slip into town some time today and no one is going to notice. But hopefully after half past nine in the morning. Because that would make sense anyway. By then you'll have been on a war footing more than six hours. You'll be getting tired. He'll know that. He'll wait. I'll be long gone.'

'We're basing a lot on your friend from yesterday actually showing up again.'

'I guess we are.'

'Will he?'

'I wouldn't be a bit surprised either way. He was that kind of guy.'

'On time?'

'Same answer.'

'What if he doesn't show up? You'll be here all day. That's the exact scenario I promised Shaw I wouldn't let happen.'

Reacher nodded.

'I don't want to put you on the spot,' he said. 'I apologize if I already have. I'll give my guy thirty minutes. That's all. If he doesn't show by ten o'clock, you can drive me to the city limit yourself. Does that work?'

'And then what?'

'Then Shaw is happy. I'll be outside the jurisdiction.'

'It's a line on the map. You could be followed. Electricians go from job to job. Also plumbers and flower delivery.'

'But at least the county will be stuck with the paperwork, not the city.'

'Your risk, I guess.'

'No, the electrician's risk. He's going to be the paperwork, not me. What choice do I have? I can't send him home to Boston with a pat on the back and a candy bar. Not under these circumstances. That would give the wrong impression entirely.'

'They'll send a replacement. They'll send two.'

'That will be the county's problem, not yours.'

'You shouldn't stick around.'

'I don't want to,' Reacher said. 'Believe me. I like to keep moving. But on the other hand I don't like to be chased away. Especially not by people who plan to throw me off a building. Which strikes me as ambitious. They seem very sure of themselves. Like I'm just a detail.'

'Don't let ego get in the way of a good decision.'

'You just trashed every general in our nation's history.'

'You weren't a general. Don't make the same mistake.'

'I won't,' Reacher said. 'I doubt if I'll get the chance. I doubt if our paths will ever cross. I'll be gone in a day. Two days max. The kid will heal up. All will be forgotten by the holidays. Life will move on. Hopefully I'll be somewhere warm.'

Amos didn't answer.

Her door opened again, the same crack, and the same head stuck in, and said, 'The black Chrysler is now cruising downtown, with no apparent destination in mind, so far obeying all traffic laws, and the squad car is still behind it.'

The head withdrew and the door closed.

'Decoy,' Reacher said.

'When will the real guy get here?'

He didn't answer.

The second arrival had many more moving parts than the first. It was a whole big production. Peter drove his Mercedes SUV to a small airfield near Manchester. Not even executive aviation. More of a hobby field. No tower, no log, no reporting requirements at all. He parked inside the fence, level with the end of the runway. He waited, with his window down.

Five minutes later he heard the distant clatter of a propeller plane. In the far distance he saw winks of light in the pale dawn sky. A twin-engine Cessna, that kind of thing, hopping and jumping, weightless on the wind. It came in low, and landed, and slowed

197

immediately to a fussy, bustling land-bound scurry, like a nervous bird, roaring with noise. Peter flashed his lights, and it rolled on towards him.

It was an air taxi, out of Syracuse, New York, booked by a shell corporation owned by a nest of ten others, on behalf of a passenger who had an Illinois driver's licence in the name of Hogan. He had arrived in Syracuse moments earlier in a charter Gulfstream out of Houston, Texas, booked by a different shell corporation owned by a different nest of ten others, on behalf of a passenger with a California licence in the name of Hourihane. Neither licence was real, and no one knew where he had come in from, prior to the wheels-up in Houston.

He climbed down from the plane and Peter helped him put his stuff in the Mercedes. Three soft bags and two hard cases. The money was in one of the soft bags, Peter assumed. The contribution. A physical weight, even in hundreds.

The plane shuddered around in place, a deafening half circle, and then it blared away down the runway and into the air. Peter drove the other way, out the gate, left and right along the back roads. The new arrival sat beside him, in the front passenger seat. He looked excited. He was sweating a little. He wanted to say something. Peter could tell. But he didn't. Not at first. He didn't speak at all. He stared ahead through the windshield and rocked in his seat, small movements, sometimes back and forth, sometimes side to side.

But eventually he had to know.

He had to ask.

He said, 'What are they like?'

'They're perfect,' Peter said.

TWENTY-FOUR

Dawn came up bright and clear, and a patrolman came by to take breakfast orders, from a diner two blocks down the street. Reacher chose a fried egg sandwich. Ten minutes later it arrived, still hot in greasy aluminium foil. It tasted pretty good. Maybe a little rubbery. Nutritious, anyway. Protein, carbohydrate, grease. All the food groups. He got more coffee from the squad room pot. No one was in there. Day watch was an hour away.

There was a feed from the radio room playing softly through a speaker on someone's empty desk. Reacher went closer and listened. There were slow blasts of static, like breathing, and call signs and code words and addresses that meant nothing, but he caught the drift. A dispatcher was talking to two separate squad cars. The dispatcher was probably down the hall, and the squad cars seemed to be circling the centre of town. One of them seemed to be right behind the Chrysler, and the other seemed to be tracking them both, from a block away. Reacher figured the regular night watch would be just one car. They were spending overtime money.

A voice that could have been Davison's broke in and said, 'Now he's in the drive-through lane for coffee.'

'That's good,' the dispatcher said. 'It means sooner rather than later he'll need to take a leak. Maybe you can get a look at him.'

No need, Reacher thought. He would be about five-ten tall, and five-nine wide, in a dark cashmere overcoat and a pink button-down shirt, with greasy black hair slicked back, and aviator shades and a gold chain around his neck. Like central casting. Whatever caught the eye.

Then a new voice said, 'The cameras at the highway cloverleaf show a Massachusetts plate heading our way. On a dark blue panel van. A Persian carpet cleaning company out of Boston. If it doesn't turn off, it's about ten minutes away.'

'Back burner,' the dispatcher said. 'We're going to get plenty of clutter. We're going to get FedEx and UPS and all kinds of things.'

The static breathed in and out. Reacher had seen Persian carpets. Mostly in old houses, or rich houses, or old rich houses. He knew they were expensive. He knew they were often treasured heirlooms. Therefore cleaning them was a delicate matter. Experts were no doubt few and far between. So it was immediately plausible that a discerning customer in Laconia would need to send to Boston for a satisfactory service. Pick-up and drop-off included, no doubt, in the same all-in-one delicate and expert price.

All good.

Except.

He topped up his coffee and headed back to Amos's office. She was at her desk, with her hand on the phone, as if she had just put it down, or couldn't remember who she wanted to call.

He said, 'I heard the radio in the squad room.'

She nodded.

'I got an update,' she said. 'The decoy is getting drive-through coffee.'

200

'And a blue van came off the highway.'

'That too.'

'Got an opinion?'

'It's a van,' she said. 'I can think of a hundred reasons why it's OK.'

'Ninety-nine,' Reacher said.

'What's wrong with it?'

'How many Persian carpets have you seen?'

'A few.'

'Where?'

'An old lady we used to visit. In a big old house. We were told to call her an aunt. We weren't allowed to touch anything.'

'Exactly. An old biddy. A rich old fussbudget. No doubt very organized. Probably she gets her mahogany polished at the same time her rug is out for cleaning. Which happens every time the latest Labrador dies. When she also has her great-grandmother's china washed. What's the earliest time of day such a grand New Hampshire lady would be prepared to receive tradespeople at her door?'

Amos said nothing.

'The van is too early,' Reacher said. 'That's what's wrong with it. It's just after dawn. It's not making a customer call in Laconia.'

'Want me to have it stopped?'

'I don't care,' Reacher said. 'I'll survive either way. But if it's the guy, you could get a nice bust out of it. He's got to be carrying. Probably a big shotgun, if he seriously expects me to get in the van with him.'

'You're about the size of a rolled-up rug,' she said. 'From a big room. Maybe this is how they move people now. Since the new cars came out, with the smaller trunks.'

Reacher didn't know if she was kidding or not.

'Up to you,' he said. 'Taking a look might put your mind at rest.'

'I would need a SWAT team, if you're right about the shotgun.'

Reacher didn't answer. She thought for a moment, and then she picked up the phone. She said to whoever answered, 'Keep eyes on the blue van from the carpet cleaner. Let me know where it goes.'

An hour later the work day was fully under way. The new watch was in. The station was bustling and crowded. Reacher kept out the way. He heard a patchwork of news, some of it from the radio feed, which was still playing softly, and some of it from people calling out updates to each other, desk to desk across busy rooms, and some of it by eavesdropping on hurried corridor conversations. The decoy in the Chrysler was still driving around, ostentatiously legal, taking scrupulous care at every four-way, yielding and deferring to pedestrians and local drivers every chance he got. He had not yet stopped for gas. Or the bathroom. Opinion was divided as to which was the more impressive feat.

But they had lost the blue van. By then they had three squad cars out, one behind the Chrysler, and two patrolling the southern approaches, and the van had been seen once, but not again. Opinion was divided between two competing theories. Either the van had parked in a carefully hidden location, perhaps an alley or a courtyard, which automatically made it suspicious, or else it had driven straight through town and exited to the northwest, perhaps to service an address in a close-by community, which automatically didn't.

Reacher wondered if the apple farmer had a Persian carpet in his house.

Amos said, 'It's nearly time for you to go.'

He said, 'Maybe I'll walk through a couple of alleys and courtyards.'

'You won't walk through anywhere. I'm going to drive you. In a marked car. No one would be dumb enough to attack a police vehicle.'

'Are you worried about me?'

'Purely in an operational sense. I want you out of here. Definitively. Once and for all. No delays. Because then my problem is solved. For avoidance of doubt I want to see it happen with my own eyes.'

'Maybe after that you should go stop the decoy and let him know it's all over. He might be grateful. He must be desperate for a leak by now.'

'Maybe I will.'

'You could tell him which way I went. Tell him I'd like to meet him. And his pal in the van.'

'Let it go,' she said. 'This ain't the MPs any more.'

'Is that how you feel?'

'Mostly,' she said.

She made a couple of arrangements on the phone, and then she grabbed her bag and led Reacher out to the lot, where she chose a black and white still wet from the car wash. The keys were in. Reacher rode in the front, cramped by the laptop and the custom compartments. He gave her directions, to the corner before the side street where the inn was. Where he had gotten out, the day before. All the way there he watched the traffic. Didn't see a blue van. Didn't see a black Chrysler, either. There was a late rush hour jam at one of the lights. Amos checked her watch. Getting close. She lit up her roof bar and slipped through in the wrong lane.

And there dead ahead was the ancient Subaru. Waiting at the kerb. On the right spot. At the right time. Inside was a familiar skinny silhouette. Blue denim, a pencil neck, and a long grey ponytail.

'Is that him?' Amos asked.

'Sure is,' Reacher said.

'Maybe I did something good in a previous life.'

She pulled in behind the Subaru. The silhouette jerked its head. Like it was suddenly staring in the mirror. Then the Subaru took off. Instantly. It disappeared out from in front of them. It howled off the kerb and blasted down the street.

Maximum acceleration.

Amos said, 'What?'

'Chase him,' Reacher said. 'Go, go, go.'

She glanced over her shoulder and stamped on the gas and took off in pursuit.

She said, 'What just happened?'

'You scared him,' Reacher said. 'Your red lights were still on. Like you were pulling him over.'

'He was stationary.'

'Maybe he thought you were busting him.'

'Why would I? Was he on a hydrant?'

'Maybe he's got weed in the car. Or secret documents. Or something. Maybe he thinks you're an agent of deep state oppression. We're dealing with an old guy with a ponytail here.'

They followed him a hundred yards behind, then eighty, then fifty, then twenty. The Subaru was doing its valiant best, but it was no match for a modern-day police vehicle. With lights and a siren. Then up ahead the Subaru turned right. It was lost to sight for ten or twelve agonizing seconds, but they turned after it, and saw it turning again, at the end of the block.

'He's heading home,' Reacher said. 'Somewhere north and west of here.'

Amos took a shortcut on a block she knew better, and came out right on the Subaru's bumper. A one-way street. Up ahead was a red light, and another small jam. Two lanes of traffic, five cars on the left, and six on the right. The tail end of rush hour. The light went green, but nobody moved. Someone was blocking the box. Not a blue van. Not a black Chrysler. The Subaru braked hard and swerved into the shorter line. Now he was the sixth car on the left, one inch behind the fifth. Amos stopped one inch behind him. On his left was the sidewalk, and on his right was the right-hand queue of vehicles, just as long, just as stopped. He was parked tighter than Paris.

Amos said, 'Technically he committed a number of offences.'

'Let it go,' Reacher said. 'And thanks for everything.'

He got out of the car and walked ahead. He tapped on the Subaru's passenger window. The old guy stared ahead for a long moment, absolutely refusing to look, rigid with principle, but eventually, and reluctantly, he glanced to his right. At which point he looked very surprised. He glanced back at the flashing lights. He was confused. He didn't understand.

Reacher opened the door and got in the car.

'She gave me a ride,' he said. 'That's all. She didn't mean to startle you.'

Up ahead the light cycled back to green, and this time the traffic moved. The guy drove forward, with one eye on his mirror. Behind him Amos pulled a wide U turn around the light and headed back the way she had come. Reacher turned in his seat and watched her go.

The old guy said, 'Why would a cop give you a ride?'

'Protective custody,' Reacher said. 'The folks from the apple farm were in town last night.'

The explanation seemed to settle the guy. He nodded.

'I told you,' he said. 'That family doesn't let things go.'

'Back there,' Reacher said. 'You shouldn't have run. Not a smart tactic. The cops will always get you in the end.'

'Were you a cop?'

'In the army,' Reacher said. 'Long ago.'

'I know I shouldn't have run,' the guy said. 'But it's an old habit.'

He said nothing more. He just drove on. Reacher watched the traffic. No blue van. They made a left and a right. They seemed to be heading north and west. Towards the apple farm itself. And Ryantown. That general area.

Reacher said, 'Did you make the arrangements?'

'They're expecting us.'

'Thank you.'

'Visiting hours start at ten.'

'Great.'

'The old man's name is Mr Mortimer.'

'Good to know,' Reacher said.

They found the main drag out of town, and two miles later turned left, on the road Reacher had seen the day before. The road that led to the place with no water. They followed it west, through woods, past fields. Reacher watched out his window. In the far distance on his right lay Bruce Jones's acres, with his twelve dogs, and then came the orchards, and Ryantown itself, overgrown and ghostly.

He said, 'How much further?'

'Nearly there,' the guy said.

Two miles later on the left Reacher saw a shape. Way far in the distance. Some kind of a new development. Long low buildings, laid out in a virgin field. There were crisp blacktop roads with bright white markings. There were newly planted trees, looking pale and slender and delicate next to their natural gnarly neighbours. The buildings were bland stucco, with metal windows, and white aluminium rainwater pipes that kinked at the bottom and ran away to spouts a yard into the grass. There was a sign at the main entrance. Something about assisted living.

'This is it,' the old guy said.

The clock in Reacher's head hit ten exactly.

The third arrival was as stealthy and self-contained as the first. The gentleman in question drove himself from a large house in a small town in a rural region of Pennsylvania. Initially he was in a car reported scrapped in western New York four months previously. He had prepared well ahead of time. He believed preparedness was everything. The whole journey had been re-hearsed, over and over in his mind. He had looked for snags and problems. He wanted to be ready. He had two overarching aims. He didn't want to be caught, and he didn't want to be late.

The plan was about anonymity, of course, and cut-outs, and un-traceability. Had to be. Stage one was to drive non-stop in the paperless car to a friend's place in back of a service station off the Mass Pike, just west of Boston. He knew the guy from a different community. A different shared interest. A tight, passionate group of guys. Secret and embattled. Loyal and helpful. They made a point of it. Like a fetish. What a fellow member wanted, a fellow member got. No questions asked.

The friend's day job was trading commercial vehicles. He bought them at auction, after they came off lease. For resale. They came and went, clean and dirty, used and abused, banged up and not a scratch. On any given day he had a couple dozen around. On that particular day he had three clear favourites. All panel vans, all ordinary, all invisible. No one paid attention to a panel van. A panel van was a hole in the air.

The best example was tidy in appearance and dark blue in colour. With gold signwriting. It had come in not long before, as a repo, from a bankrupt carpet cleaner in the city. Once a very upscale operation, by the look of it. Persian rugs. Hence the gold signwriting and the high standard of maintenance. The man from Pennsylvania loaded his stuff in it, and started it up. He set the GPS on his phone. He drove north. The route took him on the highway for a spell, then off near Manchester, New Hampshire, and onward to the back of beyond, through a small town named Laconia.

Where he got scared. Where he nearly quit. He saw two cop cars, clearly eyeballing everyone coming in from the south. Searching. Staring at him. As if they knew all about him ahead of time. As if someone had dropped a dime. He panicked and pulled over in an alley, and stopped in a loading bay behind a store. He checked his e-mail. His secret account, on his secret phone. The webmail page, with the translations in the foreign alphabets.

There was no cancellation message.

No warnings, no alerts.

He took a deep breath. He knew the scene. Any such community had a failsafe. An emergency one-click button, first thing to get to, guaranteed, no matter what else was going down. It would generate an automatic message. Maybe innocuous, to be on the safe side, but to be understood as a code. The children are under the weather today. Something like that.

There was no such message.

He checked again.

No message.

He backed out of the alley and drove on. He was quickly out of town. He didn't see the police cars again. He relaxed. Straight away he felt better. In fact he felt good. He felt he was earning it. He was facing dangers. He drove through woods and past horse fields and cow fields. On his left a shallow turn led away through apple orchards, but his phone said not to take it. He kept on straight, ten more open miles, and then the woods came back, for another ten. The van rushed along, almost brushing the trees. They met overhead. It was a green and secret world.

Then his phone told him the final turn was fast approaching, in half a mile on the left, a thread-like track curling away an inch into the forest. He took it, and thumped onward over blacktop missing some of its surface. He ran over a wire, that he figured rang a bell somewhere.

Two miles later he came out in a clearing. The motel was dead ahead. There was a Volvo wagon outside what must have been room three. As anonymous as a panel van. There was a guy in a lawn chair outside room five. No visible means of transportation. Outside room ten was a blue Honda Civic. Weird-looking plates. Maybe foreign.

He met Mark in the office. For the first time, face to face. They had corresponded, of course. He got room seven. He parked the van. The guy in the lawn chair watched. He put his bags in the room, and then he stepped back out to the light. He nodded to the guy in the lawn chair. But he strolled the other way, through the lot, to room ten. Important. Like a ceremony. His first look. At nothing much, as it turned out. Room ten's window blind was down. There was silence inside. Nothing was happening.

TWENTY-FIVE

Reacher thought the old people's home was a cheap but sincere attempt to provide a decent place to live. He liked it. Not for himself. He didn't expect to live long enough. But other people might enjoy it. The décor was bright. The atmosphere was happy. Maybe a little forced. They were welcomed at the reception desk by a cheerful woman who spoke to them as she would to the bereaved, except not exactly. A little livelier. A unique tone. Maybe part of her training. Maybe learned in role play class. As if visitors to an old people's home made up a unique demographic. Not the recently bereaved. The soon to be. The pre-bereaved.

The woman pointed and said, 'Mr Mortimer is waiting for you in the day room.'

Reacher followed the guy with the ponytail down a long and pleasant corridor, to a set of double doors. Inside was a tight circle of wipe-clean armchairs. In one of them was a very old man. Mr Mortimer, Reacher assumed. His hair was white and wispy, and his skin was pale and translucent. Like it wasn't really there at all. Every vein and blotch stood out. He was thin. His ears were old-man big and full of hearing aids. He was strong enough to sit up straight, but only just. His wrists looked like pencils.

There was no one else in the room. No nurse, no attendant, no carer, no companion. No doctor. No other old people, either.

The guy with the ponytail walked over and bent down and crouched low, eye to eye with the old man, and he stuck out his hand and said, 'Mr Mortimer, it's good to see you again. I wonder if you remember me?'

The old man took his hand.

'Of course I remember you,' he said. 'I would greet you properly, but you warned me never to say your name. Walls have ears, you said. There are enemies everywhere.'

'That was a long time ago.'

'How did it end up?'

'Inconclusive.'

'Do you need my help again?'

'My friend Mr Reacher wants to ask you about Ryantown.'

Mortimer nodded, pensively. His slow watery gaze panned across and tilted up and stopped on Reacher.

He focused.

He said, 'There was a Reacher family in Ryantown.'

'The boy was my father,' Reacher said. 'His name was Stan.'

'Sit down,' Mortimer said. 'I'll get a crick in my neck.'

Reacher sat down in the chair across the circle. Up close Mortimer looked no younger. But he showed some kind of spark. Any weakness was physical, not mental. He raised his hand, bent and bony, like a warning.

'I had cousins there,' he said. His voice was low and reedy, and wet with saliva. He said, 'We lived close by. We visited back and forth, and sometimes we got dumped there, if times were hard at home, and sometimes they got dumped on us, but overall I need to tell you my memories of Ryantown might be patchy. Compared with what you might be looking for, I mean, about your father as a boy, and your grandparents maybe. I was only a visitor now and then.'

'You remembered which kids got sick.'

'Only because people talked about it all the time. It was like a county-wide bulletin, every damn morning. Someone's got this, someone's got that. People were afraid. You could get polio. Kids died of things back then. So you had to know who to stay away from. Or the other way around. If you got German measles, you got loaned out to go play with all the little girls. If they were laying blacktop somewhere, you got sent to go sniff the tar. Then you wouldn't get tuberculosis. That's why I remember who got sick. People were crazy back then.'

'Did Stan Reacher get sick?'

The same bent and bony hand came up. The same warning.

'The name was never listed in the county-wide bulletin,' he said. 'As far as I recall. But that doesn't really mean I knew who he was. Everyone had cousins in and out all the time. Everyone got shunted around, when the wolf was at the door. It was like Times Square. So in my case what I'm saying is, there was always a rotating cast of characters. People were in and out, especially kids. I remember Mr Reacher the mill foreman. He was a well-known figure. He was a fixture. But I couldn't swear in a court of law which of the kids was his. We all looked the same. You never knew exactly where anyone lived. They all came running out the same four-flat door. About nine of them from the foreman's building, I think. Eight at least. One of them was a pretty good ballplayer. I heard he went semi-pro in California. Would that be your father?'

'He was a birdwatcher.'

Mortimer was quiet a beat. His pale old eyes changed focus, looking back years ago. Then he smiled, in a sad and contemplative way. As if at the strange mysteries of life. He said, 'You know, I had completely forgotten about the birdwatchers. How extraordinary that you should remember and I didn't. What a memory you must have.'

'Not a memory,' Reacher said. 'Not a contemporaneous recollection. It's a later observation. Projected backward. I assume he started young. I know he was a member of a club by the age of sixteen. But you said birdwatchers. Was there more than one?'

'There were two,' Mortimer said.

'Who were they?'

'I got the impression one of them was someone's cousin and didn't live there all the time, and one of them did. But they were together plenty. Like best friends. I guess from what you tell me one of them must have been Stan Reacher. I can picture them. I got to say, they made it pretty exciting. I guess truth to tell the first time I ever met them I was probably ready to stomp them for being sissies, but first of all I would need to bring an army, because they were the best fighters you ever saw, and second of all pretty soon they got everybody doing it, quite happily, taking turns with the binoculars. We saw birds of prey. One time we saw an eagle take something about the size of a puppy.'

'Stan had binoculars?'

'One of them did. Can't say for sure which one was Stan.'

'I'm guessing the one who lived there all the time.'

'Can't say for sure which one that was. I was in and out pretty random. I would find one of them gone from time to time. Or both at once. Whoever you were, you were missing sometimes. You got sent away, to eat better, or avoid an epidemic, or take a vacation. That's how it was. People came and went.'

'I'm wondering how he afforded binoculars. When times were tough.'

'I assumed they were stolen.'

'Any particular reason?'

'No offence,' Mortimer said.

'None taken.'

'We were all nice enough kids. We wouldn't break into a store. But we wouldn't ask too many questions either. Not if something came our way. Nice kids got nothing otherwise. I suppose the thought of anything worse would have been in our heads because of his father. Whichever one was Stan. We all thought Mr Reacher the mill foreman was a bit dubious. So I guess we went ahead and assumed like father, like son. Even though I didn't know exactly who Stan was. I suppose that's the power of rumour. I was only a visitor. It felt like local knowledge.'

'What kind of dubious?'

'Everyone was scared of him. He was always yelling and scream-ing and throwing punches and knocking people down. Looking back on it, I suppose he drank. He thought people didn't like him because he was the foreman at the mill. He was half right. All he got wrong was the reason. I guess we other kids imputed all kinds of villainy to him. Like in a storybook at school. Like Blackbeard or something. No offence. You asked the question.'

'Did he have a beard?'

'No one had a beard. It would catch on fire in the mill.'

'Do you remember when Stan left to join the Marines?'

Mortimer shook his head.

'I never heard about that,' he said. 'I guess I'm a year or two older. I was already drafted.'

'Where did you serve?'

'New Jersey. They didn't need me. It was the end of the war. They had too many people already. They cancelled the draft soon after that. I never did anything. I felt like a fraud, every July Fourth parade.'

He shook his head, and looked away.

Reacher said, 'Any other memories of Ryantown?'

'Nothing very exciting. It was a hardscrabble place. People worked all day and slept all night.'

'What about Elizabeth Reacher? James Reacher's wife?'

'She would be your grandmother.'

'Yes.'

'She sewed things,' Mortimer said. 'I remember that.'

'Do you remember what she was like?'

Mortimer was quiet for a moment.

Then he said, 'That's a difficult question to answer.'

'Is it?'

'I wouldn't want to be discourteous.'

'Would you need to be?'

'Perhaps I should say she kept to herself, and leave it at that.'

'I never met her,' Reacher said. 'She was dead long before I was born. I don't care either way. We don't need to walk on eggs.'

'Talking about your grandfather is one thing. He was a public figure. Being foreman at the mill. Talking about your grandmother is different.'

'How bad was she?'

'She was a hard woman. Cold. I never saw her smile. I never heard her say a nice thing. She always looked cross. Kind of sour. They deserved each other, that Mr and Mrs.'

Reacher nodded.

He said, 'Anything else you can tell me?'

Mortimer went quiet so long Reacher thought maybe he had fallen into a geriatric coma. Or died. But then he moved. He raised the same bent and bony hand. This time not a warning. This time an appeal for attention. Like a comedian calming a crowd, ahead of a punch line.

'I can tell you one thing,' he said. 'Since you jogged my memory. And since your dad might have been involved. I remember one time there was a big hoo-hah about a rare bird. Some big deal. First time it was ever seen in New Hampshire. Or some such thing. The birdwatching boys wrote it up for the birdwatching club. For the minutes of the meeting. Or the report on proceedings. Whatever you call it. One of them was club secretary by then. Can't say which one. The report was about all the things going on that might influence the bird being there, or not. It was very impressive. I believe it got picked up for a hobby magazine. The Associated Press said it was the first time Ryantown was ever mentioned outside the county.'

'What bird?'

'I don't remember.'

'Pity,' Reacher said. 'It must have been a big sensation.'

Mortimer's hand came up again.

Excitement.

'You could find out,' he said. 'Because of the birdwatching club. All their old ledgers will be in the library. They have a collection. All of those old clubs and societies. Part of history, they tell me. Part of the culture. Personally I thought television was better, when it arrived.'

'Which library?' Reacher asked.

'Laconia,' Mortimer said. 'That's where those clubs were.'

Reacher nodded.

'Probably takes three months to find anything,' he said.

'No, it's all right there,' Mortimer said. 'There's a big room downstairs, with shelves like the spokes of a wheel. The reference section. They get anything you want. You should go. You could find out about the bird. Maybe it was your father who wrote the note. It's a fifty-fifty chance, after all. Him or the other kid.'

'The downtown branch of the library?'

'That's the only branch there is.'

They left old Mr Mortimer in his wipe-clean armchair and walked the long pleasant corridor back to the desk. They signed out. The cheerful woman accepted their departure with grace and equanimity. They walked back to the ancient Subaru.

Reacher said, 'Do you know the library in Laconia?'

The guy with the ponytail nodded.

'Sure,' he said.

'Can you park right outside?'

216

'Why?'

'So I can get in and out real fast.'

'It isn't raining.'

'Other reasons.'

'No,' the guy said. 'It's a big building in a parcel all its own. It looks like a castle. You have to walk through the gardens.'

'How far?'

'Couple minutes.'

'How many people will I see in the gardens?'

'On a nice day like this, there could be a few. People like the sun. They got a long winter coming.'

'How far is the library from the police station?'

'Sounds like you have a problem, Mr Reacher.'

Reacher paused a beat.

'What's your name?' he asked. 'You know mine, but I don't know yours.'

The guy with the ponytail said, 'The Reverend Patrick G. Burke, technically.'

'You're a priest?'

'Currently I'm between parishes.'

'Since how long?'

'About forty years.'

'Irish?'

'My family was from County Kilkenny.'

'Ever been back?'

'No,' Burke said. 'Tell me about your problem.'

'The apple farming folks aren't the only ones mad at me. Apparently I upset someone in Boston, too. Different type of family. Different type of likely reaction. The Laconia police department doesn't want its streets shot up like the Saint Valentine's Day massacre. I'm supposed to stay out of town.'

'What did you do to the people in Boston?'

'I have no idea,' Reacher said. 'I haven't been in Boston in years.'

217

'Who are you exactly?'

'I'm a guy who followed a road sign. Now I'm anxious to get on my way. But first I want to know what bird it was.'

'Why?'

'I don't know why. Why not?'

'Aren't you worried about the people from Boston?'

'Not really,' Reacher said. 'I don't suppose they'll be hanging out at the library, reading a book. It's the cops I'm worried about. I kind of promised I wouldn't come back. I don't want to let them down. One in particular. She was an army cop too.'

'But you want to know about the bird.'

'Since it's right there.'

Burke looked away.

'What?' Reacher said.

'I never saw a police officer in the library gardens,' Burke said. 'Never once. Chances are they would never know you were there.'

'Now it's you getting me in trouble.'

'Live free or die.'

Reacher said, 'Just make sure you park as close as you can.'

Twenty miles to the north, Patty Sundstrom once again took off her shoes, and stepped up on the bed, and balanced flat-footed on the unstable surface. Once again she shuffled sideways, and looked up, and spoke to the light.

She said, 'Please raise the window blind. As a personal favour to me. And because it's the decent thing to do.'

Then once again she climbed down and sat on the edge of the mattress, to put her shoes back on. Shorty watched the window.

They waited.

'It's taking longer this time,' Shorty mouthed.

Patty just shrugged.

They waited.

218

But nothing happened. The blind stayed down. They sat in the gloom. No electric light. It was working, but Patty didn't want it.

Then the TV turned on.

All by itself.

There was a tiny crackle and rustle as circuitry came to life, and the picture lit up bright blue, with a line of code, like a weird screen on a computer you weren't supposed to see.

Then it tugged sideways and was replaced by another picture.

A man.

It was Mark.

The screen showed him head and shoulders, ready and waiting, like an at-the-scene reporter. He was standing in front of a black wall, staring at a camera.

Staring at them.

He spoke.

He said, 'Guys, we need to discuss Patty's latest request.'

His voice came out of the TV speaker, just like a regular show.

Patty said nothing.

Shorty was frozen in place.

Mark said, 'I'm totally happy to raise the blind, if that's really what you want. But I'm worried you won't enjoy it as much the second time around. It would help me ethically if I could double-check your positive consent.'

Patty stood up. Put her hands to her shoes.

Mark said, 'You don't need to get on the bed. I can hear you from there. The microphone is not in the light.'

'Why are you keeping us here?'

'We'll discuss that very soon. Before the end of the day, certainly.'

'What do you want from us?'

'Right now all I need is your positive consent to raise the window blind.'

'Why wouldn't we want that?'

219

'Is that a yes?'

'What is going to happen to us?'

'We'll discuss that very soon. Before the end of the day, certainly. All we need right now is a decision on the window blind. Up or down?'

'Up,' Patty said.

The TV turned itself off. The screen went blank, and the circuitry rustled, and a tiny standby light glowed red.

Then inside the window unit the motor whirred and the blind came up, slow and steady, with warm sunlight pouring in underneath. The view was the same. The Honda, the lot, the grass, the wall of trees. But it was beautiful. The way it was lit. Patty put her elbows on the sill and her forehead on the glass.

She said, 'The microphone is not in the light.'

Shorty said, 'Patty, we're not supposed to be talking.'

'He said I didn't need to get on the bed. How did he know I got on the bed? How did he know I was about to right that minute?'

'Patty, you're saying stuff out loud.'

'It's not just a microphone. They have a camera in here. They're watching us. They've been watching us all along.'

Shorty said, 'A camera?'

'How else could he know I just stood up, ready to get on the bed? He saw me do it.'

Shorty looked around.

'Where is it?' he said.

'I don't know,' she said.

'What would it look like?'

'I don't know.'

'It's a weird feeling.'

'You think?'

'Were they watching when we were asleep?'

'I guess they can watch whenever they want.'

'Maybe it's in the light fixture,' he said. 'Maybe that's what he meant. Maybe he was saying it's the camera in the light, not the microphone.'

Patty didn't answer. She pushed off the sill and stepped back to the bed. She sat down next to Shorty. She put her hands on her knees and stared ahead through the window. The Honda, the lot, the grass. The wall of trees. She didn't want to move. Not a muscle. Not even her eyes. They were watching her.

Then right in front of her a man peeked in the window.

He was on the boardwalk outside, craning around. Peeking in, one eye. Then he stepped more into view. He was a big guy with grey hair and a rich man's tan. He stood square on and stared. A frank and open gaze. At her. At Shorty. At her. Then he turned away and waved. And beckoned. And spoke. Patty couldn't hear what he said. The window was soundproof. But it looked like he said, their blind is up now.

In a happy and triumphant tone of voice.

Another man stepped into view.

And another.

All three men looked in the window.

They stood shoulder to shoulder, an inch from the glass.

They were staring, and judging, and evaluating. Their eyes were narrowing in contemplation. Their lips were pressing together.

They were starting slow, satisfied half smiles.

They were pleased by what they saw.

Patty said, 'Mark, I know you can hear me.'

No response.

She said, 'Mark, who are these people?'

His voice came out of the ceiling.

'We'll discuss that very soon,' he said. 'Before the end of the day, certainly.'

TWENTY-SIX

The library was a handsome construction, built of red and white stone, in a revival style that would have worked equally well on a college campus or in a theme park. As promised it was surrounded on all sides by landscaped gardens, with trees and bushes and lawns and flower beds. Reacher took a paved path from a gate near where the Reverend Burke parked the Subaru. Inside there were people strolling, and people sitting on benches, and people lying flat on the grass. No one looked wrong. No one stood out. No police anywhere.

Up ahead on the street beyond the gardens beyond the building was a white panel van. Parked at the kerb. Diametrically opposite the Subaru. The other side of the square. It had ice blue writing on the side. Every letter had a loaf of snow on top. An air conditioning repairman. Reacher walked on. Two minutes, Burke had said. A wild overestimate. It was going to be closer to fifty seconds. So far four people had passed him by on the narrow winding path, almost cheek to cheek, and four people had looked at him, from static positions on benches and lawns. Three others had paid him no attention. Eyes closed, or in a dream.

He went up the steps and in through the door. The lobby had the same red and white stone inside as outside. Granite, he thought. In the same ornate style. He found the stair to the basement. He came out in a big underground room with shelves like the spokes of a wheel. The reference section. Just like old Mr Mortimer had promised. They get anything, he had said.

There was a woman at a desk. She was half hidden behind a computer screen. Maybe thirty-five. Long black hair, in a cascade of tiny curls. She looked up and said, 'Can I help you?'

'The birdwatching club,' Reacher said. 'Someone told me you have the old records.'

The woman pattered on her keyboard.

'Yes,' she said. 'We have those. What years?'

Reacher had never known Stan when he wasn't a birdwatcher. There was no before and after. But neither was there in the way Stan had talked about it. He had sounded like he had been a birdwatcher for ever. Which was plausible. A lot of people started a lifelong hobby at a very young age. He could have joined the club right then. But he wouldn't have been trusted to write the minutes. Not as a kid. He wouldn't have been taken seriously by the hobby magazine. He wouldn't have been elected secretary. Not until much later. So as a starting point Reacher gave the woman four consecutive years, from when Stan was fourteen, up to when he left home to join the Marines.

'Take a seat,' she said. 'I'll bring them to you.'

He sat down at a study carrel, one of many pushed together in the centre of the room. Three minutes later the woman brought him the records. Which was three months faster than Elizabeth Castle could have gotten him a property file. He decided if he ever saw her again he would point that out.

The records were in four large ledgers with maroon marbled covers, stained and faded by time. Each book was an inch and a half thick, and the edges were marbled too, in curling, feathery patterns. Inside, the pages were numbered, and lined, and faded, and brittle, and covered in neat fountain-pen handwriting, gone watery and pale with age.

He asked, 'Should I be wearing white cotton gloves?'

'No,' the woman said. 'That's a myth. Generally does more harm than good.'

She walked back to her desk. He opened the first ledger. It continued from where the last ledger must have left off. The year Stan was thirteen. The first page of the new book jumped right in with the minutes of the next meeting. It was held in the back room of a downtown restaurant. Stan Reacher was not listed as present. Much time was taken up debating whether to change the club's name. Currently it was the Society of Laconia Birdwatchers. A faction thought the Laconia Audubon Society would be better. More upscale and scientific. More professional, less amateur. Much discussion ensued but no recommendation was made.

Stan Reacher was not present at the next meeting, either. It seemed to have wasted a lot of time with a guy banging on about restating the club's fundamental purpose, which in his opinion should be accurately maintaining a comprehensive register of competent binocular repairers. This, he felt, would bring maximum value to the members. Reacher was glad Stan hadn't been present. He would have needed a lot more patience as a kid than he ever displayed as an adult.

He put the first ledger aside, and tried the second. It was an identical book. He opened it at random, in the middle. Where he found a handwritten essay about hummingbird migration. It was labelled as a Report on Proceedings, and it was written, very neatly, by someone named A. B. Smith. It was like a scholarly article, recapping the work of others, before venturing a new opinion at the end. About how a baby hummingbird could be born in North America, and then fly alone two thousand miles and land on a spot the size of a pocket handkerchief. Mr or Ms Smith figured it must have been born with a fixed instinct, directly inherited from the parent, mysteriously transmitted at a cellular level by a mechanism as yet unknown. DNA, Reacher thought. Twenty years in the future. He knew the end of the movie.

He tried the third book. He opened it at random, and leafed ahead, and a minute later he found the meeting where his father was elected secretary. Right there. Stan Reacher, nem con. Which was short for the Latin *nemine contradicente*, which meant no one spoke against, which meant no one else wanted the job. Easy to see why. But Stan slowly got control. The meetings got faster. There was more talk of birds than names or binocular repairs. The fountain-pen writing was neat. But not Stan's. Not even a juvenile version. He must have delegated the clerical duties. Like later in life. Why the Corps invented clerks, he would say. But the content sounded like him. *The secretary ruled immediately that it was an inappropriate subject for discussion. The secretary set a two-minute time limit on discussion of the motion.* In other words, shut up, and hurry up. Like later in life. Why the Corps invented captains.

Reacher turned the pages. Another meeting, and another. And then another Report on Proceedings. There were maps and pictures and diagrams, done in coloured pencils. There were columns of text, done in ink. The title, carefully lettered, was *An Historic Sighting Over Ryantown, New Hampshire*. The article was respectfully submitted by S. Reacher and W. Reacher.

The birdwatching boys. Both Reachers. Cousins, probably. Like old Mr Mortimer said. Everyone had cousins in and out. Maybe their fathers were brothers. Living nearby. Or second cousins, or once removed, or whatever it was when it got complicated. Stan and . . . who? William, Walter, Warren, Wesley, Winston. Or Winthrop or Wilbert or Waylon.

The bird was a rough-legged hawk.

It was thought to be gone, but it came back. No doubt about it.

There was no issue with the identification. There was a clue in the name. It was a hard bird to mistake. The question was why it came back.

The answer, according to S. and W. Reacher, was vermin. Settlements like Ryantown attracted rats and mice like magnets, where they were poisoned, so the hawks either got nothing to eat, or they died from consuming toxic flesh. Naturally the few survivors went elsewhere, not to return until years later, when the government started commandeering every kind of basic item for the war effort, including steel and rubber and aluminium, of course, and gasoline, but also all kinds of other things. Such as rat poison. The military needed it all. For unspecified reasons. None was available on the civilian market. Like so many things. The result was the rats and mice in Ryantown grew plump and healthy. So the hawks came hustling over from wherever they had weathered the chemical storm, and they got back to work. Respectfully submitted.

W. Reacher was not listed as present at the next meeting. Or the meeting before. Reacher flipped through the pages, forward and backward, and never saw the name. Not once. Not on the committee, not among the membership, not at events, not on days out.

Cousin W. was not a joiner.

Reacher closed the book.

The woman at the desk said, 'Did you find what you needed?'

'It was a rough-legged hawk,' Reacher said. 'In Ryantown, New Hampshire.'

'Really?'

She sounded astonished.

'Because of no more rat poison,' he said. 'A new abundance of prey. I think it's plausible. As an integrated theory.'

'No, I mean it's amazing because someone else looked at that exact same thing about a year ago. I remember. It was about two boys, right? A long time in the past. They recorded the hawk and wrote an explanation. It was reprinted in an old magazine a month or so afterwards.'

She pattered at her keyboard.

She said, 'Actually it was more than a year ago. It was an ornithologist from the university. He had seen the historic magazine reprint, but because it came from a handwritten manuscript, he wanted to see the original. To be sure of the accuracy. We talked a little bit. He said he knew one of the participants.'

'One of the boys?'

'I think he said he was related to both of them.'

'How old was this guy?'

'Not old. Obviously the boys were from a previous generation. Uncles or great-uncles or something. The stories were clearly passed down.'

'He had stories?'

'Some of them were pretty interesting.'

'Which university?'

'New Hampshire,' she said. 'Down in Durham.'

'Can you give me his name and number?'

'Not without a good reason.'

'We might be related too. One of those boys was my father.'

The woman wrote out the name and the number. Reacher folded the paper and put it in his back pants pocket, next to Brenda Amos's business card. He said, 'Can I put the books away for you?'

'My job,' she said.

He thanked her and went back up the stair to the lobby. He stood for a moment. He was all done in town. He had nothing more to see. On a whim he crossed to the main staircase, which was inside a wide tower, just like it would be in a castle. He went up as far as the second-floor windows, for a last look around. It was a good vantage point. He saw the Subaru in the distance, small and dull, still parked, patiently waiting, about sixty yards away. He crossed the hall and in the opposite direction he saw the air conditioning truck. Still there, with its icy letters, and their snowy caps.

Plus three guys standing next to it. Sixty yards away. Tiny in the distance. Up close, maybe not so much. Every single passer-by was smaller. They were wearing some kind of one-piece jump suits. Hard to make out. He needed binoculars. Like the guy in the committee meeting. The jump suits looked tight. Short in the arms. Did HVAC guys need to be big? Probably not. Probably better to be small, for attics and crawl spaces.

They looked impatient.

Reacher crossed to the left-hand window.

Trees, bushes, a quiet street beyond.

With a cop on the sidewalk, just shy of the four-way.

The cop was alone and on foot. He was crouching. In a particular way. He was in the unmistakable stance of an armed man holding himself back from a corner. Until ordered to advance. Which implied a degree of coordination. With who?

He crossed to the right-hand window.

A mirror image. Trees, flowers, a quiet street, and a cop holding ready to roll his shoulder around the corner and take aim.

He went back to the centre window with the view of the truck. There were streets beyond it, left and right, radiating away. Plenty of parked cars. Some base models. Cheapskate buyers, or police unmarked. The three guys were probably surrounded. But not by an overwhelming force. Solo guys on the left and right flanks implied no more than two more anywhere. Four people, max. A very light force.

He crossed back to the left-hand window. The cop was inching towards the corner. No doubt his earpiece was counting him down. He crossed to the right-hand window. Same story. Still a mirror image. Synchronized. Seconds to go. It was a very bad plan. No way could Amos have been involved. Or Shaw either. He had looked smart enough. This was some uniform captain's mistake.

On the right the cop rolled around the corner.

Reacher hustled across the hall.

Same thing on the left.

A very bad plan.

He crossed back to the centre window just in time to see the air conditioning guys do the one and only thing they needed to do. They clambered through a flower bed and stepped into the library gardens. They turned the physical situation inside out. Like peeling off a T-shirt. Now everyone else was behind them. In front of them and all around them was a risk of collateral damage so great it was prohibitive. Like a smart move in chess. Mate in two.

They kept on walking. Slow. Always aware of the geometry around them. Not their first rodeo. Behind them the police response was halfway competent. The cops on foot sprinted back the way they had come, down the quiet side streets, to retake the flanks. Way back two more cops were running up. Then fanning out. Not entering the gardens. Staying on the street. Establishing a cordon. One cop per side of the square. Because common sense said the three guys would have to come out sometime.

But for the moment they kept on walking straight. By then they were about halfway to the library. Going slow. Just strolling. Which made sense. Because their next obvious move was to reverse direction at high speed and turn the situation inside out all over again. If they did it soon, they could make it back to their van more or less completely unopposed. The cops weren't ready yet. Then they could get the hell out of Dodge. Could three squad cars stop them? Probably not.

But they didn't reverse direction. They kept on coming. They kept on strolling. Now they were three-quarters of the way to the library. Reacher hustled from window to window. The cops were now in position, one per side, weapons drawn, each one near a gate. But each one also looking mindful of the fact that the three guys hadn't needed a gate to get in. Any low-enough flower bed would do. They knew. They were keeping their eyes open. Not the worst Reacher had ever seen.

The three guys kept on strolling. Did they have alternative transportation up ahead? Three guys could have driven in with three different vehicles. They could have parked them in strategic locations. Or was the black Chrysler their back-up? It had three empty seats, after all. There was no sign of it. Not in the first window, or the second, or the third, or the fourth.

The three guys kept on strolling. Now they were very close to the library. Maybe they were interested in architecture. Or Romanesque coloration. Red New Hampshire granite, white Maine granite, in intricate striped patterns. Like something in Rome or Florence.

Reacher craned his neck and watched them come up the steps to the door, right below him. He backed away to the top of the stairs and watched them enter the lobby. They were obvious phonies. Their jump suits were way too tight. Borrowed, for the occasion. Along with the van. No doubt someone owed someone else a favour.

They were each about six-two, and broad, with big hands and big feet, and wide necks, and hard faces as clenched as fists. They might have been in their early forties. Not their first rodeo. Two had black hair and one was grey. They came in and kept on strolling. Maybe they planned to walk straight through and out the other side. Which made sense geometrically. It was the most direct line between the top end of the gardens and the bottom.

They didn't walk through.

They stopped dead in the centre of the lobby.

Maybe they wanted to borrow a book. Maybe they had seen a review. Or maybe not. Maybe finally the black Chrysler had been pulled over. For an infraction during a lapse in concentration. Or on an old Massachusetts warrant. While Reacher had been in the basement, reading about the rough-legged hawk. Possibly Chief Shaw had been burning up the phone lines again. He had already established a relationship.

Protocol dictated the decoy in the Chrysler would have gotten off a last-minute warning he was about to be shut down. In which case the three guys would assume he would rat them out. That would be the commonsense operational baseline. Hope for the best, plan for the worst. Not just Reacher's strategy. Now they would make their own arrangements. A crowded public building was a good first step. It would give them breathing space. Because the cops would be cautious.

But worst case, it was also a good second step. And third, and fourth. It could withstand a siege. It held a plentiful supply of hostages. Maybe they would choose the city employees first. For extra leverage. A long, tense standoff. TV cameras in the streets. Negotiators on the phone. Pizza sent in, and the oldest librarian sent out in return.

How likely was that?

Not very.

But, plan for the worst.

We don't want trouble here.

Better to nip it in the bud.

Reacher came three steps down. Loud on the stone. A certain tempo. The three guys looked up. At first out of habit and instinct, and then surprise, and then wary recognition.

Reacher held up his right hand. Knuckles out. Which seemed to mean nothing to them. Maybe they hadn't drawn the same conclusion as Amos and Shaw. Maybe they hadn't gone as far in their reasoning. It seemed they preferred to rely on basic biometric data, including height and weight, and eyes and hair, and last seen wearing. Which in Reacher's case was a combination unlikely to recur frequently in nature.

Hence the recognition. It was wary because they were out on a limb. Their mission had already failed. It could only get worse. But they were trained not to quit. That kind of guy. Some kind of ancient competitive instinct. Which is why Reacher stayed on the stairs. They had to look up. And he was bigger than them anyway. Let their ancient competitive instincts deal with that.

All around them people melted away, instantly, like oil and water. A different kind of ancient instinct. Reacher had seen it a hundred times. On sidewalks outside bars. On dance floors. There would be a crackle of aggression, and suddenly a vast hole would open up. Suddenly there would be a wide perimeter. Which is exactly what happened. Suddenly the lobby was empty. No one was there. Except the four interested parties. Three downstairs, and one halfway up.

They had left their guns in the truck, Reacher thought. When they abandoned ship. Their overalls were tight. Made for much smaller men. The fabric was stretched. Any heavy metal objects would stand out in their pockets. Clear as day. Like an X-ray. They had nothing. Up close it was obvious.

They took another step. Reacher saw sudden inspiration in their eyes. Sudden delight. He knew why. For them he was two birds with one stone. He was a civilian hostage, to guarantee their passage out of town, and he was also the prize their bosses had demanded in the first place. He was good news on both ends of the deal.

But then they hesitated. Again Reacher knew why. They had left their guns in the truck. They had to execute an unarmed capture. An uphill three-on-one assault. No great tactical difficulty. The problem lay in the casualty estimate. Which was likely to run around 33 per cent. Which was easy to write down in a war plans memo, calmly, dispassionately, in bureaucratic language. But which was hard to contemplate up close and personal. When the war plan was you. The nearest guy would get kicked in the face. No doubt about that. They knew. Not their first rodeo. Missing teeth, a busted jaw. Who wanted to be the nearest guy?

They waited.

Reacher helped them out. He came down one more step. A subtle difference. Still higher, still bigger, but closer. Maybe close enough to swarm. All three together, all at once. So much press and crowding there wouldn't really be a nearest guy. Or a farthest guy, or a guy in the middle. They would all be one single unit, like a new species of animal, huge, weighing six hundred pounds, with six hands and six feet.

Which all might have worked, if Reacher had stayed down a step. But he didn't. They charged and he stepped back up to where he was before, and he kicked the nearest guy in the face. And then he twisted and hit the left-hand guy with his elbow, and twisted again and hit the right-hand guy with the same elbow coming back. Gravity and New Hampshire granite finished the job. All three guys went down backward in a slack tangle and rattled their bones and cracked their heads. Afterwards the last one looked best off. He was still moving. So Reacher stepped down and kicked him in the head. Just once. The irreducible number. But hard. To discourage further participation.

Then the lobby door opened and Brenda Amos walked in.

TWENTY-SEVEN

Amos was in plain clothes, obviously, being a detective, but more than that she was acting a part. She wasn't a cop, creeping in slow, forewarned and forearmed. She was a regular person, breezing in fast, without a care in the world. She was coming in undercover. No doubt she had volunteered. Or even insisted. Why not? Someone had to clean up someone else's mess. She had been an MP. What else was she good for? She was carrying a purse. It looked expensive. Probably a knockoff seized from a market. In it would be her badge and her gun. Maybe a spare magazine. But on the outside there was no suggestion. She was just a lady who lunched, come in to borrow a book. She was bright, and vague, and cheerful.

Then she wasn't.

She stopped.

Reacher said, 'I guess this seems like a coincidence.'

She looked at the guys on the floor.

Then at him.

She didn't speak. He knew why. She didn't know which feeling was uppermost. Was she mad or glad? Both, of course. She was mad at him, for sure, one hundred per cent, but also her problems were solved now, because under the new relative circumstances her inadequate four-man crew was suddenly as good as an armoured division. All they had to do was put cuffs on three groaning and dizzy men. Which made her glad. With exactly equal intensity. A full-on hundred per cent. Which made her mad all over again, this time at herself, for being glad about such a terrible thing.

'I apologize,' Reacher said. 'I needed to find out about a bird. I'm going now.'

'You need to,' she said.

'Apologize?'

'To go now,' she said. 'This was nice, but dangerous. They'll react.'

'Because they have a code?'

'Next time they'll send someone better.'

'I would hope.'

'I'm serious,' she said. 'Not good for you, not good for me.'

'I got what I need,' he said. 'I'm out of here.'

'How?'

'In the Subaru. It's waiting for me. At least it was five minutes ago. You might have scared it away. Like last time.'

Amos took a radio from her bag and called in the question. A second later a voice that could have been Davison's cut in on a blast of static and said, yes, the Subaru was still at the kerb, engine off, driver behind the wheel. She thanked him and clicked off. She looked at the guys on the floor again.

She said, 'Why did they come in here?'

'I'm hoping it was to find a bathroom where they could strip off their jump suits. Then they could have scattered three different directions, looking normal in civilian clothes. They might have sown some confusion. That was the percentage play. But in case they had something worse in mind, I figured it would be safer all around if I got my retaliation in first.'

Amos said nothing. He knew why. Mad or glad, still not sure. Then she got back on the radio and ordered all four of the street cops to head for the library. As fast as possible. Repeat, abandon current positions, hustle straight inside the building.

Then to Reacher she said, 'And you go get in the Subaru, right now this minute.'

'And get out of town?'

'By the fastest possible route.'

'And never come back?'

She paused.

'Not soon,' she said.

He stepped over an arm and a leg and went out the door he had come in through. He walked the same paved path, past people strolling, and sitting on benches, and lying flat on the grass. He went out the gate and crossed the sidewalk to the Subaru. He tapped on the glass, politely, and then he opened the door and got in.

Burke asked, 'Did you find what you were looking for?'

'It was a rough-legged hawk,' Reacher said.

'I'm glad you know now.'

'Thank you.'

'I saw cops in the gardens. Just now. First time ever. Guys running in from all sides. Just when I told you it never happens.'

'Maybe there was a big emergency. Maybe there was an unpaid fine.'

'I'll drive you to the highway now, if you like.'

'No,' Reacher said. 'I'm going back to Ryantown. One last look. You shouldn't come with me. You can let me out at the end of the road. You shouldn't be involved.'

'Neither should you. Not there, of all places. They'll be waiting.'

'I would hope,' Reacher said again. 'I more or less promised I would come. I like to be taken as a man of his word.'

236

'The highway would be better.'

'I'm guessing you didn't always think so. A couple times, at least. Maybe more. At various points in your life. Starting maybe forty years ago.'

Burke didn't answer. He started the car and pulled out in the traffic. He made a turn that Reacher thought was right for Ryantown. He settled in. He felt the snap of new paper in his back pants pocket. The note from the librarian. The ornithologist. His name and number. From the university, down in Durham.

He fished around and pulled it out.

He said, 'Do you have a cell phone?'

'It's an old one,' Burke said.

'Does it work?'

'Most of the time.'

'May I borrow it?'

Burke found it in his pocket, and handed it over, blind, his eyes on the road. Reacher took it. It was an old one for sure. Not like a tiny flat-screen TV. It had real buttons. It was shaped like a miniature coffin, and it was as thick as a candy bar. He got it working. The signal was good. They were still in town. He dialled the ornithologist's number. Down in Durham. It rang and rang, and then an assistant answered. The guy was in a meeting. Couldn't be disturbed. Reacher left a message. Ryantown, the hawk, the rat poison theory, and how the S. of S. and W. Reacher was his father. He said the number he was on might be good for another hour or two. After that, maybe they could catch up some other time.

He clicked off, and gave the phone back to Burke.

Who said, 'It might have been tin causing the problem, you know, not rat poison.'

'The birds came back at the height of production. During the war. When the mill was running full blast night and day.'

'Exactly. When the government was the customer. Quality was carefully monitored. Impurities were not allowed. The process was cleaned up considerably. And efficiency was encouraged, too. There was much less waste.'

'I think it was the rat poison.'

'Because your dad wrote it.'

'Because it makes sense.'

'Why would the government take all the rat poison in the first place?'

'I know the end of the movie,' Reacher said. 'The military foresaw sooner or later it would require immense storage facilities, literally hundreds of square miles in hundreds of countries, full of food and bales of clothing, all the things that rodents like, so someone ordered ahead, plus hundreds of thousands of other weird items they thought they could or might possibly, conceivably one day need. That's what the military does. That's what it's good at. Some of that stuff is still there today, all around the world.'

They drove on, out of the woods, past the first of the horse fields.

The fourth arrival was as complex as the second. Once again it involved private air transportation. Which at a certain level was still as anonymous as hailing a cab. Ironically not at the top, with the glossy Gulfstreams and Learjets and executive airports, but down on the grimy bottom rung, with grass fields and short-hop prop-driven puddle-jumpers, as battered as city taxis, resprayed just as many times, but which flew below a certain altitude, literally, where there were no logs or reports or flight plans or manifests. Everything was visual. No reason to talk to a tower. No requirement to have a radio, even.

Two or three or four such rides could be daisy-chained together, to cover unfeasible distances in total secrecy. Which was the strategy the fourth arrival had employed. He landed for the last time at a flying club near Plymouth, New Hampshire. From where originally, no one knew. Steven had tried to trace his home ISP. But he couldn't. One moment it seemed to be inside NASA, in Houston, Texas, and then the next moment inside the Kremlin, in Moscow, Russia. And then Buckingham Palace, in London, England. An ingenious piece of software, made for a guy who valued his privacy, and could pay the price for the very best. Which obviously this guy could. Steven drove out to meet him, and the first thing he saw was the bag with his money.

It was a soft leather duffel. Maybe not the best quality. Certainly not monogrammed. It was anonymous. Therefore disposable. Steven figured there would be two main ways to do it. He figured some guys would prefer to count it out, one solid brick of bills after another, handed over, one by one, more real that way. Others would just drop a bag and leave it there. A dull dusty thump, and then they would walk away. Without a word. Without a backward glance. Playing it cool. Hence disposable bags.

The guy had two more pieces of soft luggage, matching, better quality, and then two hard cases. Steven helped him unload. The guy insisted on moving the big pieces himself. He was a rangy character, tall and solid, maybe sixty years old, with snow-white hair and a brick-red face. He was in jeans and battered boots. From somewhere out west, Steven thought. Montana, Wyoming, Colorado. For sure. Not Houston or Moscow or London.

They packed the stuff in the Mercedes, and Steven drove south, on a road that stayed mostly in the trees. The guy didn't talk. Thirty minutes later they turned in at the mouth of the track. Between the frost-heaved posts, minus their signs. They ran over the bell wire. They drove on through the tunnel. Two miles and ten minutes later the guy was putting his bags in his room. Then he stepped back out, to the boardwalk, to the parking lot, to cast an eye over a small group of other guys, who seemed to be gathering nearby, forming up like a welcome committee, shuffling closer, casually, getting ready to say hi. The first guys in. The early birds.

There were three of them so far. First they all nodded, by way of

239

introduction. Then they started talking. Initially about how they got there. A neutral subject. They shared some details. They were partly secretive and partly what-the-hell friendly. One said he had driven down in a Volvo wagon. He turned and pointed at it, parked outside his room. He implied most of the year he lived in a house in the woods. He was a pale, wiry man, in a red plaid shirt. Maybe seventy years old. Not naturally a talker, by the look of him, but right then buoyed up with suppressed excitement. He looked a little feverish. A little damp around the mouth.

He was from Maine, the fourth arrival thought. He said drove down, which meant south, which meant he lived to the north. His car said Vermont, but it was sure to be phony. The other big state. A house in the woods.

The second guy didn't say where he was from, but he offered a long story about charter flights and phony licences. A long enough story to include just about every kind of vocal sound necessary to prove the guy had lived a long time in the south of Texas. Not a native. He was about fifty. He was a solid guy, restrained by natural country courtesy, as polite as a salesman. But excited, too. The same kind of fever. The same kind of tremor.

The third guy was handsome as a movie star, and built like an athlete. Like a tennis player, maybe, loose and rangy. The kind of guy who was great in college and got no worse for twenty years. He had a certain kind of confidence. Like he belonged. Like he was accustomed to admiration. He said he drove up in a car that didn't exist, and did the last lap in a van. He pointed to it. Persian carpets. He was from western New York or Pennsylvania, the fourth man thought, given his voice and his manner, and the route implied, and the distances, and the way he said drove up.

The fourth man asked, 'Have you seen them yet?'

The second guy said, 'Their blind is up. But right now they're hiding in the bathroom.'

'What are they like?'

'They look great.'

'Can you be more specific?'

'I think they're going to be real interesting.'

The man from Maine took over and said, 'They're both twenty-five years old. They're both strong and healthy. They seem to have a close emotional relationship. We looked at some tapes. She gets impatient with him from time to time. But he catches up in the end. They solve problems together.'

The second guy said, 'She's the brains, no question.'

'Are they good-looking?'

'Plain,' the good-looking guy said. 'Not ugly. They both have muscles. He's a farmer and she's a sawmill worker. They're Canadian, so they had healthcare growing up. You could call her strapping. That might be the right word for the woman. For him, not so much. His name is Shorty for a reason. He's compact. But high quality. I have to say, I was very pleased when I saw them.'

'Me too,' said the man from Maine.

'I told you,' the second man said. 'They look great.'

'How many more players will there be?'

'Two more,' the guy said. 'For a total of six. If they make it.'

The fourth man nodded. Rules were rules. If you got there late, you got there never. *Room Ten Is Occupied*. The clock was ticking from the get-go. There was a cut-off point. No excuses. No exceptions. Hence the air taxis, daisy-chained together. Unfeasible distances.

He said, 'Why is there no window in their bathroom?'

'Don't need one,' the second man said. 'There are cameras in there. Go over to the house and take a look.'

TWENTY-EIGHT

The Reverend Patrick G. Burke insisted on driving as far as his restraining order would permit, which was all the way to the forty-year-old fence, beyond which the road no longer ran anyway. He said he would wait there. Reacher said he didn't have to. But Burke insisted. In turn Reacher insisted he turn his car around. Nose out, not in. Ready for a fast getaway, in a forward gear. If necessary. Worst case. Turning around in the narrow fenced space made for an awkward manoeuvre. Back and forth, shoulder to shoulder, many times. But eventually the task was accomplished. The Subaru sat like a dragster at the start of the strip.

Reacher further insisted Burke keep his engine running. Yes, pollution. Yes, the price of gas. But better than fumbling the key. Better than the car not starting. When the time came. If necessary. Worst case. Burke agreed. Then Reacher insisted he feel free to take off without him. Immediately, no warning, at any time at all, for any reason or none, whatever his gut or his instincts told him.

'Don't second-guess it,' Reacher said. 'Don't overthink it. Don't wait even half a second.'

Burke didn't answer.

'I mean it,' Reacher said. 'If they come for you, it means they got past me. In which case you really don't want to meet them.'

Burke agreed.

Reacher got out of the car. He closed the door. He swung his legs over the fence. He set out walking. The weather was the same. The smells were the same. The heavy ripe fruit, the hot dry grass. He heard the same buzz of the same insects. Overhead was a hawk, on the thermals. Two more, in the far distance, widely separated. Too far away to tell what kind. Stan would have said it was typical raptor behaviour. Each one claimed an exclusive slice of the action. My street corner, your street corner. No trespassing. Like tough guys everywhere.

Reacher walked on, looking straight ahead. Refusing to glance left, at the top of the rise, where they might be waiting and watching. Refusing to give them the satisfaction. Let them come to him. He walked on. He got halfway across the orchard. Where he had knocked the kid down. There was no sign. No evidence. Maybe a little scuffed grass, from tensed-up footsteps. Maybe in a TV show they would make something out of it. But not in the real world. He walked on.

He made it all the way to the second fence. Undisturbed. All around was peace and quiet and silence. Nothing was moving. Straight ahead the leaves were darker, and the smell was ranker. The sunless shadows looked colder. He glanced back. Nothing doing.

He climbed over the fence.

Ryantown, New Hampshire.

He walked down Main Street, like the day before, stepping between swaying pipe-thin trees, stumbling now and then on tipped-up stones, passing the low remains of the church, and the

243

school. He picked his way onward, to the four-flats. To the right-hand foundation. To the remains of the kitchen, in the far back corner. The fragment of tile. He pictured his grandfather, like a clean-shaven Blackbeard, yelling and screaming and throwing punches and knocking people down. Probably drinking. He pictured his grandmother, hard and cold and sour. Never smiling. Never saying a nice thing. Always looking cross. Angrily sewing the kind of bed sheets she would never get to use.

He pictured his father, crawling around on the floor. Or not. Maybe sitting quietly in a corner, staring out the window. At a teeming patch of sky.

Your dad joined the Marines at seventeen, Carter Carrington had said. *Got to be a reason*.

He stood there for a long moment more, and then he said his goodbyes to the place. He turned and retraced his steps. Out the kitchen, through the hallway, past the trees, through the lobby, out the street door.

No one there. Nothing but peace and quiet and silence, all over again. He walked back up Main Street. He stopped at the school. Up ahead the street bent around to meet the church. Without sixty years of trees the vista would have been wide open. A person would have seen a big patch of sky. Maybe right there was their birdwatching spot. Where they saw the hawk. Maybe the binoculars belonged to the school. A grant from the county. Communally owned. Not to be taken away. Or maybe a kindly teacher had found them in a junk shop, and laid out a couple of bucks.

He walked on. He passed the church. He got back to the fence. Ryantown's city limit. Ahead of him was the orchard. Where the road used to be. A straight shot, a hundred yards, to the parked Subaru. Which was still there. It was clearly visible in the distance. Between it and him were only two points of interest. The more distant was Burke himself. He was standing in the space between the back of his car and the safe side of the fence, and he was hopping from foot to foot, and jumping up and down, and waving his arm.

The second point of interest was fifty yards closer. Halfway across the orchard, strung out across the width of the stolen road, was a line of five men.

Overhead the hawk circled slowly.

Reacher climbed the fence. He left the mossy tangle of unchecked nature behind him, and walked between orderly lines of pruned and identical trees. Up ahead the five men stood still. They were shoulder to shoulder, but not quite touching. They looked like a singing group, about to start up with a tune. Like a barbershop quartet, plus one. Maybe an alto, two tenors, a baritone and a bass. In which case the bass would be the guy in the centre. He was bigger than the others. Reacher was pretty sure he hadn't seen him before. Also he was pretty sure the older guy was standing on the big guy's right. The middle generation. Better jeans, cleaner shirt, greyer hair. The other three were the same as the night before. Minus the one that got popped. Big healthy specimens, but no military service or prison time or secret sessions with Mossad.

He walked on.

They waited.

Way beyond them in the distance Burke was still hopping up and down and waving his arm. Reacher wasn't sure why. As a warning it would always be too late. Because of the linear geometry. He would see the problem before he saw the warning. Which made no sense. Maybe Burke was offering tactical advice. Do this, then do that. But Reacher couldn't understand the semaphore. And he felt it would probably be superfluous anyway. No doubt a man like Burke had many and various talents, but brawling didn't seem to be one of them. Not so far.

Maybe it was just general agitation.

Reacher walked on.

245

The guy in the centre of the line of five was tall and wide and shaped like an artillery shell. He had a small head set on a thick bull neck fully four inches wider than his temples. Below that his shoulders sloped down, smooth and fast, like a sea creature. He had a big barrel chest, which made his arms and legs look short. He looked young, and fit, and strong.

He was a wrestler, Reacher thought. Maybe once a high school star. Then a college star. Now an apple picker. Was there a big leagues for college wrestlers? If so, the guy hadn't made it. That was clear.

But still, he was big.

Twenty yards to go.

They waited.

The wrestler was staring dead ahead. He had tiny dark eyes set back deep in his tiny head. Not much expression. Altogether passive. Hence his relative lack of success in the post-college world, perhaps. Perhaps he lacked drive. Perhaps he failed to interpret the world around him. In which case, too bad. He was going to have to suck it up. He had been warned. Obviously. He had been drafted as a replacement. There was a clue in the word. He knew what he was getting into. He could have declined.

Fifteen yards to go.

The older guy was glancing left and right at his troops. He looked mostly excited. He was about to see some real good fun. But he was a little anxious too. In a faraway corner of his mind. Which he knew was crazy. How could they lose? It was a slam dunk, surely. But he couldn't shake the feeling. Reacher saw it in his face. He helped it along, any way he could. The slow walk. The long strides, the loose shoulders. The hands away from the sides. The head up, and the eyes hard on the guy. The primitive signal, learned long ago.

Ten yards out.

The older guy couldn't shake the feeling. It was right there in his face. Suddenly he looked like he was working on a contingency plan. A potential change of tactics. Just in case. As an alternative. He looked ready to shout new orders. Which made him a legitimate target. Even though he was fifty-something and soft. He was a commander in the field. Rules of engagement. They were what they were. He was going to have to suck it up too.

Reacher figured the other three would run away. Or at least they would back off, palms out, and they would stammer their way through some kind of not-our-idea plea deal. Loyalty had its limits. Especially to promises of menial labour from people who were pretty much assholes anyway.

They would run.

Five yards to go.

Reacher believed in staying flexible, but also having a plan, and in his experience it was about fifty-fifty which got used in the end. On this occasion the plan was to never slow down, to arrive at full speed, and to head-butt the wrestler mid-stride. Which would check all the boxes. Surprise, overwhelming force, general shock and awe. With a convenient ethical twist. Literally. It would leave the older guy perfectly situated for a left hook, which was Reacher's weaker hand, which was about as humane as he could see how to make it.

But it turned out flexibility was better. Because of the wrestler. He dropped into some kind of combat stance. Like a theatrical pose. Like a photographer was egging him on. Telling him to bring it. Maybe for the front page of the local newspaper. *High School Star Wins Trophy*. That kind of thing. The guy was giving it his best shot. Wasn't really working. He looked like a fat kid pretending to be a grizzly bear. Stubby arms, like claws. At the ready. Kind of crouching, knees bent, feet apart.

So Reacher modified the plan. On the fly. West Point would have been proud of him. He preserved the essentials, and altered only the details. He never slowed down. He arrived at full speed. But instead of head-butting the guy, he kicked him in the balls. A sudden target of opportunity. Because of the feet apart. He got him with pace, and momentum, and a vicious scything upswing, and a dead-on perfect connection.

A football would have left the stadium.

It came out both good and bad.

The good part was it put him exactly where he should be. Ready for the left hook. Which he delivered. It was short and choppy by classical standards. Not elegant at all. Not much more than a whipped-in clout. But it was effective. *Bang*. Daddy went down sideways. His command influence was terminated.

The bad part was the wrestler was wearing an athletic protector. A cup. Smart kid. He had interpreted the world. He had prepared. Even so, he had taken a heavy blow. Like a blunt cookie-cutter smashing down on tough and gristly dough. But he wasn't disabled. He was still on his feet, stumping around, breathing hard. Shock, yes. Awe, not so much. Which meant the other three guys didn't run away. They didn't back off, palms out, pleading. Instead they crowded in a step, a blocking manoeuvre, to let their quarterback recover behind them.

Reacher thought, damn. The vagaries of chance. He should have stuck to the original plan. The guy wasn't wearing a football helmet. He wanted to back off a pace, to reset the geometry, but he didn't let himself. It would send the wrong message. Instead he hit the guy crowding nearest. A solid shot to the gut. Which doubled the guy over, his face on his knees, puking and gasping, so Reacher hit him again, with an elbow chopped down hard against the back of the guy's head, which planted him face first in the grass. Game over right there, so Reacher stepped left and lined up the next guy. No delay. Nothing to be gained by standing around shooting the breeze. Better just to set them up and knock them down.

But the next guy was barged out the way. By the wrestler coming through the line. His hands were out and his body was all swelled up with rage. He shoved the last guy out the way. He was coming on like a dump truck. Then he planted his feet. He crouched. Face to face. Like the start of a bout. He glared. He snarled.

Reacher thought, OK, then.

He knew squat about wrestling. He had never tried it. Never felt the need. Too sweaty. Too many rules. Too much like a last resort. He believed a fight should be won or lost long before it came to rolling around on the floor.

In the distance Burke was still jumping up and down and waving his arm.

The wrestler moved. His body turned like a single rigid unit, and he thumped his right foot down, just ahead of where it had been before. Then he turned the other way, just as rigid, and he thumped his left foot down. Like sumo. Now he was half a step closer. He was maybe a couple inches shorter than Reacher. But probably twenty pounds heavier. He was a big solid guy. That was for damn sure. He was all hard sleek muscle, smoothed out into a fluid shape, as if by passage through air or water. Like a bull seal. Or a mortar shell.

A replacement. Not exactly, Reacher thought. The guy was an improvement. He was there to strengthen the roster. He was specialist talent, drafted in for the occasion. After the lessons of the night before. Maybe he had been borrowed from a friend of a friend. Maybe he was a nightclub bouncer. In Manchester. Or even Boston. Maybe that was the big leagues, for college stars.

Reacher decided to stay clear of his arms. Wrestling was all about grabbing and grasping and grappling. The guy was probably good at it. Or at least experienced. He probably knew all kinds of follow-up tricks. He would know a dozen different ways to get his opponent down on the mat. Which would be a fate best avoided. A horizontal struggle would be a problem. Too much bulk. It could end up like trying to bench-press a whale. Fortunately the guy's arms were not long. The exclusion zone was not large. There was some scope for action. Something could be done.

But what exactly? For once in his life Reacher wasn't sure. The head-butt was still a possibility, but risky, because it meant stepping right into the bear-claw grasp. And maybe the guy knew enough to twist away and take the blow on his neck, which up close looked about as sensitive as an automobile tyre. Body shots could be delivered, fast right-left-right combinations, like working with the heavy bag, but the guy was built with the kind of slabby construction that would feel like punching a bulletproof vest. With about as much effect.

The wrestler moved again. The same dramatic manoeuvre. Again like sumo. Reacher had seen it on the television. In the afternoons, in motels. Grainy orange pictures. Huge men in fancy loincloths, blank and oiled and implacable.

Now the guy was a whole step closer.

Overhead the hawk circled slowly.

Too late Reacher realized what the guy was going to do. Which was to barge forward, leading with his stomach, again like the sumo on the television, except in that case the other guy was also doing the exact same thing, so they met in the middle with a loud slap, but Reacher wasn't moving at all, which meant the other guy had all the momentum to himself, which meant Reacher was about to get hit hard. Like getting run over by a tractor tyre.

He ducked and twisted and flung a Hail Mary right hook into the guy's side, which landed hard, and therefore according to Isaac Newton's laws of equal and opposite reactions took some momentum out of the equation, but the guy's barrelling bulk was basically unstoppable, and Reacher was spun around and bounced away, and then he had to twist again to avoid a bear claw swinging out towards him. He staggered backward, flailing his arms, trying to stay on his feet.

The wrestler charged again. He was nimble, for a guy built like

250

a walrus. Reacher ducked away and got a weak jab into the guy's kidney as he passed. It made no discernible difference. The guy reversed direction with a neat one-two shuffle and came barrelling back again, hot and fierce and feinting left and right, looking to get a grip. Best avoided. Reacher stepped back, and again, and the guy came on, and Reacher launched a straight right to the guy's face, which was like punching the wall of a rubber room, and then he ducked away, low down under the bear claw's swing, and came back up and twisted and got a hard left hook into the guy's back, before bouncing away out of range.

Now the wrestler was breathing hard. He had run around a little and taken two and a half decent body shots. Soon he would be stiffening up. Reacher stepped back. Underfoot the ground was lumpy. On his left was a windfall apple, bright like a jewel on the sunburned grass. The two surviving guys from the night before were creeping nearer, smelling blood.

Overhead the hawk was still circling.

The two surviving guys formed up and fanned out, a step ahead of the wrestler. Flank support. Or a chase-down crew. Maybe they expected him to run.

The wrestler dropped down into his combat stance. Reacher waited. The wrestler charged. Same as before. A low-down swarming thrust, off bent and powerful legs, and a high-speed waddle, leading with the stomach, aiming to use it like a battering ram. Reacher swayed left, but his foot caught in an undulation and the guy hit him a glancing blow with his charging shoulder, which felt like getting run over by a truck, twice, first with the original impact and then immediately again with its equal and opposite echo as he hit the ground, right shoulder first, then his head, then his body, then a tangle of limbs.

The guy was nimble and came straight back. Reacher rolled away, but not fast enough. The guy got in a kick that caught him high on the back and rolled him faster. A rare position for Reacher

251

to be in. But not unknown. Rule one was get the hell up, right now. So was rule two. And three. Staying down was one foot in the grave. So he waited until he rolled face down and then sprang upright like he was a gym rat showing off after fifty push-ups. Now he was breathing hard. And swelling up with anger. He was pretty sure kicking wasn't in the rules of wrestling. The game had changed.

He thought, OK, then.

The wrestler dropped down into his combat stance again. And Reacher saw what he should have seen before. Or would have seen before, if the game had changed a little sooner.

He waited.

The wrestler charged. A low-down swarming thrust, off bent and powerful legs. Reacher stepped in and kicked him in the knee, just as hard as he had kicked him in the cup, with the same scything upswing, and an equally perfect connection. Plus the guy ran right into it. He brought all his own momentum to the party. A football would have left two stadiums. The result was spectacular. The knee was any heavy guy's weak spot. A knee was a knee. A humble joint. It was what it was. It didn't get bigger and stronger just because a guy chose to spend a whole semester lifting weights. It just got more and more stressed.

In this case it more or less exploded. The kneecap shattered or dislocated and maybe a whole bunch of stuff was severed inside, because the guy went down like his strings were cut, and then the same rule-one instinct bounced him upright again, immediately, howling, standing on one leg, waving the bear claws for balance. The two surviving guys stepped back a pace. Like the stock market. Investments can go down as well as up. Behind them in the distance Burke was standing still and watching, peering anxiously, pressed up tight against the fence.

From that point on Reacher opted for brutal efficiency. Style points no longer mattered. The wrestler threw a despairing bear

252

claw at him, and Reacher caught it and jerked him off balance, and he went down again, awkwardly, clumsily, whereupon Reacher kicked him in the head, once, twice, until he went still.

Reacher stood up straight, and breathed out, and in, and out.

The two surviving guys stepped back another pace. They shuffled in place and tried to look aw-shucks sheepish. They raised their hands, palms out. They patted the air in front of them. Surrendering. But also distancing themselves. Making a point.

Not our idea.

Reacher asked them, 'Where did you find this tub of lard?'

He kicked the wrestler one more time, in the ribs, but gently, as if merely to indicate which particular tub of lard he was talking about.

No one answered.

'You should tell me,' Reacher said. 'It's important to your futures.'

The kid on the right said, 'He came up this morning.'

'From where?'

'Boston. He lives there now, but he grew up here. We knew him in high school.'

'Did he win trophies?'

'Lots of them.'

'Get lost now,' Reacher said.

They did. They ran south, at a sprint, up the slope, knees and elbows pumping. Reacher watched them go. Then he picked his way through the vanquished and walked on through the orchard. Burke was waiting at the fence. He held up the hand he had been waving. In it was his phone.

'It kept trying to ring,' he said. 'But there's really no service here. So I walked back to where I got half a bar. It was the ornithologist. He was returning your call, from the university. He said it was his only chance to talk, because he's tied up the rest of the day. So I ran back here and tried to attract your attention.'

'I saw,' Reacher said.

'He left a message.'

'On the phone?'

'With me.'

Reacher nodded.

He said, 'First I need to call Amos at the Laconia PD.'

TWENTY-NINE

The fifth arrival was as unobtrusive as the first and the third. In the back parlour Mark and Steven and Robert heard the bell ring, from the wire across the blacktop. They watched the screens. Robert lined up three different views of the track. They waited. Two miles took four minutes at thirty miles an hour, and six minutes at twenty. Call it five minutes on average, depending on how fast a person was prepared to drive, and what kind of vehicle they had. The surface could be jolting.

It was five minutes and nineteen seconds exactly, according to the digital clocks in the bottom right-hand corners of the screens. They saw a pick-up truck come out of the trees and into the light. Robert used a joystick and zoomed the close-up camera tight on it. It was a Ford F150. Single cab, long bed. Dirty white paint. Close to a base specification, three or four model years old. A working-man's vehicle. A tool of a trade.

Robert tightened the shot some more, to check the licence plate. It said Illinois, which they all knew was bullshit. The guy was from New York City. His office ISP was unbreakable, but his home

255

wifi was wide open. He ran a fund on Wall Street. He was one of the new faceless super-rich no one had ever heard of. Mark was keen to impress him. He thought Wall Street could be a key market. The right kind of people, with the right kind of needs, and the right kind of money.

They watched him drive through the meadow, and bump down off the track into the motel lot. They saw him stop outside the office. They saw Peter come out to greet him. They shook hands, and exchanged pleasantries. Peter gave him a key, and pointed. Room eleven. The absolute prime location. Significant in every way. Their bed and your bed were almost touching. Head to head. Symmetrical. Separated only by the width of a wall. Just a matter of inches. Room eleven was the VIP enclosure, no doubt about it. An honour not to be given lightly. But Mark had insisted. Demographics were important, he had said.

Robert clicked mice and tapped keyboards and arranged the screens so they could see just about everything at once, all around them on the walls, one picture overlapping the next, some of the angles different, like a clumsy attempt at virtual reality. They saw the Wall Street guy park his truck beyond the dead Honda. They saw him detour for a look in room ten's window. Nothing doing. He walked back. He looked like Wall Street. Decent haircut, fit from the gym, tan from a lamp and weekends at his wife's summer rental in the Hamptons. He was dressed well, even though they supposed he was trying not to be. To match the everyday truck. His closet had failed the challenge. His luggage was two hard cases and a soft nylon duffel, all of them dusty from the open bed.

Plus, last of all, from the passenger seat, a plastic bag from a New York deli, stuffed with what were either potatoes or rolls of money.

Meanwhile the first four arrivals were gathering close by, forming up, sliding from screen to screen, getting ready to talk, or try to, or at least to rock from foot to foot until someone said something. Male bonding. Sometimes a slow process. Robert turned up the sound. There were hidden microphones all up and down the length of the motel. Aided by what was painted to look like a TV dish, but was really a parabolic microphone, as sensitive as a bat's ear, aimed down the row, at the patch of dirt outside room ten's window. Where folks were likely to cluster. Overkill, electronically, but Mark had insisted. Consumer feedback was important, he said. The more raw and unfiltered the better. Best of all when they didn't know anyone was listening.

They listened. The voices were tinny and a little distorted. There were guarded greetings, the same as before, and the same war stories from the road, about getting there on time and undetected, and the same description of Patty and Shorty themselves, as specimens, in terms of their health and strength and general appeal.

Then the consumer feedback turned a little negative. Mark looked away, disappointed. On the screens a small schism had opened up. There were two opposing factions, separated by one vital difference between them. Arrivals number one, two and three had actually seen Patty and Shorty through their window. Live and in the flesh. Right there. After their blind went up. Arrivals number four and five had not. By then Patty and Shorty were hiding in their bathroom. Which had no damn window. So theirs was a two-point complaint. If everyone was starting out equal, like they should, free country, level playing field, and so on and so forth, then wait until everyone had gotten there, surely, and then raise the damn blind like a ceremony. Like a special occasion. With everyone lined up to witness it. Or at least put a window in the damn bathroom. One thing or the other.

In the parlour Mark said to the others, 'I don't see how we could put a window in the bathroom. Not with plain glass, anyway. Too weird. But anything else wouldn't work. You couldn't see in.'

257

Steven said, 'We could use a plastic sheet on the outside. Some kind of design on it. So it looked pebbled from the inside. Then we could peel it off when we're ready.'

'You're dodging the issue,' Robert said. 'We screwed up with their blind. Simple as that. The guy is right. We should have left it down until everyone got here.'

Mark said, 'Patty wanted to see the sunshine.'

'What are we now, social workers?'

'Her mood might prove critical.'

'How's her mood now?'

'Relax,' Mark said. 'Think outside the box. What's done is done. And as it happens we did it at the exact halfway point. Three saw them, and three won't. We could think of it as a reward for punctuality. Like a bonus threshold. Like we're offering something. We could call it marketing.'

'Punctual means on time, not early. We should treat them all equally.'

'Too late.'

'Never too late to fix a mistake.'

'How?'

'You get on the mike with Patty and Shorty, and you remind them you warned them about this earlier, and you say but maybe they didn't realize exactly what they were getting themselves into, so now for their own comfort we have taken a unilateral decision to close their blind again for them. And we do, right away. They'll hear it. They'll come out of the bathroom. Meanwhile we apologize to arrivals four and five, and we tell them we'll have a proper ceremony later. After Patty and Shorty have calmed down again. When we're all assembled. Maybe as the sky goes dark. We could suddenly raise the blind and light up the room both at the same time. I bet we would catch them right there on the bed. It would look like Saks Fifth Avenue on Christmas Day. People would come from miles around.'

258

'That doesn't solve the problem,' Mark said. 'All it means is three people will have seen them once and three people will have seen them twice. That's not equal.'

'Best we can do,' Robert said. 'As a gesture. Which could be important. We can't let this become an issue. You know how they talk in the chat rooms. Word of mouth can make you or break you. We should be seen to go the extra mile to put this right.'

Mark was quiet a long moment.

Then he glanced at Steven.

Who said, 'I guess.'

Mark nodded.

He said, 'OK.'

Robert clicked a switch labelled *Room Ten, Window Blind, Down.*

His voice came out of the ceiling. Like before. In the bathroom it was just as loud as it had been in the main room. He said, 'Guys, I apologize. Most sincerely. My fault entirely. I wasn't clear enough when we spoke earlier. About the downside of seeing the view, I mean. So we put it right for you. The blind is down again now and will stay down as long as you want. I'm sure you'll be more comfortable that way. Again, I apologize. I was thoughtless.'

Patty said, 'What do you want with us? What's going to happen to us?'

'We'll discuss what we want with you before the end of the day.'

'You can't keep us here for ever.'

'We won't,' Mark said. 'I promise. You'll see. Not for ever.'

Then there was a small electronic pop and the ceiling went quiet again.

In the silence Shorty said, 'Do you believe him?'

'About what?' Patty said.

'The blind being down again.'

259

She nodded.

'I heard it,' she said.

Shorty got up stiffly, from his spot on the floor, and he opened the door, just a crack. He knew right away. There was no bar of daylight. Just gloom.

'I'm going through,' he said. 'It's uncomfortable in here.'

'They're going to raise it again.'

'When?'

'Probably when we least expect it.'

'Why?'

'Because they're messing with us.'

'Soon?'

'Probably not. They'll wait a while. They'll want us to build up a sense of security.'

'So it's safe for a spell. Right now. Then later we could nail up a sheet.'

'Could we?'

'Why not?' Shorty said.

In the past she would have objected purely on the grounds of good manners. Being Canadian. Both the sheet and the wall would be damaged, surely. But now all she said was, 'Do you have nails and a hammer?'

'No,' Shorty said.

'Shut up, then. Save your breath to cool your porridge.'

'Sorry,' he said. He stood at the door for a moment. Then he went through. He was sore from sitting with his butt on one kind of cold tile, and his back on another. He lay down on the bed and stared up through the dark at the ceiling. Somewhere there was a camera. He couldn't see it. The plaster was smooth all over. So it was in the light fixture or the smoke alarm. Had to be. Probably not the light fixture. Too hot, surely. Secret spy cameras were presumably delicate. Circuit boards, and tiny transmitters.

So it was in the smoke alarm. He stared at it. He imagined it staring back at him. He imagined smashing it with a hammer. He imagined fragments raining down. He imagined the hammer still in his hand. What would he smash next?

He got up off the bed again and went back in the bathroom. He closed the door. He set the faucet running in the sink. Patty watched him from her spot on the floor. He bent down low, close to her ear, and he spoke in a whisper. He said, 'I was thinking, suppose I had a hammer, what would I do?'

'Nail up a sheet,' she whispered back.

'I meant after that,' he said.

'What after that?'

'I would come in here. This is the back of the building. All the action is at the front. The bullshit with the blind, and people looking in. Maybe no one is watching the back. The wall is nothing but a skin of tile, then half an inch of wall board, then a six-inch void between the studs, maybe packed with insulation, plus maybe a vapour barrier, and then cedar siding nailed on sixteen-inch centres.'

'So?'

'If I had a hammer I would bust my way through. We could walk away.'

'Through the wall?'

'A proper demolition crew could do it in a second. That would be routine.'

'Then it's a shame you don't have a hammer.'

'I figure we could use the suitcase on the tile. Like a battering ram. We could swing it, with the new rope handle. Like one, two, three. I bet the tile would come off all in a sheet. Then I could kick the rest of the way through.'

'You can't kick through cedar siding.'

'Don't need to,' Shorty said. 'All I need is to pop it off the studs from the inside, where it's nailed on. With sudden outward force. Which should be easy enough. Then it would fall away by itself.

All I would need to actually kick my way through would be the wall board. Which should also be easy enough. That stuff ain't strong.'

'How wide of a gap would there be?'

'I think about fourteen inches, effectively. We could step through sideways.'

'With the suitcase?'

'Something we got to accept,' Shorty said. 'We need to be realistic. The suitcase stays here until we capture a vehicle.'

Patty said nothing for a moment.

Then she whispered, 'Capture a what?'

'Some of these guys peering in the window must have driven here. Which means there must be cars in the lot now. Or maybe they all got picked up in a Mercedes SUV. In which case it's still out there, neatly parked somewhere, all warmed up and ready to go. If we can't find it, no matter, because there are plenty more in the barn. Which ain't far away. I bet all the keys are hanging up on a neat little board.'

'So first we destroy their property and then we steal their car.'

'You bet your ass we do.'

'This feels as crazy as the quad-bike thing.'

'The quad-bike thing wasn't crazy. It worked perfectly. You know that. We saw it working perfectly, every minute, beginning to end. It was something else that didn't work perfectly. We didn't know they had cameras and microphones. We didn't know they were cheating.'

'Just theoretically,' Patty said. 'How long would it take to kick through a wall?'

'Not long, if we kept the hole a limited size. If we kept it low down to the ground. If we were prepared to crawl out, hands and knees.'

'How long in minutes?'

Shorty closed his eyes. He visualized. Eight kicks, six with the toe, to crack the wall board in strategic locations, and then two mighty blows with the flat of the sole, to punch it all out. Call it eight seconds overall. Plus then time to tear the insulation out, handful after handful, a blur, like a dog digging up a treasure. Call it another eight seconds. Or ten. Call it twelve seconds, to be on the safe side. So far a total of twenty. But then came the siding. Popping it off the studs would not be easy. It was fixed on with big nails shot out of a gun. Heavy blows would be required. The problem was the angle of attack. He would have to direct low karate-style kicks through a narrow opening. Kind of sideways and downward. Not practical. Hard to develop maximum power. Better to lie on his back. A downward stamping motion would translate to maximum outward force. Over and over again. Eight times at least.

He said, 'One minute, maybe.'

She said, 'That's pretty good.'

'If the tile comes off all in a sheet.'

'What if it doesn't?'

'We would have to bust off every piece separately. Just to get to the wall board in the first place. Then from that point onward it would be a minute. Except probably two, because by then we would be tired, from busting off the tile.'

'How long altogether?'

Shorty said, 'Just hope it comes off all in a sheet.'

She said, 'Are we really going to do this?'

'I vote yes.'

'When?'

'I say right now. We could run straight for a quad bike. Might be better than a car. We could ride it through the trees. They wouldn't be able to follow.'

'Except on another quad bike. They have eight more.'

'We would have a head start.'

'Do you know how to drive a quad bike?'

'How hard can it be?'

Patty was quiet another long moment.

'One step at a time,' she said. 'First we'll test the suitcase on the tile. We'll see if it comes off all in a sheet. If it does, then we can go ahead and make a final decision. If it doesn't, we can go ahead and forget it anyway.'

Shorty opened the bathroom door and glanced across the room at the suitcase. It was still where he had put it down, all those hours before. After he had watched Karel drive away in the tow truck.

He whispered, 'They'll see me get it. Because of the camera.'

'They don't know what's in it,' Patty whispered back. 'We're allowed to take our own stuff in the bathroom, surely. We might need it. We might choose to sleep in here, what with people looking in the window all the time. That would be perfectly natural.'

Shorty paused. He nodded. He went to get the suitcase. Cool as a cucumber. Perfectly natural. He strolled over, and hefted it up, and strolled back. He put it down, and closed the door. Then he breathed out and flapped his hand to ease the pain in his palm.

They picked their spot. To the left of the sink. A blank patch of wall. No outlets. Therefore no hidden cables inside to snarl things up. No pipes inside, either. The water came and went all in one place, on the other side of the room. Perfect. Plain sailing.

They pulled and shoved the suitcase until it was in position. They stood facing each other, with the case between them. They bent down over it, and they grabbed the rope with all four hands. They lifted the case, six inches off the floor, to clear the baseboard at the bottom of the wall. They moved away a step, and they set the suitcase swinging, gently, back and forth, back and forth. It was a big sturdy item. Very old. A plywood shell, covered in heavy leather, with reinforcements on the corners. They perfected their rhythm. They let the weight do the work. On each swing they made one arm short and one arm long, to keep the suitcase exactly level, like a piston, so its blunt end would hit the wall square on.

'Ready?' Shorty said.

'Yes.'

'On three.'

They swung once, and twice, gathering momentum, and on three they stepped in towards the wall and accelerated the weight as hard as they could.

The case smacked against the tile.

The result was not what Shorty expected.

His instinctive prediction had been that the wall board would flex inward a fraction, which would cause the skim coat to crack off. The tiles were cemented to the skim coat. If the skim coat flaked off, the tiles would come down with it. In sheets. Gravity would see to that.

Didn't happen.

Instead half a dozen tiles shattered into pieces. Some of the broken bits rained down on the floor. Others stayed up on the wall. Like random coin-sized fragments, still solidly glued to separate coin-sized daubs of adhesive. A cheap job. The tiler had buttered three or four knobs of cement on the back of a tile, and then pressed it into place. One after another, over and over. All the un-buttered voids behind them had made them shatter on impact. But the wall board itself hadn't flexed at all.

They put the suitcase down. Shorty pressed his thumbnail in the space between two surviving fragments. The skim coat was right there, dry and smooth and creamy. It was hard and rigid. He scraped at it. It powdered a little. He pressed harder, with the ball of his thumb, and then with his knuckles, and then harder still, with his fist. The wall board didn't yield. Not even a tiny fraction. It felt solid.

'Weird,' he said.

'Should we try again?' Patty asked.

'I guess,' he said. 'Real hard this time.'

They backed off as far as the width of the room would allow, and they swung the case once, through a big healthy arc about a yard long, and then again, and on three they staggered sideways and smashed the case into the wall as hard as they could.

Same result. A couple more orphan fragments fell off the wall. Nothing more. It was like hitting concrete. They felt the shock in their wrists.

They dragged the case out the way. Shorty tapped on the wall, experimentally, here and there, in different places, like knocking on a door. The sound it made was strange. Not exactly solid, not exactly hollow. Somewhere in between. He stepped back and kicked out hard. And again, harder. The whole wall seemed to bounce and tremble as a single unit.

'Weird,' he said again.

He picked up a jagged shard of tile and used it to scrape at the skim coat. He made a long furrow, and deepened it, working back and forth, stabbing and scraping. Then he made another furrow, and another, in a wide triangle, missing some of the still-stuck fragments, including others inside the lines. Then he stepped back and kicked out again, hard, aiming carefully. The scored-around triangle of skim coat flaked off and fell to the floor. Under it was revealed the papery surface of brand new wall board. He attacked it with the shard of tile, furiously, hacking and gouging, spraying dust and curls of torn paper all around. Then he stepped back again, and kicked, and kicked, and kicked, in a frenzy of frustration. He kicked the wall board to fragments and powder. He pulverized it. He reduced it to nothing.

But he didn't kick his way through it. He couldn't. It was backed by some kind of thick steel mesh. Which came into view, section by section, as the wall board in front of it was destroyed. It loomed up through the cloud of dust and particles, white and ghostly and tightly woven. It was a net, with steel filaments as thick as his finger, running up and down and side to side. The holes they made were grudging and square. About big enough to put his thumb in, but nothing better.

He used the shard of tile to cut more wall board away. He found a place where a bright green ground wire was soldered to the back of the mesh. Like an electrical connection. A very neat job. A random yard away he found another. Same thing. A ground wire, soldered to the back of the mesh.

Then he found a place where the mesh was welded to a prison bar.

There was no doubt about it. He knew from the size, and the shape, and the spacing. Like on every cop show ever made. There were floor-to-ceiling prison bars built inside the wall. The mesh was spot welded to it, here and there, like a curtain. Like a sheet nailed over a window. He knew why it was there. Because of the ground wires. Because of a long-ago memory of a build-your-own electronics kit he had gotten at Christmas. When he was a kid. From his uncle. Same uncle who gave him the Civic, as a matter of fact. The mesh wasn't there for reinforcement. It was there because it made the room a Faraday cage. Room ten was an electronic black hole. Any radio signal trying to get in would splinter every which way through the mesh, and then drain away to ground, through the many carefully soldered wires. Like the signal never existed at all. Same thing for a signal trying to get out. Didn't matter what kind of signal it was. Cell phone, satellite phone, pager, walkie-talkie, police radio, whatever, it wasn't going to happen. The laws of physics. Couldn't be ignored.

A signal couldn't get out because of the mesh.

A person couldn't get out because of the bars.

Patty took a look over his shoulder and said, 'What is all that stuff?'

Shorty tried hard to think of something cheerful to say, but he couldn't, so he didn't answer the question.

THIRTY

Burke and Reacher drove back to the turn, where they headed south towards Laconia. Not all the way. Just a few miles. Far enough to get bars on Burke's old phone. They pulled off on the shoulder of a wide left-hand curve. Ahead of them were fields and trees, and presumably the town itself on the other side of them, in the far distance, through the haze. Reacher took out Amos's business card, and dialled her number. It rang twice and dumped to voice mail. She was away from her desk. He clicked off and tried again, this time with her cell number. It rang five times, and then it was answered.

Her voice said, 'Interesting.'

He said, 'What is?'

'You're calling on the Reverend Burke's phone. You're still with him. You're still in the vicinity.'

'How did you know this is the Reverend Burke's phone?'

'I saw his licence plate this morning. I checked with county. Now I know all about him. He's a troublemaker.'

'He's been very nice to me.'

'How can I help you?'

'Something made me think about guys getting drafted in from Boston. Seems to be a regular habit around here. I was wondering how you were doing with that.'

'Why?'

'Did anyone show up yet?'

Amos didn't answer.

Reacher said, 'What?'

'Chief Shaw is talking to the Boston PD again. They're calling in some favours. The word on the street is five guys are working out of town today. There's no sign of them at home. Their absence is conspicuous. It's a reasonable assumption they've been sent our way. In which case we know all about the first four. They were the guy in the Chrysler and the three in the library. It's the fifth guy we need to worry about. He left Boston much later than the others. We assume in response to a panic call from here. We assume he's their cleanup hitter. The ultimate sanction.'

'Has he arrived?'

'I don't know. We watch what we can, but we're sure to miss something.'

'When did he leave Boston?'

'Long enough ago to be here by now.'

'With my description,' Reacher said.

'That doesn't matter any more,' Amos said. 'Does it?'

Then she paused.

Then she said, 'Don't you dare tell me you're coming back to town. Because you ain't, major. You're staying away.'

'Relax, soldier,' Reacher said. 'Stand easy. I'm staying away. I'm not coming back to town.'

'Then don't worry about your description.'

'I was wondering exactly what it said. I was thinking back to exactly what the kid can have seen. The lighting was kind of patchy. It was an alley. There was a lamp over the door, but it was shaded. Like a cone. But even so, let's assume he got a pretty good look at me. Although it was the middle of the night and most of the time he was mad as hell and spoiling for a fight, and then he was unconscious, basically. Therefore his grasp of detail is not likely to have been impressive. So what would a kid in his position say afterwards? I'm sure it hurt to talk. By that point his teeth were in poor condition. I'm sure he had facial bruising. Maybe his jaw was busted. So what few words would he choose to mumble? Just the basics, surely. A big guy, with messy fair hair. I think that's what he must have said.'

'OK.'

'Except at one point I spoke to the cocktail waitress. She asked if I was a cop. I said I was once upon a time, in the army. The kid might have remembered. It's the kind of thing people add to descriptions. To flesh them out. To suggest the type of person, not just their appearance. Which would have been important to the kid. He needed to save face. He wanted to be able to say sure, he lost the fight, but only because he went up against a trained Special Forces killer. Like an excuse. Almost like a badge of honour. So actually I think he must have said, a big guy, messy fair hair, used to be in the army. That's what the guys in the library saw. A simple three-point check list. Size, hair, army. That's what they've got. Not very nuanced or exact.'

Amos said, 'Why does any of this matter?'

'I think the description fits Carter Carrington too.'

Amos said nothing.

'I think it's close enough to be awkward,' Reacher said. 'Certainly he's bigger than the average guy. He's imposing, physically. His hair is all over the place. Across a room, he has a certain look. I thought he was army. Turned out he wasn't, but I would have sworn. I was placing bets on where he did his ROTC.'

'You think we should warn him?'

'I think you should put a car outside his house.'

270

'Seriously?'

'Maybe a job for Officer Davison. He seems to be a capable young man. I would hate for something to happen. Because of me. I don't want Carrington on my conscience. He seems like a nice guy. He just got a new girlfriend.'

'Protecting him would be a huge diversion of resources.'

'He's an innocent bystander. He's also the guy who goes to bat for you.'

'I think he would refuse on principle. Precisely because of that. He'll say he can't accept special treatment. The optics would be terrible. The threat is against someone else, after all, who might or might not have a slight physical resemblance. He would look corrupt, and vain, and a coward. He won't do it.'

'Then tell him to get out of town.'

'I can't just tell him. Doesn't work that way.'

'You told me.'

'That was different.'

'Tell him there's something wrong with the story.'

'What does that mean?'

Reacher paused a moment, to let a truck roar past on the road. A tow truck. Heading north. It was huge. It was the kind of thing that could haul an eighteen-wheeler off the highway. It was grinding along slow and noisy in a low gear. He realized he had seen it before. It was bright red and spotlessly clean. It had gold stripes all over it. Its passage rocked the Subaru on its springs. It growled away into the distance behind them.

Reacher put the phone back to his ear.

He said, 'Carrington will get the message. He'll know what I mean. Tell him to see an opportunity where others might see a crisis. He could take a short vacation. Somewhere romantic. Rates are down after Labor Day.'

'He has a job,' Amos said. 'He might be busy.'

'Tell him I'm happy to listen to him about census methodology.

Tell him he should listen to me about staying-alive methodology.'

Amos said, 'I was feeling pretty good until you laid this on me. We have a bad guy in town, OK, but never mind, because the bad guy has no target. Now you tell me he does have a target after all, kind of, sort of, maybe.'

'Call me if you need me,' Reacher said. 'This number should be good another hour or two. I would be happy to come back to town and lend a hand. You could give my regards to Chief Shaw, if you like, and make him the offer.'

'Do not come back to town,' Amos said. 'Under no circumstances.'

'Never?'

'Not soon,' she said.

Reacher clicked off the call.

Lunch hour was long gone, and Burke said he was hungry. He said he wanted to go get something to eat. Reacher offered to pay, as a way of saying thank you for all the driving around. So they headed east towards a lake, where Burke said he knew a bait shop that had soda pop and sandwiches, at the head of a trail that led to the water, mostly used by fishermen carrying poles. It was a decent drive, and at the end of it the destination was exactly as advertised. It was a shack with an ice chest outside, and glass chiller cabinets inside, humming loudly, some of them full of stuff for people to eat, and others full of stuff for fish to eat. There was a yard-wide deli counter, with a choice of chicken salad or tuna, on white bread or a hot dog roll, plus a bag of potato chips, plus a bottle of cold water, all for a penny less than three dollars. Soda pop was extra.

Reacher said, 'I told you I was paying. You should have picked out somewhere expensive.'

Burke said, 'I did.'

He got tuna and Reacher got chicken. They both stuck with

water. They ate outside, at a government-brown picnic table near the head of the trail.

'Now give me the message,' Reacher said. 'From the ornithologist.'

Burke didn't answer right away.

Something on his mind.

In the end he said, 'Obviously it's you he really wants to talk to. He seems extremely excited. He said he was completely unaware that Stan had kids.'

'Who is he, exactly? Did he tell you?'

'You know who he is. You called him. He's a professor at the university.'

'I mean how is he related?'

Burke took a long drink of water.

'He explained in great detail,' he said. 'The short version is you count back four generations on your father's side. Not your father himself, not your grandfather, not your great-grandfather, but your great-great-grandfather. Who was one of seven brothers. Who all had numerous children, grandchildren, great-grandchildren, and great-great-grandchildren. Apparently you and the professor are both in there somewhere.'

'Plus about ten thousand other people.'

'He said he wants to talk to you about Stan. He said he feels a connection, because of the birdwatching. He said he wants to meet with you face to face. He said he has an idea he wants to discuss with you.'

'Five minutes ago he didn't know I existed.'

'He was very insistent.'

'Did you like him?'

'I felt pressured by him. In the end I took the liberty of telling him in my estimation you would likely move on very soon, not being the type of passer-by likely to put down roots, in which case it might prove very difficult to arrange a face to face meeting, simply because of scheduling issues alone.'

'But?'

'He said we simply must make it happen.'

'And?'

'He's coming tomorrow.'

'Coming where?'

'I was unable to suggest an exact rendezvous. I felt I shouldn't speak for you. I didn't know your preferences. In the end he offered a suggestion. I'm afraid I took the liberty of accepting on your behalf. I felt rushed. He put me on the spot.'

'What was his suggestion?'

'Ryantown.'

'Really?'

'He said he knows where it is. He was there for research. I tested him on a couple of things, and he knows his stuff.'

'What time tomorrow?'

'He said he'll be there at eight o'clock in the morning.'

'In a ruin in the woods.'

'He said it was appropriate.'

'For fighting a duel, maybe.'

'Appropriate was his word, not mine. And Ryantown was his suggestion, not mine.'

'Did you like him?' Reacher asked again.

'Does it matter?'

'I would like to hear your personal opinion.'

'Why would I have one?'

'You heard him talk. You got a sense of the guy.'

'I'm giving you the message,' Burke said. 'That's what I promised. Don't ask for editorial comment. It's none of my business.'

'Suppose it was.'

'It's not for me to say. I wouldn't want to influence you one way or the other.'

'When people say that, it means they would, really.'

'He sounded very eager.'

'Is that a good thing or a bad thing?'

'It could be both.'

'How?'

'Look, he's a professor at the university. An academic. I respect that tremendously. I was a teacher myself, don't forget. But it's different now. They have to promote themselves all the time. It's not just publish or perish any more. They have to be on social media. They need something new every day. I would worry that some tiny part of what he wants is a picture of you in Ryantown, for a blog post or an online article. Or to re-launch the research he did before. Or some combination. Absolutely can't blame him. He needs to feed the beast, or his students will rate him low. Visuals are important. Hence the early start. The morning light will be atmospheric. You could stare moodily into the sky, looking for the lost bird.'

'You're a very cynical man, Reverend Burke.'

'It's different now.'

'But everyone takes pictures. Everyone puts stuff online. It's no big deal. It's not a reason to worry about meeting a person. You're overselling it. You're trying to head me off at the pass. You should tell me what's really on your mind.'

Burke was quiet a long moment.

Then he said, 'If you meet with him, he'll tell you something upsetting.'

'We don't need to walk on eggs,' Reacher said.

'Different kind of upsetting.'

'What kind?'

'I heard him talk. I felt not everything he said made sense. At first I wasn't sure he was getting it straight. Then I thought I was misunderstanding the ancestry jargon.'

'What wasn't straight?'

'He kept referring to Stan in the present tense. He was saying, Stan is this, Stan is that, Stan is here, Stan is there. At first I assumed that ancestry buffs talk that way. To bring the subject alive. But he kept on doing it. In the end I asked him.'

'Asked him what?'

'Why he was talking that way.'

'What did he say?'

'He thinks Stan is still alive.'

Reacher shook his head.

'That's crazy,' he said. 'He died years ago. He was my father. I was at his funeral.'

Burke nodded.

'Which is why I thought it would upset you,' he said. 'Obviously the professor is either mistaken or confused. Or a crank of some kind, with a bee in his bonnet. All of which can be distressing, after a family bereavement. Naturally there are sensitivities involved.'

'It was thirty years ago,' Reacher said. 'I got over it.'

'Thirty years?'

'Give or take,' Reacher said. 'I was a company commander in West Germany, with the CID. I remember flying back. He was buried in Arlington Cemetery. My mother wanted that for him, because he fought in Korea and Vietnam. She thought he deserved it.'

Burke said nothing.

Reacher said, 'What?'

'Coincidence, I'm sure,' Burke said.

'What is?'

'The professor said the family story has it that Stan Reacher was working away from home for a very long time, completely out of touch, but then finally he retired, and he came back to live in New Hampshire.'

'When?'

'Thirty years ago,' Burke said. 'Give or take. Those were the professor's exact words.'

276

'That's crazy,' Reacher said again. 'I was at the funeral. The guy is wrong. I should call him back.'

'You can't. He's tied up the rest of the day.'

'Where is this old guy who came back to New Hampshire supposed to be living now?'

'With the granddaughter of a relative.'

'Where exactly?'

'You can get it from the horse's mouth first thing tomorrow.'

'I'm trying to get to San Diego. I need to get going.'

'Are you upset about what he said?'

'Not upset at all. Just not sure what to do. I don't want to waste time talking to an idiot.'

Burke was quiet a moment.

'I feel I shouldn't dissuade you further,' he said. 'My only worry was emotional strain. In its absence, I suppose you could give the professor the benefit of the doubt. It might be an innocent error. A simple transposition of two similar names, or something. You might still enjoy talking to him. About Ryantown, if nothing else. He knows a lot about it. He did research there.'

'I would need a motel,' Reacher said. 'I can't go back to Laconia.'

'There's a place north of Ryantown. About twenty miles. I told you about it. Supposed to be good.'

'Deep in the woods.'

'That's the one.'

'Sounds perfect, under the circumstances. If I gave you fifty bucks for gas, would you drive me there?'

'Fifty bucks is too much.'

'We've done a lot of miles. And there are tyres to consider, and general wear and tear, plus a share of the overhead. Insurance, for instance, and servicing, and repairs.'

'I would take twenty.'

'Deal,' Reacher said.

They climbed out of the picnic table and walked back to the Subaru.

Karel was the sixth and final arrival. He worked the morning as normal, starting early, out at the highway, where he got instantly lucky with a semi-serious fender bender, which then became doubly lucky, because both insurance companies hired him to haul the wrecks. Which paid the rent for the day. The rest was icing on the cake. There were no more crashes, but he got three separate breakdowns. Which was pretty damn good for the time of year. And then a fourth, he thought for a happy moment, after he had clocked off and was heading north, when he saw an old Subaru stalled on the shoulder. But it turned out nothing. Two guys in it, admiring the view, one of them talking on the phone. A little burble of fumes coming out at the back. The old Subaru was running fine.

Twenty miles later he slowed to a crawl, and he turned hard left, into the narrow opening. Into the mouth of the track. Which was barely wider than the truck itself. Leaves and branches brushed and battered both sides. The huge tyres bounced and slapped through the potholes. He slowed again, barely a walk, idling in his lowest stump-pulling gear. The wire was up ahead. Across the blacktop. The warning bell. He wanted all three axles to ring it separately. That was the code. *Bing, bing-bing.* Hence the low speed.

He rolled slowly over the wire. And stopped. He set the brakes. He shut down the engine. He opened his door against the press of the foliage and dropped his bags down ahead of him. Then he squeezed out sideways and locked the door from below. He gathered his luggage, and hauled it ten yards along the track, and set it down in a neat array. He turned and looked back. His truck was jammed in. There was no space either side. Obviously not for a car. Not for a quad bike, even. A pedestrian, maybe, leading with a shoulder, getting whipped in the face by branches.

278

It was a perfect roadblock.

He turned again and looked ahead and waited. Four minutes later Steven showed up in his black SUV. The Mercedes. He looked out the window at the truck. To the left of it, to the right of it, below it, above it. As if he was judging it. As if there was a whole lot of choice exactly how to position it. Karel loaded his bags. Steven backed up to a hole in the trees and turned the car around. They drove on.

Karel said, 'Happy so far?'

Steven said, 'Shorty smashed up the bathroom.'

'A small price to pay.'

'Mark wants a favour. We screwed up with their window blind. Now we got tension between the guys who saw them already and the guys who didn't. Their heads would explode if they knew you had actually talked to them. Or been in the same room as them. Or touched them, or something.'

'I didn't touch them,' Karel said. 'And I wasn't in the same room. I stayed outside. I talked to them, sure.'

'Mark wants you to act like you didn't. He wants you to balance it out, three and three. He thinks that will keep the situation under control.'

'Got it,' Karel said.

They drove out through the meadow. Peter was in the office. Karel got room two. OK with him. The room didn't matter. He put his bags inside. He said hi to the other guys. They were all gathering. They stumped around and swapped stories. Karel made out he had never been there before. He told them he was Russian, just for the fun of it. He asked all the right wide-eyed questions about Patty and Shorty, as if he had never seen them before. He found himself secretly agreeing with some of the answers. Then the two guys who hadn't seen them yet got a little disgruntled all over again, which Karel quelled simply by siding with them. The natural three-and-three balance calmed things down. Maybe Mark was right.

Then Peter stuck his head out the office door, and called down the row to say everyone was invited to walk over to the house, for a cup of coffee, and an introductory briefing, and a look at the video highlights from the last three days. So they all wandered over, just strolling, feeling good. Starting to believe. The party was complete. All six of them were present. They were sealed off from the world. It was real. It was happening. It wasn't a scam. Deep down they all thought it would be. But it wasn't. It was true and it was hours away. First sheer relief welled and bloomed, like a tide, and then buzzing excitement took over, a little breathless, a little gulped, to be resisted, to be controlled, because nothing was certain yet, because disappointment was always possible, because chickens should not be counted.

But they were starting to believe.

THIRTY-ONE

Burke and Reacher drove back on the same road, west towards Ryantown. Reacher watched the bars on Burke's old phone. When they dropped from three to two he asked Burke to pull over on the shoulder, so he could call Amos again, before service ran out completely. He dialled, and she answered, on the third ring.

She said, 'Where are you now?'

'Don't worry,' Reacher said. 'I'm still out of town.'

'We can't find Carrington.'

'Where have you looked?'

'His home, his office, the coffee shop he likes, the lunch places he goes.'

'Did he tell his office he would be out?'

'Not a word.'

'Does he have a cell phone?'

'He's not answering.'

'Try the city records department,' Reacher said. 'Ask for Elizabeth Castle.'

'Why?'

'She's his new girlfriend. Maybe he's hanging out over there.'

He heard her call across the room, Elizabeth Castle, city records.

He asked, 'Any sign of the guy from Boston?'

She said, 'We've been running every plate we've seen, in and out of town. We have automatic software now. Nothing yet.'

'Want me to come back to help?'

'No,' she said.

'I could walk around and flush the guy out.'

'No,' she said again.

He heard someone shouting a message.

She said, 'Elizabeth Castle is not at work either.'

'I need to come back to town.'

'No,' she said, for the third time.

'Last chance,' he said. 'I'm about to head north to a motel. I'm going to lose cell service.'

'Do not come back to town.'

'OK,' he said. 'But in exchange I need you to do something for me.'

'Like what?'

'I need you to look at ancient history on your computer again.'

'I already have plenty to do today.'

'It only takes a minute. You have a really good system there.'

'Are you flattering me?'

'Did you design the system?'

'No.'

'Then no, I'm not. All I'm saying is it won't take much time. Otherwise I wouldn't have asked. I know you're extremely busy.'

'Now you're respecting me to death. What would I be looking for?'

'Check the files after that thing with my father, seventy-five years ago. The next twenty-four months, until September 1945.'

'What happened then?'

'He joined the Marines.'

'What would I be looking for?'

'Something unsolved.'

'When do you need it by?'

'I'll call you back as soon as I can. I want to hear about Carrington.'

They passed the wandering turn that led away through the orchards to Ryantown. They stayed on the back road, heading north. Reacher watched the phone. The bars went out, one by one. For a moment the screen said it was searching, and then it gave up and said no service. Up ahead were miles of fields, and then more woods, far in the distance. A left to right wall. Burke drove on towards it. He said he thought the motel entrance was about five miles in. On the left side. He remembered the signs. There was one each way. They said *Motel*, in plastic letters painted gold. They were mounted on gnarled old posts.

Five minutes later they drove into the trees. The air felt cooler. Sunlight sparkled through the leaves. Reacher checked the speedo. They were doing forty. About five miles would take about seven or eight minutes. He counted time in his head. The trees grew thicker. Like a tunnel. No more sunbeams. The light turned green and soft.

Burke took his foot off the gas at seven minutes exactly in Reacher's head. Burke said he was pretty sure the turn was coming up. Ahead on the left. Pretty soon. He remembered. But they saw no signs. No plastic letters, no gold paint. Just a pair of twisted old posts, leaning over a little, and the mouth of a track. Left and right of it on the main drag were unbroken walls of trees, both up ahead and far behind.

'I'm pretty sure this was it,' Burke said.

Reacher hitched up and pulled his map from his pocket. The

one he had bought at the old edge-of-town gas station. He unfolded it and found the back road. He checked the scale and moved his finger. He showed Burke. He said, 'This is the only turn for miles around.'

Burke said, 'Maybe someone stole their signs.'

'Or they went out of business.'

'I doubt it. They were very committed. They had a business plan. I heard something about them, as a matter of fact. From the county office. They were extremely ambitious. But they got off to a bad start, as it turned out. They got in a fight about a permit.'

'Who did?'

'The people developing the property. They said any motel keeper depends on opening on time at the start of the season. They said the county was unreasonably slow with the permit. The county said the developer had started work without permission. They got in a fight.'

'When was this?'

'About a year and a half ago. Which is why they were upset about their timetable. They wanted to open the following spring. Which is also why they can't be out of business yet. Their plan showed a two-year reserve.'

A patrol car responded to the county offices because a customer was causing a disturbance. He claimed a building permit was slow coming through. He claimed he was renovating a motel somewhere out of town.

He gave his name as Mark Reacher.

Reacher said, 'I really need to go take a look at this place.'

Burke turned in, over broken blacktop that was missing altogether in whole table-sized patches. The light was greener still. Branches dipped in close, from both sides, some of them limp and broken, still fresh, as if a large vehicle had brushed by not long ago.

They found the large vehicle thirty yards later. It was stopped

284

up ahead, tight against the trees on both sides, blocking the track completely.

It was a tow truck. Huge. Red paint, gold stripes.

'We just saw this thing,' Reacher said. 'And I also saw it yesterday.'

A yard behind its giant rear tyres was a wire, laid side to side across the road. It was fat and rubbery. It was the kind of thing they had at gas stations.

Reacher wound his window down. There was no noise from the truck's engine. There were no fumes from its exhaust. Burke stopped the Subaru six feet before the wire. Reacher opened his door. He got out and walked forward. He stepped over the wire. Burke followed him. Reacher made sure Burke stepped over the wire too. He didn't like wires on roads. Nothing good ever came of them. Best case surveillance, worst case explosions.

The truck had a long sloping haunch at the back, with a short sturdy crane and a giant tow hook. It had lockers with gleaming chrome doors. Reacher squeezed down the driver's side, leading with his left shoulder, keeping his left elbow high, keeping the twigs away from his face. He slid past the owner's name, which was Karel, proudly painted a foot high in gold letters. He made it level with the cab. He stepped up on the bottom rung of the ladder and tried the driver's door. It was locked. He stepped down again and forced his way around the hood to the front of the truck. Ahead of him the track ran on through the woods. The surface remained the same. Worn blacktop, missing in places, randomly covered in grit, gravel, dirt, and leaf mould. There were tyre tracks here and there, some of them ancient, some of them recent. Twenty yards farther on there was a hole in the trees. Like a natural recess. It had brand new tyre tracks. Two tight V shapes. Like a car had backed in to turn around. Which made some kind of sense. Because the tow truck driver didn't seem to be around any more. Possibly a car had driven down to pick him up. It would have stopped nose to nose with the truck, and then backed up and turned and driven away forward.

Reacher looked ahead.

He said, 'I'm going to go take a look at what they got up there.'

'How?' Burke said.

'I'm going to walk.'

'Your map showed this track is more than two miles long.'

'I need a place to sleep. Also I'm curious.'

'About what?'

'I think the guy who got in the fight about the permit was a kid named Reacher.'

'How do you know?'

'It was in the police computer. A squad car had to go calm things down. A year and a half ago.'

'Are you related?'

'I don't know. Maybe as much as I am to the professor from the university.'

'Do you want company?'

'We could be walking two miles back again, if we don't get lucky.'

'That's OK,' Burke said. 'I guess now I'm curious too.'

They set out together. By geographic map-making standards the land was dead flat, which made walking easy, but up close and personal the track was uneven and pitted, which made it hard. Every step was an inch and a half higher or lower than the one before, which meant any step could become a stumble. At one early point they passed through a grassy ring, where no trees were growing. It was maybe sixty feet wide. It seemed to curve away, in both directions, as if it ran in a circle all the way around. As if it defined an inner part of forest. A woods within a woods. It was like a giant crop circle, but carved out of sixty-foot maple trees, not stalks of corn. All the way across they felt the warmth of the sun. Then the cold green shadow claimed them again. They had crossed the boundary. Now they were in the inner forest. They were in the woods within the woods. They were walking towards its centre.

Two miles would have taken Reacher thirty minutes, but they took Burke forty-five. They came out of the trees together, and they saw the track run on ahead, through a couple of grassy acres, to what looked like a dirt parking lot in front of what was indisputably a motel. It had an office at the left-hand end, and a station wagon and a panel van and a compact car and a pick-up truck, all parked at intervals outside the rooms.

They set out walking towards it.

They were instantly detected. Two separate ways. Robert had copied a facial recognition algorithm from a photo chip and coded it into the close-up camera. As soon as the algorithm detected a face among the trees it rang a bell and flashed a light, like a distant early warning. Like radar. Persons approaching. But by chance Steven was watching the right screen anyway, as part of a disciplined rotation through the points of the compass. The movement caught his eye. He saw two men step out of the shadows and into the sunshine.

He said, 'Mark, look at this.'

Mark looked.

And said, 'Who the hell are they?'

Robert zoomed the camera all the way. The image trembled with distance, and wavered with haze. Two guys were walking towards the lens. Head-on. Seemingly making no progress, because of the extreme telephoto. One guy was small and old. Slightly built, and slow. Denim jacket, grey hair. The other guy was huge. As wide as a door. Hair sticking up all over. A face like the side of a house.

He looked rough.

Mark said, 'Shit.'

287

Steven said, 'You told us he wouldn't come here. You said he was a different branch of the family. You said he wouldn't be interested.'

Mark didn't answer.

Then Peter buzzed through from the office. His voice came out of the intercom speaker. He said, 'But actually it turns out the guy was interested enough to walk two whole miles past the roadblock. Good call, bro.'

Again Mark didn't answer.

He was quiet a long moment more.

Then he said, 'Keep everyone inside the house. Give them all another cup of coffee. Show them another video. Keep the doors closed. Make sure no one leaves.'

THIRTY-TWO

urke and Reacher stepped off the last of the blacktop on to the dirt of the motel lot. By then they had a pretty good close-up view of what was waiting ahead. Reacher heard Amos's voice in his mind, talking about LSD in her coffee. Now he knew what she meant. Because up close the panel van parked second in line from the motel office turned out to be blue. A dark, dignified shade. Enhanced and explained by curls of gold writing. Persian carpets. Expert cleaning. A Boston address. A Massachusetts licence plate.

The biggest déjà vu in history.

Except not exactly, because he hadn't actually seen the van before. He had only heard about it on the radio. It had been caught by the cameras, coming off the highway, too early for a residential customer. Whereas he had actually seen the tow truck before. That was for damn sure. Two separate times. That really was déjà vu all over again. He had squeezed past a truck he had seen twice before, and then the very next vehicle he came upon was a van he had heard about on a police dispatcher's broadcast. He slowed half a step, automatically, thinking. Burke got a step in front of him, and walked on ahead, slow but unflagging.

Beyond him Reacher saw that the station wagon parked first in line was a Volvo, with a Vermont plate on the back. The small compact was blue, probably an import, with a plate he didn't know. The pick-up truck was a workhorse. It was the kind of thing a carpenter would use, to get boards in the back. It was dirty white. It had what he thought was an Illinois plate. Hard to be sure, given the distance. It was last in line. It was outside of what would be room eleven. The Volvo was outside of three, and the carpet van outside of seven. The small blue import was outside of ten. Ten's window blind was down, and five's lawn chair had been used. It had been scooted out of line.

They walked on towards the office, which had a red neon sign. They went in. There was a guy behind the counter. In his late twenties, maybe, with dark hair, and pale skin, and a slight look-away shyness in his manner. He had an air of intelligence. He was educated. He was healthy and fit. Maybe a college athlete. But a runner, not a weightlifter. Middle distance. Maybe a master's degree in a technical subject. He was wiry, and coiled, and shot through with some kind of nervous buzz.

Reacher said, 'I need a room for the night.'

The guy said, 'I'm really sorry, but the motel is closed.'

'Is it?'

'I took the signs down at the entrance. I hoped I would save people a wasted trip.'

'There are plenty of vehicles here.'

'Work people. I'm way behind with the maintenance. There are things I really need to fix before the leaves turn and the tourists come back. Turns out the only viable way to do it was close for two weeks. I'm really sorry about that.'

'Are you doing all the rooms at once?'

'The plumber turned the water off. The electrician is messing with the power. There's no heat and no AC. I'm way below code right now. I wouldn't be allowed to give you a room, even if I could.'

'You got Persian carpets?'

'They're organic jute, actually. I'm trying to be sustainable. It should last ten years, but only if you clean it carefully. It would be a false economy to use a regular commercial crew. These guys get Boston prices, believe me, but the spreadsheet says it should be worth it in the long term.'

Reacher asked, 'What's your name?'

'My name?'

'We've all got one.'

'Tony.'

'Tony what?'

'Kelly.'

'Mine is Reacher.'

The guy looked blank for a second, but then he focused, as if he was snagging on an odd coincidence.

He said, 'I bought this place from a family called Reacher. Are you related?'

'I don't know,' Reacher said. 'I guess everyone is related if you go back far enough. When did you buy it?'

'Nearly a year ago. It was halfway renovated. I got it open in time for the season. But now I have some catching up to do.'

'Why did they sell?'

'A grandson took it on, but honestly, I think he found it wasn't for him. He was more of an ideas guy. There was a lot of detail involved. He got in trouble with permits, I think. Pretty soon he decided it wasn't worth the hassle. But my spreadsheet told me it was. So I bought him out. I like detail.'

'Is the electrician from Vermont, or the plumber?'

'The plumber. They have the best three-season guys in the world up there. Costs me more to bring them south, but my spreadsheet tells me it would be penny wise and pound foolish not to.'

'Same thing with the electrician from Illinois, I suppose.'

'Actually that's slightly different. There's unemployment out there, so they work for less, which offsets getting them here, so it's a wash in terms of cost. But it's way better in terms of how they do the job. These guys are auditioning, basically. This is a whole new market. There's infinite work here, at their hourly rates. They want word of mouth recommendations. So their quality is excellent. Plus they already know their way around motels like this. There are more of them in the Midwest than here.'

'OK,' Reacher said.

'I'm really sorry about the wasted trip,' the guy said.

Then he stopped, and defocused again, and said, 'Wait.'

They waited.

The guy glanced out the window.

Then he said, all in a rush, 'How did you get here? I completely didn't think. Don't tell me you walked. But you can't have driven. I just realized. The wrecker is stuck.'

'We walked,' Reacher said.

'I am so sorry. Today has been one damn thing after another. The last guest I had before I closed abandoned a broken-down car. Apparently it wouldn't start, so he called a cab and disappeared. Naturally I wanted the car towed, and today was supposed to be the day, but it turned out the tow truck is so huge it got jammed in the trees.'

Then the guy looked out the window again, left and right, checking.

He said, quieter, 'Or else he just doesn't want to scratch his paint. I have to say, I'm not very satisfied. The trees on both sides of that track are trimmed precisely according to Department of Transportation guidelines. I'm pretty much a detail guy. I take care of things like that, believe me. Any highway-legal commercial vehicle should fit just fine.'

Then he stopped again, struck by another new thought, and he said, 'Let me drive you back. At least that far. I assume your car is parked behind the truck. It's the least I can do.'

Reacher said, 'What was wrong with the abandoned car?'

'I don't know,' the guy said. 'It's pretty old.'

'What's the plate on it?'

'Canadian,' the guy said. 'Maybe one-way airfare is cheaper than the disposal fees they charge up there. I'm sure there are environmental regulations. Maybe he drove the car here just to dump it. It would be a simple profit and loss calculation.'

'OK,' Reacher said. 'You can drive us back now.'

'Thank you,' Burke said.

The guy ushered them out of the office, and locked the door behind them, and asked them to wait in the lot. Then he jogged away, towards a barn, maybe thirty yards distant. It was a blunt square building, with nine quad bikes parked outside, in a neat three-by-three formation. Beyond the barn was a house, with heavy furniture on wide porches.

A minute later the guy drove out of the barn in a black SUV. It was medium-sized, and shaped like a fist. Probably European. Maybe a Porsche or a Mercedes-Benz. Or a BMW. Maybe an Audi. It was a Mercedes. It stopped right beside them. Reacher saw the badge. It had a V8 engine. The guy at the wheel waited, expectantly, so Burke climbed in the front, and Reacher got in the back. The guy crunched through the lot and thumped up on the blacktop and speeded through the meadow.

He said, 'You should head east towards the lake country. You'll find plenty of options there, I'm sure.'

They re-entered the woods through the same natural arch they had come out of. The guy drove fast. He knew there was going to be no oncoming traffic. The two miles that had taken Burke three quarters of an hour took the Mercedes three minutes. The guy stopped nose to nose with the tow truck. The light was dim and green and the red paint looked soured, like blood. The trees were tight on either side, pressing in with bent boughs and leaves spread like fingers. The lower canopy flopped down, level with the top of the windshield. The truck was in firm contact with the surrounding vegetation, certainly. But it was not physically restrained, surely. Not with the torque of its giant motor and the traction of its giant tyres. The guy wasn't stuck. He was worried about his paint. Understandable. It must have cost a buck or two. Multiple coats of red. Miles and miles of gold pinstripes, all done by hand. His name, Karel, fortunately short, spelled out in expensive copperplate, like a letter from an old Victorian aunt.

The guy at the wheel apologized again for their wasted trip, and he wished them good luck, and Burke said thank you, and got out, and Reacher followed him. Burke squeezed down the side of the truck, and Reacher went after him, elbow high, but then he stopped where the cab towered over him, and he turned around to watch. The Mercedes backed up smartly, and the guy reversed into and drove out of the natural hole in the trees, neatly, crisply, and fast. As if he had done it before. Which he had. He had picked up the truck driver.

Reacher stood for a second more, and then he turned again and blundered his way back to where Burke was waiting, on the other side of the fat rubber wire, next to the Subaru's front fender. They got in the car and Burke backed up slowly, craning his neck, all the way to where the track met the road, where the wide gravel mouth gave him room to turn, either way.

'East to the lakes?' he said.

'No,' Reacher said. 'South until your cell phone works. I want to call Amos.'

'Something wrong?'

'I want an update on Carrington.'

'You asked a lot of questions at the motel.'

'Did I?'

'Like you were suspicious.'

'I'm always suspicious.'

'Were you happy with the answers?'

'The front part of my brain thought the answers were fine. They all made perfect sense. They were all plausible. They all had the ring of truth.'

'But?'

'The back part of my brain didn't like that place very much.'

'Why not?'

'I don't know. Every question had an answer.'

'So it's just a feeling.'

'It's a sense. Like smell. Like waking up for a prairie fire.'

'But you can't pin it down.'

'No.'

They drove on, south. Reacher watched the phone. Still no service.

Afterwards Peter nearly collapsed from tension. He let the two men out, and then he backed up and turned and hustled home as fast as he dared. He drove straight to the house. He ran through to the parlour, where he leaned on the wall, and then he slid down until he was sitting on the floor. The others crowded around him, crouching eye to eye, silent, as if in awe, and then they all burst out in a fist-pumping hiss of triumph, like a winning touchdown had been scored on TV.

Peter said, 'Did the customers see anything?'

'Nothing at all,' Mark said. 'We got lucky with the timing. The customers were all in here. Thirty minutes earlier would have been a problem. They were still milling around in the lot, shooting the shit.'

'When are we going to explain the situation to Patty and Shorty?'

'Do you have a preference?'

295

'I think we should do it now. The timing would be right. It would give them enough hours to make some choices, and then start doubting them. Their emotional state will be important.'

'I vote yes,' Steven said.

'Me too,' Robert said.

'Me three,' Mark said. 'One for all and all for one. We'll do it now. We should let Peter do it himself. As a way of thanking him for his performance. As a reward.'

'I vote yes on that too,' Steven said.

'And me,' Robert said.

Peter said, 'First let me get my breath back.'

THIRTY-THREE

Patty and Shorty had migrated to the main room, and were sitting on the bed. The blind was still down. They had skipped lunch. They couldn't face it. Now they were hungry. But eating would be an act of will. The last two meals from the carton. The last two bottles of water.

They looked away.

The TV turned on.

All by itself.

The same as before. The same tiny rustle as the circuit came to life. The same bright blue picture, with the same line of code, like the screen you weren't supposed to see.

It was replaced by a man's face.

Peter.

The weasel who had screwed with their car.

He said, 'Guys, you've been asking what's going to happen, and we think now is the time to bring you up to speed. We're going to give you as much information as we can, and then we're going to let you think on it, and then we'll come back later for questions and answers, just in case something wasn't clear. Are you with me so far? Are you paying attention?'

Neither of them answered.

Peter said, 'Guys, I need your attention. This is important.'

'Like fixing our car?' Shorty said.

'You fell for it, pal. That's why you're here. Your own fault. Since then you've been bitching and moaning about what we want with you, and now I'm going to tell you, so you need to face front and listen up.'

'I'm listening,' Patty said.

'Come sit side by side on the end of the bed. Show me how you're paying attention. Watch my face on the screen.'

Patty was still for a second. Then she shuffled around. Shorty followed her. Didn't want to, but he did all the same. They sat shoulder to shoulder, like the front row at the movies.

'Good,' Peter said. 'Smart move. Are you ready to hear what happens next?'

'Yes,' Patty said.

Shorty said, 'I guess.'

'Later this evening your door will unlock. At that point you will be free to walk away. But I mean that literally. No vehicles of any kind will be available. None at all. Every single key will be hidden where you won't find it, except of course your own, which you still have, but your car doesn't work anyway, as you mentioned. All the other vehicles here are too new to hot wire. So get used to it. You'll be walking, literally, on your own two feet. Do not waste time trying to avoid it. Are you with me so far?'

'Why are you doing this?' Patty said. 'Why keep us here and then just let us go?'

'I told you I would give you as much information as I could. I said you should think on it. I said you should save your questions for later. Are you with me so far?'

'Yes,' Patty said.

Shorty said, 'I guess.'

'All around this piece of forest is what looks like a firebreak. It's a hoop about sixty feet across, with no trees growing. Did you see it on the way in?'

There was a bar of bright pink open sky.

'I saw it,' Patty said.

'It's not actually a firebreak. Mark's grandfather cleared it for a different purpose. To keep the inner forest primeval. It's a seed break, really, not a firebreak. It runs all the way around. Doesn't matter which way the wind is blowing. Invasive species can't make it across.'

'So what?' Shorty said.

'You walk all the way there, through the woods, in any direction, and you step out in that gap, in any location, and you've won the game.'

'What game?'

'Was that a question?'

'I call bullshit, man. You can't tell us we're in a game, and then not tell us what kind.'

'Think of it like a game of tag. You have to make it all the way to the seed break without getting tagged. Simple as that. Walking, running, creeping along, whatever works for you.'

'Tagged how?' Patty said. 'By who?'

The TV turned off.

All by itself. The same dying rustle of circuits, the same blank grey screen, the same standby light glowing red.

Burke's old phone showed a bar, but Reacher wanted to wait for two. He figured the signal might fluctuate, plus or minus. Starting with just one bar would be a problem, when it came to the minus part. His experience was with army comms, which always failed first and fastest. Presumably civilians had better stuff, as always, but presumably not radically better.

Burke ignored him and drove on south, and after five minutes of silence he asked, 'How's the back part of your brain doing now?'

Reacher checked the phone.

Still one bar.

He said, 'The back part of my brain is worried about the organic jute carpets.'

'Why?'

'He said he was trying to be sustainable. He sounded partly proud, and partly apologetic, and partly defiant. A very typical tone, for people into things other people think are weird. But he was clearly sincere, because he was putting his money where his mouth was, by paying Boston prices for specialist cleaning. As if he really wanted to make the experiment work. At that point he presented a coherent picture.'

'But?'

'Later he said maybe the Canadian guy had dumped his car to avoid recycling fees at home. Or whatever. He said, I'm sure there are environmental regulations. He said it with a kind of smug sneer. Just very slightly. He sounded like a regular person. Not like a guy who would use organic jute. Or even know what it was. Then he showed up in an SUV with a V8 motor. And he drove it pretty fast. In a boyish way. He seemed to like thumping up and down over things. Not like a guy who would use organic jute. That guy would drive a hybrid car. Or electric. I felt the picture was no longer coherent. I felt now it was out of focus.'

'What does the front part of your brain say about it?'

'It says follow the money. The guy is paying a Persian carpet cleaner to take care of his rugs. All the way from Boston. That's hard cash. That's solid evidence. What have I got? A feeling? A sneer I might have misheard? Maybe he needs the SUV for the snow. A jury would say the bulk of the evidence is all one way. He's a good guy. He wants to save the planet. Or at least help a little bit.'

300

'I agree with the jury,' Burke said. 'Better to trust the front of your brain than the back.'

Reacher said nothing.

He checked the phone.

Two bars.

He said, 'I'm going to call Amos now.'

'Want me to stop?'

'Does it help the phone?'

'I think it does. I think it locks on better.'

Burke coasted a spell and pulled over where the gravel was wide.

Reacher dialled the number.

'Call me back in ten,' Amos said. 'I'm real busy right now.'

'Have you found Carrington?'

'Negative on that. Call me back.'

The payment process turned into a ritual of understated magnificence. It started casual and became exquisitely formal. It felt ancient in its origins. Greek or Roman at least. Maybe tribal. Steven stayed in the parlour, watching the screens, and everyone else walked back to the motel, a bustling crowd of nine, six customers excited but restrained, plus Mark and Peter and Robert behind them. The customers went to their rooms. Mark and Peter and Robert went to the office. Where the process evolved, out of nothing. There and then. They had no plan. No thought had been given. There was a danger of jinxing. In the end it was a five-second commonsense decision. The obvious thing to do.

But epic in its drama. In its psychological freight. Mark sat behind the counter. Peter stood at the end. Side on. Halfway between. As if independent. Like a witness.

Robert was the escort. He went to get them. One at a time. The legend was born right there. He knocked on the door, and they came out and went with him. He was the Praetorian Guard, and

301

they were the great gentlemen. They were the senators. They went with him, down the boardwalk. They had no choice. He stayed a respectful half step behind. In the office he stood at the door and saw nothing.

One by one they stepped forward and paid their tribute, to Mark, with Peter as a witness, to the transaction, to their bending of the knee. Some counted out bricks of money, prolonging the moment. Others set their bags on the counter, and stepped back, expecting instant and unquestioning acceptance. Which they got. The money would be there. All of it. They couldn't afford to cheat. Then one by one Robert walked them back, and knocked on the next door along. Both casual and formal, like the deadly business of an ancient republic.

Karel got a healthy discount, for helping out the day before, but the other five paid sticker. At the end of the ritual Mark chose the two biggest of the abandoned bags, and Peter packed them. Not easy. To get five and a half bags' worth of cash into two actual bags required ingenious layering. The others crowded around. Mark counted out loud as Peter stacked the bricks. But not in numbers. At first he said, *overhead, overhead*, as the first few bricks went in, and then *profit, profit, profit*, as the rest went in. They turned it into a kind of whispered chant. Quiet, so the sound wouldn't carry. They hissed *profit, profit, profit*. Then they carried the bags back to the house, past all the windows, kind of hoping the great gentlemen were watching them do it. Watching their tribute, humbly and justly given, being carried away by the victor.

Peter had said they should think on it, and they had, not because he told them, but because it was their natures. It was the Saint Leonard way. Engage brain. Think before you speak. Begin at the beginning.

Patty whispered, 'Obviously they're tricking us somehow. It must be impossible to get to the break in the trees.'

'It can't be impossible.'

'It must be.'

'Against how many people?'

'We've seen three. There are twelve rooms, less this one. Nine quad bikes. Pick a number.'

'You think they'll use the quad bikes?'

'I'm sure they will. I think that's why Peter emphasized we would be walking. To make us feel helpless and inferior. Like underdogs.'

'Call it nine people, then. They can't cover it all. It's a huge area.'

'I saw on the map,' Patty said. 'It's about five miles across, and about seven from top to bottom. Shaped like an oval. This place is about half a mile off-centre, towards the east. It's about equal north and south.'

'Then it might be possible. There would be one of them every forty degrees of the circle. They could be a hundred yards apart. If we got in the space behind them, we'd be home free.'

'It can't be possible,' Patty said. 'Because then what? We make it to a road, we get a ride, we call the cops and the FBI, because of the kidnapping and the false imprisonment, and they pay a visit, and they see the battery cable and the prison bars and the locks and the cameras and the microphones. I don't think Peter and his buddies can afford for that to happen. They can't afford for us to get out of here. Doesn't matter how we try. Any method at all. They really cannot afford for us to make it. They must be totally confident we won't.'

Shorty didn't answer. They sat side by side in the gloom. Patty had her hands palm-down on the bed, under her legs. She was rocking back and forth, just a little, and staring ahead at nothing. Shorty had his elbows on his knees, and his chin propped in his hands. He was sitting still. Trying to think.

Then all at once the room lit up bright, every fixture, every table

303

lamp, like a movie set, and the motor whirred and the blind rolled up in the window. Outside they saw a line of six men. On the boardwalk. Shoulder to shoulder. An inch from the glass. Staring in. Karel was one of them. The weasel with the tow truck. Three of them they had seen before. Two were new.

The six of them stared on and on. Openly, frankly, no inhibition at all. From her to him, and him to her. They were judging, and evaluating, and assessing. They were reaching conclusions. Tight grimaces of quiet satisfaction appeared on faces. There were slow nods of appreciation and approval. There were gleams in eyes, of enthusiasm.

Then on some unspoken cue they raised their hands and clapped, long and loud, a standing ovation, as if they were a respectful audience saluting star performers.

But somehow in advance.

THIRTY-FOUR

Ten minutes later Reacher dialled Amos again. She answered. She sounded out of breath.

He said, 'What's up?'

'False alarm,' she said. 'We got a maybe on Carrington. But it was two hours old and nothing came of it. We still can't find him.'

'Did you find Elizabeth Castle?'

'Her neither.'

'I should come back to town,' Reacher said.

Amos paused a beat.

'No,' she said. 'We're still in the game. The computer is watching the red light cameras. Nothing that came in from the south in the second wave this morning has gone back out again yet. We think Carrington is still in the area.'

'Which is why you need me there. No point coming back after they take him away.'

'No,' she said again.

'What was the maybe?'

'Allegedly he was seen entering the county offices. But no one else remembers him, and he isn't there now.'

'Was he alone, or with Elizabeth Castle?'

'It was hard to say. It was a busy time of day. Lots of people. Hard to say who was with who.'

'Was it the census archive?'

'No, something else. The county has offices all over town.'

'Did you get a minute for ancient history?'

She paused again.

'It was longer than a minute,' she said.

'What did you find?'

'I need advice before I tell you. From Carter Carrington, ironically.'

'Why?'

'You asked for unsolved cases. I found one. It has no statute of limitations.'

'You found an unsolved homicide?'

'Therefore technically it's still an open case.'

'When was it?'

'Within the dates you specified.'

'I wasn't born yet. I can't be a witness. Certainly I can't be a perpetrator. Talking to me is no legal hazard.'

'It has implications for you.'

'Who was the victim?'

'You know who the victim was.'

'Do I?'

'Who else could it be?'

'The kid,' Reacher said.

'Correct,' Amos said. 'Last seen face down on the sidewalk, late one September evening in 1943. Then later he shows up again, now twenty-two years old, just as much of an asshole as he was before, and he gets killed. The two files were never connected. I guess there was a lot going on back then. It was wartime. Detectives came and went. They didn't have computers. But today's rules say the first file makes a material difference to the second file. Which it does, no question. We can't pretend we haven't seen it. Therefore we're obliged to re-open the homicide as a cold case. Just to see where it goes. Before we close it again.'

'How did the kid get killed?'

'He was beaten to death with a pair of brass knuckles.'

Reacher paused a beat.

He said, 'Why wasn't it solved?'

'There were no witnesses. The victim was an asshole. No one cared. Their only suspect had disappeared without a trace. It was a time of great chaos. Millions and millions of people were on the move. It was right after VJ Day.'

'August 1945,' Reacher said. 'Did the cops have a name for the suspect?'

'Only a kind of nickname. Secondhand, overheard, all very mysterious. A lot of it was hearsay, from the kind of people who pick things up from casual conversations on the street.'

'What was the nickname?'

'It's why we have to re-open the case. We can't ignore the link. I'm sure you understand. All we're going to do is type out a couple new paragraphs.'

'What was the name?'

'The birdwatcher.'

'I see,' Reacher said. 'How soon do you need to type out your paragraphs?'

'Wait,' she said.

He heard a door, and a step, and the rustle of paper.

A message.

He heard a step, and a door, and on the phone she said, 'I just got an alert from the licence plate computer.'

She went quiet.

Then she breathed out.

'Not what I thought it was,' she said. 'No one left town. Not yet. Carrington is still here.'

'I need you to do something for me,' Reacher said.

He could still hear the paper. She was reading it.

'More ancient history?' she said.

'Current events,' he said. 'A professor at the university told me thirty years ago an old man named Reacher came home to New Hampshire after many years on foreign shores. As far as I know he has been domiciled here ever since. As far as I know he lives with the granddaughter of a relative. I need you to check around the county. I need you to see if you can find him. Maybe he's registered to vote. Maybe he still has a driver's licence.'

'I work for the city, not the county.'

'You found out all about the Reverend Burke. He doesn't live in the city.'

He could still hear the paper.

'I called in favours,' she said. 'What is the old man's first name?'

'Stan.'

'That's your father.'

'I know.'

'You told me he was deceased.'

'I was at the funeral.'

'The professor is confused.'

'Probably.'

'What else could he be?'

'The funeral was thirty years ago. Which was also when the guy showed up in New Hampshire after a lifetime away.'

'What?'

'It was a closed casket. Maybe it was full of rocks. The Marine Corps and the CIA worked together from time to time. I'm sure all kinds of secret squirrelly shit was going on.'

'That's crazy.'

308

'You never heard of a thing like that?'

'It's like a Hollywood movie.'

'Based on a true story.'

'One in a million. I'm sure most CIA stories were very boring. I'm damn sure most Marine Corps stories were.'

'Agreed,' Reacher said. 'One in a million. But that's my point. The odds are better than zero. Which is why I want you to check. Call it due diligence on my part. I would be failing in my duty. You're about to re-open a cold case with no statute of limitations, with a one-in-a-million possibility your main suspect is still alive, living in your jurisdiction, and is related to me. I figured I should clarify things beforehand. In case I need to call him. Hey pops, get a lawyer, you're about to be arrested. That kind of thing.'

'That's crazy,' Amos said again.

'The odds are better than zero,' Reacher said again.

'Wait,' she said again.

He could still hear the paper.

She said, 'This is a weird coincidence.'

'What is?'

'Our new software. Mostly it counts who enters and who leaves, using licence plate recognition technology. But apparently it's running a couple extra layers underneath. It's looking for outstanding warrants, and tickets, and then it's running a page for general remarks.'

'And?'

'The van we saw this morning was illegal.'

'Which van?'

'The Persian carpet cleaners.'

'Illegal how?'

'It should have been showing dealer plates.'

'Why?'

'Because its current owner is a dealer.'

'Not a carpet cleaner?'

'They went out of business. The van was repossessed.'

Patty and Shorty went back to the bathroom, but gave up on it pretty soon. The smashed tile and the powdered wall board made half of it uninhabitable. They drifted back to the bed again and sat side by side, facing away from the window. They didn't care if the blind was up or down. They didn't care who was watching. They whispered to each other, short and quiet, nodding and shrugging and shaking their heads, using hand signals, discussing things as fast and as privately as they could. They had revised their basic assumptions. They had refined their mental model. Some things were clearer. Some things were not. They knew more, but understood less. Clearly the six men who had looked in the window were the opposition team. Their task was to win a game of tag. In thirty square miles of forest. Presumably in the dark. Presumably with three of the assholes out in the woods with them, as referees, or umpires, or marshals, for a total of nine quad bikes, with the fourth and final asshole stuck in the house, watching the cameras and listening to the microphones and doing whatever the hell else they did in there. That was their current prediction.

Thirty square miles. Six men. In the dark. Yet they were confident of success. They couldn't afford to fail. The quad bikes would help. Much faster than running. But still. Thirty square miles was ten thousand football fields. All empty, except a random six, and each of those with just one man.

In the dark.

They didn't get it.

Then Shorty whispered, 'Maybe they have night vision goggles.'

Which sparked a cascade of gloomy thoughts. They could ride around and around, in an endless giant circle, a mile or two out, one by one, like an endless pinwheel, one or other of them passing any given spot every few minutes. Meanwhile Patty and Shorty would be coming in from the side, at a right angle, like crossing a one-way street. They would be slow. They might be visible for five whole minutes, side to side, beginning to end. Would the pinwheel spin slower than that?

Or would they simply be followed from their very first step out the door?

So many questions.

Including the biggest question of all. What kind of tag would it be? Probably not the schoolyard kind. Not a slap on the shoulder. Not a beanbag. Six men. Thirty square miles. Quad bikes and night vision. Confident of success.

Not good.

Which led to the biggest decision of all. Stick together, or split up? They could go different directions. It would double their chances. More than. If one of them got caught, the other would benefit from the diversion.

One of them might get away.

Reacher sat in the Subaru on the wide gravel shoulder. If the organic jute wasn't true, then nothing was true. Told you so, said the back part of his brain. The tow truck wasn't there for an abandoned car. Not the way the story was told. Elizabeth Castle said taxis wouldn't drive out that far. The abandoned car was invented. It was part of a fantastically elaborate bullshit story. Along with the alleged plumbers and electricians, and maintenance, and water, and power.

The tow truck was a roadblock.

Burke said, 'What are you thinking?'

'I'm wondering where the people were. We saw one guy, but there were four vehicles parked. So overall I'm thinking something weird is happening up there. But then I'm thinking, how bad could it be? It's a motel. But then I'm thinking, it has a road-block. And I guess bad things could happen at a motel with a roadblock. Possibly very bad things. But I lose the phone if I go up there. And I want to hear about Carrington. And Elizabeth Castle. It's my fault they're together. And I think Amos is going to call me. She wants me back in town. This time she paused before she said no. A significant amount of time. Sooner or later she's going to ask me.'

'What could you do there?'

'I could walk around. They have my description. I'm the real thing. Carrington is a pale imitation. It would take the pressure off him. Now the bad guy would be coming after me.'

'Doesn't that worry you?'

'He wants to take me back to Boston. He wants to throw me off a building. That would be a long and complicated operation. I don't see how it could end well for him.'

'What kind of bad things could happen at a motel with a road-block?'

'Your guess is as good as mine,' Reacher said.

The last of the day was fading, so the outside lights were on, up and down the boardwalk. The six men were starting to lay out their gear. All six doors were open. All six rooms were lit up bright. Guys wandered in and out, as if absentmindedly, holding bits and pieces. There was an element of display involved. Not that there was much latitude for showing off. The rules were tight. Everyone started equal. The playing field was level. Everyone got a randomly issued identical quad bike. Like a lottery. Everyone used the same night vision. Standard practice. The course owner got to specify the exact device. Mark picked generation two army surplus. Which was the industry consensus, and a plentiful unit. Clothing and footwear were not restricted, but those experiments had been conducted long ago, by different people, and now everyone dressed the same. Nothing in the soft bags was worth a second look.

312

The hard cases were a different story. Strange, ungainly, suggestive shapes. Again, not restricted. A personal choice. Or factional, or ideological, or faith-based. Anything was permitted. Or any combination. Recurve, reflex, self, long, flat, composite or takedown. Everyone had a favourite and a theory, backed by a little experience and a lot of wishful thinking. Everyone was planning improvements. Everyone was tinkering.

There were plenty of sideways glances, when the hard cases came out.

The last of the day was fading, so the view from the gravel shoulder was changing. It was dimming and going grey. In his mind Reacher replaced it with the motel. As they first saw it. The close-up view of what lay ahead. Bright sunshine. The office on the left, the Volvo wagon outside of three, the fake carpet van outside of seven, the small blue import outside of ten, and the long-bed pick-up truck outside of eleven. Plus room five's lawn chair, slightly out of line.

Burke said, 'What?'

'It's a back of the brain thing,' Reacher said. 'You prefer the front.'

'Tell me anyway.'

'What do they need, to make a bad thing happen?'

'Theologically?'

'In practical terms.'

'There could be many things.'

'They need a victim. Can't do a bad thing without one. Maybe it's a young girl. For example. She was lured there, and trapped. Maybe they're going to force her to make a porn movie. The motel is a convenient location. Certainly it's remote.'

'You think it's porn?'

'I said for example. It could be a lot of different things. But all those things require a victim. Everything has that in common. A victim, on the premises. Somehow captured and held there, immediately available, when the rest of the party gathers.'

Burke said, 'On the premises where?'

'Room ten was qualitatively different,' Reacher said. 'Two separate ways. First the car. The only foreign plate. Also smaller and cheaper and worn out. Therefore probably a young person's car. Possibly far from home and vulnerable. Secondly the bedroom window. The blind was down. The only one out of twelve.'

Burke said nothing.

Reacher said, 'I told you, it's a back of the brain thing.'

'What are you going to do about it?'

'I don't know.'

'You should go take another look.'

'Maybe.'

'Carrington is a grown-up. He can take care of himself.'

'He's completely in the dark. He knows nothing about any of this.'

'OK, the cops can take care of him. They don't want you there anyway. The lady detective is not going to ask. Trust me.'

Reacher said nothing.

He dialled Amos's number.

It rang four times.

She said, 'Nothing yet.'

'How do you feel?' he asked.

'Rush hour is over. Downtown is quiet. We have eyes most places they need to be. And after all, the description is of someone else entirely. This is only a theory. Overall I would say I feel reasonably OK.'

'On a scale of one to ten?'

'About a four,' she said.

'Would it help if I was there?'

'Honest answer?'

'On a scale of one to ten.'

314

'Is there a number smaller than one?'

'One is the irreducible number.'

'Then a one,' she said.

'What about without the rules and the bullshit?'

'Still a one,' she said.

'OK, good luck,' he said. 'I'm going out of cell phone range. I'll check in when I can.'

THIRTY-FIVE

O nce again the TV turned on all by itself. The tinkle, the blue screen, the smeared transition to a man's face against a black wall. This time it was Mark. Head and shoulders. Waiting. He looked away and asked if something was working. Which evidently was, because they heard the whole exchange. Mark looked back at the camera. At them. Eye to eye. He stared. He waited. He smiled.

He said, 'Guys, we promised a follow-up session, for questions and answers. Just in case something wasn't clear, when Peter explained it earlier. So here we are.'

Patty said, 'Tell us about the tags.'

'Come sit on the end of the bed again. We'll have a full and frank discussion.'

Patty shuffled around. Shorty followed. Didn't want to, but he did.

Mark said, 'Patterns of consumption are changing. Aspirational expenditures are no longer limited to bigger and better physical objects. A bigger house, a bigger diamond, a better Monet. Now there's a new category. People buy experiences. They buy tickets for the moon. They visit the ocean bed. Some of them pay to act out their fantasies. For once in their lives. Some of them are harmless. Some of them are sick. They gather on the internet. They find secret message boards. That's where we advertise.'

'What message boards?' Patty said. 'Who are these people?'

'You've met Karel,' Mark said. 'The other five come from one particular web site. It has a fascinating ambiguity in its name. Very clever underground marketing. Is it describing its members, or is it describing the activity it promotes to its members? Is it a mistake, or is it a nod and a wink? It's purely a matter of emphasis. There are no grammatical rules to help you.'

Patty said, 'What's the name of the site?'

'Bow Hunting People.'

'What?'

'Which I hope answers your question about the nature of the tag. The game places no restriction on the type of bow. Except no mechanical draw, and no crossbows, obviously. Probably they'll use medium-length composite recurves. They're hoping to be mobile. They learn a lot from the deer hunting world. They'll use broadhead arrows, probably. Maybe barbed, but that will depend where you are. If they see you early, they might just track you for a spell. Then they'll shoot to wound. They want you to last all night. They paid a lot of money.'

'You're insane.'

'Not me,' Mark said. 'I'm just catering to the grubby end of the market. Their desires are their own business.'

'You're talking about murdering us.'

'No, I'm talking about giving you the chance to get away from here scot free. I'm your best friend right now. I'm trying to help you.'

'You can't afford for us to walk away.'

'Now you're just making excuses. Don't quit before you start. It's a big world out there. There are only six of them.'

'Do they have night vision?'

'Well, yes.'

'And quad bikes.'

'Which mean you can hear them coming. Don't you see? You're not completely helpless here. Choose your direction carefully, stay alert, listen hard, try to predict from the sound which way the bikes will go, and then slip in behind them after they're gone. It might be possible. Presumably someone will do it sooner or later. It's only two miles by the shortest route. As you know. Straight down the track. But I would advise against. Even alongside, in the trees. Too obvious, surely. Someone would be lying in wait.'

No one answered.

Mark said, 'More advice, if I may. Check your door from time to time. The clock starts ticking as soon as it unlocks. It's your responsibility to know. No further announcements will be made. When it opens, I suggest you depart immediately. Give it your best shot. Look on the bright side. It's a big woods. Bowhunters like to get within forty feet. Closer if they can. Shooting arrows in a forest is hard. There are always trees in the way.'

No one spoke.

Mark said, 'More advice, if I may. Please don't plan to sit in your room. It might feel smart, but it's faulty strategy. It never works. As soon as they realize what you're doing, they'll move in, until they have you surrounded. You'll have six guys at your door. They'll be disappointed. They didn't get their sport. They'll take it out on you. They'll make you last all night, but not in a good way.'

No one spoke.

Mark asked, 'Did you talk about splitting up and going solo?'

Shorty looked away.

'I know,' Mark said. 'Tough choice. The percentage play would be go for it. Problem is, you would never know what happened to the other person. In their final moments, I mean.'

*

318

Burke drove north. The phone died bar by bar. Reacher laid down the law. Burke was to let him out at the mouth of the track, and then go home and stay home, safe and secure. Never to return. Not saying yes and then doubling back and waiting. Not following on foot, just to see what was happening. None of that. Go home, stay home, forget all about it. No argument. No discussion. Not a democracy. That was the deal.

Burke agreed.

Reacher asked him again.

Burke agreed again.

They drove into the trees. It was already full dark under the canopy. Burke used his headlights. The twisted posts showed up five miles later. Right on time. Right where they should be. Burke stopped the car. Reacher got out. Burke drove away. Reacher stood on the road and watched him go. Eventually his tail lights disappeared, way far in the distance. Silence came down. There was thin moonlight on the road, from a grey night sky. Under the trees was darkness. Reacher set out walking. Alone in the dark.

Patty tried the door. She hoped it wouldn't open. Not yet. They weren't ready. They were leaning towards staying together. At least at first. As long as they could. But they hadn't said so out loud. Not yet. They were leaning towards heading west. Directly away from the track. The opposite direction. A longer route out. Counterintuitive. Maybe a good idea. Maybe predictable. They didn't know. They hadn't committed. Not yet. They had debated taking a map from the car. In the end they decided not to. It was a compass they needed. They were worried about getting lost in the woods. They might walk in circles for ever.

The door was still locked.

Patty stepped back and sat on the bed.

*

319

Two minutes later Reacher arrived at the tow truck. Its hard bulk loomed up out of the gloom. The darkness made its paint look black. Its chrome looked dull and grey. He knelt behind it and felt ahead for the fat rubber wire. He found it and logged its position in his mind. He stepped over it. He forced his way along the side of the truck, leading with his shoulder, elbow high, one side of him sliding easy on the waxed and polished paint, the other side of him getting pelted and scratched with twigs and leaves. He came out at the front and felt his way around to the centre of the radiator grille. Which was the centre of the track. He lined himself up and set out walking. Two miles to go.

They heard the quad bikes start up. First one, and then another. The distant shriek of a starter motor, the nervous bark of a high-strung engine, the fast and anxious idle. Then a third machine, and a fourth. The noise beat back off the barn wall. Then a fifth and a sixth. Then all of them, growling and rumbling and buzzing, milling about, snicking into gear, accelerating away one by one, across the grass, on to the track, turning right, away from the house, towards the motel.

For a second Shorty wondered who had gotten the bike they had pushed to the road and back.

Patty tried the door.

Still locked.

The bikes formed up into what sounded like single file. They drove through the lot. Shorty turned and watched out the window. A procession. The boardwalk lights were still on. The bikes drove by, left to right, one by one. The riders were all dressed in black. They all had bows slung across their backs. They all had quivers full of arrows. They all had weird one-eyed night-vision goggles strapped to their heads. Some of them were blipping their engines. Some of them were up out of their saddles, raring to go.

They all rode away.

For a second Shorty wondered who had bet on the west.
Patty tried the door.
It opened.

THIRTY-SIX

P atty pulled the door all the way open, and stood staring out, from one inch inside the threshold. The outside air was soft and sweet. The sky was dark as iron.

'This is crazy,' she said. 'I don't want to go. I want to stay here. I feel safe here.'

'We aren't safe here,' Shorty said. 'We're sitting ducks here.'

'We're sitting ducks everywhere. They have night vision.'

'There are only six of them.'

'Nine,' Patty said. 'You think the assholes are going to be impartial?'

'We can't stay here.'

Patty said nothing. She put her hand out the door. She opened her fingers. She felt the air. She pushed it and cupped it, like swimming.

'We'll go to Florida,' Shorty said. 'We'll have a windsurfer business. Maybe jet skis too. We'll sell T-shirts. That's where the money is. Patty and Shorty's Aquatic Emporium. We could have a fancy design.'

Patty looked back at him.

'Jet skis need servicing,' she said.

'I'll hire a mechanic,' he said. 'Regular as clockwork. I promise.'

She paused a beat.

'OK,' she said. 'Let's go to Florida.'

They took nothing except the flashlights. They hustled out between the dead Honda and a pick-up parked next door. They tracked around room twelve, and came back on the blind side, along the back wall, to where they guessed their bathroom was. They pressed their backs against the siding. West was dead ahead. A faint grey acre of grass, and then a wall of trees, low and black beyond it. They listened hard, and they looked for lights. They heard nothing, and they saw nothing.

They held hands and set out walking. Fast, but not running. They slipped and stumbled. Soon they were out in the open. Shorty imagined weird one-eyed night-vision goggles turning in his direction. Zooming in, and focusing. Patty thought, *If they see you early, they might just track you for a spell.* They fixed their eyes on the dark horizon. The wall of trees. They hustled on towards it. Closer and closer. Faster and faster. They ran the last fifty yards.

They slipped between the first trunks and stopped dead, bent over, breathing hard, gasping, for air, from relief, with primitive joy at having survived. Some kind of ancient victory. Making them stronger. They stood up again. They listened. They heard nothing. They moved deeper into the woods. On and on. Slow going, because of vines and low stuff around their ankles, and because of stepping left, and stepping right, around all the trees. Plus it was dark. They didn't risk the flashlights. Not yet. Because of the night vision. They figured it would be like setting themselves on fire.

Five minutes later Patty said, 'Are we still heading west?'

Shorty said, 'I think so.'

'We should turn south now.'

'Why?'

'We were out in the open an awful long time. They could have been watching from a distance. They saw us heading west, so now they think we're going to continue heading west.'

'Do they?'

'Because unconsciously people project spatial things in straight lines.'

'Do they?'

'So we need to turn off one way or the other. North or south. They can project us west all they want. We'll never show up. I like south better. If we find a road, it's a straight shot to town.'

'OK, we should make a left turn.'

'If we're really heading west right now.'

'I'm pretty sure,' Shorty said.

So Patty turned what she hoped was exactly ninety degrees. She checked it carefully. She was shoulder-on to Shorty. She was sideways on to the way they had just been walking. She set out in the new direction. Shorty followed. On and on. The same slow progress. Grabby vines, and whip-like saplings. Sometimes fallen boughs, propped diagonally across their path. Which meant a detour, and a long look back, to make sure they hadn't gotten turned around.

Way far in the distance they heard a bike. Maybe a mile away. A short trip. It started up, it rode a minute, and it shut down again. The faintest sound. Repositioning, maybe. For what? On what basis? Patty stopped walking, and Shorty bumped into her.

She said, 'Do they ride them all the time, like horseback, or do they get off and approach on foot?'

'I guess I don't hear them buzzing around all the time, so yeah, I guess they park them and fan out on foot.'

'Which means we won't hear them coming. Mark was bull-shitting.'

'There's a surprise.'

'We're in trouble.'

'It's a big woods. They need to get closer than forty feet. That guy was real far away. He was shit out of luck.'

'We should turn southwest now,' Patty said.

'Why?'

'I think from here it would be the fastest way to the break in the trees.'

'Won't they guess?'

'We can't worry about that any more. There are nine of them. Between them they can guess everything.'

'OK, we should head half a turn to the right.'

'If we're really heading south right now.'

'I'm pretty sure,' Shorty said. 'More or less.'

'I think we got turned around.'

'Not by much.'

Patty said nothing.

Shorty said, 'What?'

'I think we're lost in the woods. Which is full of archers who want to kill us. I think I'm going to die surrounded by trees. Which I guess is fair. I work in a sawmill.'

'You OK?'

'A bit light-headed.'

'Hang in there. We're close enough for government work. Turn half right, keep on going, and we'll reach the clearing.'

They did all those things. They turned half right, they kept on going, and they reached the clearing. A minute later. But it was the wrong clearing. They were behind the motel again. The same grey acre of grass. A different angle. But only slightly. They were coming out of the woods about twenty yards from where they ran in.

Reacher heard motorcycle engines far in the distance. First a swarm, like a whole bunch together, buzzing faintly, right at the

325

edge of silence, then individual machines about a mile away, some driving by, some slowing down. Not the clumsy bass beat of American machines. The other kind of motorbike noise. High revs, gears and chains, all kinds of cams and valves and other parts howling and thrashing up and down. The quad bikes, he assumed. There had been nine, neatly parked in three rows of three. In front of the barn. Now they were out and about, revving and squirming their way through the trees.

Hunting, said the back part of his brain.

OK, said the front part. Maybe a protected species. A bear cub, or something. Highly illegal. Maybe that was the victim.

Except a bear cub didn't drive an import or hide with the blind down.

He stopped in the dark and shuffled off the track. He stood six feet in the trees. Way up ahead he heard a bike. Not moving. Idling in place. Waiting. No headlight. Then it shut down. The silence became total again. Overhead where the canopy was thin there were slivers of steel-grey sky. Moonlight on low cloud.

Reacher moved up through the trees, following the track, six feet from its edge.

Patty sat on the ground, with her back against a tree. She stared across at the motel. The blind side. The back wall. Where they had started.

'You OK?' Shorty said again.

She thought, *If they see you early, they might just track you for a spell.*

Out loud she said, 'Sit down, Shorty. Rest when you can. This could be a long night.'

He sat down. The next tree.

He said, 'We'll get better at it.'

'No, we won't,' she said. 'Not without a compass. It's impossible. We tried three straight lines and ended up walking a pretzel.'

'What do you want to do?'

'I want to wake up and find this has all been a horrible dream.'

'Apart from that.'

'I want to go east. I think the track is the only way. Alongside, in the trees. So we don't get lost. Any other direction is futile. We could wander all night.'

'They know that.'

'They always knew. They knew sooner or later we have no alternative but to try the track. Our last resort. We should have known too. We were stupid. Thirty square miles with six guys was always ridiculous. What kind of game is that? It's a lottery. But it isn't thirty square miles. It's a narrow strip either side of the track. That's where all the action will be. It's inevitable. They're waiting for us there. The only gamble for them is what angle we approach from. And when.'

Shorty was quiet a long moment. Breathing in, breathing out.

Then he said, 'I want to try something.'

'What kind of something?'

'First I want to see if it's possible. I don't want to look stupid.'

She thought, short odds, Shorty.

Out loud she said, 'What do we need to do?'

'Follow me,' he said.

In the back parlour Steven tracked the GPS chips inside their flashlights. They were beefy transmitters, powered by a parasitic feed from the four brand new D-cell batteries, with long antennas taped inside the aluminium cases. Currently they were moving from the edge of the forest towards the back of the motel. Medium speed. Walking, not running. In a precisely straight line, which was in stark contrast to their previous navigational performance, which had been chaotic. They had been staggering uncertainly south of west from the get-go, in a tight curling line they evidently thought was straight. Their left turn looked good temporarily, but they wandered again, almost in a circle, and then their final turn brought them back to where they had started. On two occasions they had crossed their own tracks, apparently without realizing.

He watched. They made it to the motel's back wall. Then they retraced their earlier steps exactly. They tracked back around the end of the building. Around room twelve. Into the lot. Past room eleven. Then they stopped, outside room ten.

THIRTY-SEVEN

Shorty raised the Honda's hood, and felt around under the battery. The stiff black wire, chopped in half, the cut ends like new pennies. He backed away, and walked through room ten to the bathroom. He grabbed up all the towels, a big messy bundle, and he carried them outside. He dumped them on the gravel, near the Honda's rear wheel.

'Check the other doors,' he said. 'Get more if you can.'

Patty started with eleven. The door was unlatched. She went in. Shorty went back to ten. He picked up the suitcase. Both hands, around the rope. He staggered out with it. He rested it a moment on the boardwalk. He heaved it down the step to the lot, and staggered with it all the way across, short uncertain steps, to the grass on the far side, the meadow before the woods. He blundered through it, his heels sinking in the soft earth, the case swishing against the seed heads. He made it thirty yards, and stopped, and dropped the case, and laid it down flat in the grass.

Then he walked back. Patty had gotten towels out of eleven, seven, and five. Altogether they had four piles. He went back to ten's bathroom and came out with a jagged shard of tile. Broad at the base, wicked at the tip. He dropped it on the towels, near the Honda's rear wheel.

He asked, 'Which room had the most stuff?'

'Seven,' Patty said. 'Lots of clothes. Lots of potions in the bathroom. That guy takes good care of himself.'

Shorty walked down to seven. He ignored the clothes and the potions. Instead he checked the wash bag on the bathroom vanity. It was black leather. He dumped it out in the sink. He found what he wanted, right there. Bottom of the bag, top of the pile. A nail clipper. The usual kind of thing. Metal. A moon-shaped pincer, and a swivel-out file.

He put it in his pocket. He walked back to the Honda. He put the shard of tile aside. He laid the towels neatly one on top of the other, like a thick quilt. He shuffled it into position, flat on the gravel, under the Honda's rear end. He did the same thing with the towels from five, seven, and eleven, under the Volvo, the Persian carpet van, and the pick-up truck respectively.

He went back to the Honda and laid down on his back. He squirmed into position. He stabbed the shard of tile into the bottom of the gas tank. Again and again. It was tougher than he expected. A flake of porcelain smashed off the tile. Shit, he thought. Please. *I don't want to look stupid.* He knew what she was thinking.

But for once in his life he got lucky. The missing flake of porcelain sharpened the tip. It added a third dimension. It made it a needle. He changed his position and seated the base of the tile in his blunt potato farmer's palm, and he stabbed it upward, as hard as he could.

He felt the tip go in.

He felt a stain of gasoline.

He widened the hole, and a minute later he had about five gallons soaked into the pad of towels. He did the same thing three more times, under the truck and the van and the Volvo. His head spun from the fumes. But he felt full of strength and energy. Full of doing, and fighting, and winning. He pulled out the dripping wads one by one and piled them on the boardwalk. All apart from one small towel, which he took with him. Soaked in gasoline. He slid it under the Honda's battery. He poked it into crevices and draped it over bolts and brackets.

Then he backed away and straightened up and shook his hands to dry them. He got in the driver's seat and put the key in the lock. He clicked it on. He clicked every switch he could find. Heated rear windshield, lights, wipers, radio. Whatever. He wanted maximum load.

He got out. He took the nail clipper from his pocket and unfolded the file. It was a thin blade maybe two inches long and a quarter inch wide, made of gritty metal, with a curl on the end, good for scraping.

He put one arm under the hood. He bent it at the elbow, and dipped down, and twisted his hand underneath, and he slid the tip of the file into the severed space between the two halves of the stiff black wire. Between the two copper pennies. He twisted the file. He completed the circuit. Metal to metal to metal. There was a furious fizzing cascade of sparks, and the gas-soaked towel went *whoomp* and burst into flames, and Shorty dropped the nail clipper and snatched his hand away, and then he ran back and forth to the boardwalk, grabbing more towels, lighting them on fire from the flames under the Honda's hood, tossing them into rooms, into eleven, into ten, on the bed, on the floor, into seven, into five, the last few anywhere, on the boardwalk, on a plastic lawn chair, outside the office door.

They walked backward across the lot. Already flames were curling out of doors and windows. Fantastic shapes were boiling under the eaves, racing laterally, stopping, starting, like breathing, then joining together and lighting the roof on fire.

Shorty said, 'They can't afford to look at it. Not with night vision.

331

It would fry their eyeballs. All we have to do is keep it directly behind us, and they won't see us coming.'

In her head Patty thought out the geometry, and she nodded, and said, 'That's pretty smart, Shorty.'

They walked east through the meadow, past their suitcase, keeping themselves exactly in line, with the fire plumb behind them, and the mouth of the track dead ahead.

Reacher found a quad bike parked on the track. It loomed up in grey filtered moonlight. He was six feet in the trees. He dodged left and right to see the whole picture. The bike was stopped on a diagonal, facing mostly back towards the motel. The front wheels were turned in that direction. The handlebar was askew. As if it had driven down, and slowed, and turned a tight half circle. But not completely. Not a full 180.

No sign of a rider.

Hunting, said the back of his brain.

OK, said the front. But where? Up ahead, surely. The guy had driven down, and swung around, and parked. When he figured he was safely beyond the far edge of the action. Like a backstop position. He had thought about it carefully. Reacher had heard him, in the distance. The guy had sat astride his idling bike, most of a minute, presumably leaning forward on his handlebars, staring ahead, calculating. Then he had shut down and gotten off, and presumably he had walked back the way he had come, to get closer to the action, to squeeze the perimeter, to improve his angles. Which meant Reacher was currently behind him. Always a good place to be. He looked ahead through the trees. He dodged left and right for a better view.

No sign of the guy.

Reacher moved up in the trees. Hard going. Vines, brambles, leafy undergrowth shrubs. Not quiet, either. But he broke up his footsteps to a staccato rhythm. Not left, right, left, right. Not like a route march. Just random scrabbling. Like an animal. Maybe a fox, digging cover. In the dark. Maybe a bear cub. Hard to tell. He kept on going.

He saw the rider.

But only just.

The guy was standing in the middle of the track, almost invisible in the moonlight gloom. He was half turned away from something up ahead. He was an extraordinary figure. He was dressed in tight black clothes, like athletic gear. He had an archery bow slung across his back. He had a quiver of arrows. Strapped to his head was a one-lens night-vision device. Like a Cyclops eye. U.S. Army. Second generation. Reacher had used them.

A night hunt, said the back of his brain. Told you so.

OK, said the front.

There was a faint glow on the horizon. Slightly red, slightly orange.

Reacher moved up in the trees. A long step, a furtive rustle, and then another. The guy didn't notice. He was moving his head, trying to see the distant glow in the corner of his eye, where it wouldn't burn too bright, but he couldn't do it. He kept flinching away. In the end he flipped the optical tube up and out of the way, and he took a look with the naked eye. He stepped back, and left, to get a better view.

Reacher stepped forward, and right.

Something was on fire, way far in the distance.

The guy was about eight feet away. To the right, and a little ahead. He was a well-built individual. With the night vision up he was as handsome as a movie actor.

A night-time bowhunter.

Of what?

There's always a victim, said the back of his brain.

Reacher moved.

The guy heard. He took the bow off his back in one fluid motion.

A split second later he had an arrow in his hand. He nocked the arrow and half drew the string, and held the weapon half ready, pointing low. He looked all around. His night vision was still in the up position. Disengaged. The arrowhead was wide and flat. It shone faintly in the moonlight. It was a decent chunk of steel. It would do some damage. Like getting hit with an axe, but harder.

Then the guy raised the bow high, both hands, as if he was about to ford a river. He used his forearm to knock his optical tube back into place. Now he had vision again. He peered around, grotesquely, mostly ahead, one huge glass eye the size of a coffee can, his head moving slowly.

Reacher stepped back, and left. He lined up the trees. He wanted a sliver of view, but a narrow one. The narrower the better.

The guy kept peering around. He covered what was ahead of him. Then he turned, to see what was to the side of him. Then he turned some more, to see what was behind him.

He looked straight at Reacher. The blank glass lens fixed right on him. The guy raised the bow and drew the string. Reacher swayed right. The arrow fired and buried itself in the tree in front of him with a ringing *thunk* that sang through the hardwood from bole to crown.

Like an axe, but harder.

The guy reloaded with fast practised movements, all right-handed, taking an arrow from the quiver, fitting it to the bow, at the head, at the feathers, then drawing back the string. Ready. Not much slower than working a bolt action rifle. Same kind of ballpark.

Reacher called out, 'Are you aware that you're shooting at a human target?'

The guy fired again. There was a thump of energy in the air as the bowstring released, and the *shish* of the arrow in flight, and then the same slamming *thunk* as it hit a tree.

Reacher thought, I guess I'll take that as a yes.

Told you so, said the back of his brain.

The front of his brain noted that in all his long and varied life, which included military service in many different parts of the world, he had never before been attacked with a bow and arrow. It was a brand new experience. But no fun so far. The night vision was the problem. He was at a huge disadvantage. He knew second generation gear pretty well. He had used various AN/PVS models. Army Navy Portable Visual Search. Like most second generation military gear they were logical developments of the first generation. Images were much sharper around the edge of the lens. Light amplification was boosted from a thousand to twenty thousand times. They gave a highly detailed fine-grained picture, monochrome, slightly grey, mostly green, a little cool, a little wispy. A little fluid and ghostly. Not quite reality. In some ways better.

A huge tactical advantage. Twenty thousand times was a big differential. He had zero times. He had almost pitch dark. It took a strenuous wide-eyed stare even to tell the difference between a tree and not a tree. There were occasional glimmers of dappled moonlight, some of them real, most of them wishful thinking. Far to the left was the orange glow in the sky. Getting brighter. He could see the gleam of the next arrowhead. It was ready to go. It was tracking left, tracking right, trying to find a line through the trees. The guy was stepping in, stepping back, going left, going right. Trying to find his shot. A three-dimensional problem. Then a four-dimensional problem, when Reacher started moving too, randomly, left, left, right, not much, really just swaying, but enough to need a new ballistic calculation every single time.

Reacher called out, 'You need to come closer.'

The guy didn't move.

Reacher said, 'Come in the trees with me.'

The guy didn't answer.

'You would if I was a deer,' Reacher said.

The guy locked on. The glassy end of the coffee can pointed

straight at Reacher. Who saw only a sliver of the right-hand edge of the lens. A chord, in geometric language. A chopped-off edge of a circle. Which in turn meant the guy saw only Reacher's right eye, and then a wide tree, and then maybe part of his left shoulder. Not a great target. Reacher knew people who could have hit it with anything from a lawn dart to a nuclear missile, but clearly the guy with the bow wasn't one of them. Because Reacher was still alive to have the thought.

'Come in the trees with me,' he said again.

The guy didn't answer. No doubt he was thinking things through. Reacher sure was. A small crowded space, with limited room for manoeuvre, especially with a bow. Tactically awkward, especially in terms of range. Anything more than arm's length, there was a tree in the way. But anything less than arm's length was game over. The bow could be grabbed, the night vision could be knocked off, and lethal weapons could be seized from the quiver. Like knives on sticks. The guy had about twenty of them.

He wouldn't come in the trees.

Reacher moved to his left. The arrowhead tracked him. Still no clear shot. Nor would there be for three more steps. After which there was moonlight, because the canopy was thin up ahead. The canopy was thin up ahead because a tree was missing. Which left a hole. Much smaller than where they turned the Mercedes. Maybe half as wide, and half as deep. But a hole all the same. Directly in Reacher's path. A room-sized space, with no trees in the way. Mathematically impossible not to find a shot. The available options would look like a route map in the back of an airline magazine.

Speed would be the critical factor. A running man might cross the space in less than a second. His critical centre mass would be sideways on. It would pass through any particular point in time and space in less than a tenth of a second. Arrows were fast, but not like bullets. Deflection would have to be calculated. The guy would have to shoot ahead of the target. Into the space where the target was about to arrive. He would have to fire the arrow in anticipation. Ahead of time. He had no choice. Like swinging at a fastball. He had to commit.

Reacher ran left, one stride, two, three, maximum acceleration, and the guy fired at where he was going to be, a cast-iron slam-dunk grand slam, except Reacher jinked to the right, just ahead of the last tree, like a running back in a broken field, and instead of entering the treeless room-sized space he came straight at the guy, who was caught fumbling his reload. Easy enough in your momma's basement, Reacher thought. Not so easy now. He barrelled straight into the guy, shoulder first. Maximum demolition. No need for finesse. The guy went sprawling, all arms and legs. Reacher kicked whichever part of him was nearest. Then he grabbed the bow, and pulled the night vision off the guy's head, and slid an arrow out of his quiver.

Then he froze.

Anything less than arm's length was game over.

They would know that.

They would hunt in pairs.

He grabbed the guy by the collar and hauled him into the trees on the far side of the track. His bow clattered on the blacktop. It came to rest out in the open. Unfortunate. It told a clear story. Like the opening frame of a movie. Reacher stopped six feet in the trees. He hauled the guy upright. He made him stand in front, like a human shield. From behind he pushed the tip of the arrow up under the guy's chin. Into the fleshy part. The guy went up on tiptoes and raised his head as high as it would go.

Reacher pushed harder.

He whispered, 'Who are you hunting?'

The guy breathed out like a sigh, which without his current tense condition might have sounded deeply contemplative, as if a subject of immense complexity had just been introduced, that would require great scholarship and debate to resolve. Even from behind Reacher could sense his lips working, perhaps subconsciously, as he rehearsed an opening statement. But he didn't speak. Instead his breathing grew panicked for a spell. Then it resolved. As if he had accepted something. Too late Reacher realized the panic must have been over the biggest complexities of all, which would include the cops coming, and the FBI, and cable TV, and the trial of the century, the whole bizarre freak show out in the open, and the shame and humiliation and embarrassment and disgust. And then the certain life sentence.

The acceptance was what to do about it.

Under the circumstances, the best thing for all concerned.

The guy flipped his feet out from under his knees, like a starfish, like a parachutist jumping out an airplane door, and he lunged forward and took his whole falling weight on the point of the arrow under his chin. Which sliced up into his mouth, through his tongue, through his palate, through his sinus cavity, and into his brain.

Then Reacher let it go.

In the back parlour Steven was losing screen after screen. Most of the cameras were on the motel, looking outward, disguised as brackets for the rainwater gutters. As the motel burned, they burned. Also all the comms hubs were in the roof space. All the radio antennas, and all the telephone links. It had been the obvious location. The motel was closest to central, with respect to the forest as a whole. It was slightly elevated. They were rebuilding it anyway. They put it all in there. Now it was burning up. Including the hidden satellite dish for the secret internet account. No way to trace that ISP. But now gone. They were alone in the world. They were cut off.

The GPS still worked, in the flashlights. That came direct to the house. Currently it showed Patty and Shorty heading for the mouth of the track. In a straight line. With the burning motel directly behind them, no doubt. Smart. It had never been thought of. Not in any of their brainstorming sessions. Not in any of their simulations. It should have been thought of. Night vision or no night vision, they would be very hard to see, against a bright moving glare directly behind them. Not until they were very close.

His final problem was customer number three's heart rate monitor. It was sounding an alarm. Not a necessary piece of equipment, but part of the terms and conditions. A private experiment, run by Robert, who wanted to test the notion that the thrill of the hunt was in the chase. He thought not, based on experience in Thailand. He thought the thrill came in the delicious hour after the prey was cornered. He wanted numbers to prove it. Hence customers were to wear monitors. Data was to be recorded. So far number three had displayed increasing excitement, with a recent huge peak, and then he had flatlined. According to his monitor, he was dead.

THIRTY-EIGHT

Patty and Shorty held hands, and somehow the palm to palm contact was better than talking, when it came to saying what they had to say. They were both feeling weird, somewhere between paralysed and frantic, sometimes breathless, caught up in a strange double flip-flop inversion. It was pitch dark, so they were safe, except for night vision, so they weren't, except night vision couldn't be used, so they were. One step they felt secure. Like little kids, hiding. They could see no one, therefore no one could see them. The next step they felt they were walking the length of a gigantic airport runway, two tiny figures all alone in the vastness, lit up by a thousand probing searchlights.

They didn't know which feeling was real.

Maybe neither.

They walked on.

They waited for arrows.

None came.

They anticipated sentries wide on the flanks. Impatient types, hoping for the best. Hoping for early contact. They planned to avoid them by coming in pretty much centrally. Pretty much half-way between any two distant outposts. With the fire behind them every step. But then at the last moment they planned to veer off course, just as far as the edge of the blaze would cover them. Then they would work around in the woods and pick up the track's direction a little farther down. Better than walking right in, they thought. Surely the mouth of the track would be watched very carefully.

Also they planned to split up. Just temporarily. Just by ten yards or so.

'Close enough to help,' Patty said.

Then she thought, far enough to get away when the other one is killed.

But out loud she said, 'Far enough not to make one big target.'

In the distance behind them the motel's roof fell in. A huge cloud of sparks rose up, and hungry new flames started in on the timbers. The fire was brighter than ever.

'Now,' Patty said.

They went south. To their right. They skipped along sideways, glancing ahead, glancing back at the fire, trying to stay covered by its white-out glow, by the very last edge of its halo, but also pushing the envelope, going as wide as they dared, and then wider, and wider still, and then Shorty ran for the woods first, as agreed. He made it. Patty waited. No sound. No shouted warning. She went after him, squeezing between the same two trees, aiming to head around the same quarter circle, back towards the track. She could hear him up ahead. She was close enough to help. She glanced behind her. She was far enough to get away. Would she? She thought, a mile in my shoes, baby. Who knew what anyone would do?

She walked on.

Then two things happened so fast and sudden her mind went blank. They came out of nowhere. Too fast to see. Two things happened. That was all she knew. And then nothing. Except Shorty was suddenly standing in front of her, and a guy was lying on the ground. Then came a painful slow motion replay, like a mental reaction. Maybe a therapeutic purpose. Post traumatic. In her mind she saw a guy looming up. Literally a nightmare vision. All in black, tight nylon, a bow, an arrow, a hideous mechanical one-eyed face. The bow jerking right, tilting down, at her legs, aiming low. *They'll shoot to wound.* Then the string drawing back, the arrowhead winking in the moonlight, then out of nowhere Shorty was behind the guy, swinging his long metal flashlight like the riot police, hitting the guy full on behind the ear, every ounce of his potato farmer bulk and muscle behind it, plus every ounce of his anger and fury and fear and humiliation. The guy went straight down. Dead, she was sure. The sound alone told her. The flashlight against his skull. She was a country girl. She had heard enough cows killed to know what it took.

Close enough to help.

It had worked.

'Thank you,' she said.

'I busted my flashlight,' he said. 'It doesn't turn on any more.'

'You can have mine,' she said. 'It's the least I can do.'

'Thank you.'

'You're welcome.'

'Keep mine for a weapon,' he said.

They traded flashlights. An absurd little ceremony.

'Thank you,' she said again.

'You're welcome.'

She looked away.

'But,' she said.

'But what?'

'They know there are two of us. They must have known we would play it like that.'

'I guess.'

342

'Which is a risk for them.'

'I guess.'

'They must have known that upfront.'

'OK.'

'I think their obvious solution would be to hunt in pairs.'

A voice said, 'Damn right about that, little girl.'

They turned around.

Another nightmare vision. Glistening black nylon tight to the skin, a complicated bow lurid with composite layers, a steel arrowhead as big as a serving spoon, a Cyclops stare through an expressionless glass circle.

The nightmare vision shot Shorty in the leg.

The bowstring thumped, the arrow hissed, and Shorty screamed and went down like he had fallen through a trapdoor. The arrow was stuck in his thigh. He was hauling on it, and jerking his head side to side, and clamping his jaw up and down, which bit his scream into separate rapid-fire gasps of agony, much faster than breathing, *ah ah ah*, like a racing heartbeat.

Patty was calm. Like Shorty had been before. When her mind was blank. Now his was. Suddenly she thought, this is how life is supposed to feel. She heard herself in her head, as if she was her own teammate, at her own shoulder, saying sure, Shorty's bad, but he won't get any worse in the next three seconds. Not medically possible. So feel free to take care of the other thing first.

Which was the guy with the bow. Who was old, she saw. Suddenly a second teammate was at her other shoulder, saying sure, you're going to notice more now, much more detail, because now you're operating at a higher level, or maybe a more primitive level, where senses are more acute, so that although the guy is dressed head to toe in shiny black, and has a machine on his face, you can tell from his posture and his movements he's about our grandfathers' age, and he's stooped, and he's sparrow-chested, and if we think back to all the older guys we've known, uncles

343

and great-uncles and so on, and the lousy shape they were in, and we adjust for height and weight, then maybe we don't have too much to worry about with this guy.

He was slow with his reload. His right elbow was slow to bend. Kind of awkward. Arthritis, maybe. He tried to compensate by scrabbling for the arrow early. He fumbled it. Patty breathed in. She felt she was at the head of a tight V-shaped formation, somehow now in motion, loud music playing, her loyal teammates marching at her shoulder, willing her on, bearing her forward, buoying her up, making her weightless.

The first teammate whispered, I think the thing to remember, when all is said and done, apart from anything else, is that this guy shot Shorty with an arrow. Which by any standards is completely out of order.

The second teammate said, the night-vision device will protect his face. Better to aim for his throat.

Keep mine for a weapon, Shorty had said.

She did it beautifully. Despite very little prior experience. She felt it all happen, at a molecular level. She sensed every compound flooding her brain. Some were complex emotions. Mostly about Shorty. Primeval feelings. Much stronger than she expected. Some were simple software downloads. Dusty old how-to manuals, left behind from savage eras deep in prehistory. She absorbed them all, and they gave her animal grace, and strength, and speed, and cunning, and ferocity, plus some kind of serene human abandon over the top of it all, that made her surrender to instinct completely. She danced across the space, trailing the flashlight behind her, shuffling her stride to perfection, swinging the flashlight ahead of her, accelerating it hard, keeping it low, the Cyclops eye coming down to track it, then whipping it up in a savage U-shaped curve, into the narrowing angle between the dropping chin and the arching neck.

It hit with a crunch she felt all the way to her elbow. The guy went down like he ran into a clothes rope. He landed on his back. She grabbed his bow and threw it away. His night vision was bound to his head with thick rubber straps. She tore it off. He was a thin, pale, sour man, about seventy years old.

His mouth was opening and closing like a goldfish.

Panic in his eyes.

He couldn't breathe.

He pointed to his throat, both hands, desperate urgent gestures.

Can't breathe, he mouthed.

Tough shit, she thought.

Then she heard Shorty whimper.

Later she knew she would have no defence, if a lawyer accused her of flying into a murderous rage. Damn right she did. Or if he asked her, sternly, did you in fact beat the victim to death with the flashlight? Damn right she did. With blows to the head, exclusively. A lot to his face. With every ounce of her strength. Until his skull looked like a bag of nails.

Then she crawled back to Shorty.

Who was quiet.

He had seen.

First things first. She got her hands under his arms and dragged him deeper into the woods. She got him sitting upright against a tree. She got his legs straight out in front. Then she ran back to the guy she had killed. She took his night vision device. She strapped it on. She hated it. It smelled of his breath and his hair, and dirty metal, and perished military rubber.

But now she could see. Luminous green, in fantastic detail. Every vein in every leaf on every tree was sharp as a pin. As if lit from inside. Glowing softly. At her feet she saw every twig and every fallen flake of bark, with exquisite precision. In the far distance she saw trees just as bright as the trees close by. It was better than daylight. It was unnatural. It was amplified, and smoothed, and gated, and displayed. She felt like Superman.

She ran back to Shorty, and got to work.

Reacher took the dead guy's night-vision device. He strapped it on and adjusted the buckles. The world went bright and green and highly detailed. He took the whole quiver of arrows. He slung it over his shoulder. Twenty knives on sticks. Better than nothing.

He moved deeper into the woods. No danger of getting lost. The track was still visible through the trees, even though it was now thirty yards to his left. It still showed clearly. Its luminosity was exactly equal to everything else. The night vision ignored shadow and distance. Every single thing got the same green and meticulous attention.

He moved up four paces and stopped. He figured the second guy would be close, but not too close. Near enough for a rapid response, far enough to escape a train wreck. Within earshot, certainly.

He turned a long slow circle. He examined every detail. Night vision was not the same thing as thermal imaging. That was a different department entirely. If the guy lit a cigarette with a match, then sure, he would show up as a sudden bright flare. But solely because of the light, not the heat. Night vision didn't know about heat. If the guy didn't light a cigarette, he wouldn't really show up at all. Certainly not as a fat orange sausage of body temperature. At best he would show up as a pale ghostly shape the same as every other pale ghostly shape. Or not show up. He was automatically camouflaged. Because everything was green.

No sign of him.

Reacher checked the other side of the track. He moved back and forth, to see through the trees. Fifty yards away, easy. Perfect detail. Better than daylight. No light and shade, no dappling, no near and far. Each tree glowed exactly the same, as if equally radioactive, in some nightmare future world. Each vine and

346

bramble was a separate delicate line, impossibly thin, like engraving on a banknote.

He saw the guy.

Leaning on a tree, about six feet from the edge of the track. Skintight clothing, dark in colour, bow in his hand, looking mostly forward up the track, but glancing back all the time, down the track, behind him. He was anxious. He couldn't hear his partner. Now he had to choose. Respond, or dodge a train wreck?

He was forty yards from Reacher. Which implied some cautious stalking. For one of them, anyway. A painstaking task. Laborious. Reacher stood still. Sometimes he believed in letting the other guy do the work.

First he took a second arrow from the quiver. One in each hand. Then he chose a tree. A thick, strong specimen. About sixty years old, he thought, judging by Ryantown. He put his shoulder against it. He was a little thicker front to back than it was wide side to side. But it was close enough. He ranged away a step and squatted down. He used the arrow in his right hand to beat and batter and scythe through the undergrowth, big dramatic sweeps of his arm, intended to replicate the sound of a staggering man falling over, maybe rolling, maybe thrashing around. It was maybe convincing. Maybe not. It could have been rare mammals mating. So to perfect the illusion he added a loud strangled gasping groan, as if in terrible pain, part stoic, part pleading, in a voice he hoped was like a guy as handsome as a movie actor.

Then he straightened up and stood sideways behind his tree.

He waited. Two whole minutes. He thought the guy wasn't fooled. But then he heard him. Close by. Very quiet. Slow and steady. Exactly on line. He was a good stalker. He was probably right-handed. Therefore the bow would be in his left. The bow would be thrust forward, half ready. The string would be halfway back. Not slack, not tight. An awkward posture. He would be leading with his left shoulder, and walking half sideways.

Reacher waited.

The guy got slower. Now he was close to where he thought he heard the noise. He was anxious. But cautious too.

He called out in a fierce whisper, 'Hey, three, are you there?'

Reacher didn't move.

The guy said, 'Where are you, man? I think I lost you somewhere along the way. We need to get moving. We got something on fire up there.'

South Texas, Reacher thought. A polite, sincere voice.

He kicked the brambles at his feet.

The guy said, 'Three, is that you?'

Reacher didn't move.

The guy said, 'Are you hurt?'

As a reply Reacher made a quiet sound in the back of his throat. He guessed the nearest word in English would be air, said long and breathy.

The guy crept closer.

And closer.

He came around Reacher's tree, leading with his far shoulder, his belly exposed, looking through a tube, which in many ways was a technical marvel, with only one significant negative, which was a lack of extreme peripheral vision. Which meant the guy came half a step too far around the tree. Before he saw. Before he froze. Reacher stabbed him with the arrow, a vicious uppercut high in the stomach, hard enough to bury the arrow up to Reacher's fist, hard enough to lift the guy up off his feet. Reacher let go of the arrow and whipped his hand back. The guy collapsed on his knees. The arrow was sticking out of his gut. Sloping down. Maybe six inches of shaft, and then the feathers.

The guy pitched forward on his face. He landed square on the feathers. The arrowhead punched out his back. It looked wet and slimy. Not red. Green, of course.

*

Steven had lost one of the flashlights. The GPS had blinked off and never returned. An impact, possibly. Currently the surviving flashlight was sixty feet in the forest, sixty yards from the track. It had not moved for many minutes. He didn't know why.

But his bigger worry was the heart rate monitors. Now four had flatlined. Now four of their customers were technically dead. Which was obviously insane. It was an equipment fault. Had to be. But better safe than sorry. Maybe someone should go take a look. The GPS showed Peter and Robert widely separated, on the flanks, at the edge of the forest. Still in neutral mode, not interfering, there for advice and reassurance alone, only if called upon, nothing more. Mark was moving, in a wide loop back towards the buildings. Not fast. He was either walking or riding slow on his bike. Too slow. They all needed to get moving. He needed to tell them. But he couldn't. The radio hub had burned up. Their earpieces were useless. They were hearing nothing. Therefore doing nothing. Watching the fire, maybe.

Then the surviving flashlight started to move.

THIRTY-NINE

Shorty's pants leg was soaked with blood. Patty couldn't tear the fabric. Too wet, too heavy, too slippery. She ran back and got an arrow. She used the edge of its head to widen the slit the first arrow had made. The new arrow was sharp. It was as good as a kitchen knife. She opened a length about six inches either side of the wound. She peeled back the sticky fabric. She took a look. The wound was vertical. The arrow had come in with one tang up and one tang down, and it had hit above his knee, about a third of the way up his thigh. Dead on central. It had speared through muscle and hit bone. She wasn't a doctor but she knew the words. Through the quadriceps to the femur. Ninety degrees from the femoral artery. Not even close. He wasn't going to bleed to death. They had been lucky.

Except she was pretty sure the impact of the arrow had broken the bone.

She felt around. There was a ledge-shaped lump on the back of his leg. Like a displaced fracture. His hamstrings were pushed out of place. He was gasping and groaning, muted, teeth clamped, and moaning, partly with pain, partly with fury. He was pale green, in the night vision. In shock, but not all the way. His heartbeat was fast, but steady.

She studied the arrow she had used to cut the cloth. The head was a simple triangle. Two wicked edges came together at the point. The body thickened gracefully in the middle, to seat the shaft. To add weight and momentum. The edges were like razors. They would slice through anything. But there were no barbs. The edges would slice right back out again just as easily. Not even slice. No further damage. The pathway was already cut.

Except Shorty's muscle had spasmed and clamped down hard. It was gripping the arrow like a vice.

She said, 'Shorty, I need you to relax your leg.'

He said, 'I can't feel my leg.'

'I think it's broken.'

'That can't be good.'

'I need to get you to the hospital. But first I need to pull the arrow out. Right now you're gripping it. You need to let it go.'

'I got no control. All I know is it hurts like hell.'

She said, 'I think we really need to pull it out.'

'Try rubbing the muscle,' he said. 'Like I had a cramp.'

She rubbed. His thigh was cold and wet and slippery. Thick with blood. He groaned and gasped and whimpered. She squeezed both sides of the wound, inching the web of her thumb closer and closer to the arrowhead, and then she pressed a little harder, both sides, gaping the wound, opening it like a mouth. Blood welled up, and spilled out in little green rivers, some one way, some the other.

'Tell me where we're going,' she said.

'Florida,' he said.

'What will we do when we get there?'

'Windsurfers.'

'What else?'

'T-shirts,' he said. 'Where the money is.'

'What kind of design?'

He paused a moment, thinking, maybe something elaborate, and she gripped the arrow's shaft, and jerked it as sharp and hard as she would getting a stuck two-by-four out of a rack at work. The arrow came out and Shorty shrieked between grinding teeth, with pain and outrage and betrayal.

'Sorry,' she said.

He gasped and he panted.

She slipped off her jacket and used the clean arrowhead to cut off the sleeves. She tied them together, end to end, with a generous knot. She folded the body of the jacket into a tight little pad, as small as she could get it. She pressed it down on the wound. She tied it on with the double sleeves. As good as she could get right then. A pressure dressing on the front, to stop the bleeding, and a splint of sorts on the back. The big knot would hold things steady. At least for a while. She hoped.

'Wait there,' she said.

She ran back to the first nightmare figure. The one Shorty had hit. The crack behind the ear. She pulled off his night vision device. Its rubber straps were slick with blood. She took another arrow from the quiver. She ran back to Shorty. She gave him the headset to wear, and the arrow to hold. For security. As a last-ditch defence.

'Now I'm going to find us a quad bike,' she said.

She took the working flashlight in one hand, and the clean arrow in the other. She ran back to Shorty's guy. She stood where she had stood before. She replayed the scene in her mind. The guy had loomed up ahead of her. The nightmare vision. Face to face. In other words, he had been walking in a southerly direction. Coming from the north. From somewhere near the mouth of the track.

She stepped over the guy, and moved on to where the voice from the dark had spun them around. *Damn right about that, little girl*. They had turned and seen him. Face to face. He had been walking in a southerly direction, too. Also coming from the north. From near the mouth of the track. They were a pair. Working together. Common sense said they would have left their bikes behind them. They would have parked way back, surely, and then ranged ahead on foot.

She stepped over her guy and set out walking, north.

Mark saw her go. He was all set to follow, but then at the last second in the corner of his eye he saw what she was stepping over. A dead man. Two dead men. Which put things in a whole different perspective. Burning the motel was bad enough. It was insured, ironically. But obviously he wouldn't risk a claim. Even a cursory inspection would call it arson. Because it was. At the time Steven hadn't understood what he was watching. To be fair, none of them had. At that point the radio was still working, and Steven had described the pads of towels, and he had described Shorty's mysterious mechanical work, under the rear end of each of the vehicles in turn, but the camera angles were bad and he couldn't see exactly what the hell he was doing, and no one else had any suggestions either, until suddenly the towels were all on fire, and he was throwing them around.

It had never happened in any of their brainstorming sessions, or simulations, or war games. Now he saw it should have. It was inevitable. If customers pushed for better specimens, this was bound to happen. Sooner or later. A really bold move would come about.

But still, no insurance claim. The cops would come, and they would sift through the wreckage, and they would find all kinds of weird shit. But rebuilding with cash would eat up half of what they were making that night. Which would be a severe blow. Although he supposed they could tell themselves they would earn it back later. And more.

But still, a blow. Were there alternatives? Suddenly he thought so. Suddenly he thought, why rebuild at all? The motel was a dump. It was nothing to him. It was a junk part of some weird old title passed down from a dead guy he never knew. He didn't care about the motel. Then and there he decided to leave it in ruins. It would be much cheaper to convert a single room in the main house. It would be much cheaper to change the signs from *Motel* to *B&B*. Six new plastic letters, a little gold paint. A different kind of invitation. Should work fine. They didn't need more than two guests at a time anyway. The customers could sleep in tents. Part of the whole rugged experience.

But dead people were a whole different category. Mark prided himself on being realistic. He felt he wasn't blinded by emotion or ruled by sentiment or misled by cognitive bias. He felt he made purely dispassionate judgements. He felt he was good at foreseeing consequences. Like speed chess in his mind. He felt he knew what would happen next. If this, then that, then the other thing. And right then he foresaw a whole lot of dominoes about to fall. The dead people would be missed, questions would be asked, data would be traced. If Robert could find people, so could the government. Probably faster.

He thought, time for plan B.

Unsentimental.

He walked back to his bike and rode it slowly to the house. The motel had burned to the ground. Only the metal cage around room ten was still standing. It was glowing cherry red. The heat was fierce. He could feel it all the way across the lot. The embers rippled in the ghostly night-time breeze, red and white and shimmering.

He rode past the barn and made it to the house. He gunned the bike up the steps and parked it on the porch. He went in the front. Straight to the parlour. Steven said hello before he stepped in the door. Without looking up. He was watching the GPS. He knew Mark was in the house.

Mark looked over Steven's shoulder. At the GPS screen. Only one flashlight was showing. Peter and Robert were still static on the flanks.

Steven said, 'Four of the heart monitors failed.'

'Four now?' Mark said.

Steven switched screens and showed him the data. It was laid out as four separate graphs. Heart rate versus time. Each graph looked like a pencil sketch of mountainous terrain. All of them showed basically the same thing. First elevated and consistent excitement, then a brief plateau of extreme stress, then nothing.

'Might be an equipment fault,' Steven said.

'No,' Mark said. 'I saw two of them dead already.'

'What?'

'Their heads were bashed in. By Patty and Shorty, I guess. Who are clearly better than we thought.'

'Where was this?'

'South of the track.'

'What happened to the other two?'

'I don't know,' Mark said.

Steven switched back to the GPS screen. The surviving flashlight was moving down the track, in the trees, close to the edge. Peter and Robert were still stationary. In a separate window the two surviving customers were showing elevated but consistent heartbeats. Excited. The thrill of the chase. But no sudden spikes. No contact yet.

'Which ones are they?' Mark asked.

'Karel and the Wall Street guy.'

'Can we tell where they are?'

'We know where their bikes are. They seem to have taken up a middle position.'

'With the front two and the back two already gone. It's up to them now.'

'Who got the back two?'

'I don't know,' Mark said again.

'This changes everything, you know. It's not the same now.'

'I agree.'

'What do you want to do?'

'Plan B,' Mark said. 'Watch carefully where the flashlight goes.'

Steven kept his eyes on the screen.

Mark pulled a boxy black handgun up and out from under his jacket. His elbow went high, because the gun was long, because it had a suppressor attached. He shot Steven in the back of the head. And again, when the body came to rest. To be sure and certain. Plan B required a lot of both.

He took the bags of cash from the closet, and set them down on the hallway floor. He opened the closet's back wall and took out his escape kit. Cash, cards, a driver's licence, a passport, and a burner phone. A whole new person, zipped in a plastic bag.

He threw Peter's and Steven's and Robert's on the closet floor.

He carried the bags of cash outside and set them down in the dirt a distance away. He came back to the porch and opened the front door wide. He sawed the quad bike back and forth in front of it until it had room to fall over. He removed the gas cap and threw it away. He squatted down like a weightlifter and grabbed the frame. He jerked the bike up and toppled it over, on its side. Towards the house. Right next to the open door. Gas gurgled out of the open tank. It made a stain, then a miniature lake.

Mark threw a match, and backed away, and grabbed the bags, and ran. To the barn. Halfway there he stopped and looked back. The house was already alight. All around the front door. The walls, the porch boards. The flames were creeping inside.

He turned again and ran on forward. In the barn he put the bags in his Mercedes. He backed it out and parked it a distance away. He ran back to the barn. To his right the house was burning nicely. The flames were up to the second-floor windows. In the barn he hustled over to where the lawn tractor was parked. To the shelf above it, where the gas cans were kept. Five of them, all lined up, filled every time someone drove the pick-up to town. Always ready. The grass had to look good. Kerb appeal was important.

Plan B. No more of that.

He emptied the cans on the floor, under Peter's Mercedes, under Steven's, under Robert's. He threw a match, and backed away, and turned and ran to his car. He set the hazard flashers going. For Peter and Robert to see. A panic signal. They already knew their radios were dead. They were looking at two brand new fires. They had no idea what was going on. They would come running.

He drove towards the mouth of the track, at a stately speed, past the glowing ruins of the motel, through the meadow, flashing orange all the way.

He stopped in the centre of the meadow.

Robert zoomed in from the right side, a wide curve out of the woods, flailing the seed heads, flattening the meadow grass under four fat tyres. He bumped up on the edge of the blacktop and manoeuvred next to the passenger side. Mark buzzed the far window down. Robert looked in. Mark shot him in the face.

Mark buzzed the window back up. Peter was approaching on the left-hand side. The same wide swooping curve through the meadow. Exactly symmetrical. Aiming to arrive at the driver's window, not the passenger's. Which meant the Mercedes itself was between him and Robert's empty bike, and the slumped figure on the ground.

Mark buzzed his window down.

Peter manoeuvred alongside.

Face to face.

The gun was too long. Because of the suppressor. Mark couldn't manoeuvre it. It snagged on the door.

Peter stopped his engine.

357

He said, 'How bad is it?'

Mark paused a beat.

'Really couldn't be worse,' he said. 'The motel burned down. Now the house and the barn are on fire. And four customers are dead.'

Peter paused in turn.

Then he said, 'That's a whole new ball game.'

'I agree.'

'I mean it's the end of everything. You understand that, right? This is going to be no stone unturned.'

'No doubt.'

'We should get out,' Peter said. 'Right this minute. Just you and me. We need to do it, Mark. The pressure will be heavy duty. We might not survive it if we stay.'

'Just you and me?'

'Robert and Steven are useless. They're a burden. You know that.'

'I need to open my door,' Mark said. 'I need to stretch my legs.'

Peter checked.

'You have plenty of room,' he said.

Mark opened his door. But he didn't get out. Instead he stopped the door as soon as the handle mouldings were clear of the suppressor, and where Peter was still nicely framed in the now-angled window. He shot him once in the chest, once in the throat, and once in the face.

Then he closed his door again, and buzzed his window up, and turned off his hazard flashers, and drove on, down the track, towards the woods.

FORTY

Reacher got through the next section of forest pretty fast, because of the night vision. He stayed six feet off the track. He made no attempt to be stealthy or quiet. He relied on the mathematical randomness of tree distribution to save him from arrows. A clear shot from distance was always going to be a hundred to one.

At one point way far away he heard four separated pops. Two groups, a one and a three. Tiny hollow pinpricks of sound. Maybe thirty seconds apart. The back of his brain said, those were suppressed nine-millimetre rounds, fired in the open air, about a mile away. The front said, or maybe they were something cooking off, possibly aerosol cans, in the fire. Which was getting brighter again. It had flared up once, when he figured the roof fell in, and then it had faded away a little. But now the glow was back, and wider, as if more than one thing was burning.

He stopped. Up ahead on the left he saw two quad bikes parked side by side, front end in, at an angle, half in and half out of the trees. Like outside a country roadhouse. The night vision showed no riders nearby. Presumably they were up ahead. On foot. Closer to the action. Like the last two. These were the next two. They were operating a multi-layered defence. One pair after another. Which was why Reacher had avoided the infantry. He didn't enjoy slogging through endless terrain.

He moved on, quieter than before.

He stopped again.

He saw a guy up ahead. On the other side of the track, about thirty feet in the trees. Small in the distance, but lit up even-handedly, like everything else. Delineated with exquisite care, in fine grey and green lines. Clothes like a scuba diver, a bow, a Cyclops eye.

No sign of his partner. Some signs of anxiety. Mostly about the glow in the sky, Reacher thought. The guy kept looking towards it, and ducking away. Maybe a crude measure of how bright it was getting. How soon he had to flinch away. The guy was tall and substantial, and his head was up, and his shoulders were square. But he wasn't comfortable. Reacher had seen his type before. Not just in the army. No doubt the guy was a big-deal alpha male at whatever it was he was good at. But right then he was out of his depth. He was twitching with confusion. Or resentment. As if deep down he couldn't understand why his staff officers or his executive assistants hadn't taken care of things for him a damn sight better.

Reacher moved up through the trees, on the other side of the track. He moved slowly and quietly. All the way to where he was exactly level with the guy. Reacher was six feet in the trees. Then came the track. The guy was thirty feet in on the other side. A straight line on a plan. But not a clear shot in a forest. The guy was too deep. He had boxed himself in. Too defensive. He had no natural avenue of attack.

Reacher walked across the track, dead on line, a hundred random trees between him and the guy. He stepped back into the woods on the other side, and he worked his way through, now twenty feet from the guy, still dead on line. The glow in the sky was amplified twenty thousand times, and it winked and danced through the leaves, like camera flashes, like a movie star stepping out of a car. Up ahead the guy was looking down. Maybe the sparkle bothered him.

Now he was ten feet away. Reacher eased his speed back to nothing. He took a good look around. A full 360. He studied the picture, section by section. Highly detailed, fine-grained, monochrome, slightly grey, mostly green, a little cool, a little wispy. A little fluid and ghostly. Not quite reality. In some ways better.

No sign of a partner.

Reacher moved on. As always he believed in staying flexible, but as always he also had a plan. Which in this case was to stab the guy in the neck with an arrow. Which would be easy enough. Because arm's length was game over. But flexibility intervened. Up close, even in glimpsed slivers between trees, it was clear the guy was worried in a particular kind of way. An elemental way. Like a billionaire whose plane crashes on an uninhabited island. Or whose car gets in a fender bender in the wrong neighbourhood. The food chain. Suddenly not as high as he thought. Maybe ready to make a deal.

Reacher rushed him, and the guy reacted by jerking his bow up, probably nothing more than animal instinct, not a considered decision, which was a shame, because just in case Reacher had to scythe his arrow down, like a knife on a stick, to slash all four of the guy's left-hand knuckles. The guy howled and dropped the bow, and Reacher stepped real close, their optical tubes colliding, and he kicked the guy behind the knees, so that he fell over on his back, whereupon Reacher flipped the guy's night vision up with his foot, and then jammed the same foot on the guy's throat, and forced the tip of the arrow between his lips, and tapped it on his teeth.

361

'Want to talk?' he whispered.

The guy couldn't answer in words, because of the arrow jammed against his teeth, or in gestures either, because of the foot jammed against his throat. Instead he kind of nodded with his eyes. Some kind of desperate plea. Some kind of promise.

Reacher withdrew the arrow.

He asked, 'Who are you hunting?'

The guy said, 'This is not what it seems.'

'How so?'

'I came here to hunt wild boar.'

'And what are you hunting instead?'

'I was deceived.'

'What are you hunting?'

'People,' the guy said. 'Not what I came for.'

'How many people?'

'Two.'

'Who are they?'

'Canadians,' the guy said. 'A young couple. Their names are Patty Sundstrom and Shorty Fleck. They got stranded here. I was tricked into it. I was told wild boar. They lied to me.'

'Who lied to you?'

'A man named Mark. He owns this place.'

'Mark Reacher?'

'I don't know his last name.'

'Why didn't you call the cops?'

'No cell service here. No phones in the room.'

'Why haven't you run away?'

The guy didn't answer.

'Why didn't you stay in your room tonight and refuse to participate?'

No response.

'Why are you nevertheless stalking around in the dark with your bow and arrow?'

No answer.

'Wait,' Reacher said.

He heard a car up ahead. He saw bright jagged shards of amplified light coming through the trees. A big vehicle with its headlights on. He flipped up his tube. The world went dark, all except for the track, thirty feet to his right. It was all lit up, like the inside of a long low tunnel. Twin high beams were punching forward. A Mercedes rolled by. It was shiny black, a big SUV, shaped like a fist. Its tail lights showed red for a moment. Then it was gone.

Reacher dropped his tube back in place. The world went green and highly detailed again. He shifted his foot on the guy's neck. To make room. For the tip of the arrow. He steadied it against the welt of his shoe, and exerted modest downward pressure. The guy tried to scream, but Reacher trod harder and stopped him.

The guy said, 'I didn't know what I was getting into. I swear. I'm a banker. I'm not like these other guys. I'm a victim too.'

'You're a banker?'

'I run a hedge fund. These other guys are nothing to do with me.'

'I guess the world has moved on,' Reacher said. 'You seem to expect better treatment because you're a banker. When did that become a thing? I guess I blinked and missed it.'

'I didn't know they were hunting people.'

'I think you did,' Reacher said. 'I think that's why you came.'

He leaned harder on the arrow, and harder, until it pierced the skin, and drove down through the neck, clipping the spine, and out again the other side, pinning the guy like a dead butterfly against the forest floor. Against a tree root, by the feel of it. Gnarled and hard. But Reacher strained and leaned and pushed until the arrow was solidly rooted, and perfectly upright, like a monument.

Then he moved on through the trees.

*

Mark stopped his Mercedes nose to nose with the tow truck. He had run the numbers. There was a maximum four people technically still unaccounted for. Who were Karel and the Wall Street guy, plus Patty and Shorty themselves. Plus hypothetically a fifth person, if the outside pair had been victims of a third party. Of the big guy, perhaps, come back again. Because he had spotted something. Because he had been unconvinced.

Peter's fault.

Four people. Or five. All up ahead. Maybe a long way ahead. He needed three short minutes. That was all. Maybe less. He needed to reverse the tow truck out to the road, high speed, into a ditch if necessary, anything to get it out the way, and then he needed to sprint back, and hop in his car, and blast off. To anywhere. North, south, east or west. Three minutes, maybe less. That was all. But, five people, in locations unknown, each location being either more than three minutes away, which wasn't a problem, or less than, which was.

But it would be hard to be less than, he thought in the end. In practical terms. Even with bikes. He ran the scene in his mind. Like speed chess. First this, then that, then the other thing. He felt he knew what would happen. It was a loud diesel engine. Everyone would hear it in the distance. At first the customers would assume the perimeter was being loosened. An on-the-fly in-game adjustment. To keep the fun coming. Patty and Shorty would think a version of the same thing. They had done well so far, so they would assume now the goalposts were being moved against them. None of them would be suspicious. Three minutes didn't matter. None of them would react at all.

Except Karel. It was his truck. He would know some kind of weird shit was going on. He might let it go, because he thought he was more or less a semi-detached member of the team now, after the last couple of days, as reflected in the generous discount, and so on. He might feel a bit *mi casa su casa* about it. He might even

364

take it as a courtesy, not to be dragged out of the game. He was there as a customer, after all, not an umpire. It wasn't his job to make on-the-fly adjustments. He might let it go.

Or he might not.

He might be more than three minutes away. Even if he reacted immediately. He would need to thread his way through the forest, possibly sixty yards or more, back to wherever he parked his bike. That could be three minutes right there.

Or not.

Realistic. Dispassionate. Overall he figured there was a good chance of success. Either Karel would let it go, or he wouldn't, multiplied by either he was close by, or he wasn't. Two coin tosses in a row. Disaster priced at four to one, success at four to three. Numbers didn't lie. No cognitive bias.

He left the Mercedes running, and he left the driver's door open. He squeezed between the trees and the truck's enormous hood. He battled his way to where the cab towered above him. He grabbed the handles and climbed the ladder.

The door was locked.

Which he had not foreseen. For once he hadn't known what would happen. Such a simple thing. It had never occurred to him. Not in a million years. He hung there, one foot on a step, one hand on a handle, swinging free, poked by trees. At first he was angry. Karel was stupid to leave the truck without the door open and the key in. Who the hell would do that? It was insane. Flexibility was everything. They might have needed to move the truck at any time. In-game management was always fluid. Everyone knew that.

Then he got worried. A sick hollow feeling. Where was the key, if not in the truck? The best case was bad enough. The best case said the key was in Karel's pocket, which meant finding the guy, and taking it from him. Which would create a delay. Potentially a long delay. Which would in turn increase his exposure to any remaining hostile elements. Not good.

But it was better than the worst case. Karel's pockets were tight. Stretch fabric, shiny black. Would he want to carry a key? Would any of them? They had left their rooms open, after all, to Shorty's great advantage, with his flaming towels. They hadn't wanted to carry those particular keys. Maybe they thought lumps and bumps in their pockets spoiled the look.

The worst case said Karel had left the tow truck key on room two's dresser. To be picked up in the morning. Now to be picked up never, or years in the future as a lucky find, ashy, melted, twisted out of shape, purpose unknown.

Mark climbed down the ladder and forced his way along the hood to his car. He reversed ten yards, and turned around in the hole in the trees, and drove back the way he had come.

Patty saw him pass by again. She had seen him leave, minutes before. If it was really him. She was only guessing it was Mark in the car. Because of the night vision she hadn't looked at the driver directly. The car had its headlights on. Way too bright. But as she ducked away she heard the hum of its engine, and the *whoosh* of its tyres. She knew it was a regular type of car. Or wagon, or SUV. She just felt it was Mark inside. Running away, she thought, the first time he passed. But evidently not, because he came back again.

Maybe it wasn't Mark after all.

She couldn't find the quad bikes. She didn't think they would be deep in the trees. The spaces were too tight. It would be too easy to get wedged in for ever. So she confined her search near the edges of the track. She expected to find them parked side by side, maybe backed half into the bushes, maybe angled, as if ready for action, but also leaving space for others to get by, as a courtesy, if they wanted to. But she found nothing.

She stopped walking. She was already a long way from Shorty. She didn't know how much further she should go. She looked ahead, carefully. She was growing accustomed to the night vision. She turned around and looked behind her. The glow in the sky was bright again. Too bright to look at directly. She half turned back and checked to the south. She saw a small nocturnal creature skitter across six feet of open ground, and dive into a pile of leaves. It was lit up the same as everything else, a pale, wan, scuttling green. Probably grey in real life. Probably a rat.

She turned all the way back around.

She looked ahead again.

There was a man in front of her.

The same as before. The same nightmare vision. Out of nowhere. Out of nothing. Just suddenly there. With a bow held ready. The string was drawn back. The arrow was aimed. But not the same as before. Not at her legs. This time higher.

No Shorty behind him.

Not the same as before.

The nightmare vision spoke.

'We meet again,' it said.

She knew the voice. It was Karel. The weasel with the tow truck. From the Yugoslav army. Who looked like a blurry face in the back of a war crimes photo. She should have known. She was stupid.

Karel asked, 'Where's Shorty?'

She didn't answer.

'Didn't he make it? Or maybe you don't know for sure. Maybe you went your separate ways. You ain't a pair right now. He ain't up ahead, because I checked. He can't be behind you, because that would be neither use nor ornament.'

She looked away.

'Interesting,' Karel said. 'Is he back there for a reason?'

She didn't answer.

He smiled under his glassy snout.

Wide and delighted.

He said, 'Is he wounded?'

No reply.

'This is exciting,' he said. 'You're out gathering roots and berries, to make a potion, to heal your man. You're worried. You're anxious to get back. This is a truly delightful situation. You and I are going to have so much fun.'

'I was looking for a quad bike,' she said.

'No point,' he said. 'My truck is parked in the way. No one gets out of here before me. I ain't dumb.'

He lowered his aim.

To her legs.

'No,' she said.

'No what?'

'Yes, Shorty was wounded. Now I need to get back to him.'

'How bad was he wounded?'

'Pretty bad. I think his thigh bone is broken.'

'Shame,' Karel said.

'I need to go see him now.'

'The game says freedom of movement depends on not getting tagged.'

'Please,' she said.

'Please what?'

'I don't like the game.'

'But I do.'

'I think we should quit. It has gotten way out of hand.'

'No, I think it has gotten to the good part.'

Patty didn't speak again. She just stood there, with her flashlight in one hand and her arrow in the other. It was the working flashlight, not even the weapon. The arrow would be good for slashing or stabbing, but the guy was ten feet away. Out of range.

He drew back the string an extra inch. The arrowhead moved backward, the same inch, towards his hand, clenched tight around the grip. The bow curved harder. It sang with tension.

It was the working flashlight.

All in one movement she dropped the arrow and found the switch and lit up the beam. It was like she remembered, from the first time, checking on the Honda's heater hoses. A bright white beam of light, hard and focused. She aimed it right at the guy. At his face. At his big glass eye. She lit it up and pinned it down. He flinched away and his arrow fired wide and low and thrashed through the undergrowth and thumped in the ground. He ducked and squirmed and twisted. She chased him with the beam of light, like a physical weapon, jabbing, thrusting, aiming always for his face. He fell to the ground and rolled over and tore the machine off his head.

She switched off the flashlight and ran through the trees.

FORTY-ONE

Patty knew running would turn out either smart or dumb, depending on whether Karel caught her or not. Simple as that. At first she was hopeful. She was running well, and she figured he might be slow to get going. He might worry a little about an ambush up ahead, with the beam of light. Like a space movie on Shorty's TV.

Then, bad news. She heard crashing feet behind her. Getting closer. She darted right and changed direction. Karel was slower to turn. She got ahead of him. He caught up again. He got to where he was just behind her. Up ahead in the bouncing night vision she saw the track. Coming up. Closer and closer. Bright and clear. She was running towards it at an angle. There were crashing feet behind her. She burst out on the track. Karel burst out after her. He planted his feet. He raised his bow.

They were lit up by headlight beams. Amplified twenty thousand times. Like atom bombs. They ducked away. Karel flipped up his tube. Patty tore the whole apparatus off her head. The world went dark, except the car. The black Mercedes. All lit up. Slowing

370

down. Mark at the wheel. He came to a stop. He opened the door. He got out. He stayed away from the headlights. He stepped forward in the shadows.

Karel raised his bow again.

He aimed the arrow at Patty.

But he spoke to Mark.

He said, 'What's on fire up there?'

Mark paused a beat.

'Everything's on fire,' he said. 'We're in a whole new ball game now.'

'We?'

'You're kind of involved. Wouldn't you say? People have died. This is going to be no stone unturned. We should get out. Right this minute. Just you and me. We need to do it, Karel. The pressure will be heavy duty. We might not survive it if we stay.'

'Just you and me?'

'You're my number one draft pick. The others are useless. They're a burden. You know that.'

Karel didn't answer.

Mark said, 'We don't have much time.'

'We have plenty,' Karel said. 'The night is still young. We can't be disturbed. No one can get in.'

'We need to talk about that. Really we need to move your truck right now.'

'Why?'

'A tactical thing. An in-game adjustment.'

'We don't need a tactical in-game adjustment. Not now. Not any more. Shorty is wounded, and I got Patty right here. The game is over.'

'OK, shoot her and then let's get going.'

'I would want to go finish Shorty first.'

'You're stalling.'

'What?'

371

'Do you even have the key?'

'What key?'

'The key to the truck,' Mark said. 'Where is it?'

'What kind of question is that? My truck is worth a lot of money.'

Mark nodded.

'Exactly,' he said. 'I'm your best friend, worried on your behalf. I hope you didn't leave the key on your nightstand. If you did, you better call a tow truck. For your tow truck. The motel burned down. That was the first thing on fire up there.'

'I got the key right here,' Karel said. 'It's in my pocket.'

'Good to know,' Mark said. He moved the long black gun out from behind his leg, and he shot Karel four times, all in the rib cage under the arm that was holding the bow.

The gunshots were loud but dull.

The long tube on the front was a silencer, Patty thought.

Karel went down on the track, in a sudden buckling heap, with the hiss of nylon, and the clatter of his bow, and the crack of his head on the blacktop.

Mark turned the gun on Patty.

He said, 'Go get the key out his pocket.'

Patty paused a beat, and then got right to it. She felt she had done worse, pulling the arrow out of Shorty's leg. The key was warm. It was no bigger than the Honda's.

'Throw it over here,' Mark said.

'Then you'll shoot me,' she said.

'I could shoot you any time. I could take the key from your cold dead hand. I'm not squeamish.'

She threw the key.

It landed at his feet.

He said, 'How bad is Shorty?'

'Pretty bad,' she said.

'Can he move?'

'His leg is broken.'

'I think you and I might be the last two standing,' Mark said. 'And I have to say poor old Shorty is shit out of luck with me. I'm certainly not going back to help him. He can stay where he is, as far as I'm concerned.'

Patty said nothing.

'Purely as a matter of interest, how long do you think he would survive?'

Patty didn't answer.

'I want to know,' Mark said. 'Seriously. Let's work it out. What is it, five days without water, and five weeks without food? Except he's not feeling great to begin with.'

'I'll go help him,' Patty said.

'Suppose you couldn't. I guess he could try to crawl his way out, but he must be dehydrating fast and feeling weak by now. Crawling might increase the risk of infection. And it would certainly increase his exposure to predators. Some of those critters like to chew on an open wound.'

'Let me go help him.'

'No, I think he should be left on his own right now.'

'Why do you even care? You said you were only catering to other people's grubby desires. The other people are out of the picture now. So you're done. Take the key and move the truck and get out of here. Leave us alone.'

Mark shook his head.

'Shorty burned my motel,' he said. 'That's why I care. Forgive me for feeling a tiny bit vengeful.'

'You made us play the game. Starting a fire was a valid move.'

'And leaving him to die is a valid response.'

Patty looked away. At Karel, lifeless on the blacktop, caught by the spread of the headlight beams. All harsh white light and jagged black shadows.

She looked back.

She said, 'What are you going to do with me?'

'Always the same question,' Mark said. 'You sound like a broken record.'

'I have a right to know.'

'You're a witness.'

'I said all along you wouldn't let us win. The game was bull-shit.'

'It served its purpose. You should see what's in the back of my car.'

'Let me go see to Shorty. Come with me. Do it there. Both of us.'

'That's romantic,' he said.

She didn't answer.

'Where is he exactly?' Mark asked.

'A ways back.'

'Too far. I'm sorry. I really need to get going. Let's do it here. Just you.'

He aimed the gun. She saw it clearly in the headlight spill. She recognized the brand from the TV shows she watched. A Glock, she was sure. Boxy, detailed, finely wrought. The tube on the front was satin finished. A precision component. It looked like it cost a thousand dollars. She breathed out. Patricia Marie Sundstrom, twenty-five, two years of college, a sawmill worker. Briefly happy with a potato farmer she met in a bar. Happier than she ever ex-pected to be. Happier than she knew. She wanted to see him again. Just one more time.

Something moved behind Mark's left shoulder.

She saw it in the corner of her eye. In the deep black shadows beyond the headlight beams. A flash of something white. Ten feet back. Suspended in the air. Eyes, she thought. Or teeth. Like a smile. She listened. She heard nothing. Just the rustle of the car's idling engine, and the soft wet burble of its patient exhaust.

Then she sensed a shape. Behind Mark's back. A dark void. Like a tree was moving.

Crazy.

She looked away.

Mark asked, 'Ready?'

'I'm glad your motel burned down,' she said. 'I just wish you had been in it.'

'That's not nice,' he said.

She looked back at him.

There was a man right behind him.

A giant. He had stepped into the headlight wash. In his left hand was a single arrow. On his head he was wearing a night-vision device with the tube flipped up. He was six inches taller than Mark and about twice as wide.

He was huge.

He was silent.

He stepped up right behind Mark's back, not more than a foot away, like two men in a crowded queue, to get in the hockey game, or get on a plane. He reached around with his right hand and closed it over Mark's wrist. He eased Mark's arm sideways, keeping it straight, keeping it level, effortlessly, like slowly and steadily opening a door, through a perfect ninety-degree arc, until the Glock was aimed sideways at nothing. He reached around with his left hand and clamped a bent elbow over Mark's upper body and crushed him to his chest. He touched the point of his arrow to the hollow of Mark's throat. Neither man moved. They looked like they were clasped together, ready to dance the tango. Except Mark was the wrong way around.

The big man said, 'Drop the weapon.'

A deep voice, but quiet. Almost intimate. As if intended for Mark's ear alone, which was only inches away. In tone it sounded more like a suggestion than a command. But with a bleak implication behind it.

Mark didn't drop it.

Patty saw muscles bunching in the giant's right forearm. Their contours were exaggerated by the harsh flat light. They looked like rocks in a bag. There was no expression on his face. She realized he was crushing Mark's wrist. Slowly, steadily, inexorably. Relentlessly. Mark yelped and breathed fast. She heard bones click and creak and move. Mark jerked and thrashed.

The big man kept on squeezing.

Mark dropped the gun.

'Good choice,' the big man said.

But he didn't let go. He didn't change the tango-dancing stance.

He said, 'What's your name?'

Mark didn't answer.

Patty said, 'His name is Mark.'

'Mark what?'

'I don't know. Who are you?'

'Long story,' the big man said.

His muscles bunched again.

Mark squirmed.

'What's your last name?' the big man asked.

Bones clicked and creaked and moved.

'Reacher,' Mark gasped.

FORTY-TWO

A hundred yards back Reacher had seen the woman light up the hunter with the flashlight beam, and then run like hell. He had seen the hunter chase after her. He had chased after both of them. He caught up in time to see the Mercedes arrive. He crossed the track in the dark way behind it, and crept up on the far side. He heard most of the conversation. The tow truck key, and Shorty, and the burned motel. He had heard the guy say he thought he and the woman were the last two standing. Her name was Patty Sundstrom, according to the banker, just before he died. Shorty would be Shorty Fleck. Canadians. Stranded.

'I got money,' Mark said. 'You can have it.'

'Don't want it,' Reacher said. 'Don't need it.'

'Got to be some way we can work this out.'

Reacher said, 'Patty, pick up his gun. Very carefully. Finger and thumb on the grip.'

She did. She came close and ducked down and grabbed the gun and scuttled back. Reacher bent Mark's arm at the elbow, ninety degrees, like he was waving, then more, until his forearm was folded back tight on his upper arm, and his hand was touching his shoulder.

Then more. Reacher pulled Mark's hand below the horizontal, scraping it down the back of his shoulder blade, two inches, four, six. Which put all kinds of stress on all kinds of joints. Mostly the elbow. But the shoulder too. And all the ligaments and tendons in between.

Reacher took his arrow away from Mark's throat, and his elbow off his chest, and Mark dropped gratefully to his knees, to relieve the pressure on his arm. Reacher changed his grip. He let go of his wrist and bunched his fist in his collar, and twisted, to make a tight figure eight, to choke him against the button.

Then he looked at Patty and said, 'Do you want to do it, or should I?'

'Do what?'

'Shoot him.'

She didn't answer.

'You said you wished he had burned up in the fire.'

'Who are you?' she said again.

'Long story,' he said again. 'I have an appointment in the morning, south of here. I needed a motel for the night. This was all I could find.'

'We should call the police.'

'Were you headed somewhere?'

'Florida,' she said. 'We wanted a new life.'

'Doing what?'

'Windsurfer rentals. Maybe jet skis too. Shorty got the idea of T-shirts.'

'Living where?'

'A shack on the beach. Maybe over the store.'

'Sounds great.'

'We thought so.'

'Alternatively you could spend three years living in a chain hotel somewhere in New Hampshire, talking to really obnoxious people, half the time bored to death, and the other half scared to death. Want to do that instead?'

'No.'

'That's what will happen if we call the police. You'll be talking to detectives and prosecutors and lawyers and psychiatrists, over and over again, including some pretty tough questions along the way, because they'll do the math the same way I have. I came in from the road, and the action was always ahead of me. So far I caught up to four of them. I'm guessing there were more to come, originally.'

'There were six originally.'

'What happened to the first two?'

She didn't answer. Just breathed in, and breathed out.

'You would win in the end,' Reacher said. 'Probably. Some kind of justifiable homicide, or self defence. But nothing is certain. Also you're foreigners. Overall it would be a rollercoaster. You wouldn't be allowed to leave the state. All they get here is the Red Sox. You need to think about this carefully.'

She said nothing.

Reacher said, 'Most likely better if we don't call the cops.'

Mark started to struggle.

Reacher said to Patty, 'He wanted to leave Shorty to die.'

She paused a long moment.

She looked down at the gun in her hand.

'Come around,' Reacher said. 'So you're pointing it away from me.'

She came and stood next to him.

Mark struggled and thrashed, harder and crazier, until Reacher hauled him upright and punched him hard in the solar plexus, and lowered him down again, not exactly still, but at least momentarily incapable of voluntary muscular control.

379

Reacher said, 'Stick the tip of the suppressor hard in his back, between his shoulder blades. About six inches below where I'm grabbing him. The safety is a little tab on the front of the trigger. It clicks in as soon as your finger is in the correct position. Then all you do is squeeze.'

She nodded.

She stood still for what felt like twenty seconds.

She said, 'I can't.'

Reacher let go of Mark's collar, and sent him sprawling with a push. He took the Glock from Patty. He said, 'I wanted you to have the opportunity. That was all. Otherwise you would have wondered all your life. But now you know. You're a good person, Patty.'

'Thank you.'

'Better than me,' he said.

He turned and shot Mark in the head. Twice. A fast tight double tap, low in the back of the skull. What the army schools called the assassination shot. Not that they would ever admit it.

They used the Mercedes to go get Shorty. First Reacher dragged the tow truck guy into the trees on one side of the track, and then Mark on the other. Out of the way. He didn't want to drive over them. Not if Shorty had a broken leg. Bumps would shake him up.

Patty drove. She got turned around and headed back with high beam headlights. She came out of the mouth of the track. She paused there a moment. Up ahead and two acres away the motel was a low pile of glowing embers. The cars in front of it were burned out and ashy. The barn was burning fiercely. The house was burning harder. The flames could have been fifty feet high.

Two riderless quad bikes stood abandoned near the centre of the meadow. There were two humped shapes on the ground next to them.

'There were four altogether,' Patty said. 'Mark, Peter, Steven, and Robert.'

'I heard gunshots,' Reacher said. 'Not long ago. Suppressed nine-millimetre rounds. I think Mark just dissolved the partnership.'

'Where's the fourth guy?'

'In the house, probably. I wouldn't have heard a gunshot from there. There won't be much left behind.'

They watched the flames for a minute more, and then Patty turned a tight left and drove across the bumpy grass close to the edge of the woods. She watched carefully. She slowed down in two separate places, and took a long hard look, but both times she looked away and drove on. Finally she stopped. She kept her hands on the wheel.

She said, 'It all looks the same now.'

Reacher asked, 'How deep in is he?'

'I can't remember. We walked a bit, and then I dragged him further. To where I thought he was safe.'

'Where did you go in?'

'Between two trees.'

'Doesn't help.'

'I think it was here.'

They shut down and got out. Without headlights the world was pitch dark. Patty put her headset on again, and Reacher dropped his tube down in place. Infinite green detail came back. Patty turned her head left and right. She looked at the front rank of trees. At the spaces between.

'I think it was here,' she said again.

They pushed into the forest. She led the way. They walked a slow curve, east and north. As if aiming to hit the track maybe thirty yards along its length. Thirty yards from its mouth. They stepped left and right around trees. Vines and bushes clawed at their ankles.

381

Patty said, 'I don't recognize anything.'

Reacher called out, 'Shorty? Shorty Fleck?'

Patty called out, 'Shorty, it's me. Where are you?'

Nothing.

They walked on. Every ten paces they stopped and called and shouted and yelled. Then they stood still and held their breath and listened.

Nothing.

Until the third time they did it.

They heard a tiny sound. Distant, quiet, metallic, slow. *Tink, tink, tink.* Due east, Reacher thought, maybe forty yards away.

He called out, 'Shorty Fleck?'

Tink, tink, tink.

They changed direction. They hustled. Trees, vines, brambles, bushes. They called out his name every step of the way, first Patty, then Reacher, taking turns. They heard *tink, tink, tink*, getting louder with every step. They followed the sound.

They found him slumped against a tree. Exhausted with pain. He had night vision on. He had an arrow in his hand. He was tapping it against the optical tube. *Tink, tink, tink.* It was all he could do.

Reacher carried him back and laid him out across the rear seat of the Mercedes. His leg was busted bad. The wound was a mess. He had lost a lot of blood. He was pale but hot. He was damp with sweat.

Patty said, 'Where should we take him?'

'Probably better to get out of the county,' Reacher said. 'You should go to Manchester. It's a bigger place.'

'Are you not coming with us?'

Reacher shook his head.

'Not all the way,' he said. 'I have an appointment in the morning.'

382

'They'll ask questions at the hospital.'

'Tell them it was a motorcycle accident. They'll believe you. Hospitals believe anything about motorcycles. They won't need to report it. It's obviously not a gunshot wound. You could tell them he fell on a piece of metal.'

'OK.'

'Get him set, and then go park the car somewhere quiet. Leave the doors unlocked and the key in. You need it to disappear pretty quick. Then you're home and dry.'

'OK,' she said again.

She got behind the wheel. Reacher got in the passenger seat, half turned around to keep an eye on Shorty. Patty turned a wide slow circle over the lumpy ground. Shorty bounced and jostled and gasped. Patty turned in at the mouth of the track.

Shorty slapped the seat beside him, once, twice, weak and feeble.

Reacher said, 'What?'

Shorty opened his mouth. No words would come out. He tried again.

He whispered, 'Suitcase.'

Patty drove on, slow and steady.

'We had a suitcase in the room,' she said. 'I guess it burned up.'

Shorty slapped the seat again.

'I took it out,' he whispered.

Patty stopped the car.

'Where is it?' she said.

'In the grass,' he said. 'Across the lot.'

She backed up, inexpertly, corkscrewing a little, and then she turned around in the mouth of the track and set out forward across the meadow. Past the abandoned bikes, and the bodies.

'Peter and Robert,' she said.

She drove on. She stopped in the lot. They could feel the heat through the windows. Reacher saw the metal cage, sticking up

383

out of the carpet of coals. Steel bars and steel mesh. Scorched and distorted. Room ten. Shorty moved his forearm, back and forth, just once, weak and vague and limp, like an old priest pronouncing a benediction, or a wounded man miming a journey. *From there to there.* Reacher got out and walked up level with the metal cage. He turned and walked to the edge of the grass. A straight line. The shortest distance between two points. He dropped his night-vision tube in place.

He saw the suitcase immediately. It was a huge old leather thing tied up with rope. It was lying flat in the grass. He stepped over and picked it up. It weighed a ton. Maybe two. He struggled back with it, lopsided. Patty got out and opened the trunk for him. He rested the case on the ground.

He said, 'What the hell have you got in here?'

'Comics,' she said. 'More than a thousand. All the great ones. Lots of early *Superman*. From our dads and granddads. We were going to sell them in New York, to pay for Florida.'

There were two bags already stashed in the trunk. Two soft leather duffels, zipped and bulging. Reacher took a look inside. They were both full of money. Both full of bricks and bricks of cash, all neatly stacked. Mostly hundred-dollar bills, mostly banded into inch-thick wads. Ten thousand bucks at a time, according to the printed labels. There were about fifty bricks in each bag. Maybe a million dollars in total.

'You should keep the comics,' Reacher said. 'You should use this instead. You could buy all the windsurfers you want.'

'We can't,' Patty said. 'It isn't ours.'

'I think it is. You won the game. I'm guessing this is what they put in the pot. Who else should have it?'

'It's a fortune.'

'You earned it,' Reacher said. 'Don't you think?'

She said nothing.

Then she asked, 'Do you want some?'

'I have enough to get by,' Reacher said. 'I don't need more.'

He hefted the suitcase up and slid it in the trunk.

The Mercedes sagged on its springs.

'What's your name?' Patty asked. 'I would like to know.'

'Reacher.'

She paused.

She said, 'That was Mark's name.'

'Different branch of the family.'

They got back in the car, and she drove through the meadow, into the woods, almost two miles, all the way to the tow truck. Reacher took the key and climbed up and let himself in. Heavy pressure. He was a bad driver anyway, and the controls were unfamiliar. But after a minute he got the lights turned on. Then he got the engine started. He found the gear selector and shoved it in reverse. A screen on the dashboard lit up, with a rear view camera. A wide-angle lens. A colour picture. It showed an ancient Subaru, parked right behind the truck, just waiting.

FORTY-THREE

Reacher climbed down from the cab, and gave Patty a wait-one signal, which he hoped she understood. Then he squeezed and slid down the side of the truck, to the rear, and out to the air.

Burke met him right there. The Reverend Patrick G. He had his hands up, palms out, in a kind of placatory *I know, I know* gesture. Patting the air. Apologizing in advance.

He said, 'Detective Amos called on my phone. She said I should find you and tell you 10-41. I don't know what that means.'

'It's a military police radio code,' Reacher said. 'It means immediate callback requested.'

'There's no cell service here.'

'We'll head south. But first move your car so I can move the truck. We got someone else also heading south. They're in a bigger hurry.'

He squeezed back to the cab, and gave Patty what he hoped was a reassuring wave from the ladder. He got the selector back in reverse. He saw a live picture of Burke backing up, so he backed up

386

after him, a little jerky, sometimes off line, fighting the trees here and there, beating most of them, getting thumped pretty hard once or twice. When he got out to the road he swung the wheel, and parked backward on the opposite shoulder, not totally straight, but not embarrassing either.

The black Mercedes nosed out after him.

He climbed down from the cab.

The Mercedes stopped beside him.

Patty buzzed the window down.

He said, 'I'm getting a ride from the guy in the Subaru. It was nice meeting you. Good luck in Florida.'

She craned up in her seat, and looked down at the road.

'We're out,' she said. 'At last. Thank you. I mean it. I feel we owe you.'

'You would have figured it out,' Reacher said. 'You still had the flashlight. It would have worked just as well. Four big batteries, all kinds of fancy LEDs. It's not just a night-vision thing. His first shot would have missed. Then you would have been in the trees.'

'But then what?'

'Rinse and repeat. I bet he didn't have a spare magazine. He seems to have packed in a hurry.'

'Thank you,' she said again. 'I mean it.'

'Good luck in Florida,' he said again. 'Welcome to America.'

He crossed the road to where the Subaru was waiting. She drove away, south. She raised a hand through her open window, like a wave, and then she kept it there a hundred yards, fingers open, feeling the rush of night-time air against her palm.

Burke drove south, on the back road. Reacher watched the bars on the phone. Burke was concerned about the lateness of the hour. He said he was sure Detective Amos would be fast asleep in bed by then. Reacher said he was sure she meant it when she sent the 10-41. Immediate callback. She could have used a different code.

One bar came up, and then a second, and then the wide gravel shoulder they had used before. Burke pulled over. Reacher dialled the number. Amos answered right away. Not asleep. There was car noise. She was driving.

She said, 'The Boston PD called to tell us the cleanup hitter got home in the middle of the evening.'

'Does he have Carrington?'

'They're making inquiries.'

'What about Elizabeth Castle?'

'Both are still missing.'

'Maybe I should go to Boston.'

'You have somewhere else to go first.'

'Where?'

She said, 'I found Stan Reacher.'

'OK.'

'He showed up thirty years ago. He lived on his own for a long spell, and then he moved in with a younger relative. He's registered to vote and he still has a driver's licence.'

'OK,' Reacher said again.

'I called his house. He wants to see you.'

'When?'

'Now.'

'It's late.'

'He has insomnia. Normally he watches TV. He says you're welcome to come over and talk all night.'

'Where does he live?'

'Laconia,' she said. 'Right here in town. Chances are you walked right by his house.'

It turned out the closest Reacher had previously gotten was two streets away, in his second hotel. He could have made a left out the door, and a right, and a left, and then found an alley like the one where the cocktail waitress lived, with a door on the right and a door on the left, in this case not to upstairs apartments, but to neat three-storey townhouses set either side of an interior courtyard.

Stan lived in the house on the left.

Amos met them in an unmarked car, out on the kerb, at the entrance to the alley. She shook Burke's hand and said she was pleased to meet him. Then she turned to Reacher and asked if he felt OK. She said, 'This could be very weird.'

'Not very,' he said. 'Maybe a little. I think I figured most of it out. There was always something wrong with the story. Now I know what. Because of something old Mr Mortimer said.'

'Who is old Mr Mortimer?'

'The old guy in the old people's home. He said back in the day from time to time he would visit his cousins in Ryantown. He said he remembers the birdwatching boys. He said he was drafted near the end of the war. He said they didn't need him. They had too many people already. He said he never did anything, and felt like a fraud every July Fourth parade.'

Amos said nothing.

They all went to the door together. More seemly, Burke insisted, given the hour. Like delivering a death message, Reacher thought. Two MPs and a priest.

He rang the bell.

A whole minute later a hallway light came on. He saw it through a pebbled glass pane set high in the door. He saw a broken-up mosaic of calm cream colours, a long narrow space, with what might have been family photographs on the wall.

He saw an old man shuffle into view. A broken-up mosaic. Stooped, grey, slow, unsteady. He walked with his knuckles pressed on a millwork rail. He got closer and closer, and then he opened the door.

FORTY-FOUR

The old man who opened the door was about ninety. He was thin and stooped inside too-big clothing, maybe favourite stuff bought long ago, back when he was a vigorous seventy. He could have started out six-one and 190, at his peak, before the start of a long decline. Now he was bent over like a question mark. His skin was slack and translucent. His eyes watered. He had strands of grey hair, as fine as silk.

He wasn't Reacher's father.

Not even thirty years older. Because he wasn't. Simple as that. Also forensically, because no broken nose, no shrapnel scar on his cheek, no stitch mark in his eyebrow.

The photographs on the wall were of birds.

The old man held out a wavering hand.

'Stan Reacher,' he said. 'I'm pleased to meet you.'

Reacher shook the old man's hand. It felt cold as ice.

'Jack Reacher,' he said. 'Likewise.'

'Are we related?'

'We're all related, if you go back far enough.'

'Please come in.'

Amos said she and Burke would wait in the car. Reacher followed the old guy down the hallway. Slower than a funeral march. Half a step, a long pause, another half a step. They made it to a nook between the living room and an eat-in kitchen. It had two armchairs, set one each side of a lamp with a big fringed shade. Good for reading.

Old Stan Reacher waved his wavering hand at one of the armchairs, like an invitation, and he sat down in the other. He was happy to talk. He was happy to answer questions. He didn't seem to find them strange. He confirmed he grew up in Ryantown, in the tin mill foreman's apartment. He remembered the kitchen tile. Acanthus leaves, and marigolds, and artichoke blossoms. James and Elizabeth Reacher were his parents. The tin mill foreman himself, and the bed sheet finisher. He said it never occurred to him to wonder whether they did a good job or not. Partly because it was all he knew, and partly because he didn't notice anyway, because he had been introduced to birdwatching by then, which had given him a whole other world to go live in. He said it wasn't about checking off new sightings on a list. There was a clue in the word. It was about watching. What they did, and how, and why, and where, and when. It was about thinking yourself into whole new dimensions, with whole new problems and whole new powers.

Reacher asked, 'Who introduced you?'

'My cousin Bill,' Stan said.

'Who was he?'

'It was a time, back then. Somehow most of the boys you hung out with were your cousins. Maybe it was a tribal instinct. People were afraid. It was tough times. For a spell it looked like the whole thing could fall apart. I guess cousins were reassuring. Any kid's best friend was likely his cousin. Bill was mine and I was his.'

'What kind of cousin was he?'

'Neither one of us could count high enough. All we knew was I was Stan Reacher and he was William Reacher, and way back we both had the same ancestor in the Dakota Territory. I suppose the truth is Bill was a waif and stray. He seemed to be based up on the Canadian border. But he was always roaming. He spent a lot of time in Ryantown.'

'How old was he, the first time he came?'

'I was seven, so he was six. He stayed a whole year.'

'Did he have parents?'

'We supposed so. He never saw them. But they weren't dead or anything. He got birthday cards every year. We thought they must be secret agents, undercover in a foreign country. Later we thought they were more likely organized crime. Whichever required a greater degree of secrecy. Which was sometimes hard to tell.'

'Was he already a birdwatcher at the age of six?'

'With the naked eye. Which he always thought was best of all. He wasn't good at explaining why. He was only a kid. Later we understood. After we got binoculars. You get a bigger picture with the naked eye. You don't get distracted by the close-up beauty.'

'How did you get the binoculars?'

'That was much later. Bill would have been ten or eleven by then.'

'How did you get them?'

The old man looked down for a second.

He said, 'You got to remember, it was a time, back then.'

'Did he steal them?'

'Not exactly. They were spoils of war. Some kid with a stupid vendetta. Bill ran out of patience. We had been reading old battle poems. He said he felt he should seize something. The binoculars and thirty-one cents were all the kid had.'

'You wrote about the rough-legged hawk together.'

The old man nodded.

'We sure did,' he said. 'That was a fine piece of work. I would be proud of that today.'

'Do you remember September 1943?'

'I guess a few things in general.'

'Anything special?'

'It was a long time ago,' the old man said.

'Your name comes up in an old police report, about an altercation on the street. Late one evening. In fact not far from here. You were seen with a friend.'

'There were altercations on the street all the time.'

'This one involved a local bully who was beaten to death two years later.'

Stan Reacher said nothing.

'I'm guessing the friend you were seen with that night in September 1943 was your cousin Bill. I think he started something that took two years to finish.'

'Tell me again, who are you exactly?'

'I'm not exactly sure,' Reacher said. 'As of right now, I'm thinking maybe your cousin Bill's second son.'

'Then you know what happened.'

'I was a military cop. I saw it a dozen times.'

'Am I in trouble?'

'Not with me,' Reacher said. 'The only person I'm mad at is myself. I guess I assumed this was the kind of thing that happened to other people.'

'Bill was a smart boy. He was always a step ahead, partly because he had a varied life. Streetwise, they would call it now. But he knew other stuff too. He was good at his books. He knew a lot of science. He loved his birds. He liked to be left alone. He was a nice person, back when that meant something. But you better not mess with his sense of right and wrong. Underneath he was a bomb waiting to go off. He had it under control. He was a very self-disciplined person. He had a rule. If you did a bad thing, he would make sure you only did it once. Whatever it took. He was a good fighter, and he was brave as a lunatic.'

'Tell me about the kid he killed.'

Stan shook his head.

'I shouldn't do that,' he said. 'I would be confessing to a crime.'

'Were you involved?'

'Not at the end, I guess.'

'No one will bust you. You're a hundred years old.'

'Not quite.'

'No one is interested. The cops filed it under NHI.'

'What does that mean?'

'No human involved.'

Stan nodded.

'I could agree with them,' he said. 'That kid was every kind of bully. He had a grudge against anyone with one brain cell more. Which was a lot of people. He was the kind of kid who hung around four years after high school, doing the same old things to younger and younger victims. But in a nice car, wearing nice shoes, because his daddy was rich. His brain was rotting away from the inside. He became perverted. He started interfering with little boys and girls. He was real big and strong. He was tormenting them. He was making them do disgusting things. At that point Bill didn't know about him. Then he came back to town and found out, that night.'

'What happened?'

'Bill showed up in Ryantown, like he often did, out of nowhere, and for his first night we came down here, to the jazz lounge. There was a band we liked. They usually let us in. We were walking back to where we hid our bikes, and then all of a sudden the kid came walking towards us. He ignored Bill and started tormenting me on my own. Because he knew me. He was probably starting up again where he left off the last time. But Bill was hearing this stuff for the very first time. He couldn't believe it. I got it to where we could walk away, but Bill didn't come with me. The bomb went off. He took the kid apart.'

'Then what?'

'Then it became a different story. The kid put out a kind of death warrant. Bill started carrying brass knuckles. There were a couple of incidents. A couple of would-be friends, trying to make their bones. We figured rich kids got that a lot. Bill kept the emergency room busy. He sent the would-be friends their way. Then it was a background thing for a while. Bill was in and out of Ryantown. Then it blew up again. One night they ended up all alone, face to face. The first I knew about it was Bill showing up later, asking for a favour.'

'He wanted to borrow your birth certificate, to join the Marines.'

Stan nodded.

'He needed to bury the name William Reacher. He felt he had to do it. He needed the trail to go cold. It was a homicide, after all.'

'And he needed to be a year older than he really was,' Reacher said. 'That's what was wrong with the story he told. He said he ran away and joined the Marines at seventeen. No doubt that's true, in and of itself. But he couldn't have done it if the Marines knew he was seventeen. They wouldn't have taken him. Not then. They already had too many people. It was September 1945. The war was over. They wouldn't want a seventeen-year-old. Two years earlier, sure, no problem at all. They were fighting in the Pacific. They needed to keep the conveyor belt going. But not any more. On the other hand, an eighteen-year-old was always entitled to volunteer. So he needed your ID.'

Stan nodded again.

'We thought it would make him safe,' he said. 'And it did, I guess. The cops gave up. I left Ryantown soon afterwards. I went bird-watching in South America and stayed there forty years. When I got home I had to sign up for all kinds of new things. I used the same birth certificate. I wondered what would happen if the system said the name Stan Reacher was already taken. But it all worked out fine.'

Reacher nodded.

'Thank you for explaining,' he said.

'What happened to him?' Stan said. 'I never saw him again.'

'He became a pretty good Marine. He fought in Korea and Vietnam. He served in all kinds of other places. He married a Frenchwoman. Her name was Josephine. They got along. They had two boys. He died thirty years ago.'

'Did he have a happy life?'

'He was a Marine. Happy was not in the field manual. Sometimes he was satisfied. That was about as good as it got. But he was never unhappy. He felt he belonged. He had a structure he could rely on. I don't think he would have chosen anything different. He kept on birdwatching. He loved his family. He was glad he had it. We all knew that. Sometimes we thought he was crazy. He wasn't sure of his birthday. Now I understand why. Yours was July, and his was originally June. He would remember that, because of the birthday cards. I guess sometimes he got confused. Although he did fine with the name. I never heard him slip. He was always Stan.'

They talked a while longer. Reacher asked about the motel, and their theoretical relative Mark, but Stan had no information beyond a vague old family story about some other distant cousin getting rich during the postwar boom, and buying real estate, and then having a cascade of offspring, all kinds of children and grandchildren and great-grandchildren. Presumably Mark was one of them. Stan said he didn't know, and didn't want to. He said he was happy with his photo albums, and his memories.

Then he said he needed to nap for an hour. That was how it went, he said, with his kind of insomnia. He took hour-long naps whenever he could. Reacher shook his ice-cold hand once more and let himself out of the house. Dawn was coming. The morning sun was not far away. Burke and Amos were sitting together, in Amos's car, on the kerb, at the entrance to the alley. They saw him

396

step out. Burke buzzed his window down. Amos leaned over to listen. Reacher checked the sky again, and bent down to talk.

He said, 'I need to go to Ryantown.'

Burke said, 'The professor won't be there for hours.'

'That's why.'

Amos said, 'I need to think about Carrington.'

'Think about him in Ryantown. It's as good a place as any.'

'Do you know something?'

'We should be looking for Elizabeth Castle just as much as Carrington himself. They're very romantic. They counted their morning coffee break as their second date. They're almost certainly together.'

'Sure, but where?'

'I'll tell you later. First I want to go to Ryantown again.'

FORTY-FIVE

They went in Amos's unmarked car. She drove, and Burke sat neatly beside her. Reacher sprawled in the back. He told them everything Stan had told him. They asked how he felt. It was a short conversation. He said nothing had changed, except a very minor historical detail. His father had once been called by a different name, way back long ago, when he was a kid. First he was Bill, then he was Stan. Same guy. Same bomb waiting to go off. But disciplined. If you did the right thing, he left you alone. A good fighter, and brave as a lunatic.

He loved his family.

A birdwatcher all his life.

Often with the naked eye, for a bigger picture.

'Did your mother know?' Amos asked.

'Great question,' Reacher said. 'Probably not. It turned out she had secrets of her own. I think neither of them knew. I think they allowed for things like that. A clean slate. No questions. Maybe that's why they got along.'

'She must have wondered why he had no parents.'

398

'I guess.'

'Do you wonder now?'

'A little bit. Because of the birthday cards. That has a certain flavour. It feels like an obscure department of a government agency. It takes care of things while you're away. It makes sure your rent gets paid. Or else they were in prison. I would have to know the return address.'

Burke said, 'Are you going to try to find out?'

'No,' Reacher said.

On their right the sky was streaked with dawn. The car was filled with low golden light. Amos found the turn to Ryantown. The gentle left, through the orchards. The sun burned around behind them, until it was low and dead centre in the rear windshield. Amos shaded her eyes from the mirror, and came to a stop at the fence.

'Five minutes,' Reacher said.

He got out of the car and stepped over the fence. He walked through the orchard. The dawn light was on his back. His shadow was infinitely long. He stepped over the next fence. The Ryantown city limit. The darker leaves, the damper smell. The sunless shadows.

He walked down Main Street, like before, between the thin trees, on the tipped-up stones, past the church, past the school. After that the trees grew thinner, and the sun crept higher. Dappled sunbeams twinkled in. The world was new.

He heard voices up ahead.

Two people talking. Lightly, and happily. About something pleasant. Maybe the sunbeams. If so, Reacher agreed. The place looked great. Like an ad for an expensive camera.

He called out, 'Hey guys, officer on the floor, coming in, make yourselves decent and stand by your beds.'

He didn't want to embarrass them. Or himself. There were a number of things that could go wrong. She could be naked. He could have his leg off.

He waited a minute. Neither thing happened. He walked down to the four-flats and found Carter Carrington and Elizabeth Castle standing side by side on the ghost of the road, halfway to the stream. They were staring at him. They were both fully dressed. Albeit in a casual manner. He was in a muscle shirt and athletic pants. She was in cut-off jeans and a T-shirt that didn't quite meet them. Beyond them were two mountain bikes, leaning on trees. Fat tyres, and strong racks on the back, for heavy packs. Beyond the bikes a two-person tent was pitched, on the gritty dirt where the mill foreman's living room used to be.

Carrington said, 'Good morning.'

'You too.'

Then no one spoke.

'It's always good to see you,' Carrington said.

'You too.'

'But is this purely a coincidence?'

'Not exactly,' Reacher said.

'You were looking for us.'

'Something came up. Turned out to be nothing. It's all good now. But I thought I should drop by anyway. To say goodbye. I'm moving out.'

'How did you find us?'

'For once I listened to the front of my brain. I guess I remembered how it felt. For me once or twice, and maybe for you guys now. Just when you think it's passing you by, boom, you meet someone. You do all the sappy things you thought you were never going to get a chance to do. You invent a new anniversary every couple of hours. You celebrate the thing that brought you together. Some people do really weird stuff. You do Stan Reacher. You already told me you talk about him on dates. You were last seen at the county offices. You were tracing Stan's birth record. You wanted to do it properly, every step of the way. Rigorously, and meticulously, like a person should. To make it yours. It's of

400

sentimental value. You got the last known address. Elizabeth already knew where it was, because she and I worked it out together, on her phone. So you went to find it. You took the heritage tour. Because that's what people do.'

They smiled and held hands.

Reacher said, 'I'm glad you're happy.'

Elizabeth Castle said, 'Thank you.'

'And it shouldn't make a material difference.'

'What shouldn't?'

'In the interests of full disclosure, I have to tell you it turns out Stan Reacher was not who I was looking for.'

'He was your father.'

'Turns out he was just a borrowed birth certificate.'

'I see.'

'I hope that doesn't put a jinx on your relationship.'

'Who borrowed the birth certificate?'

'An obscure cousin with no known antecedents. A blank space on the family tree.'

'How does that make you feel?'

'Absolutely great,' Reacher said. 'The less I know, the happier I get.'

'And now you're moving on.'

'It was nice to meet you. I wish you both the best of luck.'

Carrington said, 'What was the cousin's name?'

'William.'

'Would you mind if we looked into him? It could be interesting. It's the kind of thing we enjoy.'

'Knock yourselves out,' Reacher said.

Then he said, 'In exchange for a favour.'

'What kind?'

'Come say hello to a friend of mine. Just a five-minute walk. I'm sure you guys know her. Detective Amos, from the Laconia PD.'

'Brenda?' Carrington said. 'Why is she here?'

401

'Theoretically there might have been a threat against you. She won't believe it's over until she sees for herself. I want you to go tell her you're alive and well, taking a break, and you'll be back in town whenever.'

'What kind of threat?'

'You slightly resembled the target of an attempted gangland killing. Detective Amos's extreme thoroughness and lateral thinking made it a concern.'

'Brenda was worried about me?'

'You're the guy who goes to bat for them. They seem to like you. It's a sign of weakness. You need to be tougher in future.'

They walked up Main Street together. Past the school. Past the church. Out to the sunny order of the orchard. Amos and Burke waited at the far fence. There were handshakes across the top rail. Assurances were given. Explanations were made. Vacation, no cell service, apologies. No problem, Amos said. Just following up.

Carrington and Castle walked back.

Reacher watched them go. He climbed the fence and stood with the others. He said, 'I decided to skip the professor. Maybe you could give him a call.'

'Sure,' Burke said.

'Back to town now?' Amos asked.

Reacher shook his head.

'I'm going to San Diego.'

'From here?'

'Seems appropriate. My dad started out from here many times. This was one of the places he lived. A whole year, when he was six.'

'You seriously want us to leave you in the middle of nowhere?'

'I'll get a ride. I've done it before. About forty minutes. That's my guess right now. Based on conditions. Worst case fifty. You guys get going. It was a pleasure to meet you. I mean it. I appreciate your kindness.'

They all stood for a moment, doing nothing. Then they all shook hands, kind of sudden and awkward. Two MPs and a priest. All buttoned up.

Burke and Amos got in the car. Reacher watched them drive away. The low morning sun boiled around them. Then they were gone. He set out walking in the same direction. Through the same gentle curve. The sun was in his eyes all the way. He made it to the north–south back road. He picked a spot, and stood in the gutter, and stuck out his thumb.

Exclusive for this Waterstones Edition

Extracts transcribed from a
conversation between
Lee Child and **John Grisham**
at the Theakston Crime Writing
Festival, Harrogate, July 2018

Lee Child: I remember reading your first book, *A Time to Kill*. It struck me as very much a father's book, in the rage, in that book, of the parent.

John Grisham: Well, yeah. The rage, the parent's retribution. When I wrote that book, I didn't have a daughter. And I'm not sure I could go back and . . . I couldn't write that first chapter, which is the raped little girl, which actually is based on a true story in Mississippi. I've always found it hard to go back and read that as I've gotten older, and I'm not sure I could write that story today. It's very violent.

Lee Child: When I look back at that book, it was clearly a Southern novel, a passionate novel, a real emotional tour de force. And then *The Firm*. It was the weirdest book for me. There was something so magnetic about it. Even the title, which was such a bland, anodyne title by itself. *[laughter]*

John Grisham: Let's talk about some of your titles! *[laughter]*

Lee Child: I remember being in the airport in Manchester, and just seeing that book and that title. It was clear that it was something more than just – The Firm. And the beginning of the book, I felt, was so dead on the zeitgeist of that moment. It was about this young lawyer who is poor, from a poor background. He succeeded at law school. He's offered this job where they're going to give him a great salary and they're going to pay off his law school loan and they're going to give him a BMW, which is like everybody's fantasy at that time.

John Grisham: You gotta love fiction. *[laughter]*

Lee Child: But it so hit the note. After the Reagan and Thatcher years, this sort of yuppie thing had come in, it just hit the spot irresistibly.

John Grisham: By the way, *The Firm*, that title was always a working title, because I really struggle with titles. It should be obvious: they're all one word titles, at least most of them. But I have a hard time every year when starting one – you probably go through this too – you want *To Kill a Mockingbird*, you know? You want a great title. You want *The Grapes of Wrath*. You want something great in the title. And it's just not there . . . They're hard to find. They've already been used.

Lee Child: Yeah. I've had long discussions about titles. I just want my new book to be called *A Very Exciting Book. [laughter]*

John Grisham: And you got Jack Reacher 13, Jack Reacher 14. *[laughter]*

Lee Child: Yeah, that's how they listed them out on Amazon, so why not?

John Grisham: Well, seriously, how do you go about finding the title, and at what point in the process do you have a title?

Lee Child: It varies. I got the title for next year's book already, but I have no idea—

John Grisham: What is it?

Lee Child: *Blue Moon.*

John Grisham: I'm not going to use it. *[laughter]*

Lee Child: That was a song. This year's book is called *Past Tense*, and it was a joke, because it's vaguely to do with the past. I was going to call it *Yesterday*, but they said there was a song called that. So I said, 'It's got to be something to do with the past.' And I thought, 'Well, I'm a writer. I can do grammar. So – *Past Tense*.' It was a joke. And they said, 'Yeah, that's great.' *[laughter]*

                The Firm was obvious film material . . . Did the movie rights sell first on *The Firm*?

John Grisham: Well, when I finished *The Firm* I sent the manuscript off to New York, but my agent was not overly excited about it. Did he show it? . . . No. He wanted me to make a bunch of changes first, a bunch of gratuitous violence and sex added to it.

Lee Child: Make it more like a Jack Reacher book? *[laughter]*

John Grisham: Reacher gets laid, but not enough. *[laughter]*

                I had a hard time with the gratuitous violence and sex, and I said, 'No. I'm not going to add stuff to the story just to spice it up. It's already good enough.' And so we butted heads. I wouldn't change anything, and he wouldn't show it around. Then in the first week in January of 1990, he called one day and said, 'We just sold the film rights to *The Firm* for a lot of money.'

                The movie came out twenty-five years ago this month. That puts some age on us. *The Pelican Brief* came out six months later. And then, six months after that, the movie *The Client* came out. So we had three big movies in a span of twelve months. That really was a very exciting time for all of us. And those movies are still on somewhere tonight. Still selling books. I'd love to make more movies.

Lee Child: Do you still get paid for them when they get shown on TV?

John Grisham: Yeah. Yeah. The movies still sell paperbacks too. Those first book deals were not that lucrative. So we're way beyond the advances. *The Firm* did okay. We all love Tom Cruise, don't we? *[laughter, applause]*

Lee Child: We do. There's one major difference – he was the right size for *your* guy. *[laughter, applause]*

So, to come back to the lawyering thing, can I point out that lots of lawyers want to become writers. I've never met a writer who wants to become a lawyer. *[laughter]*

John Grisham: Nor have I. There's a lot of dissatisfaction in the profession. Whether it's big firms, mega firms where the pressure is enormous – the money is big, but so is the job and the pressure . . . not fun.

The most fun I had with practising law was using the law degree as a tool, sometimes as a hammer, to help people. I did a lot of volunteer work with kids who got into trouble. And it's the cases I never got paid for that I remember as doing something real for society. But again, I had a wife and kids; you've got to make a living. So I did that for about ten years. And then as soon as *The Firm* sold and things went crazy I had no problem walking out of the law office without turning off the lights.

I was thirty-five, thirty-four when I started writing – how old were you?

410

Lee Child:	I was probably forty when I started writing. And therefore probably forty-two when the first book came out. So a little bit later.
John Grisham:	So it wasn't a childhood dream?
Lee Child:	No, no. I mean, I loved reading. I loved books. But to be honest I was about thirty-five before I even enquired where books came from. I just sort of thought they were there. I just loved entertainment. Ideally, I would have been one of The Beatles. That was my dream.
John Grisham:	All right, I have a question for you. After twenty years, twenty-one years of Reacher – I've read most of your books, not all of your books, might as well tell the truth – have you ever done a non-Reacher book?
Lee Child:	No.
John Grisham:	Are you going to?
Lee Child:	When anyone else asks me that, my answer is, 'You want me to?'
Audience:	NO! *[laughter]*
Lee Child:	No, they always say, they want more Reacher. You know, I thought about writing a book about how my mother was mean to me while I was growing up on the Upper West Side, but I pickled that one. *[laughter]*
John Grisham:	Yeah. So . . .
Lee Child:	I'll tell you a story about a vacation I took in 1994, maybe? I went cycling in France.

So we were sitting on this car ferry with all these truck drivers, and they were all reading your book. All of them. Truck drivers reading your book. When I got home, so was my neighbour across the street, an extremely refined |

411

lady who was a retired principal of a very posh girls' school. I'd never seen a broader spread of audience than that, which obviously explains the numbers you were selling. I was impressed, as a reader. And now, as a writer, I want to know . . . how do you do that?

John Grisham: I'll tell *you* a story. I grew up in a very strict, conservative, Southern Baptist household with two parents who were both there. The family had modest means, but we were always very, very well loved and they were great parents.

My mother was very skittish about me writing for a popular audience. I'm not sure she ever finished *A Time to Kill* because she just couldn't get past the first chapter. And there were some curse words in there. And I said then I'm not going to write another book that's going to embarrass my mother.

So I wrote *The Firm* without the gratuitous violence, the sex scenes. And over the years many people tell me or write to me to say, 'I finished this book at three o'clock in the morning, exhausted' – which I love hearing *[laughter]* – 'and, once I finished, I realized I could give this book to my eighty-year-old mother or my fifteen-year-old teenager.'

You too have refused to use bad language in your books, and I respect you for that because it's very rare. But that's one reason the books have appeal to all people. I can't imagine truck drivers being impressed by that *[laughter]* but that has been a big factor.

Lee Child: I find that the absence of those words is never

412

noticed, while their presence is. Most people would think, if you asked them, they would think, 'Yeah, there's a lot of four-letter words in the Reacher books.' Well, actually, there are none. And I'm not entirely sure why, but I too must have had a hundred thousand letters saying 'I'm glad there are no four-letter words in these books'. And I have never had a single letter saying 'Please put some in'. *[laughter]*

John Grisham: So a couple of reviewers some years ago said something like 'The most unrealistic thing about this book is the language'. But it didn't bother me. My goal is to be ignored by critics. They never liked me, I don't like them, so . . . We write popular fiction, you know, not whatever they want.

Lee Child: The problem with that is that it's also unrealistic if you put the swearing in, because if you actually listen to how people talk, they use those words so frequently. Many times in a sentence. As nouns, verbs, adverbs. A constant stream. That's just how people talk. And if you were therefore to make it sound more realistic, the book would be a thousand pages long. *[laughter]* I think it's actually linguistically much safer not to have them there at all. More authentic.

John Grisham: Keep in mind, though, you do live in New York City. Where the language can be a bit rougher than the genteel South. *[laughter]*

Lee Child: The genteel South. Yes, obviously for the English context, America's kind of flipped upside down. Where—

John Grisham: In many ways, these days. *[laughter]*

Lee Child: With great respect, the south is seen differently than the north in some ways in Britain, and it's the reverse in America.

So you'd been living this absolute dream. I mean, it must have been insane for five years. Immense success. Unbelievable success. Money, presumably . . . but then the story is that you went back to court. To try a case. Because some years previously, when you were still a lawyer, you had promised somebody you would take their case. And it took a long time to filter through, and you went back to fight it, even though you obviously didn't need to. You had a whole different career by that point.

John Grisham: Sure didn't want to. Trial work is stressful when you do it. And I had not seen a courtroom in seven years.

A month before *The Firm* was published, a friend of mine brought me the case and said, 'Hey, this is interesting, we have to do this case.' A railroad worker had been killed on a job, crushed between two cars. It was really a potentially promising case. And I had chased those cases for ten years as a lawyer. So I signed the case up.

And then *The Firm* came out, and three to four years went by, with all the craziness, and I wanted that case just to go away. I didn't have time for it. I didn't need the money, I sure didn't want to go back to court in a small town in Mississippi. I was rusty with trial work.

We won the case, but I walked out of that courtroom saying 'Never again will I voluntarily enter a courtroom'. I do get dragged in a few times for lawsuits, though. You don't get sued, do you?

414

Lee Child: Not seriously, but I do get claimed against. It seems to be a sort of underground conspiracy that every time a book comes out, I probably get ten or twenty allegations that I've stolen someone else's story. And would I like to settle for ten thousand pounds? *[laughter]*

John Grisham: Every time?

Lee Child: Yeah, every time. And I just ignore it and nothing ever happens. *[laughter]*

John Grisham: I don't get it with every book, but I've been sued several times. It's never pleasant. I've never lost a case ever. I've never been near a trial; I always scare them off. Never settled, never paid a dime.

I wrote one book of non-fiction. Ten years ago – twelve years ago. About a wrongful conviction. And I made the mistake of writing about people who were still alive. And a few of them took offence, and they filed lawsuits against me, claiming defamation, slander, all that. Our laws are vastly different than the laws over here. And we were able to prevail. But again, it's not something you want to deal with.

Lee Child: Sure.

John Grisham: Avoid the lawyers if you can. *[laughter]*

Lee Child: Yes, well, I have definitely experienced that.

John Grisham: My son's a lawyer. We talk about the law all the time. That's where my stories come from. I read newspapers, magazines, I'm always on the prowl for some story about a case or a trial or a law firm or a Supreme Court decision or a judge . . . It's all about the law. That's where the stories come from.

Lee Child: But the lawyers that you write about, they seem so foreign to the British experience.

415

John Grisham: Well, in the US most lawyers are honest, hard-working people who represent clients well and don't make a lot of money . . .

Lee Child: Come on, tell the truth. *[laughter]*

John Grisham: The truth is nobody wants to read about those guys. You want to read about the lawyer who steals the money, fakes his death, and does something horrible . . . that's what you want to read about.

Lee Child: Those crazy one-man-band lawyers, *The Rainmaker* types of lawyer, I know they exist but they're so exotic compared to the British experience . . .

John Grisham: My number one rule for writing popular fiction – and I have a ton of them – is, I never write the first scene until I know the last scene. I don't need to, because I have an outline, I know where I'm going. Most writers, like you, will say I don't do an outline, I want the story to take over the characters and see where it goes. I cannot do that. I literally sit down once I have the beginning and the ending, and hopefully it's not predictable. And then I need to figure out some way to maintain the suspense, in three hundred pages, which is the hard part. The fun part's just writing the book. The fun part's to finish the damn book. *[laughter]*

There are good days and bad days; but there aren't many bad days. When you're in a jam with Reacher, you're probably having more fun, right?

Lee Child: Yeah, I'm completely different than you. I don't want to know the end. If I knew the end I'd get bored with the story. Sure, I do run into a dead end sometimes, but that's Reacher's problem, not my problem. *[laughter]* He's got to fix it. And that extra challenge is good. I wouldn't like to know the ending until . . . This one I just finished writing, right up until ninety-five per cent of the way through the book, I just thought there is no way I can rescue this book. This is my first complete catastrophe. And yet Reacher figured it out for me in the end. *[laughter]* It's good. I hope you read this one. *[laughter]*

John Grisham: I cannot imagine doing it like that. Last fall I was touring and met Sue Grafton . . . we lost her, that was a tragedy.

Lee Child: Just let me say that I asked Sue Grafton to be at this festival this year and she agreed. But we lost her, and that was a big tragedy indeed.

John Grisham: Let me tell you, we had the same conversation of how much do you plan, how much do you outline? And she said she was like you, she didn't want to know the ending either. And she said that in the middle of every book, she was terrified, to the point of almost being unable to go on writing, that she was not going to be able to get to the end of the book and solve the mystery. I told her I thought she was crazy and I'll say the same thing to you. *[laughter]*

Lee Child: Sue Grafton had one of the great all-time lines about research: she said she was completely confident about the facts in her books. She said, 'I know it's true, because I made it up myself.' *[laughter]*

John Grisham: I asked her about Hollywood, and she said, 'I was out there for fifteen years writing screenplays:

417

	I don't talk to those people, I know those people, I don't like those people, they're not getting my stuff.' That's a pretty smart lady . . .
Lee Child:	Yes, tough. But as you know, movie money can be pretty seductive.
John Grisham:	Yes. So, back to you, you start each book on a certain day each year?
Lee Child:	First of September.
John Grisham:	I start on the first of January. Each New Year I start the first word of the first chapter on January the first. How long do you give yourself?
Lee Child:	I give myself between eighty and ninety working days.
John Grisham:	So, six months?
Lee Child:	Yeah, because not every day is a working day. So – six or seven months.
John Grisham:	My deadline is July the first. So also about six months. And I don't work every day. I love to work in the winter – January, February, March. Bad weather, days are short, it's fun to . . .
Lee Child:	That's when I do most of mine too, because usually I'm lazy at the beginning, and then January, February, March is when I'm approaching the deadline.
John Grisham:	Where do you work?
Lee Child:	In the back room of my apartment.
John Grisham:	In New York?
Lee Child:	Yeah, in New York. Where it's very quiet and peaceful. *[laughter]*
John Grisham:	It must be a big apartment.
Lee Child:	Yeah. I'm living the dream.
John Grisham:	There's plenty of rooms?
Lee Child:	Yeah, there are plenty of rooms. I really can

work anywhere. I mean, it doesn't really matter much anyway because you're working in your head.

[addressing audience] Do we have any glaring issues? Any questions? I once asked that – 'Does anyone have any questions or issues?' – at an event in New York, and a woman who sat just right here said, 'I have an issue. I think you're a very deceitful and dishonest man.' And I said, 'Really? Why?' She said, 'Your author photograph must be twenty years old.' *[laughter]*

John Grisham: I've got a unique question that I'm going to now hit you with: how often do you update your author photo? *[laughter]*

Lee Child: Well, the sad part of that first story is it was actually a brand new photo. *[laughter]* I must have had a pretty bad night. I promised her I'd use a different author photo on every subsequent book. What I did not tell her was that they'd all come from the same session. *[laughter]* So yeah, every two to three years.

John Grisham: Yeah, me too. Are you tempted to stop it, because we're ageing? You were born fifteen weeks before me, by the way, so you're older than I am.

Lee Child: Yeah, we're the same age. Let's get that established right away. *[laughter]*

John Grisham: Don't you hate it when someone will have kept your first book from twenty years ago, and then your latest book, and laugh about the author photo? Watching you age?

Lee Child: My first book had a black and white old photo. I came in and somebody said, 'Oh, I thought you had grey hair.' *[laughter]* I thought, well that's charming. But no, I'm going to transition into a sort of grizzled, haggard photo. *[laughter]*

John Grisham: To go back to my rules for writing popular fiction. A common mistake that young writers make is in the first chapter they hit you with twenty paragraphs. You know, you bought the book, you can't wait to dive into it. And before you know it you're making notes. In the first five pages you have fifteen characters. That's not uncommon. And, to me, that's a mistake.

I don't like prologues either. Because the prologue is usually some very dramatic event, a missing child or a predator is about to strike – and right when they get to the big moment, they stop and go to chapter one. And chapter one is completely unrelated to the prologue. And chapter two doesn't relate to chapter one. And in chapter three, at page thirty, they slam you back to the prologue. Which you've forgotten by then. It's just not good planning . . . do you use prologues?

Lee Child: No. I mean, not really. A prologue is really a confession that chapter one isn't interesting enough. It's just faulty structure. If chapter one isn't exciting, then make it more exciting.

John Grisham: I agree.

Audience: What's your response to adverse criticism? Do you read your reviews?

Lee Child: If it's a critical review I do immediately and temporarily get a feral type of aggressive response. It's fortunate the critic is not standing in front of me. *[laughter]* But I get over it pretty quickly, and just think, 'My life is great, how's your life going?'

420

John Grisham: Back in the early days when I had a pretty thin skin, I was insecure, I'd read like five nice reviews of a book and then one bad one and the one bad one would make me want to kill people, but you learn to ignore it. You want to reach a point as a popular author where the critics just ignore you. Because it doesn't matter. It doesn't affect your popularity.

Lee Child: Reviews aren't so powerful now. In the old days there would be a handful of actual reviewers, and yeah, they were powerful. But now we get tens of thousands of online reviews, so there's so much noise: who really cares? Reading Amazon reviews, wow. I've had sequential reviews: 'This is the best book I've ever read', then the next review, 'This is the worst book I've ever read'. So how can you really take it seriously? I read a review that said, 'I *hated* this book, I'm *sorry* I read it, I wish I could *un*read it.' *[laughter]*

John Grisham: But he had bought it. *[laughter]*

So, now this is serious. The Reacher series is twenty-two years old now. Do you catch yourself making mistakes, or places you can't remember?

Lee Child: All the time. I screwed up the sequence of Reacher's alleged promotion while he was in the army. When I checked back, in the books, he was a lieutenant, then a captain, then a major, and then a captain again. So I actually turned that into a plot point, in the eighth book; so it looked like for eight books I'd been carefully plotting this arc. *[laughter]*

Audience: Are there any things that you have to do, like a touchstone or talisman, something that you need

421

to do to get yourself in the right frame for writing when you get stuck?

John Grisham: Yeah. You've got to make yourself write a page a day; you've got to consider it a career, a job, whatever else you're working at full time. Unless you got fired like Lee. *[laughter]* That's what pays you, your real job. But you've got to find a certain time each day, a certain place. It doesn't matter when. Early, late, lunchtime; it doesn't matter when you do it. But you've got to go to that place at that time and sit down and for thirty minutes, sometimes fifteen, sometimes an hour, you've got to write at least a page. And if you're not doing that, it's not going to happen.

Lee Child: Like you, I wrote my first one in pencil and on paper. And then with the proceeds I bought a computer to write the second one. And it came preloaded with a lot of stuff including a game called Minesweeper. I got into this ritual that I would have to get to the expert level of Minesweeper within three hundred seconds before I could stop. And I realized that was a compulsion. And then I bought an iPod for music, and at the time they only worked with Apple computers, so I had to get an Apple computer, which did not have Minesweeper on it. That's when I gave that ritual up.

So my main piece of advice is . . . my longest held belief is that nothing of value is ever achieved in the morning. So, I write in the afternoon and the evening, and I suggest that nobody does anything in the morning.

John Grisham: Hm. I write only from seven to eleven a.m.